THE CRITICS LOVE AMANDA SCOTT!

MY ENEMY, MY LOVE

He held her gaze, looking deep into her eyes. One hand still touched her arm. Feeling rough wool beneath his fingertips, and mentally dressing her in silk, he moved his hand to her shoulder. When she did not resist, he grasped her other shoulder and pulled her toward him. "I have waited weeks to do this again." He kissed her, gently at first, then harder, willing her to respond.

Her lips were soft against his. Her hair smelled of violets and wood smoke, reminding him of the evening he had found her at Castle Stalker. He heard her soft moan. Her lips firmed against his, then parted, and she kissed him back hungrily. For those few moments, it was as if they were alone in the world.

Raising his head at last, reluctantly, he looked down into her eyes. "I think you are more dangerous to me, Diana Maclean, than a whole army of rebels."

"Am I, my lord? I cannot think why." With that, she slipped from his grasp and disappeared into the darkness.

HIGHLAND SECRETS

Amanda Scott

Zebra Books
Kensington Publishing Corp.

http://www.zebrabooks.com

ZEBRA BOOKS are published by

Kensington Publishing Corp.
850 Third Avenue
New York, NY 10022

First Printing: October, 1997
10 9 8 7

Printed in the United States of America

To Terry and Jim.
Just because.

One

The guard's keys rattled against the heavy wooden cell door, creating a strange echo in the chilly, stone-vaulted corridor of the prison. Before unlocking the door, the burly, grizzled man leered over his shoulder at the plump, silent laundress behind him.

"Mind ye behave, lass," he said suggestively. "Ye dinna want me tae leave ye locked in wi' her ladyship, or teach ye proper manners wi' the sting o' me cat."

"Aye, ye'd like that, ye fousome auld flit," the laundress muttered with a grimace that showed a mouthful of blackened teeth. Shifting her large bundle to her other shoulder, barely missing his head as she did, she waited with scarcely veiled impatience for him to open the door. The hood of the dingy, dark-gray wool cloak she wore against the winter cold was drawn low, concealing her face, but her tone left no doubt of her irritation when she added, "The gentry looks after its ain, ye ken. Ye'll no want her complaining tae your governor aboot any lack o' respect."

"Och, an she'll be doing that anyways, won't she? Got a tongue on her sharp as a needle. I canna repeat what she's said about Argyll, and him a duke! Dinna be long now," he added, pulling open the cell door. "I'll be a-locking of this after ye, so raise a shout when ye want tae be let oot again."

Silently she stepped past him into the cell, noting a squint in the door above her eye level that told her he might keep watching after he shut the door. Taking a chance, she pulled her handkerchief from her sleeve and stuffed it into the hole, then watched to see if he would push it back. When it stayed put, she turned to face the cell's occupant. Bobbing a curtsy, she said in quiet, much more refined tones than those she had used with the guard, "I bid you good day, madam."

The light in the cell was dim and gray, coming as it did through high, barred vents from an overcast sky. The slender, middle-aged woman sitting on the lone wood bench narrowed her eyes, then stiffened, leaning forward to see her visitor more clearly. With patent disbelief but in a reassuringly firm voice, she said, "Diana?"

Grinning, Diana Maclean dropped the bundle to the floor and stepped nearer, pushing back the wool hood to reveal her glossy dark curls and sparkling hazel eyes. "Aye, it's me," she said ungrammatically with a chuckle of relief, "though you would do better to call me Mab or some such thing, in case that wretched turnkey overhears us. But we must make haste, Mam. Are you well?"

"Aye, as well as anyone could be in this horrid place. I've not known whether to wish for company or be glad they have left me alone, but at least they did not stuff me into that odious room over the portcullis where they kept the Duchess of Perth and her daughter for a full year after Culloden. They say the Tolbooth is worse than this, too, but I find that hard to believe, and so I told Argyll the last time I wrote to him. Odious man. At least they let me keep a proper chamber pot. Most folks have to make do with a bucket." She was still looking at Diana as though she could not believe her eyes. "What's that on your teeth?"

"Boot blacking," Diana said, slipping off her cloak. "It tastes terrible, but Neil said the turnkey might try to kiss me, and I thought if he did, black teeth might put him off. As to your being alone," she added, "be glad you are, and that they did not secure you with irons and shackles. I'd never have dared to do this if they had, but thank heaven, Neil was easily able to learn that you had a cell all to yourself."

"Aye, because they've freed every other woman of rank," Lady Maclean said bitterly, "and I've tongue enough still to scorch the ears of any fool trying to house a less suitable female in here. But what are you doing here? I am glad they've allowed you to visit, of course, but why the blacking and those dreadful padded clothes? Your rank alone ought to protect you from that detestable turnkey."

"I hope you don't think the clothes too dreadful, Mam," Diana said, stripping off the faded blue dress she wore and the bulk of her plump figure with it, "because you must put them on. Quick now," she added, straightening her shift. "We must make haste, for Neil is outside the gate, waiting to take you to Glen Drumin."

Lady Maclean still had not moved, and now she looked puzzled. "Are you out of your senses, child? You cannot mean to take my place here."

"That is exactly what I mean to do, Mam. I've another dress in the laundry sack, which you will wear under this fat-laundress costume of mine, and I'll put on the clothing you take off. Fortunately that brown stuff frock is not notable enough to make the guard wonder why his prisoner is still wearing it instead of a clean one."

"I doubt he notices much," her ladyship agreed, "but surely you and Neil did not come to Edinburgh alone, Diana."

"No, Dugald Cameron and some others came with us," she said. "They've got a coach to take you from the city, and once beyond its walls, there are horses to speed you to MacDrumin. He will keep you safe. After all, he's successfully hidden his smuggling from the English authorities and their Scottish lackeys for years."

"But dim as that turnkey is, he'll see the difference between us in a blink!"

"No, he won't. He never saw my whole face, and if you take care, he will not see yours either. He expects a plump woman to leave with a bundle, and that is what he will see. The only attention he paid me was when he tried to put his hand on my backside. I growled at him that all he would get if he forced his attentions upon me was a dose of the French pox, so I doubt he'll attempt to molest you."

"Diana, you never said such a vulgar thing to him!"

"I did. There was no time to worry about decorum. You've been here nearly six weeks now, and all on a whim. Campbells like the Duke of Argyll and Red Colin Glenure seem to see naught amiss in ill-treating women when they can no longer lay hands on our menfolk. However, I will *not* allow you to stay here when I can help you escape. We Macleans look after our own. The fact that the only men left to us now are boys and young lads like Neil does not mean our ways must change. Now, pray, do as I bid you. Mary assured me that she felt no undue alarm when she heard our plan, and in any case, this is no time to argue its merits."

"I suppose not," Lady Maclean said, standing at last and allowing Diana to help her remove the stuff gown. "It will be good to have fresh clothing on, I can tell you. They would not let me have visitors, but even Argyll is not so lost to his senses as to deny me an occasional clean dress. Oh, Diana, do you really imagine your plan will serve? Even if Mary believes in it, it seems far too rash and daring."

"Don't think about that," Diana advised, making quick work of the gown's buttons and laces. "Think only about reaching Glen Drumin in safety."

"But I don't know that I should go to Glen Drumin," Lady Maclean said, frowning thoughtfully. "Really, my dear, do you think that wise? The MacDrumin is our cousin, to be sure, but an Englishman owns his estates now, you know."

"Yes, of course I know, Mam," Diana said, waiting while she stepped out of the gown before handing her a fresh one from the bag. "The Earl of Rothwell has owned MacDrumin's land since shortly after the defeat at Culloden, but Rothwell and Cousin Maggie spend their winters in London or at his estate in Derbyshire, and will not return until summer. We'll have whisked you away long before then, and mayhap even have arranged for your pardon. After all, you did nothing to harm anyone, only cutting down a few trees."

"You forget they say that I have refused to submit to the *proper* authorities," Lady Maclean said bitterly. "How they expect any self-respecting Scotswoman to bend a knee to German George is more than I can think."

"Aye, but we need not discuss that now," Diana said hastily, adding once she had fastened up the new gown, "Here, let me fling this laundress costume on over your head. You'll feel a bit burdened in it, I expect, but you need wear it only till you are safe in the coach. Neil has a bonnet for you, too, with a widow's veil."

"You've gone daft, Diana. I should not let you do this." But she held up her arms obediently so that Diana could slip the costume on over her fresh gown.

"You have no choice, Mam," Diana said, smiling as she retrieved the stuff dress, stepped into it, and pulled it up. "If we waste time arguing, I'll undoubtedly be caught and identified. Then they'll clap me in here with you, and much as you might think you would enjoy my company—"

"That will do, miss. Here, turn round and let me fasten that for you. Did you say you spoke to the guard when you came in? That was foolish. What if he makes it necessary for me to speak and recognizes the difference in our voices?"

"He won't do that if you just mutter at him. Oh, and I used broad dialect, too," she added, grinning over her shoulder. "I know you were used to scold whenever we aped the speech of the lower orders, but you must admit that our skill has proved useful more than once. Your voice is enough like mine so that if you remember not to come the gentlewoman over him, he will not hear any difference."

Turning, Diana looked critically at the now-plump Lady

Maclean, then reached to push curling salt-and-pepper curls back from the older woman's forehead. "Cover your hair with the hood, Mam. He did not see mine, but he has seen yours, and we must give him no hint that aught is amiss."

Obeying, Lady Maclean said, "What about you? He'll see you at once. Really, Diana, I cannot simply leave you like this."

"Yes, you can."

She spoke with more confidence than she felt, but for her mother's sake, she did not betray her fear. Giving Lady Maclean a quick hug, she tousled her own hair a little more, stepped to the door, and pulled her handkerchief from the squint. Then, shouting for the guard before she had a chance to lose her nerve, she turned to the bench, raised the handkerchief to her face, and sat down.

Trying to imitate her mother's earlier posture, she slumped forward, so as to look tired and depressed. The handkerchief concealed her face. Her hair remained uncovered, but in the dim gray light, she did not think he would note a difference between what he saw now and what he had seen before.

Hearing the keys rattle against the door, she fought down rising panic and avoided looking at Lady Maclean. It was not the first time circumstances had forced that stately dame to play a role other than her natural one, however, and Diana did not fear any foolish mistake. Still, she would feel boundless relief if no one raised a hue and cry within the next few minutes.

The cell seemed darker when her mother had gone, leaving her with her thoughts. She felt little of the triumph she had expected to feel. In truth, she felt only surprise that their ruse had succeeded, despite her cousin Mary's assurance that there would be no trouble.

Upon arriving at the castle, Diana had crossed the drawbridge over the dry ditch without incident, for the two guards had been chatting and showed no interest in her or in anyone else. Walking between the high stone walls of the inner barrier, she had seen three more soldiers guarding the portcullis gate, but they had shown interest only in the elegant crested carriage that had drawn to a halt there. With no more than a glance at her bundle and costume, one of the men had waved her on.

She had visited the castle only once before, years ago, but Neil and Dugald had given her excellent directions, and she strode along with as much confidence as if she had really been the laundress coming to collect prisoners' clothes. Neil had a way with the lasses, although Mam would not approve of his latest flirtation any more than the girl's father did. He had learned of the laundress through some means of his own, and he and Diana had pieced their plan together accordingly.

The crested carriage rattled by as she passed the powder magazine, but she had not caught even a glimpse of its occupant as it moved on up the hill toward the new governor's house and parade ground.

Keeping the house on her right, as Dugald had instructed, she followed the path uphill and around, through the old archway known as Foggy Gate, to the hilltop site of the original castle. To her left lay the shot yard and powder house, to her right the governor's garden and the palace close.

Crossing the garden, she had felt her confidence surge. She felt no fear. Neil had been the reluctant one, but Diana felt only contempt for Argyll's men, knowing they tended to dismiss women as harmless and weak. Not one had paid her any heed when she walked briskly into the close.

A soldier at the entrance to the great hall directed her to the prison vaults beneath it, where the turnkey, although he had never seen her before, had willingly guided her to Lady Maclean's cell.

Half an hour passed without any alarm before she began to consider how she would get out. She and Neil had talked at length about the fact that she might not get out at all, and despite the show of confidence she had put on for him and for her mother, she knew she might be there for some time. It would be horrid, she knew, but better by far that she suffer than that Lady Maclean should continue to do so.

The cell was nearly bare. Its only furnishings were the hard bench on which she sat, the chamber pot, and a shelf containing a pitcher and mug. The whole place smelled nasty, and the taste of the blacking on her teeth made it worse. Since she had no reason now not to remove it, she got up to look into the pitcher, intending to dampen a corner of the threadbare blanket on the floor to scrub her teeth. A large cockroach floating in the water banished that intent.

Fighting a wave of nausea, she scrubbed her teeth with her sleeve and, perversely, wondered when they fed the prisoners. Not that she could imagine eating their food if it matched the rest of her dreadful surroundings, but come mealtime, someone was bound to discover her.

The next hour crept like a century. The bench was hard, there was no pillow, and when she picked up the blanket, it smelled like vomit, making her glad that she did not yet need the foul thing for warmth.

Getting up again, she began to pace, but in the close confines of the cell, she found the exercise frustrating and tiresome, and sat down again.

A constant low hum assaulted her ears—moans and whining punctuated by occasional crashes or bangs, even a shriek once, though that was not repeated. The solid door muffled the sounds, however, so when she heard men's voices nearby, she jumped up to see if she could hear anything of interest. To her surprise, she had no sooner reached the door than she heard the unmistakable sound of a key in its lock. She barely had time to leap back before the door swung inward.

The turnkey said cheerfully, "I've brung visitors, me lady. There she be, me lor—Ay de mi!" The man crossed himself and put out both arms to check the two well-dressed men behind him. "Dinna touch her, me lords! She must be a witch or worse, for by all that's holy, I swear I niver seen that wench afore."

Diana ignored him. Watching the other two, she stood straight, squaring her shoulders and giving back look for look.

The older one, a dark-haired, long-faced man, gaped at her. The younger man was taller and more powerful-looking, with broad shoulders and a narrow waist. His hair was also dark, but his eyes were gray, their irises light like pale granite with black rims around them. He looked steadily at her, and although his chiseled countenance revealed no particular expression, Diana found it as hard to meet his gaze as she imagined it must be for a rabbit to meet the predatory stare of a fox.

She looked back at the older man, finding it easier to meet his dark frown than the other's steady inspection. This was not how she had imagined her unveiling. The pair were not guards or soldiers. Both wore elegant clothing and carried themselves like men of substance and authority, especially the younger one.

The elder, looking irritated and confused, said, "Where is Lady Maclean?"

Glancing back at the younger man, certain that of the two he was the more dangerous, Diana collected her wits. Making a deep curtsy, she instilled as much awe in her voice as she could when she said, "She be gone, your honor, but dinna be wroth wi' me. I couldna help it. I swear tae ye, I couldna!"

The older man said brusquely, "Turnkey, who the devil is this female?"

"Did I no just tell ye, sir, that I've niver seen the wicked wench afore? This be magic, I warrant, and black magic at that."

"Don't be a fool," the younger man said, his voice deep and vibrant with the accents of wealth, education, and a natural authority. "She passed through neither these stone walls nor the iron bars of that grating yonder. There is only one way into this cell, turnkey, and that is through this door. You must have let her in yourself."

"Och, but the only one I let in were the laundress, me lord. I swear it on me blood and bones, and I let her oot again m'self. Only her ladyship were within."

The older one said, "What have you done with Lady Maclean, wench?"

Diana did not look up or speak. Her courage was fast deserting her, and it was only too easy to let her hands shake, and show other signs of incipient panic.

Before she knew anyone had moved, a large hand clasped

her shoulder. Its warmth, even through her dress, and its size and strength, set her nerves afire and stopped the breath in her throat. She could not have spoken if she had wanted to.

"Tell Governor MacTause what happened, lass. You are the laundress, are you not?" Though his tone was gentle, a certain imperious note in it, added to the overpowering awareness of his hand on her shoulder, held her speechless.

When the governor uttered an exclamation of shock, echoed by the turnkey, the young man said, "It is the only logical explanation. Only the laundress came in, and only one person has left. Therefore, since this is not Lady Maclean, she must be the laundress. Your dangerous Jacobite tree-cutter has escaped, MacTause."

"But, me lord," the turnkey protested, "this wench don't look at all like the laundress! That one were as round as an onion."

"Padding, I'll wager. Who put you up to this, lass?" The hand on her shoulder twitched, as if it wanted to shake her.

Feeling tongue-tied for perhaps the first time in her life, Diana bit her lip, wishing fervently that she could weep at will like Mary. All her cousin had to do was widen her eyes, let her face crumple, and huge tears would spill down her cheeks. But although such a skill might aid her now, Diana lacked it, and when she looked up into the gentleman's face, she knew that if she tried to lie to him, her tongue would betray her. His gaze was too penetrating, his intelligence too plain. She looked quickly down again.

The turnkey growled, "You just leave the wench tae me, your lordship. I'll soon have the truth out of her. The claws o' me cat will—"

The hand tightened on her shoulder, but his voice remained calm when he said, "That won't be necessary. She has been frightened already, and you can see with half an eye that she is no hardened conspirator."

Governor MacTause said grimly, "Then just how do you propose to make her tell what she knows, Calder? I remind you, she has helped an important prisoner to escape, and the law is quite clear about such a crime.''

"As to the importance of your prisoner,'' Lord Calder said, "I dispute that, as you know, for we have more pressing matters on our plate than making war on women. That is precisely why I asked to see this dangerous prisoner of yours. You and his grace have kept her ladyship locked up for no good cause that I can see, other than that his grace don't happen to like her.''

"She broke the law,'' MacTause said, "and in any event, it is not my business to determine who stays and who leaves.''

"It is your business to see prisoners treated properly, however. To house any woman of quality in a place like this—'' He broke off abruptly, then added in a more even tone, "We will not pluck that crow again. As to how I shall learn what this young female knows, why, I shall ask her. Look at me, lass.''

Reluctantly, Diana forced her gaze to meet his. His eyes were like flints. His thick, dark eyebrows nearly met above the bridge of his nose, and the bones of his cheeks showed prominently. His chin was strong and well formed. His lips—

He said sternly enough to stand the fine hairs on the back of her neck on end, "Tell me the truth now, or you'll find yourself in an abundance of trouble. If you are truthful, I promise no one will harm you.''

"Now, see here, Calder—''

"Do you deny my authority, MacTause?''

"No, of course not, my lord. I merely wish to point out—''

"We can discuss your wishes later at length, sir. Just now I want to hear what this young woman has to say.'' He paused, watching Diana and waiting.

Still overconscious of his hand on her shoulder, Diana licked dry lips, then said in words scarcely above a whisper, "I dinna ken what ye want of me, your lordship. Aye, sure, ye canna think they told me aught but what they wanted me tae do. I . . . I were sore affrighted, sir. Deed, and I be affrighted the noo, as weel!''

That last bit, at least, was no lie. Lord Calder, whoever he was, was no one with whom to trifle. Despite his sensible attitude about her mother's imprisonment, every instinct screamed at her to be wary of him. She fell silent again, waiting.

When he did not speak at once, she felt as if he were peering into her soul and seeing the truth written there in flaming letters, but when he spoke, he said only, "You see, MacTause. Clearly, some damned Jacobites forced the lass to help free her ladyship. She cannot know more about them or she would tell us. She is poor and uneducated, and she's practically shaking in her boots with terror. I say we send her off about her business. We'll gain naught by punishing her for this."

"But she helped a felon escape! We've not had an escape since I came to the castle, my lord. Surely, you cannot mean to let her off with no punishment at all."

"I doubt you'd get anything but the labor for your pains," Calder said, removing his hand at last, "but if you must punish her, deny her any future access to the prisoners. Hunger teaches a harsh lesson, sir, and the lass doubtless counts on income from doing their laundry to feed herself and perhaps a family as well."

"But, me lord," the turnkey protested, "this lass—"

"Silence, you," the governor snapped. "Had you done your duty, the Jacobite woman would still be locked up. I've a good mind to order you flogged."

"You'd be wiser to do nothing in haste, MacTause," Calder said when the turnkey shuddered. "Little said is soon amended, you know, but once we begin throwing blame about, there is no telling where it will stick. 'Tis better, I think, to send the lass on her way with a warning and a fright, after which I shall undertake to explain to his grace that no one could have avoided what occurred. No doubt he will order his men to pursue her ladyship, but that we cannot help."

"She is a dangerous Jacobite traitor," MacTause repeated stubbornly.

Diana's fists clenched. Pressing them into the folds of her gown, she kept her gaze fixed on the stone floor of the cell lest they detect her fury in her eyes.

Calder said calmly, "The widow Maclean is only a woman, MacTause. Even the most dangerous Jacobites have proved powerless against Argyll and the Crown."

She dared not look at any of them. She did not doubt that Calder and MacTause assumed she was the usual prison laundress or that the turnkey had tried to tell both men that he had never laid eyes on her before that day. The next few seconds increased her tension, for the governor could easily order her whipped. He seemed to perceive a threat in Calder's words, but not knowing where the younger man derived his authority, she could not guess how much influence he wielded.

Abruptly MacTause said, "It shall be as you wish, my lord. Turnkey, take her up to the guard in the hall, and tell him to evict her from the castle. He is to learn her name and inform the guards at the entrance that she is not to step foot inside these walls again. Do you understand me?"

"Aye, your worship," the turnkey said grimly. "Come along o' me, wench."

"Take care, turnkey," Lord Calder said. "She is not to be harmed."

Unable to believe her luck, Diana did not breathe easily until she was outside the main gate. But when she found Dugald Cameron awaiting her there, her spirits soared until she felt utterly euphoric.

"I did not expect anyone still to be here," she said, grinning and tucking her hand in the crook of the huge Highlander's arm. "Did Mam get away safe?"

"Aye, they've got her outside the city gates and on her way," Dugald said. "I stayed 'cause I knew the laird would have me head if I left afore I learned what had become o' thee. We'd best make haste the noo though," he added. "We'll no catch them up, but your Neil did say he'd wait atop Firthin's Hill to see could he spy us a-coming. We didna think to see thee out so soon, Mistress Diana."

"Nor did I," Diana admitted. "A certain Lord Calder is visiting the governor, and it was he who set me free. Do you know aught of him, Dugald?"

"Nay, lass. Did they just turn thee out then?"

"I had to give the soldiers a name," she said, chuckling. "I said I was Mab MacKissock."

"MacKissock?"

"Aye, 'tis one of the Campbell septs. Let them blame some misbegotten Campbell for Mam's escape."

Dugald laughed heartily, and Diana laughed with him, feeling exultant in her unexpected freedom.

Rory Campbell, Lord Calder, watched the burly turnkey lead the girl away, wondering why he felt reluctant now to let her go. One look into her golden eyes had told him she was no practiced traitor, and in any case, she was too young to have been part of the troubles that had ended at the Battle of Culloden six years ago.

She looked no more than seventeen, and since girls of her class aged quickly, she was probably younger. He had not asked her age because he had not wanted to show too much undue interest. MacTause was no particular friend of the Duke of Argyll's, but he might find occasion for comment, and Argyll's temper being uncertain at best, Rory had no wish to annoy him more than he already had.

He had tried his late father's first cousin enough by disagreeing with him about keeping Lady Maclean in prison. As the duke had pointed out, furiously, Rory did not know her and Argyll did. But Rory's duties included administering Highland estates that had been forfeited to the Crown, and he believed the Highlanders would prove easier to rule if the English and his Campbell kinsmen would stop persecuting the few remaining Jacobites for no greater crime than believing a Stewart had more right to the throne than the man they called the second German George.

Unfortunately, the Highlands were humming again with rumors of another uprising, just as they had two years before when the young Pretender—the upstart they called Bonnie Prince Charlie—had ordered 26,000 muskets, then slipped across the Channel from Antwerp to confer with supporters in London. Obsessed with his dream of restoring the Stewart monarchy, he had visited the Tower, looked over its defenses, and had been overheard to say that the gates could be blown in by a petard. Naught had come of that visit, but rumors were rife again, and if trouble came, the task Rory faced would prove uncommonly difficult to accomplish.

As youngest baron of the Scottish Court of Exchequer, he believed he could accomplish his duties more easily if previous owners of the lands he administered would cooperate with his factors and bailies instead of trying to block them at every turn. The best course seemed obvious, but Argyll disagreed and, as chief of Clan Campbell—not to mention Lord Justice General of Scotland, Privy Councilor, and Keeper of the Great Seal—the duke deserved and demanded Rory's obedience and respect. Still, Rory knew no one would be less amazed than Argyll to learn that he had come to meet Lady Maclean and judge for himself just how dangerous she was.

"Will you stay the night, my lord?"

MacTause's question jerked him from his reverie. They had been walking silently back toward the governor's house, and lost in his thoughts as he had been, Rory had paid little heed to his surroundings and none to his companion.

Realizing that to make an unnecessary enemy was foolish, he smiled and said, "I must get back to Perthshire, sir. My plate is full these days, and much as I'd like to accept your offer, I cannot." When the older man bit his lip, looking worried, he added matter-of-factly, "What comes of today's event is more important than the event itself, you know. I'll tell his grace you took quick action to see that such an escape cannot occur again."

"You may be sure of that, my lord."

Rory took his leave, hoping MacTause would heed his warning with regard to the turnkey. To flog him would do no good. To show mercy would be much wiser, for the man would take good care never to let a pretty face sway him again.

As he settled into his comfortable carriage, he felt a twinge of pity for the golden-eyed laundress. Though he had saved her from whipping or worse, he feared she would soon find herself destitute or forced into the stews to survive. Since she was attractive enough to make him wish he were the sort to take such women to his bed, she would not starve on her back, but such a life would be sadly short.

He put her firmly out of mind then but found to his surprise that her image frequently intruded upon his thoughts in the days and weeks that followed. Busy as he was, he could not forget her. Thus, when administrative duties for the Exchequer took him into the western Highlands six weeks later, he was pleasantly surprised, albeit astonished, to find her employed as a maidservant at Castle Stalker, island fortress of the Lords of Lorne and presently the strongest and most impenetrable of the many Campbell strongholds in the Highlands.

His first thought was that her Jacobite friends must have helped her find work after she lost her livelihood, but he rejected that thought the moment it entered his mind. Not only had MacTause discovered that her name was MacKissock, which was nearly as good as being a Campbell born and bred, but no Jacobite had access to Stalker. Moreover, he doubted that respectable Highlanders of any political persuasion would encourage an innocent young female to work there. Located half a mile from the mainland on a sea-girt rock, guarding the strategic point where Loch Linnhe met the Lynn of Lorne, Stalker's purpose was strictly military and its primary occupants were rough Campbell men-at-arms.

Rory decided then, logically, that Mab MacKissock must have grown up in Argyll, which was strongly Campbell country, and was perhaps kin to Stalker's captain. However, he was able to indulge himself in that comfortable conclusion only until his host informed him that a dangerous Jacobite prisoner had escaped the previous night from a high tower room previously believed to be escape proof.

Two

While Diana helped serve the guardsmen their supper in the hall, she kept an eye out for Patrick Campbell, captain of Stalker's garrison. Slapping a roving hand absent-mindedly, she moved to serve the next man, chuckling when he made a joke but maintaining a careful mix of levity and distance. The last thing she wanted was to draw too much unwanted notice. She had been lucky to find a position in the castle. She did not want to cast herself into the suds through stupidity.

Since Patrick Campbell's wife occasionally visited him at Stalker, he had, over time, hired several maidservants to accommodate her needs, and he retained them even in her absence to cook and serve meals. Patrick's wife being a lady of uncertain temper, the maidservants were safer under his eye than one might expect in a castle full of soldiers, but Diana knew that she must stay alert.

Nothing less than her present mission would have drawn her to Castle Stalker, the Campbell stronghold that presented such a menacing presence in that part of Argyll known as Appin country, long controlled by the Stewarts of Appin. She had been there for less than a week, but even in that short time two incidents had occurred that made her wish she could carry a dirk to defend herself. She dared not, however. Since Culloden, the battle that had ended the Jacobite rebellion six years before, British law had forbidden Highlanders to carry weapons, and penalties were severe if one were caught. Many folks still carried them, of course, although most had made a great show of turning theirs in at Stalker when first bidden to do so, exchanging them for receipts from Patrick Campbell's elderly predecessor. To a man they had kept these official documents, and many displayed them prominently to prove their law-abiding nature, while storing the rest of their weapons in places unlikely to draw notice from nosy Campbells or their ilk.

The garrison's responsibility during the rebellion had been to protect and care for the military supplies stored there and to transmit intelligence, for which armed boats from Fort William called every other day. Somewhat cramped within Stalker's walls, the garrison had once numbered a sergeant, a corporal, and twenty men, all under the command of their own captain. Since the end of the rebellion, however, the number had fallen to twelve men and a sergeant, and Captain Patrick Campbell was responsible as well for Castle Dunstaffnage, overlooking the south end of the Lynn of Lorne.

Two other maids served in the castle, as well as a female cook. Diana knew that the two girls bestowed favors as well as food upon the soldiers, but she liked them and was uncritical of their behavior. They were friendly, and when she had explained that she lacked sexual experience and did not wish to submit to any man before marriage, they cheerfully helped divert any soldier who showed interest in her. The men themselves were cautious, knowing their captain would take a dim view of anyone forcing himself on a maidservant.

Patrick Campbell had been out of the castle most of the day with a party searching nearby woods and glens, but Allan Breck remained free. Had they caught him, the news would have spread even faster than had the news of his escape.

The problem now was to get herself away. She had hoped to do so as soon as she learned his whereabouts in the castle and had given him the means to signal Neil, Bardie, and the others. But she had reckoned without Patrick Campbell's strong sense of duty to the maids under his protection. When she had tried to leave, the ferryman had told her firmly that lassies were not allowed to go across the water without permission, even on their half days out, and certainly not at night when they might meet with wildcats in the mainland woods, or worse.

Having recognized the man as a Bethune of Craignure from her childhood home on the Island of Mull, she had dared to press him a little, admitting that she, too, was a Craignure Maclean, and glibly explaining that her granny was sick. Her effort went unrewarded, however, despite his recognition of her as one of his clan.

"For 'tis an unco resemblance ye bear tae the young Mistress Diana," he told her, "but still, I dassn't take ye, lass. Yon vexsome Campbells would have me head. Moreover, how will ye be getting back after? I canna sit on a rock and wait for ye."

Since the last point was unanswerable, she had pressed him no more, though she felt sorely tempted to tell him that she was Mistress Diana herself, and demand the help to which her rank entitled her from any loyal clan member. But since she had not wanted him to lose either his head or his position in such distressed times, and since he assured her he would tell no one she had even hinted at a wish to leave, she decided to say no more. That she was still free indicated that he had kept his word, and she hoped he would stay silent if someone questioned him more closely once they began to investigate the details of Allan's escape.

Nearly twenty-four hours before, she had made her way to her cousin's cell high in the tower and had given him her white scarf. No one had seen her do so, for at the time, one of the other maids had been entertaining the guard at the foot of the steps. Diana was certain that neither man nor maid would admit the interlude and that the former would insist he had never taken his eyes off the steps, so she felt confident they would do her no harm. There had been a good deal of upset that morning when the guard discovered Allan's escape, but since he had escaped through a once-barred window, using a rope that the guard swore must have flown up to him by magic, they were still trying to figure out how he had done it.

She knew his secret, but knowledge did not lessen her amazement at its success. That Bardie was strong enough and clever enough to climb the tower in pitch dark was not so amazing, because the little man had more muscle and sinew in his shoulders and arms than most men of greater size had in their whole bodies. The amazing part was that he had done so with a coiled rope slung around him, using a pair of dirks as handholds by plunging first one, then the other into the wall as he ascended. She had seen him practice on a rock cliff in Lettermore Woods, but she had not believed him when he had said it would be just as easy to climb the tower.

The thought of the Campbells' expressions upon discovering that their captive had flown, apparently by pushing the bars out of his window and weaving a rope out of air, made Diana smile. The expression froze, however, when she glanced up as she served the next man and saw Lord Calder on the threshold of the great hall, looking right at her. She had no idea how long he had been there.

The heat flooding her cheeks warned her that her face had reddened. Thus, when the lad she was serving reached up and pinched her breast, she did not hesitate to twitch away and snap, "If ye dinna want tae wear this stew, ye misbegotten maggot, keep your hands tae yourself. One more finger on me bubbies or me arse, and I'll upend this entire potful over your head."

"Aye, Mab, that's telling him!"

While the men around them roared with laughter, she shot a sidelong glance at the doorway. Calder still stood there, but he was no longer alone or looking her way, for Patrick had returned, and the two were talking. Another man joined them, who was clearly Calder's servant, and the interplay between the three told her that Patrick also considered Calder his superior. She wondered if Patrick would tell him of the escape, and for the first time she questioned her wisdom in using the name MacKissock. The first time, in Edinburgh, it had been simply a whim, a wish to cast what blame she could on the traitorous Campbells. But now, awareness that Calder might easily have learned what name she had given brought a surge of dismay.

Feeling trapped, she racked her brain, trying to think what to do. She could not turn tail and run. That much was certain, for there was no easy way off the islet. The current between it and the shore flowed swiftly whenever the tides were running, and although she could swim, she was not a strong enough swimmer to make such an attempt other than foolhardy. The ferryman would not take her either, she was sure, even if she were to confess her true identity. Loyalty or not, he had made it clear the night before that he thought any female going into the woods at night was a fool. He would never allow the daughter of his late chieftain to do so.

Glancing at the doorway, she saw with relief that Calder was still talking to Patrick and seemed to take no more interest in her. When his servant departed toward the upper regions and Patrick shouted to one of the other maids to bring them supper at a table by the fire, Diana breathed more easily. Calder had not looked her way again. If he had not recognized her, even if he were to learn about Allan Breck's escape, he would have no cause to wonder at her presence unless through some incredible mischance Patrick Campbell mentioned her name and Calder both recognized and remembered it.

Careful not to look at him again, she moved about, collecting empty platters for the scullions to clean. Then, by finding a string of tasks to do in the scullery, she managed to stay out of Calder's sight for the next half hour, and when she returned to the hall, he and Patrick Campbell had gone elsewhere. Feeling lighter of heart, she turned her mind again to escape. With Calder near at hand, she dared not wait until her half day. That much was certain.

* * *

Diana would not have felt nearly so relieved had she known that Rory had been surreptitiously watching her the entire time she remained in the hall. Though generally skilled at judging others, he felt mystified by her. His first sense of relief at seeing for himself that she had not starved as a result of her banishment from Edinburgh Castle had vanished when Patrick told him that the notorious Jacobite Allan Breck had escaped. Concealing his feelings then had taken every ounce of a considerable skill developed over the past two years in the Barons' courtroom. He did not trouble to hide his displeasure from Patrick, however, once the two men retired to that gentleman's private chamber to relax by the fire with their brandy.

"You're angry," Patrick said, eyeing him warily. "I don't blame you, and I shudder to think what Argyll will say, not to mention Cumberland. Thank heaven the latter is in London," he added, referring to the royal duke who had wreaked havoc in the Highlands after the rebellion of 1745.

Keeping his tone flat, Rory said, "Cumberland's absence from Scotland is of little consolation just now."

"Well, if the English did not keep pressing us to ferret out the few remaining rebels and punish them, I think the troubles would soon ease, Rory. As it is, pockets of discontent remain to plague us. In Appin, Macleans and Stewarts respond to any pressure to yield by standing their ground more firmly. Ardsheal still rules here as if he were in Scotland, rather than exiled in France with the other rebel lairds."

"He is able to do so," Rory said pointedly, "because until recently you have allowed his most active courier to move about wherever and whenever he wishes."

"That's not fair," Patrick said, his tone that of the schoolmate he once he had been, rather than that of a dutiful subordinate. He flushed, adding quickly, "I don't mean any disrespect—"

"I know you don't. How did Breck get out of the tower cell?"

"Damned if I know." When Rory shot him a skeptical look,

Patrick shrugged. "Oh, I can tell you he managed to remove two bars from the window and tie a rope to the other two. I can also tell you that he climbed down the rope and probably swam ashore. What I cannot tell you is how he got the rope or dislodged the bars from the window. We found them on the ground, not in the cell. But that window is high in the cell wall. I cannot believe the man simply knocked them out."

"There was no deterioration in the stonework around the bars?"

Patrick grimaced. "The whole castle is deteriorating, like the rest of our Highland fortresses. The only place in Scotland that has seen improvement these past six years is Inveraray Castle, which I'm told, has become the pride of Argyll's holdings. That is as it should be, of course, since it is the ducal seat. Still and all, I'm lucky even to get oatmeal to feed my men. But so it has always been, even during the rebellion." He paused, apparently reflecting on what he had said. Then, with a rueful twinkle, he added, "I ought not to speak so candidly, I know. Doubtless it comes of seeing so little of you these past six years. I feel as if no time has passed, as if we still can speak as schoolmates."

"We can," Rory said, smiling at him. "We are not only friends, Patrick. We are loyal members of the same clan."

"Of which Argyll is chief," Patrick reminded him soberly.

"Aye, but he would never demand that one Campbell betray another."

"So long as that policy suits his purpose."

Rory was silent.

After a moment, Patrick said, "I take full responsibility for Breck's escape, of course. I'll send word of it to Argyll at once."

"You do that," Rory said. "I shall also write to him. I'll tell him that, if he wants to keep prisoners here, he must send material to repair the tower properly, because a man seems to have pushed the bars out of his window with his fingertips and climbed to the ground as if he had walked down an outer stairway."

Patrick's sigh was audible. "Thank you, my friend. If there is anything I can do to express my gratitude . . ."

"There is," Rory said, grinning at him and ignoring the wee voice in his head that wondered more persistently with each passing moment why he did not tell Patrick about the very odd serving wench he had hired, a wench who might well have had a hand in the escape. Instead, he said, "I have been without female company for weeks now, and when you accosted me earlier, my eye had just fallen upon the most winsome creature."

Patrick looked surprised. "You want a serving wench?"

"Not just any serving wench. I've a notion this one is unusual."

"Oh, aye, I know the one, the dark-haired one with eyes as bright and alert as a sparrow's. I did not know her before she came here, but she's a MacKissock, I think she said. When she laughs, her eyes twinkle like stars reflected in the loch."

"Faith, man, have you an interest in that direction yourself?"

"Lord, no! My wife would whack off my pintle with a claymore. She hasn't seen the wench yet, but I think she'll take to her well enough. One of the others left, so when Mab showed up looking for work, I took her on. I've had no complaints. The lads like her, and she has a knack for setting them at a distance. *I* like that."

Again the wee voice spoke, but Rory knew now that he had no intention of describing his first meeting with Mab MacKissock. Not yet. The wench intrigued him and he wanted to confront her himself, to unmask her, and . . . and then what? He put the question out of his head. First he would see her and talk to her. With that in mind, he said with a laugh to Patrick, "I doubt she will dare keep me at a distance. Will you send her to my chamber?"

"Aye, if you like. I don't recall your having a taste for maidservants," he added with a twinkle. "I do remember a lass in Edinburgh when we returned from school, but she was more buxom than young Mab, and a saucy creature besides."

Rory chuckled. "I'll thank you to leave ancient history in

the past where it belongs, old friend. That was years ago, when we both were young and foolish.''

"I'll warrant there have been a few since then, however."

"Perhaps, but you will also recall that there was a war of sorts and that I have shouldered duties since then that keep me far too busy for dalliance."

"Oh, yes, your august position." Patrick was relaxing more, reverting again to irreverent school chum. "How long do you mean to stay here, by the bye?"

"Not long. I stopped only to bring messages from Inveraray, and to see how you are getting on. It's been years since I've come this far west, and I promised to visit my uncle Balcardane on Loch Leven. I stayed with him for six weeks, you'll remember, when I was eleven. I sent word ahead, and I expect to put up there for perhaps a month or so."

"Business?"

"Aye. There was trouble last year over a few of the factors in Appin country, one in particular, because Cumberland and others of his ilk in London think Highland-bred factors have shown undue favoritism to the Highland rebels."

"But the Barons confirmed the factors, did they not? I'd have heard else."

"We did confirm them. Argyll just wants to be certain we did right. He is still Lord Justice General of Scotland, you know, and thus a member of the Barons' Court, though he rarely sits with us. The factor in question is a Campbell."

"Aren't they all?" Patrick said with a wry smile.

"Not all."

"Oh, aye, some do not bear the Campbell name, but would you have me believe any of them are outsiders, Rory?"

"There are, in fact, two Stewarts. Although the Campbells are the only clan any Englishman trusts, you must know that does not mean a prick's worth in the present political climate. There are many who do not trust any Scotsman at all."

"So you have come to pull a few chestnuts out of the fire for his grace."

Rory shrugged. "I have come to test the heat of the coals,

perhaps. I do not yet know if there are any chestnuts to rescue. But I must tell you, my friend, the escape of Allan Breck will not make my task any easier.''

Patrick shifted uneasily but met Rory's steady gaze without flinching. ''Damn but I wish you would roar at a fellow instead of sticking pins in him,'' he said. ''You've been like that since childhood, you know, and it's damned irritating. I know I mucked this up for you. Didn't do my own career much good either, and I own that I hope nothing brings Argyll within spitting distance of this place for the next six months at least. Receiving the next letter will be bad enough. I don't want to hear him bellow what he thinks of my character for all and sundry to hear.''

''His judgment is sound, I think.''

''If that's your tender way of telling me I deserve to hear whatever he chooses to bellow at me, I don't deny it,'' Patrick said. ''But he is attached solely to his own interest, you know. One rarely hears anyone praise his honor or his principles.''

''I trust you do not speak so freely to anyone else,'' Rory said.

Patrick grinned. ''I do not, and unless you have changed considerably, my friend, I take no risk in speaking my mind to you.''

''I am Argyll's man.''

''So you are, and so you have always been, but you were once a lad who thought for himself, Rory. Some moments ago you said I could still treat you like a schoolmate. I trusted you then, you know. Have you altered so much over the years that you would advise me to trust you no longer?''

Guilt nibbled at his conscience when an image of Mab Mac-Kissock leapt to his mind's eye, but Rory smiled and shook his head. ''I still think for myself,'' he said, ''and you can still trust me to hear your thoughts without prejudice. I might wonder about your judgment, however, if I had not already seen from the moment of my arrival how well in hand you have everything else here.''

''Thank you for that. It means a lot just now.''

A companionable silence fell as both men sipped their brandy and stared into the fire, although Rory was uncomfortably aware that he had equivocated. Not that Patrick could not trust him where Argyll was concerned. He had never been one to carry tales of others to the duke, nor did Argyll expect that of him. But he had been careful not to assure Patrick that he could simply trust him. He could not do that unless he meant to open the budget about Mab MacKissock. Considering that Patrick was very likely housing a Jacobite traitor, the least he might expect was that Rory would warn him of what he knew. Yet he was oddly reluctant to do so, and oddly eager to meet the wicked wench face to face again.

Knowing all this, he forced himself to sit quietly with Patrick until they had both finished their brandy. Not until the captain offered to refill his glass did he shake his head and say, "I'm for bed, my friend."

Patrick chuckled. "In that case, I shall order a warming pan taken to your chamber at once, sir."

"An excellent notion," he said, his loins stirring at the thought.

"Unless . . ." Patrick's eyes were twinkling. "Will your Thomas already have thought of a warming pan? I could order hot milk instead."

"Hot milk! You deserve that I should ruin you with Argyll for making such a suggestion. Not only will Thomas not have ordered a warming pan, he will call me a mollycoddle if he thinks I have sent for one. As for a composer, he mixes the finest toddy this side of heaven. Warm milk, indeed."

Patrick was still chuckling when they left the chamber. Parting from him at the narrow, twisting stone stairway that connected the several floors of the castle, Rory made his way to the chamber allotted to himself.

There he found that Thomas had turned down his bed, a service he believed due to Rory's rank. Thomas himself sat cleaning Rory's leathers before the small fire he had built in the arched stone fireplace to take the damp from the chamber.

"It's damned smoky in here," Rory said.

"Aye, it is," Thomas agreed. Shooting a look at his master, he said, "Make your complaints tae Patrick Campbell if ye dinna like it. I canna blow it up yon chimney, and if I open yon shutter, it only makes it worse."

"Did they give you a chamber of your own?" Rory asked him.

"Nay, then, this isna Inveraray. I'm tae sleep in the hall wi' the lads, but I'll no die of it. There'll be less smoke there at least. Are ye for bed the noo?"

"I am, so finish with those things or take them away. I've a visitor coming."

"Have ye now?"

"I have, and I'll thank you to keep that look off your face, Thomas MacKellar. Remember who is master here unless you want to seek a new position."

"Aye, and who will clean your leathers then, me laddie?" Thomas rolled his eyes, adding piously, "If the old laird could but hear ye, talking tae the most loyal man in your service as if he were nae more tae ye than a carking carfuffle."

"A *what?*"

Thomas appeared to have gone suddenly deaf as he busied himself with dignified dispatch, picking up the leathers and his tools.

"You mind your tongue, Thomas MacKellar, and help me off with these boots before you go," Rory said, trying to speak firmly while fighting his amusement. He sat on a stool near the bed and put out one foot expectantly.

Thomas looked at him. Then, with a sigh, he put down the things he had gathered and knelt at Rory's feet. Catching the heel of the proffered foot in one hand and the instep with the other, he tugged, muttering, "Nae doot ye'll dizzy yourself if ye tug them off yourself, or mayhap ye've et too much and canna bend in the middle. Or ha' ye wearied yourself wi' our long day's journey, and all?"

"That will do, Thomas."

"Aye, sure." Pulling off the second boot without another word, Thomas picked up both of them. Awkwardly collecting the other gear, he moved toward the door. When he reached it, he looked back to say with grave dignity, "If ye've any further need of me, my lord, ye have only tae shout."

"Be sure I will," Rory retorted, "but I shall wait until you are sound asleep before I do. 'Tis what you deserve for treating me as if I were still the eight-year-old lad I was when you first came to me."

Thomas winked. "I'll bid ye a good nicht then, my lord."

"Good night, you old fraud."

When Thomas had gone, Rory knelt to stir up the fire, adding peat from the basket near the hearth in the hope that if it burned fiercely it would smoke less. When he stood, he saw for the first time that Thomas had put a flagon of wine and a pewter goblet on the bench in the window aperture. Picking up the flagon, he saw that it was the same excellent brandy he and Patrick had shared, and feeling much more in charity with his manservant, he filled the goblet half full. Then he opened the shutter that Thomas had closed and bolted before his arrival.

Pale moonlight glinted along the dark waters of Loch Linnhe from a quarter moon rising at the upper end of the loch. On its west coast, the mountains of Morven rose black and solid looking, except for a single light that glowed from a cottage or house. He could hear the water below lapping at the rocky shore of the islet, and looking down, he thought of Allan Breck and wondered where the villain was just then, and what mischief he was brewing. A chilly breeze drifted into the room, its salty tang mixing with smoke that persisted in eluding the chimney.

Breathing deeply of the fresh air, he sipped his brandy and savored the mysterious beauty of the loch. If he lived to be a hundred, he hoped such things would never fail to stir him. The Highlands were magnificent by day or by night.

A light scratching at the door was the only warning he had before it opened. She stood on the threshold, and he knew at once that he ought to have asked Patrick to think of something other than a warming pan for her to fetch. She held the long-handled, hot-coal-filled implement like a weapon of defense, and the way her eyes glittered, he did not doubt for a moment that she was thinking of using it as one.

Three

Diana stood still, knowing the instant her gaze met Calder's that he remembered her. She had suspected it when Patrick himself had ordered her to bring a warming pan to this chamber instead of relaying the order through someone else, but she had not dared to make excuses. Patrick had seemed amused, which meant he did not yet suspect her of helping Allan, and that meant Calder had not told him about her mother's escape from Edinburgh Castle. It was a pity, she thought, that her scruples forbade bashing his lordship over the head with the warming pan, and that circumstances prevented her instant departure from Castle Stalker.

The stillness grew unnerving. The warming pan felt heavy in her hands, and she jumped when a spark cracked in the fire. He seemed to fill the room, but still he did not speak. Instead, he watched her, perhaps waiting for her to say something, to condemn herself with her own tongue. He looked thoughtful but wary as his gaze flicked from her face to the warming pan and back.

Drawing a breath to steady herself, she said with forced calm, "I didna mean tae disturb ye, my lord. The master said

I was tae bring the pan and warm your bed.'' The instant the words left her tongue she wished them unsaid. With heat flooding her cheeks, she added hastily, ''That is, he said I were tae thrust this here warming pan beneath yon kivers ... and ... and—'' She broke off, unnerved even more by the enigmatic glint in his eyes.

He said quietly, ''I do want my bed warmed. Shut the door.''

She kicked it shut with her foot, shuddering at the dull thud of finality that cut off her last chance of escape. The red-gold firelight, flickering candles, and a haze of acrid smoke in the air made her fancy she had entered the devil's realm. Licking dry lips, she turned resolutely toward the narrow, curtained bed.

''One moment.''

The two words, softly spoken, stopped her in her tracks, but she did not look at him. She could scarcely breathe.

''My goblet is empty,'' he said. ''You may pour me more wine.''

Glancing at him, she caught sight of the flagon on the bench. ''The tappit hen sits yonder, behind your lordship,'' she said. ''Aye, and ye must ha' mistook it fer aught else. Ye can pour the wine yourself in half the time.''

''I do not wish to pour it myself. Must I complain to Patrick Campbell that his servants are slothful?''

''I dinna ken *slothful,*'' she said, lifting her chin, ''but if ye aim tae call me shiftless, I doot the master will believe ye. He kens weel that I work hard.''

''He kens little about you at all, Mab MacKissock,'' he said.

She swallowed hard, saying nothing.

''You know, do you not, that aiding a felon to escape is an offense for which you can be hanged.''

His words stirred a shiver of terror, but she dared not submit to it or she was finished: Collecting her wits and looking right at him, she said fretfully, ''But ye did let me go! I didna ken the lady's crime were sae great as that, nor mine neither.'' Relief flooded her when he frowned. So he was uncertain yet of her present guilt.

Watching her narrowly, he said, "I am speaking of the escape of one Allan Breck last night from this castle. He represents certain cowardly rebels who fled after Culloden to take up residence in France, and may mean to stir a new uprising. This is by no means the first time he has returned to make mischief here in Appin, but it is the first time we have caught him. I think you helped him escape."

Controlling her countenance with difficulty, for by nature she was open and frank, she said, "Och, now, how could I? I've naught tae do wi' any prisoners."

"You had better put that pan down on the hearth before you spill its contents on the floor," he said, retaining that narrow-eyed, suspicious look.

"I'm tae put it in your bed."

"I don't want it in my bed. If I've judged your character correctly, you'd spill a coal or two and I'd find myself burnt to a crisp by morning."

"In the event, you'd not find yourself at all," she retorted. At once she wished she had kept silent. Something about him stirred her to behave as she would with an equal, and one whom she liked at that. Surely it was not just his handsome face or well-built body, and just as surely, she was a fool if she let whatever it was seduce her into betraying herself. She must remember that she was a lowly serving girl, who owed him all due respect.

"Put that thing down as I bade you, and come here."

"Please, sir, I must do my task and get back tae the kitchen afore the master sends someone tae fetch me."

"He won't do that."

"I'm a good girl, sir. I came only to—"

"To warm my bed," he interjected. "Is that not what you said?"

"Aye, but not in the manner ye would wish," she said firmly.

"You are a most disobedient wench," he said with a sigh. "I have given you two orders, both of which you have brazenly ignored, and now you dare refuse the service that your master sent you here to perform. If I complain to him, you will get a good hiding, which, in my opinion, is exactly what you deserve.''

She knew he was right about what would happen to her, and she would get more than a hiding if he told Patrick Campbell about Edinburgh. Forcing a note of submission into her voice, she said hastily, ''I will set the warming pan on the hearth, sir since that is where you wish it, and I will gladly fill your goblet.''

''I thought perhaps you would,'' he murmured.

Swiftly she moved to set the long-handled pan on the hearth, but when she straightened, she found him standing between her and the bench where the flagon sat. He was more than a head taller than she was and much broader across shoulders and chest. Her gaze met the top button of his buff leather waistcoat. Staring at it, she moistened her lips again. ''Do ye mean tae let me pass, sir? I canna fill the goblet if I canna reach yon tappit hen.''

''I would first exact a price for your impertinence, Mab MacKissock.''

She looked up then and saw a new glint in his eyes. The firelight reflected in their gray depths warmed them, stirring again the odd fancy that she played with the devil. She could not seem to look away. She feared him, feared the power he held over her both with his rank and his knowledge of what she had done in Edinburgh. Yet she wanted to touch him, and she found the danger of her position exhilarating. He had not unmasked her, so he did not want her to die for her sins, and apparently he was willing to believe that she had not helped Allan escape.

''Well?'' he said.

''What price?'' But she knew. She knew perfectly well, and when he held her chin in one warm hand and tilted her face up, she did not resist. He surprised her by pulling off her mobcap with his other hand, freeing her dark curls to spread over her shoulders. His expression warmed with appreciation as he bent toward her.

His lips were warm, too, and soft against hers. Then they

firmed and pressed harder, and she felt a stirring in her body, a tingling deep within unlike anything she had felt before. Shocked by her feelings, she pulled back.

Calder smiled. "So you did not lie about being inexperienced," he said. His hand still held her chin, his fingers warm and strong.

"I do not lie!" The words came unbidden, spoken more fiercely than she had intended. Indeed, she had not meant to speak them at all, for in view of her present position, the declaration was ludicrous. Yet his suggestion that she might lie had offended her as much as such a charge ever had. Even in her recent activities, she had tried never to tell an outright falsehood. She was not a good liar, for one thing. She had too much tendency to say what she thought. For another, it was a matter of honor. The Campbells and the English authorities had none. Far better to defeat them without employing their own wicked methods. Hoodwinking them was one thing, outright wickedness another.

"I find it hard to believe that you have not deceived Patrick," he said wryly. He released her chin but still regarded her with sardonic suspicion.

Remembering her role, she said more calmly, choosing her words with care, "Misfortune ha' come upon me, sir, but I try tae do what's richt."

He stood aside. "Fetch the flagon then, Mab MacKissock, though I think you need the brandy more than I do. I'll give you a sip or two to relax you, and then you can warm my bed." His smile made it impossible to mistake his meaning.

Her hand shook when she picked up the pewter flagon, and she nearly spilled the brandy when he held out his goblet. It was one thing to slap away the hand of an impudent young soldier but quite another to resist the attentions of a noble guest in her master's house. Remembering Calder's threat to complain about her made her hand shake even more. Patrick Campbell would not hesitate, she knew, to order her whipped for insolence or obstinacy.

"You may put that down now," Calder said gently.

She did not want to step past him again, though she would have given much for a breath of fresh air from the open window to clear her head. But since it was not the smoke that had made her dizzy, the cool, clean air would doubtless do little to steady her. She felt a pulse beating in her throat, and her chest felt tight.

The last thing she wanted was to be ravished by this, or any, man. Neither did she wish to be beaten, however, and above all, she did not want to anger him into revealing what he knew of her to Patrick. If they began to ask questions about her, the maidservant and soldier whose illicit activities had allowed her to slip up to the tower might well admit their sin. Then the ferryman would own that she had begged him to take her across the water. She could not afford such questions.

"MacKissock is a common enough name in Perthshire," he said suddenly, "but I do not know any MacKissocks in Argyll. Who is your father?"

If she never heard the name MacKissock again, she decided, it would be too soon. Still clutching the flagon, thinking rapidly, she said, "My father is dead, sir. Most of the men in my family are dead." That was certainly true, and her eyes welled with unexpected tears at the thought.

"Don't weep," he said, reaching for her. "Have a sip of my brandy instead. It will calm you. Truly, I did not mean to make you sad."

Involuntarily, she stepped back until the warmth of the fire behind her warned her that she could go no farther. "Ye are kind, sir," she said, "but I mustna ha' any. If they smell it on my breath, I'll be in a peck of trouble."

"Not if I compel you to drink it." With his hand open but still outstretched, he took a step toward her.

Afraid a spark might set her skirt afire if she got any closer to the hearth, she skipped sideways, forgetting the long handle of the bed warmer until she kicked it. The pan tilted, its lid flipped up, and hot coals spilled to the hearthstones, scattering.

Calder, still moving toward her, jumped back again with a

yell and an oath, hopping on one foot in obvious pain. He wore only stockings on his feet.

Appalled, she cried, "Och, ye've burnt yourself!"

"Aye, and you spilled those coals on purpose!" Still hopping, he held the sore foot now with both hands, and she could see smoldering wool.

With presence of mind, she doused it with the remains of the brandy.

"Good God, what are you doing now? That's damned expensive brandy!"

"Would you rather have a charred foot?"

"You might have set my whole leg afire, wench! Have you never seen a flaming pudding at Christmas? What do you think makes the flames?"

"Brandy does, of course," she said tartly, "but not when it's poured over the pudding in a veritable waterfall." When he glanced at her in surprise, she realized she had forgotten her accent and added hastily, "I dinna ken why that is, sir, but 'tis quite true, I promise ye."

"True enough, I expect," he said, putting his brandy-soaked foot to the floor in a hesitant way at first, then more firmly. Taking the flagon from her, he put it back on the window bench. "Now I shall have to send for more brandy."

"Your stocking is all wet," she said.

"Aye, it is." The look he gave her boded no good.

"I . . . I'll fetch more brandy."

"You'll stay where you are. I have not finished with you yet."

"Please, sir," she said, feeling more desperate by the minute. " 'Tis sorry I am that ye burnt your foot, and sorry about the brandy, but I dinna want tae lie wi' ye, and I dinna want tae drink spirits. 'Tis wicked, the devil's ain brew, that. Ye can force me tae do your bidding, but I beg ye will not. Our minister says—"

"Spare me what your minister says," he said. "I've no wish for an unwilling bed partner. I just thought you might enjoy discovering what you have missed."

She held her tongue. She had thought him angry, but he did not seem so now, and the feeling of being trapped was dissipating in the face of his calm. He could still complain of her to Patrick, but she began to think he would not, and from that it was no great step to wonder if she could somehow exploit his evident attraction to her. She had dissuaded him rather easily from his intent to ravish her. Perhaps she could influence him just as easily to help her.

When he sat down on the window bench and pulled off his wet stocking, she took courage in hand and said, "Please, my lord, I didna mean tae offend ye. I ha' been affrighted the whole day long, since they learned of that rebel's escape. I ha' been here less than a sennight, ye see. I feared they would think I had helped him."

"As I thought," he said, watching her. "But you say you did not."

Though he spoke the words evenly, his tone did not fool her. With a deep sigh, she looked at her feet and said sadly, "Och then, ye dinna believe me. 'Tis but a matter of time now before Patrick Campbell sends for me, and I warrant he'll no believe me neither. These Campbells, they do be a fierce lot, ye ken."

"I do. I am a Campbell myself."

The admission shook her, though she ought to have known, she told herself, keeping her countenance with difficulty. The authority he displayed in Edinburgh ought to have told her. He was clearly a Scot, not an Englishman, and nowadays in Scotland, the only men with his air of distinction and authority were Campbells or their ilk. And here she was, pretending to be one of them. No wonder he had asked about her father. She nibbled her lower lip, trying to think how best to respond.

He said gently, "I thought you said you were a Campbell yourself."

"Aye, sure," she said, "but not from the same branch as Patrick. And not all Campbells be as fierce as these," she added, glancing at him from under her lashes.

"What do you want, Mab MacKissock?"

Hesitantly, as though she feared to anger him—which, in fact, she did—she said, "I didna ken what manner of household this were when I came. I hoped tae get work, but I did think Patrick Campbell's wife were a-living here with him, and would look out for the maids. Being amongst all these men frightens me, my lord. I doubt any lass could keep her innocence if she remained long beneath this roof."

"I repeat then, what do you want?"

"Do ye mean tae stay long at the castle, my lord?"

"I leave at dawn," he said, "for Balcardane."

"Balcardane?"

"Aye, my uncle is the Earl of Balcardane. Do you know his estate?"

She did, but she said thoughtfully, " 'Tis a castle on Loch Leven, is it not? I ha' family hereabouts, too, ye see. If I could but travel wi' ye as far as"—she thought swiftly—"as far as Glencoe . . . mayhap ye could explain tae Patrick Campbell that I be afeared tae tell him I want tae go. I ken weel that if I just up and leave before my half day, he will think 'tis because of that rebel escaping. And just the thought o' them asking me questions . . ." She looked into his eyes, widening hers as innocently as she could. "I'd be ever sae grateful if ye could, sir."

He stood up again, and suddenly she felt smaller and not nearly so confident. Her throat tightened, and she had all she could do to maintain eye contact with him. Then it occurred to her that she would be wiser not to maintain eye contact. No maidservant in her right mind would do so. With relief she looked down, forcing herself to breathe evenly, waiting to hear what he would say.

It surprised her to hear amusement in his voice when he said, "If we burn the place down, Patrick's not likely to listen to either of us."

Her gaze flew to him again, and she saw that he was looking at the floor behind her. Glancing back, she saw the scattered coals. Only one still glowed, and she stepped hastily upon it, saying, "I'll fetch the hearth broom."

He said nothing while she swept the coals into the fire.

When she straightened, he said, "I'll take you to Glencoe on one condition."

"Condition?" A tingling sensation shot up her spine.

"Aye, that you stay here with me tonight."

"But—" The tingling increased.

"No buts." With a crooked smile, he said, "I'll do your bidding but only if I can do it without having to answer to Patrick's mockery. He will never let me hear the end of it if you leave now, because he will know that you refused me and that I allowed it. He will wonder why I did, and indeed, I wonder at that myself."

"Ye said ye wouldna take me against my will," she reminded him.

"I meant it, but that does not mean I will enjoy hearing Patrick fling my generosity in my teeth. He will call it a want of resolution."

"He would dare?"

"He would. We went to school together. He lacks all proper respect."

He held her gaze, and as if he had said the words aloud, she knew he was thinking that she also lacked proper respect. To keep him from dwelling on the thought, she said, "I can sleep by the hearth, sir, if ye wish."

"I don't wish that at all." He hesitated, but glancing at the narrow bed, he frowned. "A pox on Patrick for not providing a larger bed for this chamber."

"I dinna care," she said. "It is no the first time I ha' slept on the floor."

"Where do you usually sleep?"

"On a pallet by the kitchen fire."

He frowned for a moment, then pulled the top quilt off the bed. "This will make an excellent pallet."

"I couldna!"

"Oh, yes, you can, and don't be thinking I shall freeze, for I won't, even if we leave that shutter open. There are two more coverlets on the bed, and I sleep warm." He began to unbutton his waistcoat, and when it occurred to her that he likely slept naked as well, she turned hastily away.

"I must fetch summat tae scrub that brandy from the floor," she said.

"Use the towel on the washstand," he said.

"I will not. 'Tis a perfectly good one, and scrubbing the floor will ruin it."

"Damn it, wench, stop arguing with everything I say, and do as I bid you!"

Without another word, she fetched the towel and ewer from the washstand, poured water onto the brandy, and wiped the floor. Sighing for the ruined towel but contenting herself with the thought that she would be beyond Patrick's reach before he discovered the infamy, she wrapped herself in the quilt and curled up on the hard floor, facing the fire. Watching the flames dance, she tried without success to keep images of the man behind her—doubtless naked now—from stealing into her mind.

Rory watched her. Clearly, she was no laundress or serving maid, despite what he had believed, for she had slipped more than once from rough dialect into more genteel tones. Perhaps she had served as a lady's maid to Lady Maclean. That would explain her willingness to risk her life for the Jacobite widow.

He wanted to confront her, even to shake the truth out of her, but since she was to leave Stalker with him, he could afford to be patient. Moreover, if he forced her to speak now, only to learn that she had served more than the token role he suspected in Allan Breck's escape, he would have to turn her over to Patrick for punishment. And Patrick, knowing he already had Argyll's wrath to face, would not be lenient. Rory doubted that Patrick would hang the wench, but he could not be certain, and even the small chance that he might was too great to risk.

To his surprise, he fell asleep at once, and to his consternation, he did not waken until Thomas shook him before dawn

the next morning. Since Rory did not instantly recall the events
of the night before, Thomas's grin caught him unaware.

"What's so funny, damn you?"

The wiry little man grinned wider. "I never knew a lassie
tae choose a hearthstone over your bed afore. Ye mun be losing
your touch."

"A blot on thy 'scutcheon to all futurity, Thomas. Fetch my
boots." He picked up the linen shirt he had cast aside the night
before and drew it on.

Thomas said, "Shall I wake her first, and send her about her
business?"

Rory did not look at him. "She goes with us."

"Does she now?"

Looking at him then, Rory saw that one of his eyebrows had
arched upward comically. "Hush your gob, Thomas," he said
sternly. "I'll have no disrespect today. Exert yourself instead
to remember my position and the deference due to it."

"Aye, sure, master." But Thomas was still looking at the
girl, who lay curled up like a kitten on the hearth, her dark
curls tumbling over her face, one hand fisted beneath her softly
rounded chin, and his response was almost offhand.

Sighing, Rory said, "I hope you've broken your fast, and
that you've brought us something to eat. I want to leave within
the hour."

"Aye, there's bread on the tray there, and ale in the flagon.
And I brought fresh ruffles for your shirt."

"I don't want them."

"Ye'll no be going tae Balcardane without them," Thomas
said indignantly. "Tae be puffing your consequence one minute
and dressing like a commoner the next. I ask ye, what of the
respect due tae me? Ye'll wear a proper wig and all, too."

"I will wear my tie-wig, plain ruffles, and no powder,
Thomas, so there's an end to it." Realizing that the girl had
wakened, he added, "Good morning. Forgive us for waking
you, but I want to be away before sun-up."

She sat up. "I am usually up long before now." Then, casting a wary look at Thomas, she added, "When must you be at Balcardane?"

"I wondered that m'self," Thomas muttered.

Rory shot him a warning look, but his henchman had already turned to take a pair of cambric ruffles from the box where he kept them. Looking at Diana, Rory said, "It won't take much above two hours to reach Balcardane, but Patrick is busy, and once I've made up my mind to leave a place, I'd as lief do so at once. Moreover, I've learned never to depend upon Highland weather, particularly at this time of year, and at the moment, it is neither raining nor snowing."

She nodded, getting up and shaking out the quilt. Ashes stirred on the hearth as she did, and she glanced at the remains of the previous night's fire. Thomas had not replenished it, knowing his master would want to depart at once.

"Have you things to collect?" Rory asked her.

She nodded. "One or two."

He knew she would want to attend to personal needs, too, as did he. "Run away and fetch what you need," he said, "and tell anyone who tries to stop you that you are following my orders. I will speak to Patrick when I have dressed."

She nibbled her lower lip, and he thought how kissable her lips were. Giving himself a mental shake, he added harshly, "Don't be long. We'll not wait for you."

When she had gone, he used the chamber pot, finished dressing, and wolfed a large chunk of bread from the loaf Thomas had brought. Then, downing a mug of ale, he said, "Have you ordered our horses?"

"Aye," Thomas said. "The lad went across an hour ago." Stalker's stables were on the mainland, the islet being too small to contain more than the tall towered castle. Few of the men possessed horses of their own, in any case, so the stables ashore were generally for the use of the captain, his family, and his guests.

Leaving Thomas to finish his chores, Rory sought out Patrick, finding him in the hall. His men, too, were up, and many had already gone to renew the search.

"You're off then," Patrick said, smiling at him.

"I am, and I'm taking the lass with me."

"You must have been more successful with her than I expected."

"She claims to have kin near Glencoe."

"I did not think she would stay. She's not like the other wenches."

"No."

Patrick fell silent, and Rory waited, knowing what was coming. Patrick was no fool. "You know," he said, "she has been here just a short while."

"Less than a sennight, she said."

Patrick nodded, holding Rory's gaze. "Someone helped Breck," he said.

"Aye, but you know well that his help came from outside," Rory said. "He did not push those bars out unaided, even if the stonework is soft."

"Someone had to tell them where to find him."

"Has she left the island since she arrived?"

"No, and that is the only reason I haven't interrogated her yet. No stranger has set foot inside these walls, what's more."

"Then I suggest you let me take her to Glencoe. I can keep an eye on her, learn where she goes and whom she meets, and then I can set someone to watch her afterward. If she knows aught of rebels, we'll soon discover it."

Patrick smiled wryly. "I should have known you were ahead of me." He held out his hand. "I'll see you again before you leave Appin, I trust."

"You will. I'll ask Balcardane to invite you to spend a night or two with us."

"I'd enjoy that. I visit Fort William from time to time, so perhaps I can stop at Balcardane on the way. As to your journey, my men have searched from here to Kentallen along the Loch Linnhe shore road, and east to Glen Creran. They will work their way south today, so you should encounter no rebels."

Rory smiled. "Do you think they would molest us if we did?"

"Most likely not," Patrick said. "We keep hearing rumors of trouble ahead, but things have been peaceful enough. Still, as the weather improves, who can say what will happen? We don't know precisely why Allan Breck has come, after all."

"His usual reason, I'm told, is to drum up more malcontents for the French."

"Aye, and to collect the so-called rents for Ardsheal and the other lairds in exile," Patrick said bitterly. "That alone might put a spark to the tinder if rebellion is in the wind. It's no wonder the folk hereabouts protest when they have to pay two landlords, their own and the government. They won't welcome you, Rory."

"I aim to keep my head low," Rory said. "I don't generally go about reciting my titles to folks, in any case. If you'd like to help, just mention now and again that I've come to visit Balcardane and renew my childhood acquaintance with the area."

Patrick nodded, and the two made their farewells. Soon afterward, as the ferryman took Rory, Thomas, and the girl across to the mainland, the sun splashed its first golden rays of the day across the deep-blue waters of the loch.

The girl protested briefly when Rory told her to ride pillion behind Thomas.

"I can quite easily walk behind you," she said. "You won't go too fast."

"Would you rather ride with me?"

Without another word, she allowed Thomas to pull her up behind him, and they rode in silence along the well-traveled but presently deserted dirt road that followed the shore of the loch. A steep, thickly wooded hillside, carpeted with lush green bracken, sloped up away from them. Stout oak and beech trees, beginning to show new spring leaves, mixed with thick evergreens overhanging the road. The woods were silent, as if the inhabitants had not yet wakened. But as that thought crossed

Rory's mind, a squirrel chattered angrily, and another answered it. Their angry debate made him smile.

As he did, he caught a glimpse of movement from the hillside, and turned his head. Something large and heavy struck him painfully, knocking him from his saddle. He lay stunned on the hard-packed ground.

Four

Diana, riding with Thomas, saw the tightly curled body hurtle out of the trees like a human cannonball toward Calder. She did not see the rope at first, and so when Bardie swung back into the dense woods again after knocking Calder from his saddle, the sight surprised her almost as much as had the attack. Feeling Thomas reach for something, she leaned forward and grabbed his hand just as three men erupted from the hillside shrubbery. They yanked him from the saddle and took his pistol. A moment later, she slid down into her cousin's upstretched arms.

Knowing better than to name names, she gave him a quick, welcoming hug and said, "Why are you still here? There are soldiers everywhere!"

"There are none here," Allan Breck said, grinning at her, his blue eyes dancing with mischief. He wore the dark blue coat and red waistcoat of his French regimentals over dun-colored breeches. "They've moved to the south," he added. "I've got eyes and ears everywhere, lass. Did you think we'd leave you behind?"

"Hush," she said, casting a glance at Calder, who was stirring, and another at Thomas, struggling angrily in her brother's grip.

Allan's servant, Fergus Gray, smashed his fist into Thomas's face, whereupon Thomas sagged in Neil's arms and the lad dumped him unceremoniously to the ground. Pulling a *skean-ochil* from his boot, Fergus turned toward Calder.

Instantly discerning his intent, Diana snapped, "No! Don't kill him. Stop him," she added urgently, clutching Allan Breck's arm.

Allan checked Fergus with a gesture but scowled at Diana and said in Gaelic, "I do not like leaving witnesses, lass. Certainly not Campbell witnesses."

"Tie and gag him," Diana said to Fergus in the same language. Then, to her brother, she said, "Do the same to Thomas, and make sure neither can free himself quickly." Knowing that Neil would obey but uncertain of Fergus, she turned back to Allan, saying insistently, "You must not kill them. Calder is close kin to Argyll, and the duke's men would punish every family in Appin to avenge his death. You were in France when the Duke of Cumberland wreaked havoc here after Culloden, but I remember how it was, and I don't want it to happen again if I can prevent it."

"She is right," Bardie Gillonie said in his gravelly voice as he slid down the hillside behind them. He, too, spoke the Gaelic. "No reason to bring the whole lot of them down on us. Speaking of Campbells," he added, glancing back anxiously over one shoulder as his feet hit the path, "I heard a whistle just now."

Diana saw with approval that Bardie kept out of Calder's line of sight. His lordship would remember her all too well, but he could not have seen Bardie before the attack, and she doubted that even Thomas, now stirring awkwardly in his bonds, had seen enough to realize how easily the dwarf could be identified. Sliding on his backside Bardie had looked almost normal, albeit shorter than most men, but on his feet, his deformity was obvious. With stunted legs too short to carry his large torso easily, his gait was lurching and ungainly.

He grinned at her, revealing surprisingly white, even teeth.

She had always thought his smile his best feature, but running a close second were the richly dark, expressive eyes set deep beneath shaggy dark brows in his overlarge head. He had a big bony nose and chin, huge hands, and amazingly muscular shoulders. Presently wearing a leather waistcoat and breeches, he was clean shaven and wore his dark hair tied back, as always, in a black bag at the nape of his short, thick neck.

"Expected you last night, lass," he said. "We had the devil's own time of it, keeping out of sight of Patrick Campbell's louts, though in fairness, there was little danger of them catching us. Never saw such a bunch of blind beggars in all my life. Must have prowled under our trees all of fifty times these two nights past. Grew downright wearisome till they went to bed and let us get some sleep."

"I could not get away before," Diana said. "They have strict rules about when females can go out. I tried to leave at once, of course, but the ferryman would not bring me across. He said Patrick Campbell would have his head for it."

Bardie frowned. "But that ferryman is a Bethune of Craignure, is he not?"

Neil said, "He is." He looked at Diana. "Did you tell him who you are?"

It occurred to her that they all had assumed neither of their captives spoke Gaelic, and she realized in a rush of alarm that such an assumption might prove disastrous. "We had better go," she said, shooting a look at her cousin.

He nodded, glancing at the captives with a speculative expression that showed he had instantly understood her caution. "Are they well tied?"

"Aye," Neil and Fergus said as one.

"Drag them into the shrubbery then, and be quick about it," Allan said. He cocked his head, listening. "Another whistle. They are coming this way. Bring that other horse," he said to Diana as he snatched up the reins of Calder's gray.

She saw then that Fergus had blindfolded his lordship, and felt some relief, hoping he had not seen any of the men clearly enough to identify later. Of them all, the one he most likely had seen plainest was Allan, and of them all, Allan would be the most careful, for his very life depended on it.

Many people in Appin country knew him, and although most would not betray him, he was well able to look after himself. That he was still alive after six years of paying cat-and-mouse visits to Scotland from France proved that much.

Still, she said, "We cannot steal their horses."

"Not steal, borrow," he said, smiling at her. "The men from Stalker are coming from the south, so we shall ride north for a mile or two before we turn the beasts loose in the woods. When they find them, they'll scour the area thereabouts, searching for these two, because I'll wager anything you like that they will pass by here without seeing them." Signing to Fergus, he said, "You'll ride with me, and you," he added with a nod at Neil, "will ride with her."

Diana said, "But what about—?"

Quickly cutting in, Bardie said, "I'll look after myself, lass. I'm as safe in the woods as anyone could be. I'm sure," he added dryly, "that himself knows that as well as anyone. Always thinks of others, he does, so large of mind as he is."

Allan shot him a sour look but said calmly to Diana, "He hates riding. You know that. He is afraid of horses and boats, and God knows what else."

"He risked his life to save yours, however. You might show more gratitude."

Ignoring Allan, Bardie said, "Don't fret for me, lass. I have my own trails, and I'll be home through the forest before anyone knows I've been away."

Allan said no more, and once Neil and Fergus had dragged Calder and Thomas well off the path, Neil mounted Thomas's horse and reached down a hand to Diana. "Hurry," he said. "I can hear them now. I thought they were all moving south, but one party must have turned back this way."

"Patrick Campbell knows Calder is riding toward Balcardane," she said, letting him pull her up behind him. "Doubtless he diverted a few men to keep an eye on him. We can be grateful he did not think to do it before now."

"Don't stand about gabbing," Allan said, reverting to English. Setting Calder's gray to a trot, he led the way with Fergus clinging behind. The last glimpse Diana had of Bardie was as he scrambled up the hillside and burrowed into the thick bracken beneath the densely growing trees. He would be safe, she knew. The woods thereabouts were too thick for riders, even for most men on foot, and if soldiers later chanced to see him in the forest, they would have no reason to accost him.

Leaning forward, she hugged her brother, saying, "I'm glad to see you, but you took a dreadful risk. I'd have got away on my own eventually, you know."

"We didn't know," he retorted. "Allan said he did not think Patrick Campbell would suspect you, but I wasn't as certain, so if we are to talk of taking chances, we'll soon be at outs with each other, Diana. Did they give you any trouble?"

"Not until last night," she said. "Some tried to take liberties, of course, but I expected that, and the only difficulty was making myself remember that I could not just tell them to keep their hands to themselves. But last night was different," she admitted with a grimace she knew he could not see.

"What was different about last night?" Neil sounded merely curious, but she was glad he was the one asking, and not her cousin. Before she had thought of an acceptable reply, he added, "I expected your greatest trouble to come immediately after they discovered Allan had got away."

"Well, it didn't, for I was lucky. No one saw me near the tower, so no one had cause to suspect me. They would have got round to me soon enough, but Calder's arrival made rather a big difference."

"Why were you riding with him today? If he is kin to Argyll, I should have thought you'd keep well clear of him."

"I don't know if you recall all that happened in Edinburgh," she said, keeping her voice low, although the chance that it would carry above the sound of the horses' hoofbeats to the riders ahead of them was slim.

"I remember that you insisted you should be the only one to go inside the castle," Neil said. "I still say—"

"It would have been foolish for you to go," she said, as she had at the time. "Men are always more suspicious of other men than they are of women. But never mind that now. I met Calder there that day."

"Good God! Is he the visitor you told us about? I didn't recall his name."

Since she had not decided how much she ought to reveal about her confrontation with Calder, she was glad when Allan chose that moment to rein in and say, "We'll leave the horses here."

They had reached an arched stone bridge over a little burn that tumbled merrily over rocks and stones in its haste to reach the loch. To their right lay a steep-sided, lushly green glen that over the centuries the rushing water had carved into the mountain. Leathery ferns hugged the base of every oak, beech, and hazel tree, and some even grew in the forks of high branches. Patches of orange, gray, and black lichen and bright green moss crept upward, even on the pines, painting their bark with color. Honeysuckle and giant ivy draped otherwise bare oak and hazel branches, and the scent of rich, damp earth drifted from the glen's dark depths.

In surprise Neil said, "You want to stop? We've gone less than a mile!"

"All the same, lad, we'll leave the horses in this wee glen and take to the ridge top. We've been fortunate not to meet anyone else, but we cannot hope that will continue. Folks are out and about now, and the last thing we want is for anyone to remember us with these horses. This gray I'm riding is too easy to describe. It's bad enough that we've had to keep to the shore road this long, but till now we've had no easy access for these nags into the woods."

By the time he finished speaking, the others had dismounted. Neil bent to get a drink, and then they quickly led both animals along the burn, up the narrow glen, into the woodland. Finding a deer trail, they followed that up away from the water for a hundred yards, then released the horses and walked on without them toward a ridge where the trees grew less densely. Still well below the crags with their treacherous scree, they wended their way along a low, winding ridge that connected several glens, some sloping west, their burns feeding Loch Linnhe, and others sloping east into Glen Creran and Glen Ure. Bardie was undoubtedly traveling in the same general direction, but they saw no sign of him.

They did not talk. Conversation would not travel far in the woods, and they could be fairly certain the enemy did not lurk among the granite boulders and open, heather-covered stretches above them, but the others knew that Allan was listening to the animals for any odd silence or chattered warning of enemies approaching.

Their own silence reassured the forest creatures that they meant no harm, and soon the anxious twittering of the birds returned to song. The cawing of the rooks grew deeper and more resonant. The only strident note came from a blackbird that erupted from a thicket with an angry scream as they approached, foolishly revealing the location of his mate's nest.

Two hours later, as they walked west down Glen Duror, accompanied by the roar of its frothing, icy river, Diana felt little surprise to see a doe heavy with fawn gingerly make her way to the bank to drink, heedless of their passage. Snowdrifts lingered in shadows, but signs of spring appeared everywhere. Buds seemed to swell before her eyes, while masses of herbs in leaf and early bloomers like the tiny forest daisies, chickweed, and dandelions created a colorful carpet beneath her feet.

She began to feel a familiar sense of homecoming. It was the first time she could recall feeling the sensation about the gray stone, slate-roofed house on the hill above Cuil Bay. She still retained strong feelings for her family's ancient home on the Island of Mull, overlooking the convergence of the Sound of Mull with the Firth of Lorne. One of the most recent Maclean strongholds to fall to the enemy, Castle Craignure had been forfeited after Culloden and her father's death. Its lands legally belonged to the Crown now, but she did not doubt that one day a Campbell would live there. They had taken over nearly every other piece of Maclean land on Mull and elsewhere. Had her mother's family not been willing to provide Lady Maclean and her children with a home, they would have had to beg for their bread.

Despite living now in Appin country, dependent on the Appin Stewarts, Lady Maclean still took an interest in her late husband's tenants. Thus, when many had been unable to find fuel for their home fires over a particularly harsh winter, she had ordered trees at Craignure cut for firewood and had refused to disburse the rents that many insisted on paying to her. Those two crimes had brought her to the notice of the authorities, specifically Red Colin Glenure, the Crown factor, who ordered her arrest. Although it was not yet safe for her ladyship to return from Glen Drumin, Mary would be waiting at home for Diana and Neil, glad to have them back again. She would not be so glad to see Allan, however, Diana thought with a sigh.

They had emerged from the thickest part of the woods, and Diana realized that in her enjoyment of the forest and the welcome signs of spring, she had allowed the distance to widen between herself and the men. She hurried to catch up.

"Allan," she said, "were you expecting to stay with us? Because if you were, I should perhaps tell you—"

"We'll stop at Aucharn," he said, cutting in without apology, as was his too-frequent habit. "We must pass right by it, and James will want to know I'm safe. I need stay in the area only the one night, Diana, because I'm for Rannoch Moor tomorrow, but there are arrangements I must make. James will help me, I'm sure."

Diana was not so certain that James Stewart would welcome Allan's arrival. Ever since the new factor had arrived the previous year to take James's place, there had been increasing enmity between the two, and she knew Red Colin would like nothing better than to learn that James had harbored a fugitive. She would leave that for James to explain, however. Making Allan realize that everyone at Maclean House might not welcome him was more important now.

She, her mother, Neil, and their cousin Mary Maclaine shared the gray stone house at the pleasure of the exiled Laird of

Ardsheal, who had the honor to be Lady Maclean's brother. The late Sir Hector Maclean's land on the Island of Mull having been confiscated—there could be no other word for it—after the tragic loss at Culloden, Ardsheal had provided his sister and her children with the house known now as Maclean House, at a peppercorn rent. That he had been able to do so was due entirely to James Stewart's having been Crown factor at the time and having agreed to allow Lady Maclean's tenancy of the house and the land surrounding it.

It was that sort of thing, Diana mused now, that had got James into trouble with the authorities and had given the powerful Barons of the Scottish Exchequer an excuse to replace him with Colin Campbell. The Campbells and the wicked Duke of Cumberland—a man even the English called the Butcher— had said James was too lenient with rebel families, and perhaps he was. But he was a fair man, too, well loved and respected in Appin country.

People did not like Red Colin. They barely tolerated him, and people across the loch on Cameron lands were actively hostile. Since his mother was a Cameron, they—quite sensibly in Diana's opinion—considered him a traitor to the clan.

They soon came to Aucharn, James Stewart's farmhouse nestled in a clearing a mile or so from the mouth of the glen. Before they had crossed the stable yard, James hurried out of the house to greet them. He was a small, wiry man in his late fifties, not much above five and a half feet tall.

"Allan, is that you?" he demanded, striding forward. "Lord bless me, lad, but you're taking the devil of a chance! They are searching high and low for you. 'Tis only by the greatest good fortune that there are no men watching this place now."

"Good fortune favors me," Allan said with a grin, putting out his hand. "How are you, James? As you might have guessed, your prodigal needs a bit of help, but I'll stay only overnight, then take myself out of your hair. I mean to visit my mother in Rannoch, and see what I can do to drum up recruits there for Ogilvy's regiment. I trust you will have the second rents for me when I return."

James grimaced. "As to that, lad, I'll do what I can, but it won't be as much as last time. Folks haven't got any extra money, and that's the plain truth. They did not mind scrimping and scraping to help look after Lady Ardsheal and her children after Culloden, but once she went to join her husband . . . Well, the truth is, folks are tired of paying their rents twice, and I can do little about that."

"Dash it all," Allan said angrily, "they should pay the rent to their lawful landlords, not to the blasted Campbells for the English Crown. Appin folk are a spineless lot, that's what. They should throw the Campbells out, beginning with that cursed devil's spawn who took your place. Where is their loyalty to their own?"

"That will do, Allan Breck," James said firmly. "After living with me for most of your youth, you should know better than to complain of such things. I know what is due to Ardsheal, none better. He is my half-brother, after all. But he is in France, playing croquet on the archbishop's lawn, not here, facing Colin Glenure."

Diana held her breath, knowing of old that her cousin's temper could flare dangerously when someone crossed his will, but although he flushed at the mild reprimand, he did not attempt to argue with James. That was not really surprising, since most people respected James. Not only did he run Aucharn farm but he was a small-scale entrepreneur with a dozen irons in the fire, and he was educated. It was to him that Appin people turned when baffled by legal and financial problems.

James was a kind man, too, and generous. Over the years, he had fostered a succession of orphan children in his household, including Allan himself, for Allan's father, a man of some notoriety and few scruples, had died when Allan was ten. As a result of James's knowledge and many kindnesses, he was well known and needed no further identification anywhere in Appin or Lochaber than "James of the Glen."

As tacksman for Ardsheal, although he was no longer the Crown factor, he was still responsible for vast portions of the estate, including Maclean House. As a natural son of the fourth

Laird of Ardsheal, he was half-brother not just to the present laird but also to Lady Maclean.

Allan said now in an offhand way, "I hope you don't mean to send me away, for I do need a place to sleep tonight, and Diana don't want me at Maclean House."

James clapped him on the back. "You know you always have a bed here with me and Margaret and the lads, Allan. Just keep out of sight, and don't frighten her by saying the Campbells know you're in Appin country. She knows never to speak your name abroad, so she won't talk out of turn."

"I thought you said they searched here already," Neil said.

"So they did, but Margaret was off walking in the woods with your cousin Mary at the time, and she never laid eyes on them."

"With Mary, was she?" Allan shook his head. "I'm surprised Mary didn't see the soldiers in a vision—aye, and me, as well—and warn Margaret all about us."

Diana said tartly, "You know Mary would not give you away, Allan, so don't say such things. You also know that her visions don't come on command, and that she rarely sees things other than extreme danger or death when they strike someone near and dear to her. Faith, she saw my father's death and those of her brothers at Culloden, which is nothing to mock, sir. I promise you, if you mean to plague her about the Sight, you'll not find yourself welcome at Maclean House now or later."

"I'll pay my respects to your mother nonetheless, my dear," he said, looking down at her in the superior way he had perfected when they were children.

"You won't, for she is not there," Diana said. "I thought someone must have told you that. Red Colin had her arrested for felling trees on our old estate, and for failing to turn over the rents people still insist upon paying her instead of him. He said she refused to show respect for the proper authorities, and he had her cast into Edinburgh Castle prison."

"He *what?*" Allan's eyes blazed, and he turned on Neil. "Why the devil did you not tell me of this outrage at once?"

"Thought you knew," Neil said with a shrug. "It's ancient

news hereabouts, and you never asked about her. You did not ask about anyone, in fact, except Diana. You spent most of last night and the night before telling Bardie and me about your grand exploits in France and how delightful it is there, and how much I should like it if I were to join Ogilvy's French regiment.''

Diana glared at her cousin. "You must not try to recruit Neil. Just who do you suppose will look after Mam and the rest of us if you take him back with you?''

"He don't want to go," Allan said, "but that is of no concern now. I cannot believe anyone would be so daft as to put your mother in prison. Red Colin has much to answer for. Someone ought to spit him and roast him to a slow turn.''

Feeling much in sympathy with that notion, Diana smiled at him and said, "You needn't take him on for Mam's sake. She is free now. I meant only that she is not at Maclean House, and won't be there for some time yet to come.''

"Where is she?''

"She is safe, Allan. You are the one who taught me never to talk about such things, not to anyone, you said, lest I let a cat out of the bag. I make it a practice to tell no one, but though you have no need to know where, I promise you she is safe.''

To her surprise, he nodded and said with a chuckle, "Good lass. Stick to that buckle and thong, and you won't go wrong. I take it then that the authorities did not release her voluntarily.''

Diana smiled. "No, they did not.''

Allan looked at Neil again. "I never would have thought you'd grow up to such advantage, lad. Who helped you set her free?''

Diana bristled but relaxed at once when she saw Neil's eyes begin to dance. "I was there," he said, "but I did not set foot inside the castle walls. Diana did it all. She insisted that we ride to Edinburgh even though snow still lay thick on the ground, especially in Glen—in the higher glens," he amended hastily with a rueful glance at his sister. Then he looked away from her again and added on a purposeful note, "The fellow that Bardie knocked off his horse earlier . . ." Though he paused and shot another apologetic look at Diana, he went on determinedly, ''You ought to know that Diana met him in Edinburgh, and he recognized her at Castle Stalker.''

Diana had definitely not wanted to discuss Calder with her cousin, but she gave Neil full marks for diversionary tactics, because Allan's eyes hardened at once with speculation. She knew he was no longer thinking about Lady Maclean's whereabouts or stewing about Red Colin's having replaced James as factor.

''What was Calder doing in Edinburgh?'' he demanded.

Diana shrugged. ''He was visiting the prison governor,'' she said, going on glibly to explain how she had freed her mother, and how Calder had believed her to be an innocent laundress. ''Even at Stalker, he did not question my being a maidservant,'' she added. She did not mention that he had asked Patrick Campbell to send her to his bedchamber, but her expression must have revealed more than she realized, for her cousin frowned.

He said sternly, ''Just how did you come to meet him there?''

''I told you, he is kin to Argyll,'' she said. ''He was visiting Patrick Campbell with messages from the duke. And, too, he said that he and Patrick went to school together when they were lads.''

''I don't like the sound of that,'' Allan said. ''What if he is searching for your mother? What if he knows who you are and hid the knowledge from you in the hope that you would lead him to her? Why were you with him this morning at all if he thought you no more than a simple maidservant?''

''Because of you,'' she said instantly.

''Here now, Miss Diana,'' James said, chuckling. ''We cannot hold Allan responsible for all the ills that befall us. How could that have been his doing?''

''Because he escaped, of course. I told Calder I was afraid that once Patrick and his men stopped searching for the missing prisoner, they would begin to wonder which of us in the castle had helped him escape. Since I was the newest maidservant, I feared they would suspect me. I also told him that I had not expected to serve in an all-male establishment, that I had believed the captain's lady would be living there with him. Since she was not, I said, I feared for my virtue.''

Allan chuckled and said, ''Clever thinking, but mind you don't do that sort of thing again. You've got a lot of spunk for a lass, and I'll warrant you can outthink most men, but you are still a lady, Diana. You ought to behave like one.''

She stuck out her tongue at him, and the others laughed.

James said, ''If you mean to stay here, Allan, you'd best get your gear inside and let Neil and Diana get on home. You and I have much to talk about, I expect, and it won't do for you to show yourself too openly.''

Allan agreed, but as Diana and Neil turned away, he said, ''When you send a message to your mother, include my regards and the laird's, will you? Tell her I'll be in Appin country or Lochaber for some time before I return to France, so if she wants to see me or to send a message to Ardsheal, she need only let me know.''

''Aye,'' Diana said, ''I'll tell her. And thank you, Allan, for rescuing me.''

''Tit for tat, lass, tit for tat.'' He kissed her on the cheek, bade Neil farewell, and strode into the house with James and Fergus Gray.

Leaving Aucharn, Diana and Neil followed the river path to the mouth of the glen, through the clachan of gray stone, thatched-roof cottages known as Inshaig. Little more than a half hour later, following the loch shore, they arrived at the gray stone house perched in a grassy meadow overlooking Loch Linnhe at the south end of Cuil Bay, which had been their home for the past six years.

They found their cousin Mary cleaning vegetables in the kitchen with the maid, Morag MacArthur. Mary saw them first and rushed to greet them, pushing loosened strands of her thick tawny hair back behind her ears. ''Thank heaven,'' she said. ''I have been having the oddest feelings these past two days, like some internal creature gnawing at my mind. It disappeared this morning, but since nothing had changed as far as I knew, I have been in something of a worry.''

Neil, hugging her, said, ''You should know better. I warrant you feared Alian would leave Diana behind, but it was no such thing. Since she was in a den of Campbells, as he said, he would have stayed for her even if Bardie and I had not been with him. He risked his life for her, Mary, just as he risks the rope every time he sets foot in Scotland. And now that they've caught him once, only to lose him, they are all the more determined to capture him again.''

''I know,'' Mary said in her soft voice, ''but Diana was risking her life, too, Neil, and much more than that.'' She looked searchingly at Diana, her light gray eyes shrewd and her gaze penetrating, but she asked no awkward questions, suggesting with her gentle smile only that Diana must be hungry.

''Famished,'' Diana told her. ''I had a bite this morning, but nothing since.''

''Well, we've got some salmon that Morag caught this morning, cucumbers that Bardie brought us from his garden, our own potatoes, and a baked custard. Not a feast, but you will both feel better after you eat. Then you can tell me the rest.''

''I'm going to wash my face,'' Diana said, walking through the kitchen to the long, narrow scullery, where she poured water from a ewer into the basin. Though she knew that Mary would want to hear every detail, she was not certain just how much she wanted to tell her about the enigmatic Lord Calder.

Five

Rory struggled with his bonds after his attackers left, cursing himself for a fool with every writhing, painful movement. He could hear Thomas grunting a short distance away, and when he finally was able to rub the gag from his mouth, he called to him in a low voice.

Another grunt was Thomas's only reply.

"Push your face against the ground, man, or hook the cloth on a branch and pull it away," he said, still taking care to talk no louder than necessary.

"Are ye hurt, lad?" Thomas asked gruffly a moment later.

"My dignity more than my body," Rory admitted. "To be taken unaware because I let Patrick lull me into a sense of safety makes me feel like a damned fool, Thomas. I should know better than to let down my guard so easily."

"Aye, ye should," Thomas agreed.

"Thank you," Rory said dryly. "What little Gaelic I remember from my boyhood proved insufficient to follow what they said. Did you understand them?"

"Enough tae ken their leader was Patrick Campbell's missing prisoner, and that the lass stopped him from murdering us. She knows ye be kin tae his grace, and fears he would exact a vengeance equal tae Cumberland's.''

"He would not," Rory said with distaste. He had no use for the Butcher and had been at one with Argyll, for once, when the duke exerted every ounce of influence he possessed to force Cumberland's recall to England from Scotland.

Thomas said, "The lass said, too, that she would have got away last night but for the ferryman. He refused tae take her off the islet.''

"Good for the ferryman," Rory said.

"Aye, but they all seemed tae think the man ought tae have taken her. He's a Bethune, they said, and one of them asked if she had told the man who she is.''

Rory frowned. He could think of no peaceful connection between the MacKissocks and Bethunes, although marriage between members of even the most contentious clans was not unheard of.

"Whisst now," Thomas said. "There's that whistling again. Like as not they are searching the woods tae the south near the castle, and they'll soon be upon us. On this steep slope, we can roll tae the road in a pig's whisper and—''

"We'll do no such thing," Rory said with a grimace.

"Ye'd rather lie here till we rot?''

"If you think I want Patrick to learn how easily they took us, you are very much mistaken. I doubt that our captors will brag of it to anyone, for they won't want word to reach the authorities any more than I do, so keep still.''

Not only did he want to avoid Patrick's gleeful mockery, but he intended to find and punish Mab MacKissock himself. Just thinking of her golden eyes and the way her skin had flushed when she realized he wanted her made his palms itch to touch her again. Only this time, he would put her right across his knee and—

The sounds of approaching horses and riders pulled him from what was rapidly becoming a most satisfactory fantasy. Irritated, he muttered, "Mind, Thomas, not a sound, or I swear I'll turn you off without a character.''

"Just how do ye think we will free ourselves if ye refuse tae shout for help?" Thomas demanded indignantly.

"Fortune always leaves some door open, Thomas. Now, hush."

Thomas growled but remained obediently silent while a party of four riders passed, and although it required more effort than Rory's words had implied, they freed themselves not long afterward.

Walking along the road at a good pace, they soon came to an arched stone bridge over a burn. Having noted that until now the steep, densely wooded bank had made leaving the road nearly impossible, Rory decided the moment he saw the narrow glen formed by the burn that his captors had left the path there. He could tell little from tracks near the bridge, because the party of four had obliterated earlier marks, but by leaping from boulder to boulder across the brook, he soon found hoofprints in the damp, peaty earth on the far side.

Following these, giving a high-pitched whistle from time to time, it was not long before he heard Rosinante whinny in response. He whistled again, and the gray gelding soon appeared with Thomas's mount trailing docilely behind it.

With ten miles to go before they would reach Loch Leven and Balcardane Castle, Rory set a fast pace. They reached Cuil Bay soon after noon, and Kentallen Inn a half hour later. Running into the party from Castle Stalker at the inn, he responded to their surprised questions by saying that he and Thomas had taken time to explore a small glen they had come upon along the way.

When one man pointed out that Glen Duror, not far from the inn, was much more worthy of exploration, Rory laughed and said, "We've dawdled enough for one day, I think. Is there not a short way to Balcardane that passes through Lettermore Woods? I seem to recall such a path from my boyhood."

"Aye, sir," the same man replied. "The turning be just past the village of Kentallen a mile yonder. Once in the woods, the right fork of the path will bring you out near Balcardane. That fork bypasses Ballachulish and the ferry, which, as you may also recall, takes one across the narrows where Loch Linnhe meets Loch Leven. The left-hand fork shoots right down to the ferry, so folks can get there—or get here from there—without having to wind all along the shore road.''

Thanking him for the directions, which he had elicited as a diversion and not because he required them, Rory was soon on his way again with Thomas.

Lettermore Woods—a dense forest of oaks, Caledonian pines, Scots fir, and larches, carpeted with bracken—was shady and peaceful, the only noise the distant cries of gulls and ospreys, a nearby twittering of forest birds, and the rustling of leaves disturbed by what little breeze slipped through the foliage. When they reached the ridge top, Rory got his first clear view of Loch Leven and Balcardane.

The great stone castle with its prominent square tower nestled snugly in a hazel grove on the hillside, overlooking the loch. Balcardane was a recent addition to the Campbell holdings, for his grandfather had acquired it only after the rising of 1715. Since most Campbell strongholds lay in country south and east of Appin, Balcardane, deep in Stewart country, provided a certain strategic advantage.

When they arrived at the castle, the porter guided Rory directly from the courtyard entrance through the great hall to a pleasant drawing room overlooking the gray waters of Loch Leven. A fire crackled in the white-marble fireplace, and the room smelled lightly of wood smoke and dried roses.

The room's lone occupant, sitting near the window with her tambour frame, was a plump lady in a rather worn but fashionably wide-skirted pink and silver striped afternoon frock and a gaily embroidered white apron. Atop mouse-brown hair arranged in complex twists and side curls, her frilly cap twitched rhythmically as she plied her needle, oblivious of the interruption.

When the porter announced Rory by his title, she looked up in surprise over wire-rimmed spectacles that had slipped down her nose and said, ''Lord Calder? Good gracious, Rory, is that you, my dear?''

"Yes, Aunt Agnes," he said, striding forward with a smile to make his bow. "Did no one tell you that I was coming to visit you?"

"Oh, very likely they did, but I rarely recall what I'm told, as Balcardane frequently reminds me," she said with a worried look as she pushed her spectacles back up where they belonged. "In truth, no one ever seems to tell me anything, or to listen to what I tell them, but then I so rarely ever talk to anyone that perhaps that is not a fair declaration to make, or a truthful one, for that matter. Oh, there you are, dear sir," she added without pausing for breath when the fourth Earl of Balcardane entered the room, frowning. "Only look who is here, sir. It is our dear Rory Campbell, only he is Lord Calder now, of course." To Rory she added sympathetically, "We were prodigiously sorry to learn of your poor papa's death, my dear. Lud, but 'tis nearly two years ago now since he died, is it not?"

"It's been three years," Balcardane snapped. "Cease your prattle, woman, and let the poor man sit down." Holding out a hand to his nephew, he said, "Good to see you, lad, good to see you. How is your mother getting on these days?"

"In excellent health when last I saw her," Rory said, shaking hands with him. "I spent the winter between Edinburgh and London with the duke, however."

"Splendid," Balcardane said, "but dashed expensive company, I'll wager."

Wearing a brown frock coat, buckskin breeches, and top boots, he was a burly man of some fifty summers with graying hair, pale blue eyes, and what appeared to be a perpetual frown. As he sat in a chair near his wife's and signed to Rory to draw up another, Balcardane inspected him with a keen gaze, but if Rory expected a polite compliment to follow, he soon learned his error.

"Those boots must have set you back thirty guineas or more," Balcardane said with disapproval. "Ought to see that your man keeps them better polished, for they are all over mud—your coat, too. Your cousin Duncan will put you to shame, damned if he won't. Dresses fine as fivepence, does

Duncan." He sighed. "Don't know how he affords it. I don't give him more than his due, I promise you."

Lady Balcardane had returned her attention to her work, but she looked up over her spectacles again to say placidly, "Duncan always looks very fine, to be sure, my lord. But it is scarcely fair to scold poor Rory for having got a bit of mud on his clothes when he has only just arrived after a long journey."

Balcardane said as if she had not spoken, "How long do you stay, lad? Hope you ain't brought a large party. Costs money to feed folks, you know."

"No party, sir, but I'd like to remain for a month or so, if I may. I have come from Inveraray by way of Kilchurn, Dunstaffnage, and Stalker, so I have an assortment of messages for you, as you might imagine. However, there is nothing so pressing that we need bore my aunt with them."

"You still gracing the court?" Balcardane asked.

"Court?" Lady Balcardane looked up again. "Have you been to court, dear? Did you make your bow to King George? How prodigiously thrilling for you!"

"Don't chatter of things you know nothing about," Balcardane growled, shifting impatiently in his chair.

"Yes, dear," she said, "but I do think it is unfair to say I chatter when as anyone can tell you, I scarcely ever say a word. As silent as a grave I am most of the time. Lud, sir, I don't know how my vocal chords stay in order, so little use as they get. Oh, Duncan," she added happily as her attention shifted to the doorway, "just see who has come to stay with us. 'Tis your cousin Rory, my dear."

A tall, raven-haired man of approximately Rory's age strolled into the room, nodded curtly at him, and said as he moved to stand with his back to the fire, "How do you do, cousin."

"Rory has been to court, Duncan," Lady Balcardane said. "Is that not thrilling? I have always thought it prodigiously unfair that they moved the court to London from Edinburgh, so we cannot enjoy court life to the extent that my dear mama did when she was young, and all her family, and your papa's, too, I expect, whilst we have scarcely ever attended a court function—well, never, in fact—because the Union occurred long before we were married, you know—in fact, before I was born, I believe, in ought three or some such year.''

"May 1, 1707, to be exact," Duncan said evenly. "You were but a babe in arms, ma'am." Turning to Rory, he added, "So you have been to court, cousin. They just keep heaping one honor after another upon you. I daresay it is a wonder that you can still stand upright under such a load."

Wondering at the edge in Duncan's voice, and the man's general surliness, Rory looked more carefully at him but said calmly, "It is true that I have been presented at court, thanks to his grace, but my aunt is laboring under a slight misapprehension. The court to which my uncle referred, ma'am, is the Scottish Exchequer Court. I have the honor to be one of five Barons of the Exchequer, you see, and have served in that capacity now for nearly two years."

"Dear me," Lady Balcardane said, putting down her work and removing her spectacles. "It is a law court then. I get them all mixed up, I'm afraid."

"Most folks do," Rory assured her, smiling. "My duties pertain for the most part to the estates forfeited to the Crown after the last rebellion. Not an onerous duty, I assure you, but I mean to take advantage of my visit here to assure myself that our administration is running smoothly in Appin, Lochaber, and Morven."

"What makes you think it ain't?" Balcardane demanded, bristling.

"Why, nothing at all, sir, but since it is my duty, I shall keep my eyes open. I don't mean to puff off my consequence. Indeed, I'd as lief you not noise my status about, for I'm just here to observe. I don't want to make anyone nervous."

"You're damned young for such duty, if you ask me, and if you've come to check up on Colin Glenure, I'll have you know that I sponsored his appointment myself. And Argyll supported me, by God."

"Yes, sir, I know, and if you have heeded recent judgments of the Barons' Court, you will know that I have also strongly supported Glenure and that we recently reconfirmed him as factor here. I must speak with him while I'm here, of course, but I did not come here to spy on anyone.''

"I daresay you could have sent him a letter for a good deal less than it is costing you to bring the news yourself,'' Balcardane said.

"I wanted to come, uncle. I seem always to stop at Inveraray or Kilchurn, so I have not seen Loch Leven or any part of the western coast since my last visit here when I was ten or eleven.''

"Eleven,'' Duncan said. "You are a year older than I am, except for a few months of the year, when two years separate us. You came in June, I remember, when I was still nine, and I did not celebrate my birthday until just after you had gone. I remember thinking that most unfair at the time.''

"Since mine is next week, I'm afraid that will happen again, cousin,'' Rory said with a smile, "but there, you see, sir. Clearly, this visit is long overdue.''

Lady Balcardane agreed with him enthusiastically—and at length—until her husband cut in to suggest bluntly that it was time to dress for dinner.

"If we are going to dress, that is,'' he muttered, getting up. "Where the devil is your brother, Duncan? He ought to be here to welcome Calder.''

Duncan shrugged, his dark brows snapping together in a heavy frown. "How the deuce should I know where he is? Ian is long out of leading strings, sir, and in any event, I was never one to hold his leash.''

"You make him sound like one of your hunting dogs, my dear,'' Lady Balcardane said, "and in truth, you have always looked after him rather closely. He will have gone into the woods, I expect, or out onto the loch in his wee boat. He frequently does such things, dear sir,'' she added, smiling fondly at her husband. "I wonder that you have to ask, really, but so it is, always. Shall I ring for someone to take you up to your bedchamber, Rory dear?''

"Don't bother,'' Duncan said. "I'll show him. You will want him in the tower room, I expect.''

Balcardane said, "Excellent notion. A good choice."

"Do you think so?" Lady Balcardane looked doubtful. "It is so high, so many stairs, you know. I daresay some people like the exercise, but I doubt that I have set foot in that room for years. The maids go up, of course, so you will find it perfectly clean and tidy, Rory dear. Indeed, I ordered them to scrub the floor only the other week. But perhaps you would prefer a chamber nearer to the ground."

"The tower room will suit me very well," Rory said, wondering at the same time if his cousin had any particular reason for putting him there.

Clearly, his aunt might have chosen another room, but he remembered the tower bedchamber from his boyhood and had no objection to it. From its windows on a clear day he would enjoy views north and east across Loch Leven, west to Ballachulish ferry, and south up the steep, thickly wooded ridge. Not, he reflected, that many days at this time of year would be clear. When he and Thomas had arrived, a thick mist the Highlanders called a *haar* was already gathering. Thinking of Thomas reminded him that he had not seen him since their arrival.

"I did not travel with a party, uncle, but I do have a manservant with me," he said. "I'd like him housed near me if he won't be putting anyone out."

Duncan said, "We can put him in the little room below the tower bedchamber, the one that opens off the half-landing."

"Didn't that used to be some sort of munitions room?"

"You have an excellent memory, lad," Balcardane said, "but we moved all those old papers to a newer wing of the castle. They were getting damp."

Foreseeing that Thomas was going to be displeased with his quarters, Rory nonetheless made no complaint, and when he entered the tower bedchamber, he found the prospect from the window so agreeable, even through the thickening gray mist, that he was glad he had kept silent.

Thomas came in a few minutes later, bearing a pot of hot water. "Just tell me they ha' blocked up the fireplace in this room tae save money on fuel, and ye'll tell me nobbut what I expect tae hear," he grumbled.

"You malign my relatives, Thomas. As you see, there is an excellent fireplace. It is at least as big as the one I had at Castle Stalker—and it does not smoke, moreover—so let me hear no more complaints from you, if you please."

Since he did not expect to be obeyed, he was not surprised when Thomas retorted waspishly, "I see plain enough that ye have got a fire, my lord. I do not have one, however, and from what I hear of his lordship's nipfarthing ways, I'd no ha' been surprised tae find that he expected ye tae stay warm with nae more than the hot air wafting past your room through yon tower chimney from below. I ask ye, who builds a tower with a stair that winds upward along a warm chimney wall but leaves a whole bedchamber tae suffer frosted walls in wintertime?"

"His lordship did not build the castle, but I collect that your room has no fireplace because the chimney goes up the other side of the stairwell."

"Did I no just say so?"

"You did. I shall wear the blue velvet with the red and gold waistcoat," Rory said. "I don't want powder, but do be a good fellow and shake out that light plaid I brought with me."

Thomas's eyebrows shot upward, and he said with disapproval, "The wearing of the plaid, as ye ken very well, is proscribed by law and has been for years past. Do ye, a baron of the court, dare flout the law in such a way?"

"I do, for if you think my uncle will not be wearing trews or full plaid at his dining table, you are mistaken. As *you* know very well, for I've heard you complain of it far too often, members of the nobility always think they are above the law. He already takes me for an upstart because of my grand position and tender years, and I do not wish to offend him when I have only just arrived. Moreover, I'll wager my new tie-wig that Duncan dons a plaid for dinner."

"He's a one, that lad," Thomas said, shaking out clothing. "They do call him Black Duncan in these parts, and not, I'm thinking, just because of that inky hair of his. Looks a mean-spirited lad tae me. Ye'd best watch your back.''

Rory had already decided that it would behoove him to do that. He did not know what had stirred his cousin's temper, but that it was volatile was clear. A peaceful man himself, most of the time, he had no wish to stir coals that might burst into flame without warning.

As he dressed, he found himself thinking yet again of Mab MacKissock and realized that he was not so peace-loving as he had thought. He still wanted to throttle the wench or beat her soundly, and if he could find her, he would certainly do one or the other. It occurred to him as he sat to let Thomas pare his nails that he was expending a good deal of mental effort on a mere maidservant. He had told himself more than once that he wanted only to see that she got her just deserts, but he knew it was more than that. Had he wanted only to punish her, he would not, he knew, keep thinking of her golden-hazel eyes, her slender but curvaceous figure, or of her eminently kissable lips. MacKissable lips.

''Your other hand, my lord, *if* ye please,'' Thomas said in a tone Rory knew he had copied from the duke's extremely pompous valet.

Recalled to the moment, he obediently held out his right hand, forcing his thoughts to matters nearer at hand. He would find Mab MacKissa—He would find the wretched wench soon enough and teach her not to make fools of her betters. In the meantime, he had to deal with his irascible uncle, his ill-humored cousin, and his duty to the Exchequer, all without stirring up a hornet's nest or worse.

Appin country had long been an unstable area and still harbored more than its share of rebels. Even if the rumors of an impending uprising proved unfounded, there were many folks who could be stirred to mischief with a single misspoken word. He knew now that Mab MacKissock was a member of that faction, and although she deserved to be served up to justice, he did not want to incite the threatened rebellion himself merely to soothe a base desire.

"For revenge," he said firmly, aloud.

"What's that ye're muttering now?"

"Nothing, Thomas, nothing at all. I shall go down now, and you may do as you please for the rest of the evening. I shan't want you again till morning."

"Ye'll undress yourself then? Or mayhap ye've spied another obliging maidservant. The good Lord knows the last one proved a superior morsel."

"That will do, Thomas," Rory said, adjusting the light plaid he wore draped over his left shoulder. It was, he knew, no more than a token gesture, but perhaps before making it, he ought to have made sure no company was to dine with them.

He knew no one would dare call him to task—indeed, no member of the gentry had yet been punished for ignoring the diskilting law—but he believed in setting a good example. His position allowed him to carry a weapon in the Highlands, and his baggage contained both a pistol and a sword, but he did not wear either on his person. To flaunt his right to bear arms would not endear him to the Highlanders. Still, he was no fool. That they might threaten him because of the Campbell alliance with the hated English government was the very reason the authorities allowed him to carry his weapons in the first place.

Not every Campbell enjoyed that right, of course, but he would have wagered a good deal that his uncle had weapons hidden on the premises, weapons he had not given up to the authorities when ordered to do so. No doubt Balcardane was certain that no one would challenge him, and he was right. No one would.

Rory learned when he joined the others that he had been wise on two counts. Not only did Balcardane and Duncan both sport full plaids at the table, but neither man had powdered his hair.

At dinner Rory met the fourth member of the family. He was pleasantly surprised to find that Ian Campbell was a quiet, conservatively attired gentleman of nineteen, with a calm demeanor and a lurking twinkle in his light blue eyes.

Ian smiled, saying, "Forgive me for being away when you

arrived, cousin. I barely remember your last visit, but I have heard much about you over the years.''

"At least some of it good, I hope," Rory said, returning the smile.

"Lud, sir," Lady Balcardane said with a laugh, " 'Tis prodigious amazing that your ears did not ring with it all. Why, my dearest Balcardane is forever singing your praises. 'A well set up lad,' he said after your visit years ago, 'quick of mind and able to hit his mark with any weapon.' And you only eleven at the time. Just to think of it!''

Rather startled, Rory said hastily, "I am glad he did not say such things to me, ma'am. My head would have swelled like a bullfrog's throat, so puffed up in my esteem as I'd have got. My father would have brought me speedily to my senses, of course," he added, turning to Duncan. "I hear you still offer excellent fishing in these waters, cousin. Do you often try your luck?''

"I've better things to do with my time," Duncan said. "Get Ian to take you. The young fool likes sitting on a bank with a rod in his hand, doing nothing and like as not forgetting even to wear a coat. Doubtless that's where he was today.''

Flushing, Ian said, "I'll show you the best places anytime you like, Cousin Rory. Pay no heed to Duncan. He would rather fight than fish, and thinks me a weakling merely because I am not as belligerent as he is.''

"Belligerent, am I?" Duncan began to push back his chair.

Ian looked wary, but Balcardane said with a laugh, "Sit down, Duncan, sit down! Would you floor your brother in front of our guest on his first night at Balcardane? If you must punish him, for God's sake do it in a good cause. Ain't nothing amiss in owning to a bit of belligerence. At least you show allegiance to your clan and don't suffer impertinence from outsiders, which is more than Ian can say. I'm pleased to see you wearing the plaid, Calder, I must say. Shows proper loyalty, that does, and I should like to see a deal more of it.''

"Indeed, my dear sir," Lady Balcardane said as Duncan settled back in his chair, "I do not know why you and Duncan become so out of reason cross with Ian. I am sure he says nothing that would anger anyone of sense. Well, not sense,'' she amended hastily, ''but of ordinary sensibility. Of course, you will both say that it is a matter between gentlemen and not anything of which I have the smallest knowledge or understanding, but Duncan, I do think your father is wise to suggest that you wait at least until you know your cousin better before—''

''Let's hear some of those messages you've brought me, nephew,'' Balcardane said, cutting in without apology. ''Been months since I was next or nigh Inveraray—or Edinburgh, come to that.''

Despite what he was rapidly coming to recognize as plain rudeness to Lady Balcardane, Rory was happy enough to divert his uncle's attention, and the rest of the evening passed in ordinary discourse. Duncan, making no secret of his boredom, left them soon after dinner to pursue his own activities, and by the time Rory retired to the tower bedchamber, he had much to think about.

That his uncle's parsimonious nature might drive more than one member of his family to distraction was clear. That Balcardane set great store by clan loyalty was equally clear, as was the fact that like most clansmen, his respect for Argyll stemmed from blind loyalty rather than real devotion to the duke.

There was nothing amiss with that, of course, but Rory suspected that Balcardane harbored a lack of confidence in his nephew's loyalty to Clan Campbell. More than once during the evening the earl had raised the subject of Colin Glenure, reiterating his faith in the man's ability to serve as Crown factor.

Rory began to wonder if Balcardane really had faith in Glenure. Not until the earl chanced to mention that the factor was a first cousin born the wrong side of the blanket did Rory understand his anxiety. Doubtless Balcardane had recommended Glenure because of their kinship, and he feared now that if Glenure failed, others might see the failure as partly his own.

Before long, these thoughts had run their course, and Rory found himself thinking idly of the golden eyes and pert manner of Mab MacKissa—

Diana lay in bed staring up through the darkness at the ceiling. Thick mist surrounded the house, so not a bit of light showed in through her window. It was as if the *haar* had swallowed the outside world. A guilty shiver passed through her at a sudden fear that Calder's bindings might have been too tight, that he and Thomas MacKellar might still be lying where she and the others had left them.

That fear dissipated quickly. Calder was a capable man, too capable not to have escaped long since. He had said he was making for Balcardane, which meant he had passed within a hundred yards of Maclean House. The dirt road between the high meadow in which the house sat and the loch shore it overlooked was the only road suitable for horses between Balcardane and Castle Stalker. Had she kept an eye on the road, she would know for certain, but there had been no opportunity to do that without arousing more of Mary's curiosity.

Mary had been curious anyway, of course, but Diana had managed to answer her questions without volunteering any unnecessary information. Neil had said little, too, because that was his nature and because his thoughts had no doubt drifted to the latest target of his amorous inclination. If Mary read more in Diana's evasions than in her words, she did not comment. And although she was quiet the next morning when Allan Breck came to tell them he was on his way to Rannoch Moor, Diana saw nothing odd in that, since Mary was not fond of Allan.

Allan's behavior gave no indication that he was aware of Mary's coolness, however. He greeted both young women with a cheerful smile, saying, "Have you errands for me? I'll be back before long, you know. I shall be here, there, and about, looking for lads ripe for recruiting."

Diana said with a chuckle, "We have few friends on Rannoch

Moor, Allan. Most folks there are a bit rough for our taste, and I daresay it is not safe for you to visit others nearer at hand with messages from us.''

He laughed and shook his head at her concerns. ''Afraid for my safety, lass? You need not be. I can look after myself. Have done these six years past, after all.''

She knew better than to remind him of his recent capture. Nor did she point out that the authorities had hitherto been unaware of his visits until they were over, or suggest that Patrick Campbell was a more able commander than most. The truth was that she gave little thought to Allan or to Patrick, for in her mind's eye she saw only Lord Calder. She did remember, however, that his lordship had excellent cause to want to hunt down Allan Breck, and perhaps one or two others, as well.

Six

Having wakened to thoughts similar to those that had plagued him before sleeping—and plagued his dreams, as well—Rory had no sooner sat down to break his fast with his uncle and cousins than he said without preamble, "Are you acquainted with any MacKissocks hereabouts?"

His uncle frowned, but Duncan said sarcastically, "Are you interested in sheep farmers, cousin?"

"I am more interested in rebels," Rory replied calmly.

Balcardane snapped, "Damme, lad, but the MacKissocks are a stout branch of the Campbell tree. If you mean to look into things here in Appin, I suggest you keep to your duty and look after the forfeited estates. Many belong to Campbells and their ilk, to be sure, but they came by them all fair and square."

Recalled to his senses, Rory said tactfully, "Many clans had members who fought on opposing sides in the last rebellion, sir, even Campbells. I asked only because I thought the MacKissab—MacKissocks—lived mostly in Perthshire."

Duncan gave a shout of laughter. "You nearly said Mac-Kissable," he exclaimed. "It's a wench, by God! But the Mac-

Kissocks are only a sept, so she's likely not of noble birth. Taken by a serving wench, I'll wager. Is that it, cousin?''

Ian's eyes twinkled as he looked from one to the other, but he said nothing.

With a hope that the dim light filtered through the lingering outside mist would not reveal his discomfiture, Rory said evenly, "I asked because I thought I'd heard the name mentioned in conversation about rebel factions. However, if you know of no such rebel family hereabouts, doubtless I was mistaken.''

Duncan looked smug, but he said nothing more, and Rory decided there was no point in giving him further grist for his mill. Turning his attention to his plate, he remained silent, thinking about the first time he had laid eyes on Mab MacKissock. He had originally believed the little traitor to be a dupe, a poor innocent exploited by wicked Jacobites. Now that he knew she was one of them, was it not likely that Lady Maclean knew her personally? He recalled wondering earlier if the wench might have served as her ladyship's maid and supposed there were odder things in life than a Campbell serving a Maclean.

Appin country contained a host of Macleans, he knew, but he knew next to nothing about her ladyship. Her case had fallen under the Exchequer's jurisdiction, because Colin Glenure had ordered her arrest, but the judgment against her had taken place in a local baron bailie's court, not in Edinburgh.

The bailie had ordered her incarceration in Edinburgh Castle because most female prisoners were held there, particularly females of rank, and had duly notified Argyll, the Lord Justice General. Argyll had approved. Rory had taken exception only because it went against his sense of chivalry to lock up a gentlewoman for doing no more than trying to keep her erstwhile tenants warm through a cold winter.

Argyll had called him some unpleasant names, but having known Rory all his life, the duke had not seemed surprised by his dislike of her arrest and subsequent confinement. Rory had gone to see Lady Maclean because he hoped to learn more to bolster his argument. Now he realized that he did not know precisely who she was or where she presently might be found. He knew only that she was the widow of a rebel Maclean chieftain and that the forfeited estate lay on the Island of Mull.

At one time all estates on Mull, and many others in Appin and Lochaber, had belonged to Macleans. Over time, either warring Campbells or the British Crown had seized a good many of them, but Appin and Mull were still Maclean country, and—not surprisingly, perhaps—most Macleans still supported the few remaining diehard rebels, if they did not actively abet them.

As these thoughts flitted through Rory's mind, Balcardane was saying to Duncan that he wanted him to tell a tenant he would not soon get his cottage rethatched, due to the expense. Rory waited until they fell silent before he said casually, "There was an escape from Edinburgh Castle some weeks ago. I was there at the time, and it occurs to me that you might know the woman who got away."

Duncan said, "So she really did escape. We heard as much but did not credit it. How the devil does a gentlewoman escape from the castle vaults?"

"She had help," Rory said. "A laundry maid exchanged places with her."

"How brave of them both," Ian said with an approving smile.

"They ought both to be flogged," Balcardane snapped, glaring at him.

Rory said, "The estate she supposedly plundered is on Mull, is it not?"

"Aye, and there's no *supposing* about it," Balcardane said. "She cut down six trees. But she's not lived on Mull these past five years or more," he added. "She is a Stewart by birth—Anne Stewart Maclean—sister to the rebel Laird of Ardsheal and widow of Sir Hector, a damned Maclean rebel and erstwhile chieftain of the Craignure Macleans. She presently holds tenancy of a house on her brother's land at the south end of Cuil Bay, where she lives with her children and an orphaned niece. That's Crown land now, I'm thinking," he added. "Glenure said so, at all events."

"Yes," Rory agreed. "A recent act annexed certain forfeited estates inalienably to the Crown. Ardsheal's was one of them."

The conversation moved to Macleans and Stewarts in general, and the centuries-long, relatively unsuccessful struggle by both clans to keep Campbells from taking their land. Both the Craignure and Ardsheal estates had been forfeited after Culloden, but Rory knew that Ardsheal, at least, had had reason until recently to hope he might regain his estate in time. The annexation had ended that hope.

"And every acre taken over legally," Balcardane added with righteous fervor.

Rory did not argue the point. He was thinking of Lady Maclean and wondering if she had been bold enough simply to return home. He asked no more direct questions, however. Not wanting to reveal his reason for speaking of her, or his deep interest in her rescuer, he took the first opportunity to call for his horse and announced his intention to refresh his childhood memories of Appin country.

"A fine notion, lad," his uncle said bluffly. "Here it is, the first day of April, and the sun's shining bright for once. I'll have Duncan or Ian take you about and make you known to such folk as ought to be honored with your acquaintance."

Duncan said testily, "I'll arrange my own day if it is all the same to you, sir. Ian can take him."

Rory said, "I'll take myself, thank you. I think I can find my way about."

"Can you now?" Duncan's tone was sarcastic again. "Doubtless you lead such a charmed life, cousin, that you need not fear that one of our less loyal neighbors, seeing you alone, might snatch the opportunity to murder you."

Balcardane chuckled, but Ian said diffidently, "You ought at least to take one of our lads along, sir."

"I thought we'd disarmed all these people," Rory said lightly.

"Well, that is the law, of course," Ian said, but his doubtful tone confirmed what Rory had suspected. Clearly, Campbells and soldiers were not the only ones who had retained weapons, legal or otherwise, in their possession.

"I shall take my man with me then," he said, "but I do not want an entourage. The less stir I make, the better I shall like it." Shooting a thoughtful look at Duncan, he added, "I comprehend your meaning well enough, you know. I hope you know that I've got no quarrel with you."

"Oh, aye, I know that," Duncan said.

His manner belied his words, but Rory felt no inclination to smooth his ruffled feathers. He had already seen enough of Duncan to know he was the prickly sort who looked for offense where none was intended. Until he had taken the man's full measure, he knew he would accomplish nothing by trying to reassure him. Ian was another matter. The lad was smiling ruefully, as if he hoped his expression would somehow ease the sting of Duncan's behavior.

When Duncan's footsteps faded away, Balcardane growled, "Pay him no heed. He's always like that, but he's a good man in a fight. I'll say that for him."

"I am glad to hear it," Rory said mildly. "He seems a bit liverish, however, and at present, I have no need of a fighter. I'm more concerned about administering the forfeited properties efficiently, and that will prove difficult if Duncan and men like him act as if the remaining rebels hereabouts are of no more concern than a hive of bees to be stirred up at will for their amusement."

"Well, I don't say he does that," Balcardane said doubtfully. "He's not one to overlook insult, but he don't go about looking for trouble either."

Ian looked about to speak, but he held his tongue, pouring himself another mug of ale instead. Balcardane pushed back his chair and got up, but although Ian stood politely when his father did, he made no move to accompany him.

Rory also stood, since he was certain Balcardane expected it. But he watched Ian curiously and felt no surprise when the lad shot him a speaking look from under his long, curling lashes. "I'll be along in a moment, sir," Rory said to the earl. "If you are going to the stable, perhaps you might just tell my man that I shall want him to accompany me."

"Aye, lad, I'll tell him."

When he had gone, Rory said, "Did you wish to say something to me?"

Shyly, Ian smiled. "I doubt you need warning from me," he said quietly, "but Duncan is not quite so harmless as my father would have you believe him."

"We are all on the same side, lad, all Campbells born and bred. I do not think I need fear your brother."

"He is called Black Duncan hereabouts," Ian said. "Folks have cause, for his temper is vicious, and he does not snap only at his enemies, I fear. He does not like to be crossed, sir, and he particularly dislikes you, you see."

"But why? I have done him no harm. I scarcely know him."

"Aye, that's true, but from the time of that first visit you made here Duncan's heard over and over what a paragon of virtue you are."

"But that's nonsense," Rory protested, nonplused but beginning to understand at last what motive Duncan had had for putting him in what the other man must have thought was an inconvenient bedchamber.

"Oh, aye, I've no doubt that it's nonsense," Ian said with a lurking smile, "but my father is prone to compare one man to another, one lad to the next. All my life I've heard what a braw lad Duncan is, because I am not of a bellicose nature, myself. I'd as lief lie on my belly and watch a parade of ants building a nest as pick up a sword and spit someone with it."

Rory chuckled. "I used to sit in the forest and hope a deer would come feed from my hand. I saw a few, but I never managed to feed one."

"Good thing for you one never got close enough," Ian said, grinning. "Deer are as like to slash with their hooves as to nibble politely from your hand."

"I expect that's true. Did your father want you to fight?"

"I was too young to take part in putting down the rebellion.

Even he agrees to that, but he no sooner says so than he will describe the heroic action of some ten-year-old lad who saved an army. I did not want to go, mind you. Indeed, I expect I'd have been an even sadder disappointment to him had I tried to take sword or pistol in hand. Duncan did distinguish himself, of course. He is justifiably proud of his skills, and constantly harasses those of us who are less skilled to learn more. Since most folks hereabouts don't dare to be seen bearing arms, his inferiors are legion.''

Rory smiled at him. ''I doubt he is as superior as all that, lad, but thank you all the same for the warning. Do you care to ride with me for a while?''

Ian flushed. ''I would be honored. Only I cannot in good faith spend more than a couple of hours with you, for I am promised elsewhere by noon.''

Rory stood. ''Then suppose we start out together and when you have had enough of my company, you may leave me to my own devices.''

''I will then, and gladly,'' Ian said, downing his ale in a gulp as he got up. ''That will please Father, too, for I'll have to take a horse if I go with you.''

''Indeed, you will, for I mean to gallop the fidgets out of Rosinante, and we would soon leave you behind. Do you not generally ride?'' he added some minutes later as they strolled across the courtyard toward the stables.

''Not often,'' Ian said, ''for I can get anywhere I like nearly as fast on foot. The woods hereabouts are too dense to ride through, so on horseback one must keep to the paths. Afoot, if a man knows the deer tracks, he can move from glen to glen right speedily, but Father says it does not look well for me to run when he can well afford to mount me. What did you call your horse?''

''Rosinante—after Don Quixote's skinny nag, in the book by Cervantes.''

''Do you tilt at windmills then, sir?''

''Not often,'' Rory said, ''but that book is one of my favorites. I don't recall many of the tracks hereabouts," he added. "What route do you recommend?"

"That depends on what you want to see," Ian said with his lurking smile. "Appin country takes up the northern half of Argyll, so we have a wide choice."

"I am content to ride where you wish. Whither do you go?"

Ian's open gaze shifted as he said with a shrug, "You don't want to spend the day riding around Loch Leven, I expect. We can go to Kentallen, or take the Ballachulish ferry across to Lochaber."

"I want to see Appin first, and although I'd like to see Cuil Bay again, Thomas and I passed through Kentallen and the Lettermore Woods yesterday."

"Then, if you like, we can take the hill pass into Glen Creran as far as Glen Ure, and follow Glen Duror back to the shore of Loch Linnhe near Cuil Bay."

Deciding it would behoove him to attend to business before setting out in search of Mab MacKissock, Rory said, "I have messages for Colin of Glen Ure. Have you time to ride that far with me?"

"Nay, but I can put you on the track, and you will easily find his house."

Thomas MacKellar had two horses ready, and a third was quickly saddled for Ian. The mist had vanished completely, leaving the day sunny and clear, and they rode uphill to the rocky pass in silence, with Thomas following a short distance behind. On the far side, twenty minutes after entering the wooded confines of Glen Creran, when they met a couple walking briskly toward them along the shady path, they drew aside and reined in, waiting for the pedestrians to pass.

"Good day to you, John Maccoll," Ian said in the Gaelic when the man doffed his cap politely. "This is my cousin, Calder. He is a Baron of the Scottish Exchequer Court and—"

"He is glad to meet you," Rory cut in, dredging the correct phrase from his memory, motivated by a certainty that his young relative was about to recite a litany of his titles and connections. The last thing he wanted was for word of his authority to fly around the area before he had had a chance to learn what he could in a more casual way. From what he had heard since coming into the Highlands, he knew that people would speak more openly if they were not nervous about his power.

He smiled and nodded at the plump middle-aged woman, who regarded him with open curiosity as she curtsied deeply. Upright again, she continued to stare.

The man, as burly as she was plump, nodded respectfully and said in careful English, "This be my wife, Sarah, my lord. It be right tae say *my lord,* is it not?"

"Aye," Ian said, switching to English, too. "He is Lord Calder, cousin to—"

"Thank you, Ian, but I'd as lief you did not burden each new acquaintance with your notion of my character," Rory said, smiling easily at the woman. "How do you do, madam? It is a most pleasant day, is it not?"

She chuckled but did not reply, and John Maccoll said, "Sarah understands English well enough, my lord, but she don't speak much, only the Gaelic."

"And I don't speak much of the Gaelic, as you clearly deduced for yourself," Rory said ruefully. "I shall have to learn to speak it more fluently if I mean to spend time here, or I shall find myself saying things I don't at all mean to say."

The man chuckled, nodded again, then said to Ian, "We've started our new thatch, lad. Tell your father, will you? 'Twill spare me a trip to Balcardane."

"Aye, I'll tell him," Ian promised. Some minutes after they had ridden on, he said to Rory, "John is one of the few my father will permit to rethatch this year. In truth, I think he'd be afraid not to permit it, for although John seems a pleasant sort, you should see him when his temper erupts. Duncan is mild by comparison."

"Does John's temper erupt frequently?" Rory asked, amused.

"Well, he has a beautiful daughter, Katherine, a dairymaid, and most of the lads take great care when they speak to her.

She and John serve James of the Glen, who was Crown factor in these parts before Colin Glenure took the post.''

"I recall James Stewart," Rory said. "We replaced him because he refused to collect rents from Ardsheal's tenants and those of other exiled lairds."

"Aye, they'd all been sending their rents to France," Ian said with a sigh. "Can't blame folks for not wanting to pay twice."

"Sending rent money to an exiled Jacobite leader is not an excuse deemed acceptable for nonpayment to the lawful authorities," Rory said wryly.

Ian shrugged. "Do you not want me to tell people who you are, cousin?"

"Don't tell any lies on my account," Rory said, "but I'd as lief you don't make a gift of information either. I know I can count on you and your father to tell me much of what goes on in Appin country, and I must speak to the Crown factors and bailies, of course. But I don't want folks worrying that I mean to stick my oar into unknown waters before I know exactly what I'm stirring up."

Ian frowned thoughtfully. "Perhaps you'd best not explain that to Duncan. He won't go about puffing off your consequence, but if he knows you don't *want* it puffed off, he will do what he can to annoy you. I've never understood exactly what it is you do, anyway, so I don't mind saying no more than that you're my grand cousin come to visit from Perthshire. Will that suit you?"

"Down to the ground," Rory told him. "Where are we now? I haven't a notion how far we are from where Glen Ure meets Glen Creran."

"Another two miles," Ian told him. "I'll leave you when we reach the opening of Glen Ure. You'll see the house from there, about halfway up the glen, and Colin and Janet will put you right when you want to leave. That track yonder leads over the hill pass into Glen Duror, so that's the one you and Thomas will take if you want to go home by Cuil Bay."

"We'll have traveled in a circle then," Rory said, smiling.

"More like a square. Glen Creran divides Appin country up the middle, and Cuil Bay marks the midway point, so you'll have made what amounts to a circuit of the northwestern quadrant. Do you want to call on anyone else in particular?"

Rory considered telling him exactly what he wanted, and asking him if he knew anyone answering Mab MacKissock's description, but he did not know the boy well enough yet to trust him. Ian seemed honest but something of a rattlepate despite his assurances.

No more than Rory wanted word of his authority in Appin noised around did he want people speculating about his connection to a young Jacobite female, or to a woman as well known as Lady Maclean must be. Thus, it took no longer than the blink of an eye to decide to keep his true purpose from Ian. He said only, "Not at present, but I shall look to you soon to teach me more about Appin country."

Ian grinned. "No one's better suited." They chatted in a desultory way until they reached the entrance to Glen Ure, a shallow, wide-bottomed glen with grassy, heather clad slopes. Ian said, "Here we are. It's the big white house yonder. Give my best regards to Colin. He is a cousin, too, you know."

"I expect you are related to a good part of the local citizenry," Rory said.

"Aye, that's a fact."

They parted, and Thomas drew alongside Rory. The distance to the house proved deceptive, for it was at least a half hour before they reached it, and at first the place seemed deserted. But when they drew rein, a boy ran from a stable behind the low built house, calling to them.

"Say he'll look after the horses," Thomas said, translating.

"I must certainly look to my Gaelic," Rory muttered.

"Aye, ye should. Do the master speak English, or do ye want me tae come?"

"Glenure is an educated man, Thomas, so just look after the horses and learn what you can from the minions. I want to know the general disposition of the local folks toward each other, as well as toward the government."

"Aye, sure. We looking for more damned Jacobites then, are we?"

"Just inquiring into local sentiment, Thomas. That will do for the present."

"Aye, then here's your man a-coming the noo."

An auburn-haired man in his twenties had emerged from the house and was striding toward them. He looked curious at first, but as his gaze swept over them and came to rest upon Rosinante, his demeanor became more formal.

"He's too young," Rory said. "Glenure's son, perhaps."

"How may I be of service to you, sir?" the young man asked.

"I am looking for Colin Campbell of Glen Ure," Rory said.

"My uncle is away upon Crown business, sir. I am Mungo Campbell."

"Do you expect him back today?"

"Och, aye, he's only out and about near Loch Linnhe."

"Then you may tell him that Lord Calder would like a word with him at his convenience," Rory said. "The Earl of Balcardane is my uncle, and I am fixed at Balcardane Castle for several weeks. Will you do that?"

"Aye." The young man looked searchingly at him. "Should I know of you?"

"Your uncle does. Tell him I have come only to confirm my belief that he is doing his duty as it should be done, to bring him news, and for no other purpose."

"Och, well, he'll be pleased about that," Mungo said, pushing a hand through his unruly curls. "Given him all manner of grief, the Barons have, saying he's like to be soft on the rebels on account of Gran's family being Camerons, and all."

Though he suspected that he might learn much from Mungo Campbell, Rory was loath to take advantage of him, so he made his farewell without further ado.

"Another rattle," Thomas muttered disapprovingly. "Do all the lads hereabouts think wi' their tongues?"

"I begin to think it may be something of a deceit," Rory said. "An insouciant manner may cover much stealth, Thomas."

"Oh, aye," Thomas said with a wry look. "Yon curly-top looks a rare conspirator, he does. Or were ye thinking mayhap on our gentle Ian?"

"Enough, Thomas. We have done our duty. Now I mean to look for a lady with a face like a benediction and a mind of truly Machiavellian scope."

"I take it ye mean tae find the lass who twisted our tails at Castle Stalker," Thomas said wisely. "That one wants hanging, and no mistake."

"Oh, not hanging,Thomas. Although by the time I finish with her, she may think hanging a better proposition."

Thomas chuckled. "A rare drubbing then, and that's grand if ye can find her, but where tae look? Ye ken fine that ye canna ask folks tae deliver her up tae ye."

"I'll find her," Rory said grimly. "The woman she rescued in Edinburgh was one Lady Maclean, sister to the Laird of Ardsheal, and she lives at Maclean House, on the south end of Cuil Bay. If her ladyship does not know her rescuer, who will?"

"What of this Glenure, then? Do we continue tae search for him, as well?"

"We'll let him come to us, I think," Rory said. "I want to take his measure, but I'd as lief he not look upon me as some sort of nemesis. Argyll and my uncle approve of him, after all, and he seems utterly loyal to the present government, but he is native to Appin country and his mother is a Cameron of Morven."

"A fierce rebel clan, the Camerons."

"Yes. That fact nearly led to his undoing, for many in London find it hard to believe that a chap whose mother hails from a clan that has remained staunchly loyal to the Stewart line can render justice on behalf of King George."

They soon reached the steep track over the pass to Glen Duror, and fell silent. Occasionally they met others, all afoot. Several doffed caps or curtsied, depending on their gender, and all greeted them politely, but Rory did not stop to talk. Except for the continual low roar from the snow-fed torrent tumbling down its center, Glen Duror was warm and peaceful, and an hour later, they passed through the clachan of Inshaig and emerged at Cuil Bay two miles south of Kentallen Inn.

Waves lapped rhythmically at the shore, and looking west and south, Rory saw the solid blue mountains of Morven and Mull in the distance, easily identifiable to one who had learned their names as a lad. Mull was more distant than it had been from Stalker, but Ben More was visible, for the day remained clear and sunny.

The breeze was stiffer than it had been in the glens, and the current looked rapid, although the many boats on the loch seemed to pay it little heed. The tide was going out, Rory decided. He had heard that the loch waters moved swiftly when the tide was running.

Turning on his saddle, he said to Thomas, "Perhaps you had better ride ahead. If you see anyone, ask how we can recognize Maclean House. I'd as lief not have to ride back to inquire at Inshaig or Kentallen Inn. We can do better than that."

"Aye, we can, but have a care. His lordship did say I wasna tae let ye out of my sight, lest ye come tae grief."

"Do you think I cannot take care of myself?" Rory demanded.

"Och, well, there was the wench and all," his henchman said.

"The wench had help, Thomas, and no one is going to attack me here in plain sight of those fishing boats, not to mention anyone on the hillside who might be looking down at us as we speak. Too many witnesses. Moreover, no matter what anyone says to the contrary, I doubt the number of rebels in Argyll is as great as all that. More than from Perthshire, to be sure, but not the entire population."

"Just have a care, will ye? I willna enjoy telling me Lord Balcardane or his grace that ye let yourself be ambushed whilst I were riding round yon countryside."

"Enough of your gab, Thomas. Get on."

Touching his cap with sour deference, Thomas obeyed, but he was soon back again. "Met a wee lass just round yonder bend," he said. "She will have it that Maclean House sits in a meadow beyond a point of land ye can see from where I spoke tae her. I'll show ye. The wee one did say five minutes, mayhap ten.''

"Not so wee if she can judge time and distance," Rory said.

Thomas grinned. "In places not so wee. Just right she is, tae my thinking.''

"Don't go bewitching all the females in Appin," Rory warned. "That is the last sort of trouble I want to deal with here.''

"Och, but it isna myself that's got wench trouble. I'm a discreet lad, I am.''

"Then choose discreet lassies," Rory retorted.

When they rounded the bend, he saw at once that they must have passed near Maclean House the previous day. Ten minutes later, they came upon a track leading inland, and soon saw a broad meadow in which a large white house sat against the steeply rising green and purple hillside. Surrounded by trees, and boasting a side garden already showing colorful spring growth, the house made a pleasant picture.

Rory began to doubt that Lady Maclean would be there. The place was too conspicuous, too much a Highland gentry household. To return here with the authorities still searching for her would have been folly. Still, someone might know of Mab MacKissock, if that was truly the wench's name. He had begun to doubt that, too, and had already worked out a good description of her to offer anyone who might help him find her. Whether they would tell him anything if they recognized her remained to be seen, but his powers of persuasion were considerable.

"They've got company," Thomas said.

Rory saw five people standing in the yard between the main house and what looked like a barn or stable. From their stiff postures and agitated movements, he knew he and Thomas were interrupting an acrimonious confrontation. Two of the participants were female, three male, and by the time he and Thomas were within hailing distance, he could hear at least two angry male voices. Because the five stood in a small circle, he could not see a single face clearly, but he felt an odd, unexplainable sense of excitement, well beyond what the little scene conveyed.

One of the women, a young one with tawny hair, turned her head and saw them, then reached out to touch the nearest man. When he turned with his mouth dropping in dismay, Rory recognized Ian. Then the other woman turned, and his wonder at Ian's presence vanished in a blink when he found himself staring in shocked disbelief at Mab MacKissock.

That she recognized him at once was clear, for she looked both defiant and frightened. As well she might, he thought grimly, but perversely, his senses focused on the bright color in her cheeks and the way her eyes sparkled.

The other two men were still arguing. One was tall and red-headed with bushy, beetling red eyebrows, and clearly had a temper to match. The other man, older and smaller, was trying to calm him but seemed close to losing his own temper. Then the wench spoke, and both men fell silent.

She turned to Rory and said curtly, "What do you want?"

"Diana!" The other young woman sounded shocked by her rudeness, but the wench paid her no heed. She kept her eyes fixed on Rory.

Realizing the instant he heard her addressed as Diana that she was not in any way the common wench he had once thought her, but seeing no reason to reveal his dismay before such an audience, he said mildly, "I have come to speak to you."

"Well, you'd better do it quickly," she snapped. "Red Colin has just served us with preliminary notice that we are to be evicted in six weeks, on Term Day, although our rent is paid in full. I daresay such treatment is what all the loyal citizens of Appin can expect now that you filthy Campbells control the Highlands."

Seven

Diana glared at Lord Calder, ignoring the others, hoping no one could tell how hard her heart was beating with fear. He had spoken mildly, and perhaps she ought to have replied in kind, but he held the power to see her hanged, and before his arrival Red Colin had made her so angry that she could not think straight. To make matters worse, when she had seen his lordship so shockingly near, the words had simply spewed from her tongue on a wave of panic. She could not take them back now, heaven knew, but help came from an unexpected quarter.

Red Colin, puffing himself up like an arrogant cock, said aggressively, "You intrude upon Crown business, sir. Who the devil are you, and what do you want?"

"I am Calder," his lordship said steadily, his eyes taking on the flintlike look that Diana remembered only too well from Edinburgh.

She did not expect the peevish Crown factor to react to the look in the same way that she had, but she was not surprised when he fell silent, scowling at Calder through slitted eyes as the latter dismounted and handed his reins to Thomas.

James, looking like a sleek, well-mannered banty rooster

next to Red Colin, held out his hand at once and said, "I know of you, of course, my lord. I am James Stewart, erstwhile factor here and still tacksman for Ardsheal's estate. Welcome to Appin country. Perhaps you can be of assistance to Mistress Diana and her family, for this is an utter travesty, as I was just telling Glenure, and—"

"I will be happy to speak with you both presently," Calder interjected. "Just now, however, I want a word with Mistress Diana, so if you would please me, James Stewart, you will leave now in peace and call upon me at Balcardane at your convenience to say what you will. Glenure, you may await me yonder near the gate. I want to speak to you when I am finished with Mistress Diana."

Though his words were polite, his tone left no room for debate, and both James and Red Colin made their bows and stepped away out of earshot, leaving Calder with Diana, Mary, and a red-faced but still silent Ian. Thomas led the gray and his own mount toward the barn.

Certain that Calder had no wish to help them, and having fully expected him to demand her instant arrest, Diana remained speechless. Perhaps he did not yet understand the extent of Red Colin's authority, for surely, if he had, he would have ordered him to take her into custody at once.

Mary and Ian were still looking at her, she noted, Mary doubtless expecting to be presented, and both wondering how she knew Calder. Gentle Ian had said that his cousin was visiting Balcardane, but since Red Colin had arrived at that very moment in their conversation, she had neither admitted her acquaintance nor requested more information about Calder.

Just as it occurred to her that he might think she had told Ian about their previous meetings, Calder said in the same mild tone he had used before, "I hope you do not mind my addressing you as Mistress Diana."

"I don't care what you call me," she blurted. Then, realizing that she would be safer if she directed the conversation, she reined in her temper and said more politely, "Pray allow me to present my cousin Mary Maclaine, sir."

As Mary made her curtsy, Diana hastened to add, "She hails from another branch of our clan, and her name is spelled differently from ours but pronounced the same way. She is the seventh daughter of a seventh daughter, but her mother and several of her sisters died when she was small. Then Butcher Cumberland and his villains murdered the rest of her family after the rebellion. Finding herself orphaned, she came with us to Appin when we moved here from the Island of Mull."

She knew she was babbling, and when his eyes began to gleam, she feared he would cut her off as ruthlessly as he had James. Determined to let him know that she had said nothing to Ian about their encounters, she said quickly, "You already know Ian, of course. You must be the grand cousin he said is visiting Balcardane."

Glancing at Ian, who regarded him the way a sparrow must regard a sparrow hawk—an attitude with which Diana felt great sympathy—Calder said, "I am."

His mild manner gave her courage. She said crisply, "I know you think you have reason to harbor ill feelings toward me, sir, and perhaps you do. But if you think I will allow you to bully anyone else in my household, you had better think again. You can prove nothing against anyone, as you must know by now, so I wish you will just say whatever it is you want to say to me and be off again."

Ian said in bewilderment, "What are you saying, Diana? Do you already know Cousin Rory? Why did you not say so before? Why would he harbor ill feeling toward you, and what could he possibly wish to prove against anyone?"

Calder's visible, albeit grim, amusement added to her annoyance with herself. That she could so stupidly dismiss Ian's presence when she had just been at pains to tell Calder he was unaware of their previous meetings just showed how rattled she was. She said glibly, "Never you mind, Ian. If I don't seem to be thinking or talking sensibly, you must blame your thoughtless kinsmen—Red Colin for upsetting me with his awful notice, and his lordship for descending upon us without warning. You called him Cousin Rory, and I knew him as

Calder, that's all. I met him in Edinburgh, but he is a Campbell, after all, and we . . .'' She fell awkwardly silent when Calder raised his eyebrows in an exaggerated expression of interest.

Speaking then for the first time since Calder's arrival, Mary said gently, ''Diana, do let Lord Calder get a word in, will you? He means us no harm.''

Seeing the flintlike eyes snap toward Mary in surprise, Diana said, ''I told you she is the seventh daughter of a seventh daughter, my lord.''

He said to Mary, ''Do you have the gift of second sight, mistress?''

Mary nodded. ''I do, sir, though it is more a curse at times than a gift.''

''She cannot control it,'' Diana said, feeling herself relax as a result of Mary's reassurance. ''If you do not mean us harm, then I hope you will heed what James of the Glen said, for Red Colin has overstepped himself this time, you see. Our next quarter's rent is paid, so he has no business serving us with an eviction notice.''

''I daresay he knows his business,'' Calder said. ''You can appeal to the Exchequer if you disagree, or to the Duke of Argyll, but it will do no good to complain to me. You cannot expect me simply to take your word over that of my kinsman, especially when I have not yet heard his side of the dispute.''

''You said you wanted to speak to me, but now you say nothing to the purpose. If you cannot help us, then go away, my lord. We want none of you or your ilk. Not you, Ian,'' she added when the young man flushed deeply. ''We don't count you an ordinary Campbell, you know.''

With a new edge to his voice, Calder said, ''I do want to talk to you, mistress, but I should prefer to do so privately.''

''Well, I don't want to talk privately to you!'' Heat surged to her cheeks at the sound of her rudeness, but the thought of being alone with him again set raw nerves afire throughout her body. Knowing they could all see her confusion did nothing to calm her. Nor did the look of intent in his eyes when her gaze collided with his.

Suddenly, the warm sunlight reminded her of the hearth fire at Stalker. The salty breeze touching her face seemed to smell of wood smoke, and hearing a sea lion bark in the distance, her imagination turned it to a distant night bird's call.

Without looking away from her, Calder said sternly to the others, "Leave us."

Her lips dried, and she struggled to look at anything but the steely gray eyes that held hers in thrall. Forcing the words out, she said, "Mary, don't go."

To her shock, however, Mary said, "Come, Ian. You heard his lordship. He wants to speak privately with Diana."

Ian said, "But, Mary, don't you think—?"

"Come, Ian," Mary repeated with uncharacteristic firmness in her voice. "I have already told you that he means her no harm."

Wrenching her gaze from Calder's to glare at them, and finding her tongue at last, Diana snapped, "How can you say that? He is a Campbell, is he not? It is indecent to leave any defenseless young female alone with a Campbell male."

Mary laughed, curtsied, and pushed Ian ahead of her toward the house.

"Traitors," Diana muttered.

"If Ian is a traitor, he is not betraying you," Calder said, still with that edge she had heard before in his voice.

"I meant both of them, for I have never known Mary to do such a thing before. Ian only stopped here to tell us he had found one of our lambs in the woods," she added, hating the defensive note that crept into her voice.

"If that is true," Calder retorted, "then he knew this morning that the lamb was missing, because he told me he had an appointment at noon."

"Well, it is true that he found a lamb," she said. It was true, although she knew Mary had expected him. But with Mary one never knew if expectation was ordinary or derived from intuition.

Calder said, "I did not come here to talk about Ian."

"He will be relieved to hear that, I'm sure."

"I do not tell tales out of school, Mistress Maclean."

She found herself wondering why his calling her Mistress Maclean sounded more like an epithet than a polite form of address. But when she looked for an answer in his expression, she wished she had kept her eyes lowered.

He was still watching her as steadily as before, and she found his gaze just as disconcerting. Remembering her concern earlier that he might not have been able to free himself from his bonds, she grimaced. Clearly, he was a man who could take care of himself. Glancing toward the gate, she saw that James had gone, but Red Colin leaned against the rail fence, watching them.

"Look at me," Calder said.

"He is watching us," she said. "You may enjoy that, but I do not."

"Then don't look at him," he said without sympathy. "Attend to me carefully instead, for I have some few things to say to you."

She felt a chill race up her spine. "I don't want to hear them."

"I don't doubt that, but you will hear them nonetheless. Thomas MacKellar told me that you saved our lives."

Surprised, she made the mistake of looking right at him again. He did not wear a wig, and the sunlight set auburn highlights dancing in his dark hair. "What made Thomas think that?"

"Don't play games with me, Diana Maclean. You will not win. Thomas said that one of your associates was about to slit his throat when you stopped him. Need I ask the identity of that would-be assassin?"

"You may ask," she said. "I will not tell you."

He nodded; looking satisfied, and she realized she had just admitted that someone among them had intended murder. When he looked as if he expected her to say more, she said impatiently, "So someone wanted to kill you. It might have been anyone, you know. Appin country does not love the Campbells."

"You are quibbling now. The leader of your little band

announced that he did not want to leave witnesses. You talked him out of murdering us.''

"So you understand the Gaelic," she said. "I was afraid you might."

Color tinged his cheeks, but he did not contradict her. Instead he said, "We did not altogether understand what you said about the ferryman. I collect that he refused to take you from the islet when you first wished to leave."

"A decision for which you will no doubt commend him."

He did not deny it but said quietly, "Someone said the man hails from Mull, from Craignure. The Lady Maclean who was imprisoned in Edinburgh is the widow of the Craignure Maclean chieftain, the same Anne Stewart Maclean who holds tenancy here. Will you deny that she is your mother?"

"I will not." She watched him, fascinated, but the way he jumped from subject to subject made her head reel. She realized that he had deduced her identity as much from her presence at Maclean House as from anything she had revealed to him earlier, but she was uncertain where the gambit was taking him now.

His nod did nothing to enlighten her. Then he frowned, saying, "So the ferryman is a member of your clan."

"From one of the septs, yes. He is a Bethune. Why do you ask?"

"He is not reliable."

"How can you say that? He was loyal enough to his master to deny me passage. You heard me tell the others so yourself."

"Did you tell him who you are? Before you answer, you might as well know that it won't matter a whit one way or the other. If you told him and he did not help you, he is disloyal to his clan and thus cannot be trusted. If you did not tell him, the likelihood is that he would have helped you if you had. Can you deny that?"

She could not. She had told Bethune only that she was a Maclean of Craignure, not that she was Sir Hector's daughter. "That is not fair!"

"Life is not fair. Patrick will hire another man. Where is your mother?"

"You cannot expect me to tell you that."

"I suppose not, although I assure you that I did not approve of her arrest."

"She was guilty of nothing more than looking after our tenants."

"They are no longer your tenants."

"No, they are Crown tenants who were being allowed to die of cold and lack of proper food," she said with heat. "Mam just did her duty. She did not shirk it merely because Butcher Cumberland and the filthy English seized our land."

"I'd take care to mind my manners better if I were you, mistress. You do yourself no good by hurling abuse at me."

"What good would it do me to be nice to you? Can you help my mother? I'll warrant you want to know where she is just so you can help Red Colin capture her and send her back to Edinburgh in chains."

"I have no such wish," he said quietly. "Indeed, from what I have learned of her crime, I believe that her conviction should be set aside. I will see what can be done about that if you like."

"I wish I could believe you meant that," she said wistfully.

"I do not make idle promises, mistress. I will do what I can for her ladyship." He paused, but before she could summon up words to express her wary gratitude, he added unexpectedly, "Do you and your household have sufficient food?"

Astonished, she said, "Aye, sir."

"And wood to keep you warm?"

"Aye." She wanted to ask what difference it would make, since Red Colin would evict them in six weeks' time, but she bit her tongue. With long experience of Campbells to guide her, she did not trust Calder's promise, but neither did she want to make more of an enemy of him than he was. She would be grateful for any help, particularly if he could arrange for Lady Maclean's safe return from Glen Drumin. Since her ladyship was presently safe, however, the threatened eviction was a more serious matter, and he had already said he would not help with that.

"Do you frequently help villains escape from justice?" he asked her.

Caught off guard again, she gasped. She saw nothing in his expression to aid her, either, although the flinty look had softened. Still, she could not answer his question without placing herself in more jeopardy.

As he had done before, he waited with an expectant air, clearly prepared to remain silent until she spoke. It was most unnerving behavior.

At last, she said, "A moment ago, you warned me not to play games, sir, but it seems to me that you do so yourself. How can I answer such a question?"

"Truthfully."

"If I say no, you will not believe me. If I say yes, you may see me hanged. I should thus be a fool to say either one."

He smiled, and her breath caught in her throat, for not only were his teeth the whitest, most even she had ever seen, but the smile lightened his countenance and brought a sparkle to his eyes. The creases in his cheeks deepened to reveal a tiny dimple near the right one. She wondered what it would be like to hear him laugh.

He touched a finger to the point of her chin, and although his touch was light, it seemed to burn. Entranced, she could not seem to make herself step away.

She said nothing, but she was aware of nothing and no one but him. She could hear his even breathing over the hush of the breeze caressing the trees and stirring the grass in the yard. She felt a pulse beating where his finger touched her chin, but whether it was his pulse or her own, she had no idea.

At last, she said in little more than a whisper, "What will you do?"

"About you?"

She wanted to nod, but she still could not move. Her breath dried her lips, and her tongue felt too big for her mouth.

Looking into her eyes, he said, "That will depend, won't it?"

"On what?" She licked her lips.

"On how much trouble you give me, mistress."

Faced with that steady, unblinking gaze, she felt an overwhelming urge to promise him that she would give him no trouble at all. She managed to overcome the impulse by sheer force of will, however, saying instead, "I make trouble only for those who deserve it, my lord. To others, I am as meek as a lamb."

He grimaced wryly and shook his head. "If only I could believe that. I don't, of course, for although it is the first day of the month, I am not such an April gowk as to fall into the same trap a third time. Take heed of my warning, mistress. You have already made me look a proper dunder-clunk for believing you in Edinburgh, and for allowing myself to be led from Castle Stalker into ambush. Do not judge my intelligence by those actions, or you will swiftly come to grief."

His expression hardened, and she could not mistake the menace in his voice when he added, "I am amazed by my restraint. You deserve, at the least, a good hiding. If Patrick Campbell learns what I know, you could be hanged. So take care, for if I catch you at such tricks again, I promise you will come by your just deserts."

Believing him, she had the good sense for once in her life to say nothing.

He waited, as he had done before, but she felt no pressure in the silence, and when he glanced toward the house again, she began to breathe more easily. Then, turning back, he said abruptly, "I hope you've got better sense than to endanger the rest of your family by embroiling yourself in any business you cannot handle."

He did not wait for a reply then but turned on his heel and strode to Red Colin, still waiting by the gate. Watching him go, Diana realized that her heart was thumping hard again. She realized something else, too, that for once Mary had been wrong. They did have something to fear from Calder, and that was Diana's unexpected and most disturbing attraction to him.

Rory did not look back. A voice in the back of his head was calling him everything he had told Mistress Diana he deserved to be called. She had done it again. If ever a wench deserved throttling, that one did, and here he was, walking away, having warned her to take care. What manner of witch was she?

Glenure watched his approach, the wary expression on his face showing Rory that at least someone was properly awed by his authority. Certainly Diana Maclean felt no awe of him. She was sassy and sharp-tongued, with no sense of her danger. And he, who ought to have brought that sense home to her in no uncertain terms, had asked instead if she got enough to eat. Just the thought of that now made him grimace with annoyance.

Glenure stepped back a pace.

"Where the devil do you think you are going?" Rory demanded.

"N-nowhere, my lord. I hope ye dinna think I've done wrong here," Glenure added hastily, "because I have not. Sir Hector Maclean—that be the Laird of Craignure, ye ken. Him being attainted after Culloden, his lands was properly forfeited, and just this past sennight, I were sent word that them lands, and Ardsheal's as well, was to be annexed inalienably to the Crown."

"Yes, I knew about Ardsheal's."

"Do ye ken as weel that the Court awarded her ladyship a hardship grant of nearly one hundred and seventy pounds after the Rising, my lord?"

"No, I did not read that in the record," Rory said. "I have sat with the Barons' Court just on two years now, you see."

"Aye, and so I thought. But since ye've met that young vixen daughter of hers, it won't surprise ye none to learn they be cut from the same bolt of cloth."

"No," Rory said with a sigh. "That does not surprise me." Seeing Thomas approaching with the horses, he gestured to him, adding, "My man will follow if we walk along together. Which way do you go?"

"Back to Glen Ure," the factor said, stepping aside to let Rory precede him through the gate. "We'll take the shore road as far as the next glen along. That will save me turning back to walk up Glen Duror. I've no wish to encounter James of the Glen again today, I can tell you."

Remembering that Diana had referred to James Stewart by that appellation, Rory said sympathetically, "He does seem to side with the Macleans."

"Aye, sure, he would then. He's close kin to her ladyship, James is, though he did come wrong side o' the blanket."

Rory said nothing.

Glenure shot him a look from under his bushy red brows. "You're thinking I bear a similar kinship to Balcardane, I expect. Well, that's true enough, though that isna the one that's usually flung in my teeth when folks dinna like what I do."

"Your mother is a Cameron."

"Aye, she hails from Morven, across the loch, and my authority extends to some few estates there, but I do my duty, my lord. None will deny that."

"Is that why you are attempting to evict Lady Maclean and her family?"

The unbecoming flush told Rory he had hit the mark, but Glenure said, "I do no more than I am told to do. Not only is her ladyship presently a felon evading the law, but she has not taken the oath. What's more, the grant she received after the Rising didn't mollify her in the least. She's a damned difficult woman, my lord. Insisted on managing her deceased husband's estate, then carried her insolence to the point of felling trees illegally and refusing to disburse her rents."

"Which is why you arrested her."

"Aye, *and* why the bailie's court sent her to prison. To teach her a lesson."

"A harsh lesson," Rory said. They had reached the road along the loch shore, but he was still feeling his way in the conversation. Uncertain of Glenure and wondering if the man would see reason if he met it face to face, he wondered, too, what imp made him want to throw obstacles in his path when he was plainly doing his appointed duty.

" 'Twas no more than she deserved," the factor insisted, "but because of it, I'm warned that her son would like to murder me. Don't believe it myself."

"She has a son?"

"Och, aye, young Neil—Sir Neil Maclean, as he ought rightly to be called. To give the lad credit, he puts on no airs, and most folks dinna call him so."

"But if he wants to murder you—"

"Rumors, my lord. I take no more stock of them than I did of rumors that the Barons would not confirm me in my post. I wait for a thing to happen. That's my way. If young Neil Maclean is a killer, I'll eat my wife's best Sunday bonnet. Now if they was to say the same of that heathenish Allan Breck . . ."

"Tell me about him," Rory invited.

Glenure shot him an oblique look. "Word is, that fox is loose again."

"He is."

Nodding, Glenure said, "Thought as much. They said he'd been run to earth, but I didna believe it. Said I'd wait and see him in chains first. Doubt I'll ever enjoy that pleasure. As slickery as an eel, is Allan Breck."

"Is he a killer?"

Glenure shrugged. "He's more a messenger, my lord. There's them that say he means to stir up a new rebellion. Don't think that myself. He isna the sort others follow. The lairds send him to collect their second-rents, and folks here send him back with messages for their exiled menfolk. He spends a deal of time on Rannoch Moor, trying to recruit the rougher lads there for Ogilvy's French army. Thinks he's a bigger noise than what he really is, does Allan Breck. He don't bother me none, nor I don't bother him."

A huge brown and white osprey plunged to the surface of

the loch so close as to startle both men, then swooped up again with a struggling salmon in its talons.

"I'll tell you what I think about Lady Maclean," Rory said, watching the bird. "I think we'd be wise to drop the charges against her." Looking at Glenure then, he added, "They are devilish unpopular, you know. She seems to have done no more than try to protect people toward whom she feels a strong sense of duty."

With a suspicious look, Glenure said slyly, "Trying to catch me out, my lord? Still thinking I might favor the damned rebels? I don't. No one seems to care a whit that I fought against them in the last rising."

"It is not my intention to question your loyalty, Glenure."

"Well, be that as it may, the woman is guilty and did not serve her full time. I willna drop the charges, my lord, and if I catch her, back she goes."

"Those two young women may become destitute if you throw them out of their house," Rory said, hoping to stir his sympathy if he could not convince him he was not testing his loyalty.

"They won't have to leave," Glenure said smugly. "Already got that worked out, I have. The good Campbell family that will move into Maclean House come Term Day will provide honest employment for both those lassies, so they willna starve or go a single night without a roof over their heads. I'm a compassionate man, I am, and if that shows disloyalty to the Crown, then so be it, my lord."

Rory found himself without a word to say. Although he had seen Diana Maclean act the roles of laundress and maidservant, he could not imagine the proud young woman he had met today working for any Campbell family to earn her daily bread. Mary Maclaine might do so without mishap, but the very thought of the quiet seventh daughter scrubbing floors or waiting on others disturbed him almost as much as the thought of Diana attempting to fill such a subservient role.

Though he would have liked to order Glenure to drop the charges and vacate the eviction notice, he lacked the authority to do either one by himself. Such actions required rulings from the full Barons' Court, and their next formal sitting was two months away. He would be back in Edinburgh by then, able to exert his influence to protect Diana and her family, but the mischief the dauntless wench might get up to in the meantime made his blood run cold.

Eight

Diana waited only until Ian had left Maclean House before declaring, "We must ask James what to do about the eviction notice, Mary."

"I did ask Ian," Mary said with a sigh. "The thought of our being evicted distresses him dreadfully. You know he cannot bear even an animal to want for warmth or food, but he does not know what we can do."

Diana sighed. "I know you love Ian, but even you must admit that he is not a man one goes to when one is in trouble. He is too young, for one thing."

"He is older than I am," Mary pointed out.

"Less than a year." Diana realized that she rarely thought of Mary being younger than herself, let alone younger than Ian. She smiled. "You seem older than anyone except perhaps old Granny Jameson. I expect that is because you are wiser than most folks. I do wish you could see into our future though. It would be a great comfort to me if you could manage to see us warm and dry in six weeks' time."

"But you know I cannot do that. I felt as if Calder would help us. You saw how wrong I was about that."

Not wanting to tell her she had been wrong about more than that where his lordship was concerned, and knowing that Mary would read the truth in her face if she did not divert her, Diana said, "He won't help us with the eviction. However, he did say he would see what he can do to make all safe again for Mam."

"Did he? That must explain why I had that good feeling about him. I do like him, Diana, even if he is a Campbell."

"Fiddle-faddle. You love Ian, and he is a Campbell."

"Yes, but you said yourself that even you do not think of him as one. He is by far the kindest, most caring man I have ever known. Folks don't call him Gentle Ian for naught, after all."

"They call him that in contrast to Black Duncan and most other men in their clan, that's all. Ian is too good-hearted even to *be* an infernal Campbell, but if you are hoping that you and he can ever be more than friends, you are more addled than even Allan thinks you are. Neither clan would allow the pair of you to marry."

"We'll see," Mary said, but she looked worried, reminding Diana yet again that, while she could occasionally catch a glimpse of another person's fate, Mary knew no more than anyone else did about her own.

It was soon time to prepare supper, and Neil came in while Morag MacArthur was helping Diana put food on the table in the little dining parlor off the kitchen. Frowning, Neil said, "Is it true that Glenure wants to evict us?"

"It is. You should have been here to see it. What a dreadful man he is!"

He shrugged. "I was helping Katherine drive some cows in for milking."

"I hope John Maccoll did not catch you making sheep's eyes at her," Diana said with a teasing smile.

"He never saw us, and I don't want to hear your thoughts on that, if you please. There is little enough for me to do here."

"Oh, Neil, you could find things to do if you but looked."

"Aye, well, tomorrow some of the lads and I are sailing to

Mull for the day to climb Dun da Ghaoithe, though I doubt that's the sort of thing you mean, but tell me about Glenure's visit. Someone at the alehouse in Inshaig said he was passing out evictions again, that he had been here and at Kentallen Inn, amongst other places.''

"It's true enough, I'm afraid," Diana said. "I mean to speak to James of the Glen tomorrow. Do you want to come with me?"

"Why should I?"

"Neil, you are our chieftain now. You have responsibilities."

"I'm a chieftain without land, Diana. That's nothing at all, and a fine fool I'd look if I went about pretending to be worth something. Moreover, if you think James would pay more heed to me than to you, you are all about in your head."

She did not press him, for she knew that he took his losses hard and did not blame him for feeling bitter. He had not fought in the rising, their father was dead, and yet the land that had belonged to their family for centuries was gone. In time Neil would come to see that his responsibility to his clan had not ended on the field at Culloden, but until that day came, she could do little to persuade him.

Thus it was that the following, misty morning she set out on her own for Glen Duror. She was not afraid to walk alone, but she took the precaution of slipping into a pocket beneath her skirt the small pistol her father had given her before leaving to follow the prince. She also tucked a *skean dhu* into her garter. It was all fine and well for foreigners to demand that Highlanders go unarmed, but if she met a wildcat, a boar, or a Campbell, she wanted to be prepared.

She had high hopes of getting excellent advice from James of the Glen, for his authority, although derived initially from the factorship and his kinship to the Laird of Ardsheal, had long since been fortified by his indisputable competence.

She knew his story well. Educated at Ardsheal's expense, he had seen service during the rising as captain of a local company. After the rebellion crumbled, when Ardsheal and others fled to France, James had come home to make peace with the government and to look after Ardsheal's wife and children. Then, when the Barons of the Exchequer took away the factorship and gave it to Glenure, Lady Ardsheal had fled to France without a word of thanks, to be reunited with her husband.

Diana did not hurry, enjoying the spring day and the cool solitude of the glen. She avoided the path by the turbulent river, keeping to deer trails instead to avoid meeting anyone who might take advantage of her solitary state. The walk took the best part of two hours, but by the time she arrived, sunlight danced on greenery wherever its rays penetrated the dense woodland. It felt warm on her face when she crossed the clearing to the house.

She had known that James might be away, looking after his various enterprises, and had been prepared to await his return, but she found him at home with his wife.

He greeted her warmly, saying, "Come you in, lass, come you in! Margaret, love, fetch out scones and jam for Mistress Diana."

"Don't trouble yourself, Margaret," Diana said, smiling at the plump, motherly woman, "but if you could ask someone to fetch me some water to drink, that would be grand. I've come to seek your advice, James."

"Aye, and didn't I expect you to come to me? I have turned my mind inside out, and I think I've got a plan. But sit ye down, and we'll talk a bit first."

His wife soon left them alone, and Diana said, "I am at my wits' end, James. Where will we go? Mam will be distraught when she learns of this."

"Now, now, didn't I say I'd got an idea? What I mean to do is to set off for the capital tomorrow at first light."

"But what can you do in Edinburgh?"

"Yesterday Colin Glenure served preliminary eviction notices, not just to you but to four other Ardsheal tenants," James said. "All are residents I introduced before he took the factorship. I tell ye, he selected them with care."

"What do you mean?"

"Not one has a standing lease or right of long-term occupation that would entitle them to stay, Diana. Even your mother's peppercorn lease is tenuous, since Ardsheal was not here when we drew it up, to make all tidy."

"That means Red Colin expects to meet few legal obstacles, does it not?"

"Aye, and he thinks any that exist will be negotiable. But each one of the five tenants has paid his quarter's rent and, as far as I know, most are willing to take the oath of allegiance. As I see it, we ought to be able to stop him."

"Why these five families, James?"

"They each bear some connection to a known rebel, Diana. Therefore, his motive for ousting them can only be to silence once and for all those voices that accuse him of secretly sympathizing with enemies of the Crown."

"It's still unfair to pick only Ardsheal families."

"He didn't," James said with a wry smile. "He chose five on Ardsheal land, but there are others, lass, including the landlord at the Kentallen Inn and at least one that I know about in Morven, a Cameron family that's kin to his mother."

"How horrid, but I still don't understand what you can do in Edinburgh."

"I mean to apply to the Exchequer for an order confirming our tenants in their holdings. A single baron can do nothing, unfortunately, but the court can help us, and once they hear what Glenure is up to, I am sure they will do what is right."

"Oh, James, if only you can succeed!"

"I'll likely be gone at least a fortnight," he said with a smile. "Don't do anything rash before you hear from me, lass, and don't, on any account, let Glenure force you from Maclean House before Term Day."

"I won't. Just let him dare try to make us leave!"

She stayed chatting until it was time for James and his family to eat their midday meal, and although she had planned to walk to the head of the glen to call on Bardie, she allowed them to persuade her to stay. Thus, it was after three o'clock before she was on her way again. Although the April dusk lingered

until nearly half past six, it was still too late to travel farther
if she was to get home before dark.

Retracing the route she had taken before, she made better
time moving downhill, but the thick undergrowth and narrow
track made speed impossible, and she knew she had plenty of
time. She had been walking half an hour when she heard a
wildcat scream a short distance ahead.

When she paused to listen, wondering what had startled
the generally shy but dangerous animal, she heard another,
distinctly human cry, followed by yet another. Snatching up
her skirt so that she could move faster, she took her pistol from
its pocket and hurried as fast as the shrubbery would allow her
toward the river path.

By the time Rory had finished breaking his fast at Balcardane
that morning, he had had a surfeit of his relatives. Ian seemed
incapable of opening his mouth without drawing fire from his
surly brother, and Balcardane apparently cared only for counting his groats. Through it all, Lady Balcardane, who had chosen
to join them in the breakfast parlor that day, maintained an
amiable flow of chatter about the weather and whatever else
chanced to attract her notice.

"That mist will clear off by noon, you mark my words,"
she said as a footman served her from a platter of cold sliced
beef. "Some bread, too, if you please," she added in exactly
the same amiable tone.

Ian said, "I mean to ride into Lochaber this morning, Father.
May I take any messages or serve you in any other way?"

"Why Lochaber?" Duncan demanded, as if his younger
brother had just announced something of a criminal nature.
"You cannot have business there."

"One of the lads told me he'd heard of a golden eagle's
aerie a few miles northeast of Onich. We are going to take a
look."

"There may even be sunlight by ten, I daresay," Lady Balcardane said.

"Nonsense," Duncan snapped, clearly startling her, but he kept his eyes fixed on Ian, and it was clear that he had not heard his mother's remark, let alone meant his response to contradict her. Oblivious, he went on, "Your friends probably saw a buzzard, that's all. There is no eagle's nest within hours of Onich. They nest higher in the mountains, on cliffs, not near the water."

"There are cliffs near the sea, too," Ian said quietly.

"Not near Onich, there aren't."

"Perhaps not, but eagles also nest in pine forests, Duncan, and you cannot deny that there is a large forest northeast of Onich."

"A wind from the northeast can chap one's skin prodigiously, my dear," his mother said. "Pray, take heed."

Balcardane said, "You can take a letter to MacLachlan at Coruanan and have a look at that horse he wants to sell. I've put off going myself to save the expense of the journey until I'd other business to take me there. It's a bit out of your way"— he ignored Duncan's snort of laughter—"but you won't let that trouble you, I warrant."

Ian glanced at his brother but said only, "No, I don't mind. Keppenach is only a couple of miles above Onich, after all."

"In the exact opposite direction from your precious aerie, if the damned thing even exists," Duncan pointed out.

Ian smiled at him. "That might distress you, but it can make little difference to me, you know. I'll take the ferry at Ballachulish in any event, and I've got nothing else to do today."

"I'll be at the Kentallen Inn," Duncan said.

"Spending your groats again," Balcardane said.

Lady Balcardane said, "I have not been across to Lochaber in months. I daresay the weather will be pleasant there today, too."

Duncan had not replied to his father's comment, but Balcardane was not content to let the matter rest. He went on to deliver a homily to his elder son on the errors of squandering money, insisting that there must be far less expensive ways to spend his time than drinking whisky with his friends at the Kentallen Inn.

Rory continued to eat his breakfast. His aunt seemed never to stop talking, and the others seemed so oblivious of her chatter that the entire spectacle became almost entertaining. Almost, but not quite.

Duncan swallowed the last of his ale and said abruptly, "I know you won't think it necessary to take a pistol with you, Ian, so for God's sake don't turn your back on any of the charming citizens of Lochaber who don't enjoy kinship with us."

Ian smiled. "I do not need to guard my back, brother. I don't count as many enemies amongst my acquaintance as you do."

"If a man is not a Campbell in these parts, little brother, he is an enemy, but if you are such a fool as to trust everyone, be it on your own head when you are struck down unaware."

"If I am unaware, I daresay even that will not trouble me. Will you attend my funeral, Duncan, and play a pibroch on the pipes?"

"Funeral?" Lady Balcardane blinked at him. "Funerals are to bury the dead, my dear. One does not enjoy a funeral until one dies, I'm afraid."

"The devil of it is that you don't believe me," Duncan snapped, pouring himself another mug of ale. "You think that smiling at people and being gentle and kind to them is enough to protect you, but it isn't, my lad, not by a long chalk. Your own clan can't protect you if you continue to approach our enemies like a damned playful puppy. You'll get kicked one of these days, and by God, you'll deserve it."

"That's enough, Duncan," Balcardane snapped. "Not but what he ain't right, Ian, lad. You stay away from them as ain't our own kind, you hear me?"

Ian smiled, and Rory said quickly into the pause that followed, "I aim to take a long walk today. Perhaps I'll tramp along with you and Duncan, Ian, since you will both be taking the road toward Ballachulish and the Lettermore Woods."

Both men looked surprised. Duncan recovered first, saying,

"I'll not be going that way, I'm afraid. I'm meeting a friend at the head of Loch Leven first, but doubtless Ian will be glad to have your company."

"I will, indeed," Ian said, smiling at Rory. "I'm leaving straightaway though. Do you want to come look at the eagles with us, sir?"

"No, thank you. I aim to walk along the ridge above Glen Creran. I want to get my bearings, so I'll come home again by way of the shore road, I expect. I just want to spend a day looking about and talking with any folks I might meet."

"You won't meet many on the ridge," Duncan pointed out.

"Well, I've got the day and all ahead of me. I'll leave you now."

"Perhaps after my cousin Archie comes to stay," Lady Balcardane said thoughtfully, "I shall ride back to Lochaber with him for a fortnight or so."

Rory stared at her, uncertain whether he ought to comment or ask who Cousin Archie was. Before he could decide, Ian said, "I'll meet you in the yard, cousin," and Balcardane snapped, "You'll take a horse, my lad."

"Not today, sir," Ian said. "We'll be on the cliffs, you see."

Balcardane looked as if he would take exception nonetheless, so Rory excused himself with careful civility and fled.

As it happened, Ian accompanied him only to the path leading to the woods, since the shore road would take him to the ferry crossing, but Rory had not really wanted company, so he did not mind. The lad gave him good directions, explaining which glens would lead him by easy paths back to Loch Linnhe from the ridge, and listing the people he might reasonably expect to meet or to call upon.

Parting from Ian, he decided to take the hill pass they had taken before, then follow the ridge top between Glen Creran and Loch Linnhe. At the head of the pass, the summit of Bidean nam Bian loomed to the east, beckoning to him. The highest peak in Argyll boasted dramatic ridges and intriguing, secluded corries. Its gorges cut deep into the rock curtain flanking Glen Creran, dropping with uncompromising steepness and exhibiting a certain alien ferocity. He recalled from his boyhood rambles that turbulent, salmon-filled rivers swept through their deepest recesses.

Bright dazzling sunlight reflecting from the summit snow cap told him the climb would be dangerous now, but the magnificent view recalled his childhood more forcibly than anything else since his arrival. Following the ridge top, he enjoyed a panoramic display of Glen Creran and Loch Linnhe. As his aunt had predicted, the mist had gone, leaving a sunny day in its passing. Small white clouds drifted in the cerulean sky, looking like a scattering of thickly wooled sheep in a vast blue meadow.

The ridge was mostly heather, grass, and granite now, and by climbing one of the nearby granite domes, he could see Lismore and beyond to Mull. To the south he saw a peak he thought might be Ben Cruachan, the ancient meeting place of the Campbells. Then, turning back to look down on Loch Linnhe, he was struck by the spectacle of the tide driving the waters into the Firth of Lorne. Currents eddied like rivers, as if the loch lay on a slope. He could almost feel the pent-up force of water swirling through the maze of black islands, then surging forth, eddying around the narrow length of Lismore, then gushing in a veritable torrent through the Lynn of Lorne into the Firth.

Nearby movement caught his eye. On a flat below, a small group of red deer grazed, but he did not think they had drawn his notice. Overhead, a golden eagle soared on high wind eddies, the deep, leisurely beats and long glides of its powerful flight making it unmistakable. It soared with its wings in a shallow vee held slightly forward, its primaries upheld. When it plunged, then swooped up again, rolling as it did, he wondered if it might be courting. Whatever it was doing, it was enjoying the day, and he thought of Ian. Smiling, he decided that neither the lad nor any friend whose opinion he respected would mistake a buzzard for the king of the skies.

There was movement below again, and this time a flash of red drew his eye to a small person who disappeared just then into a wide, dark gash in a sweeping granite slab to his right.

Curious, Rory descended, keeping his eye on what had appeared to be only a black scar on otherwise gray rocks just above the tree line.

As he neared the spot where he had seen the person, he realized it was an opening to a small glen. The song of a bubbling burn competed with that of the birds, and a few moments later, he found himself surrounded by cool greenery. A rutted path followed the burn, and he strode along, amazed to find this pleasant sanctuary in what had looked like a sea of granite boulders, grass, and heather.

He came upon the little house unexpectedly. It looked like any other house with its stone walls and thatched roof, but it was smaller all around, including its low front door. As he approached, a man appeared from the far side, walking with a lurching gait. He stopped when he saw Rory.

The man was no more than forty inches high, with stunted legs and a thick torso. Over shirtsleeves, he wore an old-fashioned crimson waistcoat that came to his knees, with brown leggings and oddly shaped half-boots beneath. His dark hair was tied back in a bag at the nape of his neck. A black cat followed at his heels.

"Good day to you, sir," Rory said. "I hope I did not startle you. My name is Calder and I've come from a morning on the ridge, looking to explore Glen Duror on my way to Loch Linnhe and back to Balcardane."

"Ye've taken a wee wrong turning then, but you're welcome enough," the dwarf said. His tone was wary, but Rory could scarcely blame him.

He knew his size intimidated men of ordinary stature and thought he must look like a giant to this one. At least the little man spoke excellent English. "You've a fine house there," Rory said.

"Aye, I built it m'self. That lout Glenure—" He broke off, then grinned, showing uncommonly even teeth. "You being kin tae him, I'd best say no more."

"You know who I am?"

"Aye, sure, I ken fine that ye be a Campbell, and that's all

I've any need tae know. I'll no give my head tae ye for washing if I can avoid it.''

"I am aware that Glenure has served eviction notices on at least one family hereabouts. Have you received one as well?''

"Nay, then, not this time. He tried that trick when he first took the factorship from James o' the Glen, but Parson told him I be a ward o' the kirk, and threatened tae shame him in public for his lack o' charity.'' He grinned again. "Want a look at me garden?''

Amused, Rory followed him around to the back of the house, where a clearing revealed a neatly tended patch of cultivated land. "You must grow enough for an army," he said.

"Aye, well, I sell enough of it tae keep m'self in snuff," the dwarf said. "I sell a bit o' the honey from my bees, too. Would ye care for a bite wi' some bread?''

"I would indeed. I've some mutton in my sack that I'll be glad to share.''

"Right then, come along. I am Bardie Gillonie, and this here's Matilda.'' He scooped up the cat and put it on his shoulder, lurching ahead to lead the way with the cat swaying but otherwise undisturbed as it clung to its perch.

Rory followed him back around to the front, eyeing the low door with misgiving and wondering if he would offend the dwarf if he suggested that they take their meal outside.

Gillonie looked back as he pushed open the door. "Ye'll fit, but ye'll ha' tae nip doon a bit or ye'll thwack your pate on the lintel.''

Rory nipped down, finding the inside of the cottage quite clean and tidy, and smelling of freshly baked bread. He had to take care not to bang his head on the cross beams, but Gillonie provided him with a stool, putting a loaf of bread, a knife, and a pot of honey on the low table beside him. While Rory took off his gloves and hat and set them aside, the dwarf turned away, then came back with two mugs. Handing one to Rory, he said, "Tae your good health, my lord.''

"And to yours," Rory said, raising his mug. Taking a swallow, he had all he could do not to choke, and it was another moment before he could breathe properly. He had expected ale, but the brew inside was some of the strongest whisky he had ever tasted. And the smoothest. He raised his eyebrows. "This is potent stuff."

"Aye, it is." The dwarf drew up a second stool and sat opposite him, resting his big hands on his knees. "Now for a bit o' pleasant discourse," he said. "Tell me what ye think about the rotation o' the earth. I'm for it, m'self, but the last chap I asked were clean against it."

Rory allowed himself to be drawn into what proved to be an absurd conversation, but to his surprise he enjoyed it, and when he saw the dwarf's dark eyes twinkling with mischief, he had a strong notion that he was being gulled. Abruptly, he said, "Don't you get lonely, living here all alone?"

"I dinna be alone. I've got Matilda, have I not?"

"Still . . ."

Gillonie made a dismissive gesture. "Got a sister in Peebles, wants tae come live wi' me and keep me house, but I keep house better nor she does. Worse, the lass lacks a quick mind like me own. She's soft in the head, is Aggie. We spent our childhood a-quarreling, and I'm no of a mind tae quarrel for the rest o' me days."

They talked of many other things, and when it was time for Rory to go, he found he was reluctant to do so. "I've enjoyed myself," he said. "How much for a pot of your honey? I believe my aunt would like it on her morning scones."

"Aye, she would, that," Bardie agreed. " 'Tis thruppence, the honey."

Making the exchange and pulling his gloves on again, Rory said, "I'll come again, if I may."

"And welcome. Mind now," Bardie added, "ye mun keep tae the path. Once past James o' the Glen's place, there'll be a fork and ye'll want the right-hand branch, or ye'll end up at the south end of Cuil Bay."

"Aye, I know. The right fork brings me out near Kentallen Inn, does it not?"

"Aye, sure. Ye'll make the inn fine afore nightfall," Bardie added with a considering glance at the sky, "but I'm thinking the dark may come upon ye afore ye reach Balcardane, and there'll no be a moon the nicht."

"Then I'll stay at the inn or hire a link boy," Rory said with a smile as he put on his hat and shook hands in farewell. "I'm glad to have met you, Mr. Gillonie."

"Call me Bardie," said the dwarf. "Ye'll do, for all you're a Campbell."

Taking his leave, Rory soon found the main glen. He strode along, thinking that although he had failed to follow through with his primary purpose for the day, he had met someone who might well tell him what went on in Appin country. He would want a few more conversations with Mr. Bardie Gillonie before he would dare trust his word, but his first impression was encouraging.

He passed a sprawling house in a clearing and decided it must be the home of James Stewart, but he did not stop. It was after three, and even if he maintained a fast pace, he knew the dwarf was right about the likelihood that it would be dark, and chilly, before he reached the castle. It was warm now, however, and he opened his coat and unlaced the top of his shirt, enjoying an unfamiliar sense of freedom.

The plain fact was that he had procrastinated like a schoolboy, enjoying the first true day of leisure that he had allowed himself in over a year. He would never have done such a thing at Inveraray. The knowledge that he would face Argyll's acid tongue upon his return would have dissuaded him. But no one at Balcardane held authority over him anymore. Here, he was wholly his own man.

Lost in thought, and walking silently on the mossy dirt path, he stepped over a fallen log without looking beyond it and trod on the tail of a large cat. Not until it screeched in fury and flew at him, turning, twisting, and apparently propelled by hidden springs, did he see the rabbit's carcass that had lain beneath it. He realized in the split second before the creature's claws struck his unprotected throat that he had interrupted a wildcat enjoying the spoils of its hunt, but by then it was too late.

The attack caught him so unaware that he staggered under the weight of the cat, crying out as he caught his heel against the fallen log and fell backward. He carried no weapon other than Bardie's honey pot in the cloth bag he had carried his mutton in earlier, and he had dropped that in the onslaught.

Thus, with only coat sleeves and gloves to protect his arms and hands, all he could do was to cover his face and try to push the beast away. Its claws were sharp, tearing right through his clothing, shredding his shirt where his coat lay open, and he wondered if the writhing beast could kill him. If he could get a firm grip, he was sure he could fling it away, but it thrashed and twisted ferociously, biting whenever hand or arm got near its mouth, and clawing savagely at any part of him it could reach. He held his arms as best he could across his throat and face, knowing that if the claws reached his eyes, they would blind him.

When the shot rang out, it nearly deafened him, but the cat took off as if it had been scalded. Then two small soft hands were touching his arms, and a voice he would know in full darkness amidst the furor on judgment day said anxiously, "It's all right now. You can put down your arms. Are you very much hurt?"

Doing as she bade him, he realized that both of his arms and his chest burned like fury. He felt damp, sticky blood everywhere. Nonetheless, looking up at his rescuer, he said grimly, "Mistress Diana, would you like to explain why a well-mannered Highland lass like yourself carries a forbidden weapon on her person?"

Nine

Suppressing a tremor of fear at Calder's question, Diana said loudly enough to be heard over the river, "You should have rolled into the water. Those cats can swim but they'd rather not, and certainly not in water rushing as fast as that is."

"That water's like ice," he said.

"So you'd rather have your eyes clawed out, or your throat slashed?"

"Why do you carry a pistol?"

"You're ungrateful as well. Do you mean to report me to the authorities?"

"Don't tempt me. Where is it?"

"Where you won't get it unless you are even less of a gentleman than most Campbells," she said. She had slipped it back into the pocket beneath her skirt, where she hoped it was not presently singeing a hole in the cloth. The barrel and firing pin tended to stay hot after one fired the thing.

Eyeing her with enough speculation to make her nerves jump, Calder said, "I do wish you would stop assuming that I am a villain just because of my surname."

"Don't you assume that I'm a rebel because of mine?"

"Aren't you a rebel?"

She smiled. "I won't answer that. If I say no, you will think me a liar, and I would have to be a fool to say yes. Do your arms hurt? There is a lot of blood."

"They hurt like the devil, and so does my chest, but I think those are the worst of my injuries. It did not slash anything of great importance."

"No, it seems to have missed both your eyes and your throat."

"Those are not the important items I was thinking about," he said with a noticeable twinkle in his eyes."

"Men," she muttered. "See here, can you get up?"

"Of course, I can." But when he attempted to do so, he staggered and had to lean on her shoulder. "Good Lord, I'm as weak as a—" He broke off with a crooked grin. "I nearly said 'weak as a cat,' but at the moment . . ."

"Not the best choice of words," she agreed, feeling weak herself and wondering at her reaction to that disarming grin. Asserting control over her wayward emotions, she went on matter-of-factly, "You got a shock, that's all, but you must clean those scratches carefully."

"They will be all right."

"Look," she said, annoyed, "that cat was one of the biggest I've ever seen around here, and some of those wounds look deep."

"I don't like fuss."

"It isn't fuss, my lord. Wildcats have got stuff in the pads of their feet that can cause terrible infection. The scent of it is so strong that one can smell it wherever they've clawed the trees. We should get help, I think. Someone ought to have heard—Ah, there's someone coming now. James, over here!"

"We heard a shot," James Stewart said, running up to them with two of his sons and his servant John Maccoll following behind. "What's amiss?"

"A wildcat attacked his lordship," she said. "He must have been all of thirty pounds or more. You remember James of the Glen, do you not, my lord?"

"I do, but are you sure that thing was only thirty pounds? It felt like a hundred and thirty to me."

"No doubt, but we do not grow them that big. They are small but very fierce, sir, and dangerous when provoked."

"I did not provoke him on purpose, mistress. I just stepped over a log."

"Onto his tail, while he was eating," she pointed out. "Very careless."

"I'll not argue that, or that his legs are like springs for him to have leapt at me like he did." He sighed. "My own legs are sagging. May I sit on that rock?"

"Yes, but you cannot sit there long." Turning to James, she said, "I want to get his lordship down to Maclean House, to Mary. Can you send one of your lads to Bardie for herbs. He'll know the ones Mary will want."

"Aye, and I'll send the other for the blacksmith at Kentallen," James said. "Your Mary knows a deal about remedies, right enough, but he'll know if aught else should be done. Moreover, someone can send word from there to Balcardane to assure them that his lordship is in good hands."

She had been about to object to sending for the smith, but like others of his ilk the man had a good reputation for healing, and in fact she did not know whether Mary would want him or not. Deciding that the decision was not hers to make, she held her tongue. When Calder attempted to stand again, she said, "We should do what we can to wash those scratches, sir. I know that is what Mary would say."

"I've no objection," he said. "Cold water might soothe them. At least that ridiculous dizziness has passed."

Diana opened her mouth to tell him she had known grown men to die after being attacked by a wildcat, but she shut it again, seeing no good to gain by sharing that news with him. Glancing at James, she saw hesitation in his expression and knew he had been thinking the same thing.

"What is it?" Calder demanded, getting up and looking from one to the other.

"Nothing, sir," Diana said. "If you are steady again now,

I think it will be best if you go down by the water and wash your arms and chest. Let me help you take off your coat." When she had, she saw with a shiver of distress that its thin wool sleeves had done little to protect his arms. She said as calmly as she could, "Your shirt is dreadfully tattered, so you might as well take it off, too. I just hope you don't take a chill when we walk down the glen."

"We'll get the shirt off when we've soaked those wounds a bit," James said, holding out an arm to help him down over the rocks to the turbulent water. "If Mistress Diana does not object to my taking my waistcoat off in her presence, my lord, you may have it to wear under your coat. My shirt would not fit you, but my waistcoat is long and very loose on me, so it ought to help keep you warm."

Seeing Calder about to object, Diana said quickly, "Never mind my presence, James. That's the very thing for him. And now, sir, don't dawdle about. You don't feel the cold yet, I expect, but you will soon enough, and I want to have you down out of this glen before then. I won't be able to carry you if you faint, you know."

As she spoke, he groped his way to a large flat boulder that jutted into a stretch of rapids tossing white froth into the air. Looking back over his shoulder at her, he smiled, and his deep voice carried easily over the sound of the river when he said with a touch of humor, "I won't faint, lass."

" 'Tis best you don't faint there," she shouted back, clutching his coat to her bosom. "For goodness' sake, pay heed to what you are doing!"

Broad pools trapped lingering late sunlight farther down, but she knew their peaceful look was deceptive. Strong currents swirled beneath the surface, and in some places narrow black gorges plunged deep between chiseled rock walls, where a victim of the river might be trapped beneath it and drowned. Despite telling him earlier that he ought to have cast himself into the water to rid himself of the wildcat, she knew that if he fell in now, it would be nearly impossible to save him. The river dropped away over a succession of granite steps that, over the centuries, rushing water had scoured and polished to ice-like slipperiness.

Feeling like a bitch with one pup, she bit her tongue and twisted her hands in the coat she held to keep from warning him again. He was a grown man, after all. Not only had he said he disliked fuss but there was no good reason for her concern.

As she watched, trying to convince herself that one Campbell more or less would make little difference to anything or anyone, he straightened and turned. His right foot slipped, missing its purchase.

Diana clapped a hand to her mouth to keep from screaming. Only when James moved swiftly to put a steadying hand under Calder's elbow did she breathe easily again, but the fear that one or the other might fall did not leave her until both men had moved away from the water toward the path again.

So intent was she on the river tableau that she did not realize John Maccoll had left them until he came bustling along the trail from the direction of James's house, carrying a bundle of cloth. In Gaelic he said, "I brought towels, mistress."

"Good," she said, taking a large one from him and giving him Calder's coat to hold. Stepping carefully from rock to rock toward the water, intending to soak the cloth, she met the other two men coming up and stepped aside to let them pass, her attention fixed on the rocks so she would not slip.

A firm hand caught her by one arm. "Let James do it, or his man," Calder said. "Those wet rocks are slippery."

She looked up at him with an impish smile. "Do you think I have never done this before, sir?"

"I think there is no cause for you to do it now," he said.

Before she could reply, James said calmly, "John, put his lordship's coat on the boulder beside you and soak a couple of those clouts in the water. While you do that, I'll help him take off his shirt so he can wash the scratches on his chest."

"Aye, master."

"Thank you," Calder said, still looking at Diana.

Standing there in his ragged shirtsleeves, he looked as big

and powerful as ever, although she thought his face had lost some of its usual color. She was not sure if he was thanking James for intervening, John Maccoll for dampening the cloths, or her for scaring off the wildcat. At the moment, it did not matter much which it was. She kept forgetting that he was a damned Campbell.

She still held the cloth she had taken from John Maccoll, and she glanced at the burly man as he moved toward the water, intending to give it back to him.

As if he read her mind, Calder said, "Keep it. I will need one to dry myself afterward. I think I am going to be glad now that the water is like ice. Just the thought of touching these scratches with those towels makes me feel dizzy again."

He was still watching her, and she had the notion that he was testing her reaction to his words. No doubt he would find it gratifying to know how her stomach churned at the thought of the pain he would endure, but she did not intend to reveal her feelings so easily. She did not understand them, and she had no wish to examine them herself, let alone allow him to do so.

He released her arm, and she stepped back carefully, certain that if she stumbled he would catch her again, and afraid that she wanted him to do just that.

Back on the rutted path, James helped him take off his wet, bloody shirt, and although Diana had intended to keep her eyes averted, she found herself glancing at the two men frequently.

Calder's broad, well-muscled chest was a veritable lacework of oozing, bloody scratches. His gaze caught hers, and she looked quickly away. Then he gasped, and she looked back to see that James had begun to clean the blood away.

Diana wanted to do it, and when Calder winced, she nearly jumped forward to snatch the cloth from James. But, catching his lordship's eye again, she kept still.

At last James said, "That will do for now, I'm thinking. I'll send John Maccoll along to see you get safe to Maclean House, sir."

"I'm grateful for your help, James Stewart," Calder said,

putting out his hand. "I'd say we've no need for Maccoll, but I'd make poor protection for Mistress Diana in this state, so I'll accept your offer with thanks."

"I can take care of myself," Diana said, the words spilling from her tongue in her relief that he seemed all right.

"Your pistol is empty," he murmured provocatively.

She saw James and John Maccoll exchange alarmed glances. Swallowing, she said, "I'm still armed, my lord, and that weapon is legal."

"Show me."

Feeling betraying heat in her cheeks, she said, "I will not."

"John Maccoll is going with us then."

"Very well," she said, adding with a direct look, "I daresay I shall be grateful for his protection."

He chuckled. "That's fact, and so will I, with greater cause." Leaving her sputtering, he turned away to let John Maccoll help him put on James's waistcoat and his own coat. Though the wool waistcoat was fashionably oversized on James, it was a snug fit for Calder, and Maccoll slipped it inside the coat so that he could don both as if they were but a single garment. Still, Calder winced as he put them on.

James moved close to Diana, saying in an undertone, "I thought it must have been his lordship's pistol we heard, my bairn. Whatever were you about to let a Campbell know you carry a forbidden weapon?"

"He might take it away from me, James, but I do not think he will give me up to the authorities," Diana said.

"But he *is*—"

"Shall we go?" Calder said. "Even with John Maccoll to protect us from each other, I'd as lief be out of this glen before dark."

"You've an hour of good light yet," James said. "Once dusk falls, it will last another thirty to forty minutes in the glen, longer in the open. You've time."

They did not tarry, and it soon became clear that Calder had no intention of coddling himself. He set the pace, and if he was walking slower than usual, Diana could not tell. As for

John Maccoll, all he was protecting them from now was an attack from the rear, for Calder had ordered him to follow Diana.

Not until they had passed through Inshaig to the shore road did Calder turn to say, "Come walk beside me. The path is wide enough, and I want to talk to you."

Reluctantly she obeyed, but before he could begin, she said, "If you mean to demand that I give you my pistol, sir, I'll tell you here and now that I won't do it."

" 'You're leaping over the hedge before you come to the stile, lass.' "

" 'Fear is sharp-sighted, and can see things underground, and much more in the skies,' " she retorted.

"God save us, a wench who has read Cervantes!"

" 'Youngsters read it, grown men understand it, and old people applaud it.' "

He gave a shout of laughter. "Ah, the fair sex."

She looked at him searchingly. "I don't think that phrase originates from *Don Quixote* like the other ones, does it?"

"I don't know if it originates there, but one can certainly find it there."

"Well, I've thought of a much better one, anyway." Shooting him an impish look, she said, " 'Those who play with cats must expect to be scratched.' "

He groaned. "Unkind, mistress. You may go whistle before I'll give you another opening for your thrusts."

She chuckled. "I think you altered that one a bit."

"I frequently do alter them," he admitted. "I find it astonishing how often something Cervantes wrote fits a modern situation. Still, I own that I'm surprised to meet a female who has memorized his work."

"Well, I have hardly memorized it all, although I have committed a number of passages to memory," she said. "I just hope you won't ask where they come in the book, because very likely I have forgotten. I know many of Shakespeare's sonnets, too, and I must tell you, I think Don Quixote was the wiser man. At least he did not insist that the only good woman is a married one.''

Chuckling, he said, ''I first encountered the don and his faithful companion, Sancho Panza, when I was a boy. My father's notion of punishment was to thrash me soundly and lock me in his library for an hour or more, depending on the gravity of my offense. I discovered *Don Quixote* on one of those memorable occasions, and soon came to look upon him as a friend to turn to in uncomfortable circumstances. As a result, I've carried a copy for years, to read in times of trial or tribulation.''

A silence fell between them, and just as Diana remembered what had begun the exchange, he said, ''What manner of weapon do you carry that you believe is legal, mistress? I can tell you for a fact that your pistol is not.''

''I know the other one is,'' she said. ''It's a *skean dhu.*'' Watching him, she wondered if a Campbell from Edinburgh would know the weapon. The Highland short dagger, derived in recent years from a skinning knife, was small enough to beat the ban, but she did not know if anyone had tested that fact in a court of law.

Calder said, ''I've seen one. They are devilish small. I'd not advise trying to defend yourself against anything of size with it, lass. As for that pistol of yours—''

''My father gave it to me,'' she said. ''It is the last thing I had from him before he died, so don't expect me to hand it over to you without a fight.''

''I won't fight you for it. I'd have to be a plutonic hypocrite to do so after you defended me with it, but don't flaunt it. Others would not be so generous.''

They were in sight of the house now, so she said only, ''We are nearly there, sir. I hope you will be as generous to my brother if he is at home and says aught to you that he should not. He is sometimes a bit free-spoken.''

''Unlike the rest of his family?''

Diana grinned at him, but in the event, Neil was not at the house.

Mary greeted her with relief in her voice. "I was beginning to think I should worry, Diana. I never expected you to be away all day. Good evening, my lord." Then, seeing Calder in better light, she exclaimed, "Faith, what happened to you?"

"A wildcat attacked him," Diana said. "Sit down, sir. You are still quite unnaturally pale."

"But no longer weak," he said, obeying her. "I wish you'd believe that."

"I'll fetch some of my remedies," Mary said, leaving them.

She had not been gone long when a pounding at the kitchen door that they could hear from the front heralded Bardie's arrival. With Mary close behind him, he lurched into the parlor, carrying a sack that he plumped down on a table. Grinning at Calder, he said, "Good day tae ye, my lord. Had I known ye meant tae wrestle a wildcat, I'd ha' gone along tae cheer ye on."

"Well met, Bardie," his lordship said with his crooked smile. "If I had known what lay in wait for me, I'd have invited you to bear me company." Catching Diana's bewildered gaze, he added, "Bardie and I took our midday meal together today. But how did you get here so quickly, sir?"

"Och, I've my own ways, I have," Bardie said, winking at Diana.

Diana had all she could do not to demand to know what they had talked about earlier, and not to send Bardie a warning look. Wondering just how much Calder knew about the group that had attacked him, she forced herself to look at Mary, fearful of giving something away in her expression if she looked elsewhere.

"I brought ye duck's weed, calf's plant, and juniper, lass," Bardie said to Mary. "If they willna serve, Mistress Diana can send one of the lads tae find nettles and another tae fish for eels."

Mary smiled at him. "First I must see just what must be done, Bardie, but thank you for bringing those things. I've got dried mariner's plant, of course, but the calf's plant will make a more potent poultice to draw off any infection that might be starting. I've already asked Morag to heat water and fetch me some barley.'' Turning to Calder, she said, ''Will you let me examine your wounds now, my lord?''

''Gladly,'' he said, ''but you ought to know that James of the Glen sent one of his sons for the smith at Kentallen. I am afraid you will find me much more trouble than my wounds are worth.''

''Oh, no,'' she said calmly. ''A wildcat's scratches easily grow corrupted, sir, and men have been known to die from them, so you must not treat them carelessly.''

Diana saw the look he shot her, and knew as if he had spoken that he realized what she had been thinking earlier. He did not argue with Mary, however, sitting where she told him to sit and allowing himself to be divested of James's waistcoat and his own tattered coat. She heard him gasp once, and she saw him wince.

Mary glanced at her. ''Do you think a shirt of Sir Hector's might fit him? This waistcoat is snug on him. Every move he makes must be painful.''

Diana had not thought of what the scratchy wool must feel like against his wounds, and she sent him a look of apology.

He smiled and shook his head. ''You make me sound like a bleating milksop, Mistress Mary.''

''Weak as a cat,'' Diana said, ''but 'thou hast seen nothing yet.' ''

Mary looked surprised. ''Thou?''

Calder chuckled. ''She is quoting from *Don Quixote,* mistress. I warrant she is hoping your poultice will make me shriek mercy for my sins.''

''Is she, indeed? The shirt, Diana.''

With a speaking look at Calder, Diana went to find him a shirt. He was larger than Sir Hector had been, and Neil had taken most of their father's remaining shirts, but she found an old one that was baggy enough so that she thought it would do. Taking it back, she found that the smith had arrived, having hurried from Kentallen in the clear expectation that he would find a dying man at Maclean House.

He was a large, muscular fellow of indeterminate years, and he looked a little put out. In Gaelic he said, "The lad did tell us his lordship had been scratched to bits, so I near killed a horse to get here."

"Thank you for coming," Diana said. Glancing at Calder in the expectation of seeing an embarrassed smile on his face, she saw instead that he was frowning.

Bardie said with a touch of belligerence, "Speak English in the presence o' your betters, man. I don't see why ye came here at all, for we've no got any use for ye. Ye must know that Mistress Mary can look after things better nor ye."

"I've healing in me hands," the smith said, his English awkward but adequate for the purpose.

"Aye, and Mistress Mary's a seventh daughter, ye auld gowk."

"Gowk, am I? See here, ye loathsome diddler—"

"That will do, the pair of you," Diana said. To the smith, she added in Gaelic, "We are much obliged to you for coming so quickly, but I do think you will find that Mistress Mary does not require your assistance."

"Aye," Bardie put in gruffly.

Morag MacArthur entered just then with a basin, and Mary, moving toward her, said to the smith in a kindly way, "I mean to use the ribbed side of calf's plant to draw out any of the remaining poison, and the smooth side to encourage healing. For the deeper scratches on his chest, I shall add calf's plant to a barley poultice."

"Aye, that's good," the smith said approvingly.

Bardie said, "Ye'll wash your hands first, lass, and take a sixpence from his lordship tae bless so he can wear it round his neck."

Mary said to Morag, "Put the basin on the table, please. There is no need for a sixpence, Bardie. That is little more than superstition, and mostly for boils."

"It canna hurt," Bardie said stubbornly.

Surprisingly, the smith said, "He is right. Best do it, mistress."

Diana said with a grin, "Have you got a sixpence, my lord? Mary will put it in the water she's just washed her hands in. Then you must wear it around your neck till the wee folk take it from you along with any remaining evil in your body."

"There's a small purse in that sack John Maccoll carried down the glen for me," Calder said. "Bring it here, Maccoll. I think I've got a sixpence."

Maccoll handed it to him, and he looked inside.

"Here you are," he said, handing a coin to Mary. Then, reaching into the sack again, he tossed a shilling to the smith. "That's for your trouble," he said. "I am glad to know who you are and where to find you if I ever have need of you."

Bowing and tugging his forelock, the smith assured him that it would be an honor to serve him. Then he took his leave.

John Maccoll said, "My lord, if you'll no be needing me more tonight, I'll walk along with him. It's time I were getting back up the glen home."

Calder hesitated, but Diana said, "Thank you, John. Sir Neil will be along soon, so if his lordship decides he must go farther tonight, he'll look after him."

Maccoll nodded, frowning, then left with the smith.

When the door had shut behind the two, Diana said, "Why did you taunt the poor smith, Bardie? He means well, and he has an excellent reputation as a healer."

"No so good as Mistress Mary's," Bardie said. "Moreover, he is a fool."

"So you told him," Diana said, "but there was no need to take him to task for speaking the Gaelic. We all understood him, after all."

"Nay then, lass, his lordship doesna speak it, and it's gey unmannerly tae speak a language your guest canna put his tongue round."

"But he does too speak it," Diana said.

At the same time, Calder said to Bardie, "How the devil did you know?"

Diana looked at him in surprise. "You said you had understood us!"

"No, mistress, you assumed that I did because I knew what you and your companions said after they attacked us. But how did you know I don't, Bardie?"

Smiling, Bardie said, "If a man speaks the Gaelic easily and meets up wi' a chappie like me in the woods, he'll no start blathering English like ye did the day, for he'd no think a Highland dwarf could understand him. Either ye thought I would, or ye canna speak the Gaelic. The choice was unco clear, my lord."

"Yes, I suppose it was," Calder agreed with a grimace.

Diana said, "I don't believe you. You must understand some."

"I do, of course," he admitted, "but not enough. I was fluent as a child, but I've not had to use it much since, you see. My man speaks it, but he is not with me every minute, so I want to gain a better command before I leave here. I find I don't like being left out when others speak a language I don't comprehend."

"That's how many folks hereabouts feel when the authorities babble English at them," Diana pointed out.

"Then perhaps they should learn to speak English," he said gently.

"If that isn't just like a Campbell, to insist that people give up their native ways, right down to their native tongue, and take up the ways of their conquerors."

"This will hurt a bit, my lord," Mary said.

When he gasped at her touch, Diana's irritation melted and she turned away, glad that Mary knew what she was doing. She was even more glad that she did not have to do it herself. She wanted to snatch him baldheaded sometimes, but the thought of really hurting him made her feel ill.

The calf's plant stung enough to make him groan, but Mary said, "It will be over quickly, sir, and I promise you, it's necessary. If the scratches putrefy, they will become far more painful than they are now."

"I don't believe you," he said. "That stuff is liquid fire."

"Bear up," Diana said bluntly, wanting to divert his attention in much the same way she had diverted Neil from childhood pains. She need not have worried, however. A greater diversion came in the person of Ian, striding in from the kitchen.

"Mary, I'm sorry, I couldn't get here sooner. I—" Seeing Calder, he broke off, clearly at a loss, then blurted, "Sir, I— Are . . . are you injured, cousin?"

"And here I thought you came rushing in to protect me from an enemy clan," Calder said smoothly. "Clearly your interest in this household is greater than I had imagined, lad. Perhaps you had better explain it to me."

The tense silence that fell must, Diana thought, have told him all he wanted to know, and may even have suggested much more.

Ten

As the silence lengthened, becoming almost palpable, Rory watched Ian narrowly. The lad was clearly disconcerted to see him, for he kept glancing awkwardly from one to another of the others in the room as if he hoped one of them would speak for him.

Bardie Gillonie grinned at him. Diana was watching Rory, and Mary had stopped with her hand halfway to his chest, holding the hot poultice she intended to place there. Her sympathetic gaze fixed on Ian, and it was she who recovered first.

"Ian calls here frequently, my lord," she said matter-of-factly. "We stopped thinking of him as a Campbell long ago, I'm afraid. We have no argument with him." Gently, she laid the poultice in place.

Rory stifled a groan. The damned thing was hot.

Ian collected himself visibly, enough to ask, "What happened to you?"

Rory began to tell him, but the others chimed in, in a near chorus, and he fell silent, letting them tell it while he watched Ian. Several times the lad looked at Mary, and his expression when his gaze fell upon her lovely countenance told Rory that he had guessed right about the true attraction at Maclean House. Instead of annoyance, he experienced a strange sense of relief, completely at odds with the strong loyalty he felt to his clan.

"Couldn't handle a wildcat, eh?" Ian said at last, smiling at him.

"Mistress Diana said it was the largest one she had ever seen," Rory said, breathing more easily as he became used to the poultice and it cooled a little.

"The cat was huge, Ian," Diana said. Then, looking at Rory, she went on with a touch of acid in her voice, "I don't know why you keep squirming, my lord. That poultice produces much less heat than a mustard plaster."

"One does not, in general, lay a mustard plaster upon an open wound, lass."

Bardie said, "He's in the right about that, he is."

Apparently deaf to their exchange, Ian said musingly, "Wildcats attack only when they feel threatened or if one provokes them. Why did you upset him?"

Glaring at him, Rory said, "I do wish people would stop taking sides with that fiendish cat. If it was stupid enough to drag its supper onto the path where a log hid it from anyone approaching, it deserved to get its tail trodden upon."

Ian laughed, as did the others, but Rory noted that his cousin still seemed wary and ill at ease. Seeing no reason to coddle him, he said bluntly, "I thought you went into Lochaber, hunting eagles, Ian. What business brings you here?"

Glancing at Mary again, Ian looked for a moment as if he would not answer, but then he squared his shoulders and faced Rory directly. "I suppose you will tell my father, but I won't deny why I'm here even so. I love Mary, Cousin Rory. I have loved her since the day I first set eyes upon her."

"And you, mistress?" Rory looked at her.

She felt the poultice. "That should be heated again, I think, sir."

"It's barely started to cool," he protested. "Answer my question."

Diana said quickly, "What difference does it make what she

feels? Neither the Campbells nor the Macleans would countenance such a union.''

Her eyes bright with tears, Mary snatched up the poultice and fled.

When Ian moved to follow her, Rory said firmly, ''One moment, lad. Surely you know that Mistress Diana is right. Your father would see you dead and buried before he would let you marry a Maclean, no matter how she spells the name.''

''Aye,'' Bardie agreed. ''That's plain fact, that is.''

''Perhaps not,'' Ian said. ''Campbells have married Macleans before.''

''In the distant past, perhaps.''

''Many times,'' Ian insisted. ''Marriage between factions is an excellent way to fortify any truce between them, Cousin Rory. You must know that.''

Rory frowned. ''First there has to be a real truce, Ian.''

''But there is! There has been no killing for six years, no rebellion, no—''

''No defiance of the lawful authorities?'' He looked at Diana.

She glared back at him, but with telltale color in her cheeks. The light outside had faded, and someone had lighted lamps in the parlor. The maidservant, he supposed. She had come in and gone out several times since his arrival.

Diana said, ''None of that matters a whit. If Balcardane did not stop it, Black Duncan or the Macleans most certainly would.''

''But, Diana—'' Ian began.

''As for your stupid notion of bolstering a truce,'' she snapped, turning on him, ''I know of at least one Campbell-Maclean union like that, that nearly took the life of the bride. Although she was the Campbell, just thinking about what her loving husband tried to do to her makes me shiver.''

''Is that the Lady Rock tale?'' Ian demanded.

''It is.'' To Rory she said, ''Back in the days when the Macleans were still struggling with the Macdonalds to fill the void left after the fall of the Lord of the Isles, they formed an uneasy alliance with the Campbells of Argyll and fortified it with more than one intermarriage. Some of those couples may have got on well enough, but Lachlan Maclean was the sort of man who only wanted a thing till he got it. Becoming bored with his wife, Lady Elizabeth Campbell, who happened to be the Earl of Argyll's sister, he began casting his eye about for a new wife. But he could not just send Lady Elizabeth back to her brother, or tell him she had somehow disappeared, so he marooned her on a rock in the Firth that disappears at high tide.''

"Pleasant fellow," Rory said, watching the way the lamp-light set highlights dancing in her ebony hair. "That's why they called it the Lady Rock, I expect."

"Right," Ian said. "It lies near where the Sound of Mull meets the Firth."

"Midway between Lismore and Craignure," Diana said. "I could see it from my window at home."

"Are you talking about the Lady Rock?" Mary asked, returning with a fresh poultice that sent a cloud of steam rising from the basin in which she held it.

Eyeing the steam with misgiving, Rory said, "Your cousin is explaining why it is unwise for Campbells to marry Macleans."

"I don't see that the Lady Rock story proves that at all," Mary said. "They had an unhappy union, to be sure, but I don't think either side behaved well."

"Though it pains me to say it, that Maclean was stupid," Diana said. "Thinking Lady Elizabeth had drowned, he reported her death to the Campbells."

"I remember that tale now," Rory said. "His announcement was premature, was it not? Unbeknownst to him, a pair of passing fishermen had rescued her and taken her to Argyll."

"That's right," Ian said.

"Well, I hesitate to confide this," Rory said, tensing as Mary laid the hot poultice across his chest. "It was one of my ancestors, the Thane of Cawdor, who avenged the attempt on Lady Elizabeth's life. He was also her brother, you see, and shortly afterward he paid a visit to your Maclean in Edinburgh."

"A visit!" Diana exclaimed indignantly. "He sneaked into

Maclean's bedchamber, taking him by surprise, then dirked him in his bed!''

"I heard it was a fair fight," Rory said calmly.

"Well, I never heard that."

Bardie said, " 'Tis some hundreds of years in the past. Stands tae reason that hereabouts they'd tell the version that makes the Macleans look best, and that his lordship would hear only the Campbell's side. 'Tis likely, I'm thinking, that there's but a whisker's worth o' truth in both stories, lass."

"Bardie's right," Ian said, a note of relief in his voice. "I only mentioned other unions because I hoped you might put the notion in my father's head, Cousin Rory. If it came from you, he'd be bound to listen."

"You give me more credit than he would, I fear," Rory said.

Ian began to protest, but Mary silenced him with a look.

"The poultice is cooling, my lord," she said, putting her hand on it. "Morag will have the next one warm by now. Ian, love, please tell her to bring it to me."

"That won't be necessary," Rory said. "I am grateful for all you have done, but I mean to get back to Balcardane tonight."

"But you cannot," Diana said. She bit her lip, and he knew that she wished she had not spoken. Still, it was a sign that she cared whether he lived or died.

He was beginning to take quite an interest in Mistress Diana, and while he knew that nothing could come of it, he was glad she had not tried to freeze him out of her life altogether. He had promised Patrick to keep an eye on her, and by heaven, he meant to do just that. Although he was as loyal to his clan as any man, he had never understood those who refused to make friends among the opposition.

"You should rest, sir," Mary said.

"I promise you, I shall," he said. "But I'll do my resting at Balcardane."

"Best let him have his way," Ian said with a sigh. "If he does not show up tonight, my father and Duncan will think you've abducted him."

"That's right," Rory said, giving the poultice to Mary and looking around for the shirt Diana had brought him.

Bardie handed it to him. "I've got a string for your sixpence, too," he said.

Rory smiled and shook his head, but the dwarf said, "Ye'll wear it, or Mary will be thinking it's her fault if ye die."

"Well, I don't want her to think that. You'll come with me, Ian?"

"Oh, aye, of course I will. I don't want your death on *my* conscience either."

"You will take horses, sir," Diana said.

"I am perfectly stout," he told her.

"Nonetheless, you will not walk to Balcardane. Ian would take the shortest, most difficult route without thinking twice about it."

"I'll take him by the long road if Mary says I must," Ian said.

"You'll take horses," Mary told him. "There are at least two good ones in the barn, Diana, if one of them can ride the bay with the white stockings."

"White Boots? Certainly. Neil will not mind." She was still watching Rory, and when he caught her eye he saw color flood her cheeks.

Mary said, "I'll tell Morag then. Take the sixpence, sir," she added, handing it to him. She had affixed Bardie's string to it, he saw.

He took it from her and tied it around his neck. It rested lightly on bare skin where he had left the shirt open at the top instead of tying its lace.

"If the coin disappears, don't fret, sir," Mary told him. "It is meant to do so, they say, for then you can be sure all the poison has left you. I'll tell Morag to have someone saddle the horses now."

Ian was helping him shrug into his coat again, without James Stewart's waistcoat, when the front door opened and another young man entered. This one was as dark as Diana, but his face was longer than hers and his eyes deeper set. For a moment

Rory wondered if he could be the fugitive who had escaped from Stalker. Even before the thought completed itself, however, he saw how young the lad was—at least a year or more younger than Ian—and knew he was not Allan Breck.

"We wondered where you'd got to, Neil," Diana said.

"I told you, we sailed to Mull to climb Dun da Ghaoithe. And don't ask if I called on any of our old tenants," he added, "because I didn't."

"Aye, you did say you would go today," she said calmly. "Make your leg to Lord Calder, if you please. This is my brother, Sir Neil Maclean, my lord."

The lad hesitated, a frown darkening his brow, but then he said, "How do you do, sir? Are you kin to Gentle Ian?"

"I have that honor," Rory said.

"Then you are welcome here. I remember now," he added, looking at his sister. "You said he was here yesterday when that villain Glenure served his notice."

"I did," Diana said coolly. "Mind how you speak of those who are not present to defend themselves, if you please."

He looked at her as if she had lost her mind. "Since when do you care what I say about Red Colin? Allan says far worse than I do, and you never reprove him."

She shot him a look from under her brows.

Flushing bright red, he said defensively, "Never mind that. When is supper?"

Rory wondered if young Neil had been among the group that assaulted him. He could not imagine Mary or Ian taking part in such an event, but it occurred to him that he could imagine Bardie helping to plan the assault, at least, if not actually taking part in it.

He dismissed these thoughts as unworthy of one who owed most of the present group a debt of gratitude, and began to make his farewells. He noted though, that when the horses were ready, young Sir Neil made no secret of his relief at their departure, even when he saw that Rory had borrowed his gelding to ride.

* * *

"You see what comes of giving a Campbell the run of this house," Neil said to Mary and Diana when the others had gone. "Now he's bringing his deuced kith and kin to call. I expect we'll soon be serving supper to Balcardane and his lady."

Diana said coolly, "I brought his lordship here, Neil. Would you have had me leave him to the mercy of a wildcat, or to the putrefaction of his wounds?"

Neil shrugged petulantly. "I don't care what becomes of him. Devil take it, Diana, are you mad? We attacked the man just a few days ago, and now we're nigh onto offering him a bed in our house. You even gave him White Boots to ride!"

Exchanging a look with Mary, Diana decided not to mention that they had wanted Calder to spend the night. Seeing him on his feet, smiling and at ease, she had known he was nearly as stout as he claimed to be. Yet she could not rid herself of the thought that for him to be out in the dark was dangerous. With a sigh, she told herself that before long she would be thinking she had acquired Mary's gift.

Her feelings about his lordship were double edged. When she chanced to think about the moment she had first seen him with the writhing, snarling wildcat clawing at him, she felt the same shiver of fear race up her spine that she had felt then. He was not a small man. He was large and clearly accustomed to taking care of himself. Yet in that moment she had known he was as vulnerable as any other man in such a predicament. He might have managed without her help to fling the cat off, and to chase it away. But one accurate slash at eyes or throat, and he would have been blinded, or dead. Either thought was too horrid to contemplate.

Helping Morag and Mary get supper to the table, she reminded herself yet again that he was a Campbell like any other Campbell, but to her mind's ear, the phrase sounded stale and inadequate, even untrue. He was as different as a man could be from any Campbell she had met before.

Calder had Ian's kindness, insofar as he had refrained from

betraying her to Patrick Campbell or, as far as she knew, to anyone else. More than that, he had treated her with consistent civility and a complete lack of the umbrage one expected to meet with in a Campbell. Ian did not count. That young man had no loyalties that anyone could discern, and no strong passion for anything or anyone except the creatures of the forest and Mary Maclaine.

Even his passion for her cousin was not what Diana would want from a man she loved. Ian clearly adored Mary. No one could doubt that. But he was content to watch her, to serve her, to be at her beck and bay, to worship her without question. If he knew she had a temper, Diana had never seen any sign of it. He certainly had none himself. She could not imagine Gentle Ian taking up a sword even to defend Mary's honor, or knocking down a man to avenge an insult. Not that she could imagine any man insulting Mary. No one did.

It was not that folks feared her. Mary's gift set her apart from other women, and although the occasional outlander might be tempted to think her a witch, even they thought her a good one because of her knowledge of the healing herbs. Local folk were soon able to convince the wary that she merely possessed a mysterious, awesome gift. Diana believed that people loved Mary, much as they did Ian, for her generous spirit and peaceful nature. But Allan Breck had insisted more than once that there was an element of real fear, too, no matter what anyone else claimed.

"They fear the lass will see their passing one day," he had said on more than one occasion. Diana wondered if he had merely spoken his own fear aloud.

"I saw Dugald today," Neil said, cutting into her reverie as he took his place at the table.

"Why did you not bring him here?" she demanded. "Did he speak of Mam?"

"Of course, he did," Neil said. "He came to say that she is homesick and wants to return. I warned him not to let her do so."

"Did you tell him about the eviction notice?" Mary asked him, putting the last of the steaming platters on the table.

"Of course I did, but I told him not to breathe a word of it to Mam."

"Oh, Neil, you should not have told him," Diana said. "I doubt that Dugald can keep it to himself. If MacDrumin or anyone else even suspects he's got a secret, they'll winkle it out of him in no time."

"No, they won't. He promised me he'll keep mum. Besides, I wanted his advice. Dugald is a knowing lad, when all is said and done."

"What sort of advice?" Diana asked with misgiving.

"Never you mind. I've got a notion how to keep Maclean House, that's all, and Dugald has promised to help me."

"Help you do what?"

"I'm not going to tell you."

"Oh, Neil, don't get into trouble."

"If that isn't just like you," he complained, "telling a man to take responsibility one minute and chafing at him about it when he does."

She apologized, but she did not forget the conversation. Her younger brother had been feeling his bitterness more and more of late. She knew he fretted at having no power to mend things for their people, and even more at losing Craignure Castle.

She thought often of the massive black strength of Craignure. Impregnable, they had thought; yet it had fallen to the enemy without a shot fired in its defense. After Culloden, a few papers signed in London had accomplished the matter, and their people on Mull had become Crown tenants, dependent on uncaring authorities.

Lady Maclean had visited the island regularly until her imprisonment, when Diana and Mary had taken over the task. Neil took them each week in his boat, so they could visit their old tenants and be sure no one lacked the bare necessities to survive. Few admitted to troubles these days, their upset having been great at her ladyship's arrest, but all were glad to see Diana and Mary when they visited.

These visits led to others, elsewhere, for many of their people had kin in Appin, and Diana never refused to pay a requested call, if only to reassure one kinsman that the other was well. For the fortnight following the wildcat's attack, she kept busy with such tasks as these and put all thought of the eviction out of her head. There was nothing she could do about it, except to trust James, and trying to think of how they would survive if he failed them only made her head ache.

She tried to put Calder out of her head as well, but that proved to be more difficult. His handsome image danced in her dreams, and she saw him pass by numerous times on the road, but he did not call at Maclean House.

At the same time, she fretted about her brother. Neil had become secretive, and when she heard that Allan Breck had left Rannoch and was in Appin again, she feared that somehow Allan would convince Neil that salvation lay in joining his regiment. Her informant was Granny Jameson, an elderly woman whom she frequently visited, but Granny had laughed when Diana mentioned her fears.

"Och, nay, lass," she said. "Allan Breck were but drinking too much whisky at the Kentallen Inn. He'll no be recruiting our lads. But what's this I hear tell aboot that buzzard Glenure trying tae turn ye oot o' Maclean House?"

"So he says," she admitted. "I don't know what we will do if he succeeds."

"Och, but I hear that be settled as well," Granny said, smoothing her white apron. Her pale blue eyes twinkled. "According tae Glenure, he means ye tae serve the new Campbell family that will live in your house."

"Does he?" Diana snapped. "Well, believe me, I'd kill myself, or him, before I'd allow him to make me any Campbell's slave."

The fortnight passed slowly for Rory. More than once, he found himself thinking up excuses that would take him to Maclean House, but he did not go. His sixpence had disappeared without a trace, and although Mary had warned him that it would, he did not believe wee folk had crept up in the night and stolen it.

He often heard about Diana as he made his rounds of the area. At first, few people would speak openly with him about anything, but he frequently encouraged Ian to walk with him, and the lad proved an invaluable companion. He numbered as many Macleans as Campbells among his friends, and if everyone did not greet Rory with unmixed delight, they were civil to him because of his kinship to Gentle Ian.

He was wise enough not to assert himself, for he knew he would learn more by being quiet and polite than by asking a lot of questions. It was Ian who first mentioned the wildcat, and who told of Diana taking Rory home for Mary to heal.

They had stopped at the Kentallen Inn one evening for refreshment, and Ian told the tale to entertain others in the common room. The atmosphere warmed with the telling, and although Rory endured some friendly teasing, he welcomed it. His Gaelic had improved. Much of his childhood vocabulary had returned, and he understood most of what was said to him now.

"Had his head near took off by a wee wildcat, eh," one of the wags said, cocking his head in mock puzzlement. "Would that be the Mistress Diana as took it off, or the wee beast in the forest, I'm wondering."

A chorus of chuckles greeted this sally, and Rory said with a friendly smile, "I do not in general speak of ladies in pubs, sir. But since I can say only good things about one who rescued me from dire peril, I do not hesitate to say that the only wildcat I have met had a great deal of fur and many sharp claws and teeth."

The man nodded, grinning, and raised his mug. "A fine lady, is the Mistress Diana. Aye, and her mother, the Lady Anne Stewart Maclean. Mistress Mary, too. I drink a toast tae their continued good health and good works, I do."

"Aye," echoed numerous others, raising their mugs. Next,

they toasted Rory and Ian, then the Highlands, the king (albeit not by name), and bonnie Scotland.

Rory found himself downing enough mugs full of ale to make him wonder if he would be able to keep to his road going home. Glancing at Ian, he saw the lad watching him from beneath his brows, amusement plain in his expression.

"Are they trying to put me out of my senses?" Rory asked in an undertone.

"Nay, but you do not have to drink it all at each toast," Ian said, grinning. "They won't take offense, for they are—most of them—sensible Macleans, Camerons, and Stewarts. You are only a weakling Campbell, after all."

"That will be enough of your sauce, lad."

"Oh, aye, I'm mum. We can leave now if you like."

"I like. You've given me most of your day, and while I am grateful, I cannot help but think you would rather be elsewhere."

They were getting to their feet as he spoke, and the others called out farewells and invited him to return. Tossing some coins to the landlord, Rory told him to give everyone another drink, thus assuring his welcome whenever he chose to return. Ian had gone on ahead, but he waited by a tree outside in the moonlight. They were afoot that night, but a friendly half moon rode high over Loch Linnhe, its reflection dancing on the waves, making them sparkle like a scattering of diamonds, and turning the mountains of Morven into looming black masses across the loch.

There was hesitation in Ian's manner when he met Rory's gaze, and in the moonlight Rory thought he could detect spots of color on the boy's cheeks. As they began to walk along the road toward the path through Lettermore Woods, Ian said, "There was no need to thank me, sir. I don't mind taking you about."

"You've been mighty generous with your time, all the same."

"You have been more kind than I deserve," Ian said. "I expected you to say something to my father after you learned about Mary and me. No one could have been surprised if you had, but I ought to have known you would not.''

"Are you so certain I haven't?'' Rory asked with a smile.

"He'd have rung a harsh peal over me if you had, and Duncan would have done worse than that." Ian sighed. "You must think me a coward. Duncan says that I'm as weak as a girl. Which is a stupid thing to say," he added on a different note. "Only think of how strong the Maclean women are, all three of them.''

"Yes, it was a stupid thing for Duncan to say," Rory agreed. "I don't think you are weak, lad.''

"You don't?''

"You have managed to make friends on both sides of a potentially explosive situation. With a host of men like you we could bring peace to the Highlands.''

"Well, I *am* something of a coward," Ian confessed with a rueful smile. "It took me nigh onto a fortnight to raise this subject with you, and I still don't know how the devil to tell my father about Mary.''

"Sometimes it takes a long time to think of just the right thing to say.''

The boy's brow cleared. "That's true," he said. "You know, you are much easier to talk to than Duncan or Father. I'm glad you came to Appin.''

"I, too," Rory assured him, thinking of Diana Maclean.

They walked along the moonlit road in easy companionship until they reached Balcardane, but there they met with a flurry of activity. Men shouted in the stable yard, and metal clinked against metal, giving Rory to know before he had fully taken in the scene that some of them were arming themselves.

"What goes on here?" he demanded of the first fellow he met.

"Cattle raid, my lord," the man said. He carried a dirk and a powder horn, and the bulk of a holster showed beneath the left flap of his jacket.

"Here?''

The man chuckled. "Aye, my lord. Master Duncan heard

they mean to take the herd grazing at the head of Loch Leven. We put them there because it's near time to move them to the upper shielings. Beltane feasting's but a sennight away.''

They found Duncan in the great hall, slinging a sword belt over his shoulder. A musket and powder horn lay on a table nearby. ''I see you know about the raid,'' he said. ''One of my lads heard a whisper and told me.'' Turning to Balcardane, who was hurrying down the stairs, he said, ''You need not go with us, sir. I can manage. We've heard of no organized raids of late, so this group is bound to be a small one.''

''Aye, you'll look after things,'' Balcardane said, ''but need you take so many men? Some of their gear is like to be damaged, and will require replacing.''

''If I take fewer men, we're like to lose it all,'' Duncan said evenly.

''I'll go with you,'' Rory said.

Duncan looked at him for a long moment, then shrugged. ''As you wish, cousin, but I'll not wait for you.''

''I'll be along as soon as I've put on my boots. Ian, tell Thomas to saddle my horse. Do you come with us, lad?''

''He does not,'' Duncan said sternly. ''He'd only get in the way or get himself killed. He'll stay here where he's safe.''

Ian did not argue with him but hurried off to obey Rory's command.

When Rory returned to the courtyard, Thomas had Rosinante saddled and ready for him. ''Watch your back, lad,'' he said tersely when Rory had mounted.

''Aye, I will, but I'm curious. Who dares to attack the Campbells?''

Thomas spread his hands, glancing around at the group of twenty or more mounted men. ''Ha'ye got your pistol at hand?''

''I have, and the dirk as well.''

Duncan shouted, and they were off at a canter, riding down-hill to the road, then east toward the head of the loch. A half moon hung low over Morven, its light sparkling on the water, against which the riders made ghostly dark shadows.

Rory rode next to Duncan. ''Won't the raiders hear us coming?'' he asked him, pitching his voice to carry above the rumble of hoofbeats on the dirt road.

"The cattle are in a glen near the head of the loch,'' Duncan said. "We have an advantage even if we don't take them unaware, for I doubt they have horses.''

Half an hour later, Rory heard cattle lowing ahead.

"They're there, right enough,'' Duncan said. Spurring his horse, he plunged ahead, but Rory caught up quickly.

Just as he picked out the entrance to a narrow glen ahead of them, a horn sounded, its three-note melody sounding eerie in the pale moonlight.

Duncan gave a shout. "They've seen us and some are mounted!''

One rider made a dash for the Lochaber side. Gathering his mount, he cleared the rushing burn that fed the loch in a magnificent arc, showing that both horse and rider knew their business well.

"I'll follow him,'' Rory cried. "You take the others.''

"Take some of my men with you,'' Duncan shouted at him, but Rory had already given spur to Rosinante and pretended not to hear.

In that brief moment when the moonlight shone brightly upon the escaping horse and rider, he had seen the flash of four white stockings. He remembered instantly that he had ridden such a horse in the past fortnight.

"Unless I miss my guess, Rosinante,'' he muttered as the gray galloped toward the crossing, "that reiver is none other than Sir Neil bloody Maclean.''

Eleven

Rory had all he could do in the next few minutes to keep Rosinante steady beneath him, for the ground turned mushy on the other side of the narrow, tumbling burn. A mist was rising, too; and to make matters worse, the moon was disappearing behind the mountains of Morven. In minutes it would be gone.

Sighting his quarry ahead, he urged Rosinante to a faster pace, and as he did, he heard the telltale sound of harder ground beneath them. The gray surged forward, proving again that it was nothing like its skinny namesake. The distance between Rory and the other rider decreased rapidly.

He saw Neil glance over his shoulder, and involuntarily did the same. No one was following them. His feelings about Neil were mixed. One moment he wanted to protect him, the next to flog him, but he dared not even shout. There was no sign of a breeze now, and the mist-clouded waters of Loch Leven lay calm and still. Voices could easily carry to the other side, less than a half mile away.

The mist changed the tones of their thudding hoofbeats, making them sound almost hollow. It drifted in patches over the land, and with Neil giving him the lead, Rory could see the ground ahead well enough to keep Rosinante at the heady pace the lad set, but soon such speed must prove dangerous. It was a miracle that one of their horses had not already missed its footing on the uneven ground.

Even as the thought entered his mind, he saw Neil draw rein and slow his pace. Rory let Rosinante close the distance before he did likewise, then saw to his astonishment that Neil was grinning. Anger surged within him, but he controlled it, waiting for the boy to speak first.

"I knew it was you," Neil said.

"I am not surprised. I recognized you, as well."

"Did you? How?"

"White Boots."

Neil looked surprised. Then his expression cleared, and he exclaimed, "How stupid of me! You rode him back to Balcardane after the wildcat attacked you. That was weeks ago, though. Fancy your remembering."

"I am not in my dotage," Rory said, resisting an urge to grind his teeth.

Neil must have heard a warning in his tone, for he said anxiously, "Are you angry? Look here, you won't tell Diana, will you, or the authorities? You did not catch me with stolen cattle, after all, and there's no law against riding at night."

"No, there is not," Rory said. Little light remained now. Only a curved sliver of moon still peeked over the mountains to the west. "You had better hope no one else recognized your horse, however, and that your confederates do not betray you. I'd have little choice then but to admit that I recognized both you and the horse."

"Would you do that?" Neil frowned. "I expect you would at that. I thought that since you were smitten with my sister you would not betray me, but I'll warrant you're a Campbell through and through, after all."

"I am that, lad, but I am also a fair man, and as you say, there is no law against riding at night. Why did you run?" He saw the boy stiffen indignantly.

"If you think I'm a coward, think again. When we heard

the horn, the men ran for cover. Not everyone with me was mounted, however, and I was afraid you might catch the ones afoot, so I flashed out of the glen, hoping to lead you all on a chase. I never thought only one of you would follow."

"I knew I could catch you," Rory said. "You should be glad I came alone. Duncan's men would not be so willing to engage in conversation with you."

Neil chuckled. "I can't deny that. Will you tell Duncan about this?"

"Not unless I must."

"I knew I was right about you, but don't tell Diana either, will you?"

"You'd best tell her yourself, lad. I've a strong notion that others will have recognized that gelding. You should know better than to ride a horse that's so easy to identify on an illegal foray."

"Are you saying you'll tell Diana if I do not?"

"I'm saying," Rory explained with more patience than he had thought he could muster, "that you are misreading the situation between your sister and me."

"She saved your life! What's more, I've seen the way you look at her."

"She's a beautiful woman. I'll warrant most men look at her."

"Well, that's a fact, but still—"

"Expect no more favors from me," Rory interjected, suppressing a new, amazingly strong emotion that gripped him at the boy's casual agreement that other men admired his sister. Refusing to recognize the feeling for what it was, he added harshly, "You may tell her, while you are about it, that we are even now. It is quite possible that she saved my life that day in the woods, but taking it all in all, I think she will admit that we are quits. She owes more to me now than I owe to her."

"I don't know what you are talking about," Neil said stiffly.

"Don't you? Oddly enough, I credited you with more intelligence than that."

"Look here, I know that you know all about—"

"Don't be a damned fool," Rory snapped. "If you are about to speak of things that lie in the past, don't. What I know or suspect, is of no consequence until you confirm it, lad. Trust me when I say you do not want to put anything into words that you might have to admit later if I have to make an official statement."

The moonlight had gone, and the scattering of stars above cast insufficient light to reveal the boy's expression, but Rory heard petulance in his voice when he said, "Oh, very well, have it your own way. I won't say another word."

"I wish I might believe that."

"What the devil do you mean by that?"

"Nothing. Go home, Sir Neil, and give thanks to God that you can do so. And next time—for I do not doubt there will be a next time—take greater care."

Angrily, Neil jerked his reins and kicked the bay's flanks.

Watching him ride away, Rory found himself sending up a little prayer that Neil would reach Maclean House safely. Turning back, he forded the burn, but instead of riding into the glen where he knew he would find the others, he turned toward Balcardane. The last thing he needed now was an angry confrontation with Duncan, although he could not doubt there would be one before the night was done.

At the castle, he found his aunt, his uncle, and Ian waiting in the drawing room. Ian looked anxious and Lady Balcardane politely inquisitive, but his uncle seemed to be his usual testy self.

"Where the devil is Duncan?" Balcardane demanded. "Did you catch them or was it all a hoax?"

"Cattle raiders," Lady Balcardane said, in much the same tone that another might comment on the weather. "I daresay they will not mind the dampness rising off the water, but it seems to seep through the very walls. Even my yarns feel damp tonight. Perhaps you might stir up the fire, Rory dear."

As Rory turned toward the fireplace, Balcardane growled, "Never mind that! Ring for a servant if you want the fire tended, madam. Where is Duncan, lad?"

"He is still at the head of the loch, I believe," Rory said, handing the poker to Ian when the younger man got up from his chair and reached for it. "Perhaps, Aunt, if I move your chair nearer the fire, your yarns will stay dry."

"Do you think so, my dear?" She looked at the pile of multicolored threads in her lap and sighed. "They are very pretty, don't you think?"

"Odrabbit it, he don't care a whit about your yarn, madam! And if it's got damp, don't think you'll be buying any more. What did you find, sir? What did you find? Did they get any of our cattle? Expensive beasts to replace, cattle are."

"As to that, sir, I don't know," Rory admitted. "I think perhaps we frightened the raiders off before they were able to take any. I chased one that rode away. Then, being uncertain that I would find the others, I came back here."

"Ye did right," Balcardane said. But he continued to fret until he heard noises heralding arrival in the great hall. "That will be Duncan, that will. Run tell him where we are, Ian, or he'll go straight off to bed."

Ian obeyed and soon returned with his brother. Duncan looked straight at Rory, his mouth set. "So you let him get away, did you?"

"I'm afraid he did get away," Rory said, pretending to misunderstand.

"So did his friends, may they rot in hell. Don't look so damned innocent."

"Duncan, please, your language," his mother protested.

"Sorry," he said in a tone that belied the word. "You recognized that horse as easily as I did," he said, advancing angrily toward Rory.

"What horse?" Ian asked.

"Bay gelding, four white stockings," Duncan said without looking at him.

"White Boots? Neil Maclean's bay?"

"You see, cousin, that horse is well known hereabouts."

"Is it? I'm afraid it's not the first I've seen with such markings. Nor will it be the last. But if you are sure, why do you not simply confront him?''

"And say what? That his horse was involved in a cattle raid? I told you to take two of my men with you. Why did you not?''

"I don't know your men," Rory said. "Since you did not shout names or order anyone to follow me, I gave chase without them. I am not as familiar with the terrain as that rider was, however. In any event, we'd be hard pressed to prove he was near any stolen cattle," he added. "Were any of them actually stolen?''

"By God, I don't believe this," Duncan said hotly. "You say you came here to be certain those who had been disloyal to the Crown were not being treated too softly by the factors. Now here you are letting one of the devils get away after he's tried to steal our cattle!" He took another step toward Rory, who braced himself.

Ian grabbed Duncan's arm. "Wait," he cried. "You're being unfair, Duncan. He said we can't prove Neil did anything illegal, even if he—'' His words ended abruptly when Duncan turned in fury and knocked him down with a single blow.

"Don't get up or I'll do it again," Duncan thundered, standing over him. "You don't know what you are talking about, you young fool. You don't even know which side you are on, because you can't think beyond Mary Maclaine's bewitching gray eyes. Oh, aye, I know all about her. Did you think I did not?''

Ian stayed where he was, looking warily up at him and rubbing his reddening jaw. "It's just as well that you do know," he said quietly.

"What's this?" Balcardane demanded. "What about Mary Maclaine?''

"Only that he'll make any excuse to visit Maclean House, that's all," Duncan said. "That'll end soon enough though, when Red Colin evicts the lot of them. Even our Ian will think twice before making a fool of himself over a serving wench.''

"She's no serving wench," Ian said, starting to get up.

Duncan shifted his weight threateningly.

"That will do," Rory said.

Duncan looked at him, his eyebrows shooting upward. "Do you think you can interfere if I decide to teach my little brother respect for his elders?"

"I think you will be happier if you don't put me to the test," Rory said evenly. He met Duncan's angry gaze and held it.

"Oh, very well," Duncan said. He turned on his heel and strode to a side table where a tray laden with glasses and a decanter of whisky stood.

Rory held out a hand to Ian, helping him up.

Balcardane glared at his younger son. "What's this about Mary Maclaine?"

"I love her," Ian said. "That's all."

"All, is it? I forbid you to set foot in that house again."

"They are to be evicted on Term Day," Ian said. Looking at Duncan, he said, "What did you mean when you said Mary will be a serving wench?"

"Colin don't want the women to starve," Duncan said smoothly. "He's made arrangements for them to earn their keep, that's all."

Before Ian could take issue and draw his brother's fire again, Rory said, "First he must make his eviction stick, I think."

"Are you saying he cannot?" Duncan smiled. "Will you order it set aside."

"I have no power to do that."

Duncan sneered. "First the Barons warn him not to show favoritism. Then one of their own comes amongst us, and does just that. I begin to think perhaps my idiot brother is not the only one with a strong interest at Maclean House."

Balcardane said angrily, "I wish someone would explain all this to me!"

Duncan ignored him, saying to Rory, "I wish you well, cousin, but you will find that neither of them bears a soft spot for Campbells. Mary Maclaine encourages Ian now, but just wait and see how she treats him after they are evicted."

"I begin to think the notion of evicting them was not Glenure's alone," Rory said, watching Duncan narrowly.

Duncan shrugged. "Think what you like."

Diana learned of the attempted cattle raid the next day, and soon discovered that her brother had been involved. When she confronted him, he did not deny it.

"Calder said you would find out," he said with a shrug. "Nothing came of it, though, so you needn't make a fuss."

"Not make a fuss! Neil, if you had been caught by the Campbells, they might have hanged you on the spot to save the sheriff the trouble!"

"No, they wouldn't. They never saw me near any cattle, and there is no law against being out and about on a moonlit night. We kept a good watch, and Dugald got all the lads away safe and sound."

"Dugald! I ought to have known, but how did either of you think a raid could possibly help matters?"

Shrugging petulantly, Neil said, "Don't blame Dugald. We were going to sell the cattle. Money always helps matters, Diana, and you are always saying I should help the clan. We might even have bribed Glenure to forget our eviction."

"He is more likely to have arrested you the moment you attempted it, and surely you did not hope to bribe Calder. What did he have to do with this?"

"He caught me. But he had to let me go," he added hastily. "He could prove nothing, after all. Still, he says you owe him more now than he owes you."

She got nothing more from him, but she soon had more important matters to concern her, for on Sunday James of the Glen returned from Edinburgh. She had received only one letter from him in the weeks he had been away, to tell her that he had been unable to present their case before the Barons of the Exchequer.

"Too few of them are in town to make up a quorum, and they do not sit again until after Term Day," he had written.

"I've met with one of them, though, and I now hope to present our case to the Court of Sessions, and not wait for the Barons."

He presented himself at Maclean House on Sunday afternoon. Diana knew from the moment he entered the parlor that he had brought them good news.

"Oh, how glad we are to see you," she exclaimed, smiling with relief.

"Whisst now, wait till ye hear it all before ye cheer, lass," he said. "We've no done with it yet, but we've made a good start."

"Tell us," Mary said, gesturing for him to draw up a chair and sit down. "Morag will bring you a mug of ale if you like."

"Aye, I'd like that fine. Me throat's as dry as a ridge-top rill in August."

Diana contained her impatience while he took the mug that Morag gave him and drank deeply of its contents, but then she said, "Now, tell us at once. Can we tell Red Colin to go to the devil, James?"

"Not just yet, lass," he said, taking a second, more modest sip of his ale.

Mary said, "Is it true that one Baron agreed to advise you?"

"Aye, it is. I knew one alone couldna help much, and I didna want to talk with a Campbell against Red Colin—Three o' the five be Campbells, ye ken. But this chap says he is certain the Barons will see justice done when next they sit."

"What about now?" Diana demanded. "Red Colin means to evict us on Term Day, and that's little more than a fortnight away!"

"I know, lass. My chappie advised that them that be most threatened—which would be her ladyship, a few Camerons, and the landlord at the Kentallen Inn—must present a proper protest to Glenure."

"Mam cannot come here to protest. Red Colin would arrest her!"

"Aye, but ye can stand for her, or Sir Neil can."

"Not Neil." She had barely spoken two words to him since

learning of the cattle raid, and in any case, she would not trust him on such a mission.

"Aye, well, Colin would listen to you best, lass," James said. He added with a self-conscious smile, "That isna the whole of my news though."

"What more then?"

"I got a solicitor to present our case before the Court of Sessions," James said. "That's the highest court in all the land, and only see what came of it." With a flourish, he extracted a sheaf of papers from inside his coat and held them out.

"What is that?" Mary asked.

" 'Tis called a sist, or a stay of execution, *sine die*. The Latin bit means till an unspecified date, so there's no end to it, not till we say there is or the court does."

"Oh, James, that's wonderful," Diana exclaimed. "How clever you are!"

"It ought to keep us going until we can present our case to the Barons' Court and get the evictions set aside."

Impulsively, Diana said, "Can we show it to Red Colin straightaway, James? Oh, how I shall enjoy that!"

"Slowly, lass, slowly. I ha' never done anything like this afore, ye ken, so I want to do it right. I'd best no be party to it myself, for it must be done peaceable and proper, with a solicitor present, and all."

"Do we know a solicitor whom we can trust?"

"I've a kinsman who will do it. I'll take it to him tomorrow. There's one thing more," he added with a note of hesitation.

"What?"

"No one is obliged to join the delegation that takes the sist to Glenure, but I'm afraid each of them who would avoid eviction must promise to take the oath."

"I cannot be sure Man would agree to that," Diana said. "What can we do?"

"Well, don't be thinking ye can whisper the oath yourself and be done, lass. The tenancy is in her ladyship's name. I know, because I drew up the papers myself. If ye act in her behalf, ye must promise she will take the oath at first opportunity.''

''I'll have to think about that, James.''

''Aye, and so I knew. We've plenty of time before we must present the sist, but I'd as lief do it quick now that I've got it in me hands.''

''I understand.'' She did, but she did not like it. Lady Maclean would hate the notion of swearing an oath of allegiance to the British king. Diana hated it, too.

''Did you glean any other news in your travels, James?'' Mary asked.

He grimaced. ''Only that our Allan is making more mischief. I met him at a dramhouse in Lochaber, and when I told him about the evictions, he said the folk of Appin are spineless for not ending Glenure's career. Spoke verra loud, he did.''

''What can he be thinking?'' Diana demanded. ''He must not make himself so visible, or he will soon have all the Campbells chasing him again.''

''Aye, but he's ale-mad. In Glen Coe, I heard he'd offered a man a good price for Colin's skin, as if it were a fox's pelt. I never could curb that lad's temper. He declares that before he returns to France he'll teach Colin a sharp lesson. I hope he'll not attempt any such daft thing, I can tell you.''

Diana hoped so, too, but knowing Allan had a tendency to talk big when he drank too much, she discounted his threats. She had to decide what to do about Red Colin and the eviction. She tried to discuss it with Neil, but he offered no help.

''Do what you please,'' he snapped. ''You will anyway.''

She did not press him, but early the next morning when Ian came to call, bringing Calder with him, she was in no mood to cope with either of them. Though she had not spoken to Calder since the day of the wildcat attack, she had thought of him frequently, and now, thanks to Neil's encounter with him after the failed cattle raid, his appearance at Maclean House put her instantly on the defensive.

Mary greeted the two men with unfeigned pleasure, saying,

"Neil has gone out with his friends for the day, so you find only Diana and me, I'm afraid."

"We did not come to see Neil," Ian said, smiling at her. "You must wonder why you have not seen me in over a sennight, so I'll confess at the outset that my father has forbidden me to set foot in Maclean House again."

"Then why have you come?" Diana said curtly, avoiding Calder's gaze.

Shooting her a look of surprise, Ian said, "Cousin Rory expressed an interest in visiting the Isle of Mull today, and perhaps climbing Dun da Ghaoithe. We thought you and Mary might like to go with us."

"Not today," Diana said. "We have more important things to do."

Looking annoyed, Mary said, "Faith, Diana, what have we got to do?"

"Beltane is but two days hence," Diana said stubbornly. "The grates must all be cleaned and new fires laid. Morag has all her baking to do, so we must help."

"We have plenty of time," Mary said. "Most of that must be done on the day, anyway. You said you wanted time to think, Diana. You can do so as easily in a boat sailing to Mull as in the parlor, or while you're cleaning a grate."

A brief silence fell before Calder said gently, "I hope you will come. Ian knows about Mull, he tells me, but not nearly as much as one who grew up there."

She met his gaze and felt warmth surge into her cheeks. It was ridiculous, she thought, the way she allowed the man to affect her. Perhaps the best thing would be to submerge herself in his company until she tired of him and could put him out of her mind as he deserved. No doubt he expected her to thank him for protecting Neil. He would have a long wait.

"Very well," she said abruptly. "We'll go. Morag will have to pack food—"

"We've got food," Ian said cheerfully, "and I've brought my boat. We sailed at dawn from Balcardane, and the wind is from the northeast, so it will give us good speed to Mull. We can return on the tide late this afternoon.''

In the boat, when they had pushed off, Mary moved swiftly to help Ian with his sails and rigging, leaving Calder and Diana alone in the stern.

"Do you know what you are doing with that tiller?" she demanded.

"Would you like to man it?" he asked calmly.

"No. If you think I am going to thank you—"

"For what?"

"For not turning Neil over to Black Duncan, or Glenure.''

"I require no thanks. Just be sure he understands that I could not have helped him had his confederates been caught and spoken against him.''

"No one was caught.''

"They were fortunate.''

"They were indeed.'' She sighed, looking at the water. He said no more, and after a few moments, she began to feel the sea's calming effect, as she always did.

From amidships she heard Mary call to Ian, and his reply. Gulls shrieked overhead. Two flew alongside the sleek sailboat, clearly hoping someone would fling them a crust. She did not look at Calder. After a moment she closed her eyes, listening to the rush of water as the boat skimmed the waves, to the flapping of sails when they luffed and the snap when they filled with air. Rigging clinked, gulls cried, and she could hear sea lions barking from distant rocks.

"What troubles you so that you must give particular thought to it?''

His voice was low and sounded almost at one with the hushing of the water. She opened her eyes and looked at him. "I must think how to prevent your kinsman from evicting us, of course. James has found a way to stop him, but it requires that Mam swear the oath. I daresay you can guess how she will feel about that.''

"Is her pride worth more to her than her home?''

"That's so easy for you to ask," Diana said scornfully. "What do you know of principle, or honor?"

"My principles and honor are intact," he retorted, glancing toward the bow as if to see if the others could overhear. "Now, answer me. Will your mother allow her pride to keep her from taking the oath if that is the only way to save your home?"

"I don't know," Diana admitted.

"Can you talk to her?"

"Not easily. She is some distance from here."

"I see. Is her presence required to prevent the eviction?"

"James says not, only her promise, which I could give on her behalf. Everyone, even Red Colin, knows she would not refuse if I promise for her."

Mary moved to sit nearby, and conversation turned to other matters until they reached the Island of Mull and beached the boat near Craignure Castle.

"They're letting it fall to ruins," Diana said, glaring at both men.

Ian said defensively, "It is not our fault. It belongs to the Crown."

She said no more, leading them instead up a sheep track behind the castle's thirty-foot curtain wall. The track followed a burn that spilled in waterfalls over rock terraces along the way up. Though Dun da Ghaoithe dominated the northeastern quarter of the island, climbing it was easy. In less than two hours they reached its stony summit, where drifting puffs of mist had begun to form.

Between the puffs, they enjoyed fine visibility. Diana pointed out the peaks of Skye in the north and scattered houses of Oban to the east, then Grass Point to the south. Looking down on a landscape spattered with cattle, sheep, and thatched white houses, she felt the onset of homesickness and a sense of sad defeat.

"I say," Ian said, "there are an awful lot of cattle down there. Do you think any of them are ours?"

"If it seems like a lot," Mary said, "it's probably because the drovers are gathering them to move them to the high pastures after Beltane. And if any of those cattle are stolen, Ian Campbell, it is only because people here have few other ways to feed themselves."

"Speaking of food," Calder said mildly, "how about breaking out what we brought, Ian? I'm starving."

Mary smiled at Ian then, and he grinned back at her.

Conversation while the four of them ate was desultory. When they finished and started back down the track, Diana moved to lead, but Calder caught her arm and said, "Let them go ahead. I want to talk to you." She obeyed reluctantly, and he said, "Tell me how James can stop the evictions."

Glaring at him, she said, "You just want to know so you can stop him."

"Have I tried yet to prevent anything you've done?"

That was unanswerable. At last she said, "He obtained a thing called a sist from the Court of Sessions in Edinburgh."

"Did he indeed? James is a wilier man than I thought, then."

"Do you even know what a sist is?"

"I do. It will delay the evictions, just as you said."

"There is a rub."

"Your mother and the oath."

"How can she swear it? Even if she were to agree, she would no sooner show her face here than they would arrest her and send her back to Edinburgh."

"Is that all that's keeping you from presenting the sist to Glenure?"

She nodded, amazed that he could think such a point trivial.

"What if I could prevent her arrest?"

"Could you?"

This time he nodded. "I never thought it was right, you know."

Without thinking, she blurted, "But you are Argyll's man."

"I am close kin to him," he said, "but you can count that a point for your side this time. Will you trust me?"

Meeting his gaze, feeling its intensity, she suddenly felt as if she were alone with him, as if the rest of the world had vanished into the mist. The look in his eyes warmed her to her toes. She reached out to touch him, feeling surprise when his waistcoat felt rough and real.

His hand clasped hers and held it against him. "I can make it safe for her to return if she will agree to swear the oath," he said quietly, looking into her eyes.

She pulled her hand back, collecting herself. "I . . . I don't know. Can I trust you? You are a Campbell first and foremost, after all."

"If you do not trust me, what then? You would be wisest to protect what little remains of your property, mistress."

They were still high enough on the mountain to have a wide view, and gazing down at what her family had lost, Diana knew he was right.

Accordingly, when the little deputation called upon Red Colin two days later, on the morning of the feast of Beltane, she and Mary went with them.

Greeting the group with astonishment, Red Colin said harshly, "Don't ask me to let you keep your homes. It's too late. I've already let them to other tenants."

"Then you must unlet them," Diana said, handing him the sist.

He stared at it in shock. "Where the devil did you get this?"

"Read it, Red Colin," Diana said, unable to keep the note of triumph out of her voice. "We have our own fair copy, so you may keep that one for yourself."

As the group turned and strode cheerfully away, Mary muttered in an undertone, "Don't gloat yet, Diana. I've got a very bad feeling about this."

Twelve

Diana stared at Mary in dismay. "What do you mean, a bad feeling?" she demanded. "What sort of bad feeling?"

"I don't know exactly," Mary admitted, pulling her cap from her head and loosening her tawny hair in a way that would have drawn censure if Lady Maclean had been present. The solicitor and the other men who had gone with them to Glen Ure walked ahead, striding rapidly to get back to work they had left to be part of the deputation. "I can't think with my hair all twisted up," Mary said.

Diana chuckled, looking fondly at her. "You look like a bairn with it spilling down your back like that."

"Well, hair needs to breathe, too," Mary said defensively, "and it's not like I keep it in a fashionable state at the best of times."

Diana laughed aloud at that, for her cousin's idea of a grown-up hairstyle was to twist it into a knot at the top of her head with bits escaping every time she moved or turned her head. No hot irons, curl papers, or powder for Mary Maclaine. "It does help," Diana said, "that your hair curls all by itself."

"Oh, aye, but it is heavy all the same, and piled all on top, it gives me a headache, so I cannot think."

"Well, think now. Your bad feelings often mean someone has died. It's not that sort is it?" She felt a rush of panic, thinking of Lady Maclean, of Neil, and oddly, of Calder. All three images collided in her mind's eye.

But Mary was shaking her head. "It's not that sort of feeling at all. I would never describe *that* as a mere feeling, Diana. A vision is far, far more powerful."

"Then what?"

"I truly cannot explain. It may be only the sort of feeling anyone gets when they think things are too good to be true. It just niffles at me, making it impossible to feel good about what we did. . . . Oh, look," she added in much lighter tone, "violets are blooming in the woods, and a whole field of bluebells."

They had left Glen Ure to follow the path up Glen Creran, and Diana had been watching the rushing river, still swollen with run-off from snow fields higher up. They had walked from sloping, sunlit granite into a shady wood, and she looked obediently beyond the velvety moss-covered bank into dimly lit fern-filled spaces under the trees until her gaze fell upon a cloud of blue covering the ground. Bluebells in countless thousands, each with its soft leaves and single spray of slender bells, made a vast blue lake amidst the greenery.

"Oh, I wish we could take some home," Mary said. "Everything will be particularly tidy today, and a bouquet of bluebells would add a touch of lovely color to festival time."

"They would wilt long before we could get them home."

"I know, and they belong in the woods. Still, they are beautiful."

They walked for some distance through cool greenery before Diana drew her cousin's thoughts back to the first topic of conversation. "If not death, then what?"

"I don't know. I wish I hadn't spoken. Something will go wrong, that's all."

Diana frowned. "There is one thing that could go wrong. Red Colin did not question the document at all. I don't think he read past the part barring the evictions, but James said everyone must swear the oath. What if Colin declares that since Mam has not taken it, we cannot stay? How could we fight him then?"

Having bent down to peer into a snow pond near the path, Mary glanced back over her shoulder to say, "If Aunt Anne could arrange to take the oath properly before Term Day, he would have nothing to declare. Would she do it?"

"I don't know, but that would be better than my making promises for her," Diana said. "Perhaps she could even return to us. Calder said he can protect her if she will swear the oath."

"Do you trust him?" Mary turned back to the pond.

Diana hesitated. "Instinct tells me to trust him, but experience warns me that I'd be a fool to trust any Campbell, especially a Campbell male."

"They say he is Argyll's man."

"Aye, well, they are close kinsmen, aren't they? But that means he can draw on the duke's influence to protect her. I have seen how men respond to him"

Mary looked back again and smiled. "You know that niffling I told you about?" When Diana nodded, she said, "It goes away when you talk of trusting his lordship. I think he is much like Ian. Come look at all the pollywags, Diana. This pond is teeming with them. I hope it doesn't dry up before they can hop away."

"Calder is not like Ian," Diana said indignantly.

Mary laughed. "Oh, not in the way you mean, but he can be kind. He is not always ruthless like Black Duncan or Balcardane, or Allan Breck."

Accustomed though she was to defending Allan, Diana did not want to bicker. "We should hurry," she said, moving on. "We haven't time to dawdle if we are going to help Morag prepare for the festival. She will be trying to clean hearths and bake Beltane bannocks at one and the same time, if I know her."

"Yes, of course," Mary said, straightening at once and hurrying to catch up.

The May first festival of Beltane was one of four ancient fire festivals celebrated in the Highlands, and although it was no longer as grand an occasion as Yule, All Hallows, or the Midsummer festival, many still enjoyed its traditions and festivities. For Highlanders whose sustenance depended upon their flocks and herds, Beltane coincided with the move to summer pastures, and since protection of their stock was of basic importance, they invoked both Christian saints and pagan deities to provide every protection imaginable.

"I know Morag wants to go into Kentallen for the fun tonight," Mary said a short time later. "Her brother Gordy is helping with the bonfire."

"Do you think anyone will try to herd cattle through it this year to purge them of evil spirits?" Diana said with a chuckle.

"No, though I daresay some of the more agile lads will leap over it," Mary said, leading the way across a stone bridge to the other side of the river, so they could begin the walk up and over the low ridge into Glen Duror. "They enjoy the sport, but do you think the folks who break up their bannocks and fling them to the gulls really think it protects their cattle from eagles and wolves?"

"I should think you would be fascinated by the more magical rites of Beltane," Diana said.

"Why, because of the Sight? There is nothing magical about that. At least, I don't think of it as magical. It is frightening, Diana. I'm glad it doesn't happen often, or I'd go mad. I'm glad, too, that I cannot see the future, although I have learned to trust certain feelings," she added with a speaking look.

"I know," Diana said, "and I mean to do something about the one you had today. I shall leave for Glen Drumin tomorrow to speak to Mam."

Mary frowned. "Do you think you must convince her to take the oath?"

"I don't know, but I want to look her in the eye when I tell her what I have done," Diana said. "I am sure Red Colin will be on our doorstep the moment he realizes an oath is required. Before that happens, I want to be out of his reach. And before

I promise for Mam, I want to know she will not object. Then, too, if I can arrange for her actually to swear the oath before Term Day . . .''

"She will honor any promise you make in her name, Diana. You know that.''

"I know, but to force her . . . Do you understand how I feel about that?''

"Aye.'' Mary hesitated, frowning again. "I don't like you going to Glen Drumin though. The hairs on the back of my neck stood up when you said that.''

"Well, I'm going, so tell them to lie down again,'' Diana said. "These odd feelings are of no use to anyone if you cannot explain or interpret them. Things happen or they don't, Mary, but one cannot complain about what does happen if one has done nothing to prevent it. And I don't mean to waste time tonight attending a village festival, either. I'll need to pack some things, and I'll need a manservant to go with me, I expect, so I shall have to arrange about him as well.''

"I think Dugald Cameron is still in Appin,'' Mary said absently.

Three yellow butterflies darted ahead of them, one with orange-tipped wings, and Diana knew Mary's thoughts were darting with them, so she did not respond at once. If Dugald were still about, he would provide better protection for her than a manservant, but if she asked Neil to find him, Neil would want to go. By the time Mary realized that Diana had not answered, she had thought of another topic of conversation, and they talked in a desultory way until they reached Maclean House.

Neil was in the kitchen when they arrived, munching one of Morag's freshly baked bannocks, and although he had wanted no part of the deputation, he was eager to know what had occurred. While they described their visit, Diana and Mary began to polish grates so Morag could tend to her baking.

Tradition demanded that enough bannocks be baked for everyone in the house, and to hand out to guests and workers. It was time to replenish the home fires, as well, and so freshly cut wood and peat lay neatly piled in baskets beside each hearth, waiting for the new fires to be laid.

When Mary went to replace the parlor grate, Diana drew Neil aside. "I want you to find Dugald and bring him here," she said quietly. "I must speak with him."

"Dugald? Don't be daft."

"Don't tell me he's gone home already!"

"No, he's still about, but if you mean to mix him into another of your mad schemes, Diana, forget it. The only reason he hasn't gone back to Glen Drumin is that he felt he ought to put a good show on his visit here, lest the damned Campbells suspect he took part in that cattle raid."

"Did any Campbell see him that night, do you think?"

"No, but they have been everywhere. If it's not Black Duncan and his men harrying folks and asking fool questions, it's Patrick Campbell and his soldiers from Stalker, still searching for Allan. Dugald tells everyone he is just visiting kinfolk, and to that end, he's been rethatching his old auntie's cottage, all innocent like."

"Well, I want him," Diana said. "I suppose I shall have to explain." She did, and as she had expected, Neil said not only that Dugald would leap at the chance to go with her but that he must go, too. "I don't think that's wise," she said.

"Don't argue with me, Diana. I am not going to let my sister ride into the remotest part of the Highlands with only one chap—even if it's Dugald—to protect her. It ain't seemly, and Mam wouldn't like it."

"Then I'll take one of our menservants along as well, and my pistol, too."

"You'll take me," he said stubbornly.

"Neil, don't be foolish. What if Black Duncan or one of Patrick Campbell's men is watching you? They did see you riding away from that raid, after all."

"We'll leave before first light. By the time anyone knows we've gone, we'll be well on our way. I'll tell Dugald to meet us at some point well beyond Fort William. That way no one will see us all together."

"What if they see you speaking to him?"

"They won't. He's bound to attend the festivities in Kentallen tonight. Everyone will. I've only to find an opportunity to slip a word into his ear."

She hesitated. "We'll all go to the village then. I had not meant to go, but if you go alone, they will watch you more closely. Morag," she added, raising her voice, "will we need more bannocks if we take a basketful with us to Kentallen?"

"Nay, mistress, I've plenty for all and to spare," the maid said placidly.

"That's settled then," Diana said, wondering if Calder would attend the Beltane festival, and trying to ignore the thrill of anticipation she felt at the thought.

The sun slipped behind the western mountains as the party from Balcardane approached the Lettermore Woods track that evening.

"I'm glad you decided to come with us, Cousin Rory," Ian said, riding beside him. Lord and Lady Balcardane and Duncan rode ahead, while a number of servants from the castle, including Thomas MacKellar, walked behind.

"You'll be leaving us soon, I expect, lad," Balcardane said over his shoulder.

"I've still a few things I want to do, sir," Rory said. "If I have not worn out my welcome, I'd like to stay a week or two longer."

Lady Balcardane said placidly, "You are welcome to stay as long as you like, my dear. It is no trouble to us, no trouble at all."

Duncan said bluntly, "Haven't you got business in Edinburgh, cousin?"

"Not presently. The duke is still at Inveraray, for I had a letter from him yesterday. They've begun to rebuild the west wing, and he approved some refurbishing of Castle Stalker, too, which will please Patrick Campbell."

"I was referring to the court," Duncan said. "Don't they meet soon?"

"Not until June," Rory said. "I'll return before then."

"I heard about the sist, you know," Duncan said.

"Did you, indeed?" He wondered if Duncan was hinting that he knew James of the Glen had failed to present his case to the Barons' Court because they had lacked a quorum. He did not know himself whether he was glad or sorry about that, for without hearing the evidence he could not say how he would have voted (had he somehow learned of James's intent and managed to be present). He did know how he would have wanted to vote, but duty demanded that he give fair hearing to all the evidence, and he did not know if he could have listened without prejudice.

All in all, he decided, it was as well that he had not known of James's intent. He was certain that James had purposely not told him. James would most likely not have expected to encounter a problem raising a quorum, and the fewer Campbells he had to contend with on the court, the better he would have thought his chances. Campbell members held the majority, after all. The others, like James, would expect Rory to vote with them against any Stewart claim. Argyll would expect that, too.

Duncan said no more about it, and Rory turned his thoughts to the evening ahead. They passed others on the road, and long before they reached the village, he found himself eyeing each new group as if he expected to see a familiar figure among them. He knew it was absurd to watch for her this side of the village, since Maclean House lay beyond it, but he could not help himself. Each time he saw a head of glossy black curls, his heart beat faster, and the sense of disappointment that followed, when he saw that the face belonged to someone else, was most unsettling.

The festivities, he soon learned, took place not in the village proper but in a large adjoining field bounded on the west by the loch, its waters looking gray and chilly in the light of dusk. The tide was running, stirring currents on the surface, and from nearby rocks jutting above the receding water, sea lions barked, their cries muffled by the chatter of the increasing crowd and lively music from fiddles and other stringed instruments. Rory found himself listening for the familiar skirling of bagpipes, though he knew he would hear none. Like the Highlanders' weapons, bagpipes had been banned as instruments of war.

Dusk had dimmed nearly to darkness before he saw her, for Ian and some other men had demanded his help with the bonfire. Turning to scan the crowd again, he saw that children, dozens of them, had congregated in one corner of the field.

Curious, he drifted nearer, to find them gathered around Bardie Gillonie, who had perched on a boulder, his short legs folded beneath him, knees pointed outward, his big hands resting lightly atop them. The dwarf was telling a story in the Gaelic, and Rory was pleased to discover that he could follow it. His command of the language had improved over the weeks so that he could understand most of what was said to him, although he could not always say what he wanted to say.

Soon he found himself as fascinated by the tale as the children were, and before long, other adults joined them. A jug of whisky made the rounds, and others soon followed. Some folks had brought mugs. Others merely took a swig when the jug came to them.

The atmosphere was merry, and other men told stories, but it was Bardie Gillonie whose tales held everyone's attention. Rory soon realized the dwarf had the gift of the ancient bards, and wondered if his name had derived in some way from an ancestor possessing the same gift. When he saw a man drop a coin into the dwarf's mug, he realized it was probably one way Bardie supported himself, and he moved forward to contribute a couple of shillings.

Bardie looked up and grinned impudently at him. "Thank ye kindly, me lord. I see yer still amongst us, and all."

"I am, indeed. That was a fine tale you told."

"Shall I tell about Lady Elizabeth and the Lady Rock?" the dwarf asked, his eyes glinting with mischief. " 'Twould entertain Macleans and Campbells alike."

"I'd not advise it," Rory said, glancing at Duncan, a short distance away.

"Och, that one," Bardie said with a grimace. " 'Tis a pity he's kin tae such a fine gentleman as yourself. A quick temper, has Black Duncan, and 'tis like tae get him murdered one day, does he no take care."

"Well, you need not sound so pleased by the prospect," Rory said sternly. "He is my cousin, I'll remind you."

"Aye, and didn't I just say what a pity that is? But he's left off watching us the noo, me lord. He's got a mind tae hunt lesser prey instead."

Following the direction of the dwarf's gaze, Rory saw Neil Maclean. Feeling his heart leap, he quickly scanned the crowd until he saw Diana and Mary, chatting with a group of local folk, amongst whom he recognized only the parson.

Bardie clicked his tongue in annoyance. "Ay-de-mi, there's trouble, that is."

Still watching Diana, Rory said, "Why should it be?"

Irony touched Bardie's voice when he replied, "Am I tae take it ye dinna ken the details of the late cattle raid, me lord, when I'm told it were yourself as chased a horseman fleeing on a bay horse with white stockings?"

"You hear a good deal," Rory said, turning reluctantly back to look at him. "Is Duncan still trying to pin that raid on Sir Neil?"

"Ye ken yer cousin better nor I do, me lord."

"Bardie, tell us a tale of the devil and his imps," cried one impatient lad.

Rory leaned closer. "Mind now, rascal, don't be telling tales of Duncan."

"Och now, would I do that?" Bardie protested, adding in a louder voice, "The devil appears in all manner of forms, me bairns, even wi' hair as black as Duncan Campbell's. But 'tis me own belief that the Earl o' Hell canna be a Scot."

"And why is that?" Rory asked, willing for the moment to act as his foil.

" 'Tis nae more than simple logic," Bardie said with a

comical look. "Even before the ban, did ye ever hear o' the devil showing himself dressed in a kilt?"

His audience erupted into gales of laughter.

Bardie went on, "Most likely Auld Clootie's an outlander and his visits tae these parts only temporary. Shall I tell ye about when the Mackay met up wi' him?"

His audience clamored for the tale, but Rory saw Diana looking his way, and quickly made his way to her.

"I had begun to think you were not coming," he said, glad to see that most of the others in her group had wandered off. "Good evening, Mistress Mary."

"Good evening, my lord," Mary said. "Did Ian come with you?"

"He did, and the rest of his family besides. He is yonder with the bairns, however, listening to Bardie Gillonie tell about Mackay and the devil."

Mary chuckled. "I like that one. Ropes of sand." She walked away toward the children and Bardie, still chuckling.

He stared after her, bewildered. "Ropes of sand?"

Diana said, "That's how it ends. The Mackay learned all the devil could teach him and then turned rebellious. When the devil reprimanded him for his insolence, the Mackay gave him such a thrashing that, in order to get away, the devil promised he would leave him alone in future and provide him with a legion of workers to do his bidding unquestioningly and without any wages."

"Sounds a good bargain for the Mackay, but I'll wager there was a catch."

"There was, indeed, for the legion of workers soon became a curse instead of a blessing. They could work so quickly, you see, that soon there was no work left for them to do. They howled for more and became such a nuisance that the Mackay, nearly out of his wits, drove them all to the seashore and set them to weaving ropes out of sand. It is said that they are still at it to this very day."

Rory chuckled. "I was wondering if Bardie got his name because of his gift for storytelling."

"The name Bardie," said Duncan, moving between them out of the gloom, "means a gelded cat, cousin, nothing more."

"That's not true," Diana snapped. "It also means bold and fierce."

"Likewise pert; shameless; or insolent," Duncan said with a wry smile. "Even you must admit such definitions fit Bardie better than yours, Diana."

"I have never given you leave to address me so informally, sir," Diana said. "I would prefer that you do not."

"Would you? You seem to have lost the rest of your family. Where has your bewitching cousin got to, I wonder?"

"I am sure I do not know. She is perfectly safe here amongst our neighbors, however. Even Campbells dare not harm her here."

Rory felt himself wince and was careful not to look at Duncan, but he found that he had underestimated his cousin.

Duncan said in a silky tone, "I hope she is not making sheep's eyes at my brother, for that will not do. And speaking of brothers, have you misplaced yours again? The last time he strayed, he nearly got shot for a cattle thief, so perhaps you ought not to let him wander about alone."

Hearing Diana gasp, Rory thought it time to take a hand. "No one would have shot him, cousin. The rule of law still applies in the Highlands, I believe."

"You should know," Duncan snapped, shooting him a speaking look.

"As you say. Someone is attempting to gain your attention yonder," he added, gesturing toward a young lady who was shyly waving at Duncan. "No doubt she requires your assistance to turn the great bannock. I can smell it baking."

Duncan glared at him, but Diana said, "If you have not taken a turn with the baking, sir, you won't prosper this year. Or do you scorn all the old ways?"

When Duncan still hesitated, Rory said with mild exasperation, "Oh, go away, do. You don't want to tempt the fates, my lad."

"Is that a threat?" Duncan demanded, bristling.

Rory returned his belligerent glare with a look of light mockery. "Go have a whisky with your friends, cousin, or search for your brother if you'd rather do that."

"He is more likely to search for mine," Diana said bitterly when Duncan had turned on his heel and walked away.

"And what do you mean by that, I wonder," Rory said, smiling at her.

"Why, nothing, sir," she said, smiling back warmly.

"Odrabbit it, nephew, if the wench is going to look at you that, you ought to kiss her," Balcardane said, clapping him on the back hard enough to make him brace himself.

Rory could easily smell whisky on the earl's breath. Shooting him a look of amusement, he said, "You would have me kiss a Maclean, uncle?"

"What difference does that make tonight? She's a winsome wench and right kissable, I'm thinking." He hefted his mug as if he were toasting them. "Kissing is kissing, I always say, and if it's festival time and a wench is pretty—" He shrugged, downed the last of his whisky, then said, "Must get some more. Mistress Diana is no enemy of ours, lad. If it weren't for her and Mistress Mary taking care of my best herdsman last Candlemas, we'd have lost the man. Didn't cost me a penny, either," he added on a note of satisfaction. Then, peering down into his empty mug, he turned abruptly and left them.

Seeing Diana's expression turn wary, Rory caught her gaze and held it, saying softly, "So I am not the first Campbell to owe his life to you, mistress."

"It was not so bad as that," she said. "The man needed our help, and no Christian women could do less, for goodness' sake."

"I know a few who would do much less," he said, unable to resist reaching out to touch her arm. Cheered by the fact that she did not instantly draw away, he added, "I have heard many tales of Mistress Diana in my ramblings. You are much respected hereabouts, I believe, and not only by Macleans and Stewarts, either."

"If that is so, sir," she said in a low voice, "it is because of my mother. She taught us to care for anyone in need. She has often shared food from our table that we could ill afford, believing others needed it more than we did." She licked her lips, and he found himself wanting to taste them.

"I think I want to meet your mother."

"You nearly did once."

"I know." He held her gaze, looking deep into her eyes. One hand still touched her arm. Feeling rough wool beneath his fingertips, and mentally dressing her in silk, he moved his hand to her shoulder. When she did not resist, he grasped her other shoulder and pulled her toward him. "I have waited weeks to do this again." He kissed her, gently at first, then harder, willing her to respond.

Her lips were soft against his, and a little salty, or perhaps it was yeast from bannocks she had eaten with her supper. Her hair smelled of violets and wood smoke, reminding him again of the evening he had found her at Castle Stalker. He heard her soft moan. Her lips firmed against his, then parted, and she kissed him back hungrily. For those few moments, it was as if they were alone in the world.

Raising his head at last, reluctantly, he looked down into her eyes. "I think you are more dangerous to me, Diana Maclean, than a whole army of rebels."

"Am I, my lord? I cannot think why." With that, she slipped from his grasp and disappeared into the darkness.

He made no attempt to pursue her, and left Kentallen for Balcardane soon afterward. His thoughts and dreams had been full of her of late. Since he knew what his desire for her could lead to if he were not careful, by the time he reached the castle, he had convinced himself that he was enjoying no more than a light flirtation.

This mild deception sustained itself until Ian burst into his bedchamber an hour later, startling him while he was writing to tell Argyll that he had decided to remain in Appin for at least another fortnight. He had no wish to reveal his true reason—that he wanted to be sure the sist prevailed and Glenure did not turn the Maclean women out of their house—so his composition had required much thought.

"What the devil," he exclaimed as ink spattered across the desk from his quill. "Have you not learned to announce your entrance like a gentleman?"

"Sorry," Ian said, hastily using his shirt sleeve to wipe up the damage. "I thought you would already be asleep, sir."

"That is your excuse for bursting into my bedchamber?"

"Well, it is nearly one o'clock in the morning, you know."

"I couldn't sleep, so I was writing a letter."

"I'm glad, for Mary said I should tell you at once."

"Mary Maclaine?" Rory's breath caught in his throat. "What is it?"

"Danger, she said. Duncan has been acting strangely, saying he means to catch Neil at some sort of mischief. He also thinks you're soft on Diana," Ian added with a sidelong look, "and he's said more than once that someone should make her less attractive to you. I warned Mary about that."

"Did you now?"

"It is *not* disloyalty," Ian said defensively. "If I can prevent bloodshed on either side, I'll do what I must. Mary has tried to talk to Neil and Diana, to warn them, but they won't listen to her. She says they mean to leave Appin tomorrow."

"To go where?"

"I don't know. She wouldn't say, but she did say to fetch you. She is afraid Duncan will follow them, and she says you can prevent trouble. I'll go with you."

"Nay, lad, you will not," Rory said firmly, getting to his feet and dusting his letter with sand. "You'll get a good night's sleep, and then you will see this letter of mine off to Inveraray in the morning. I'll attend to Mistress Diana then, too. She will be asleep now and won't be going anywhere before sun-up."

"But Mary said *at once,* and she has the Sight!"

"Did Mary know, when she said that, that I had already left for Balcardane?"

"No," Ian admitted, "and she had gone home before I realized why I could not find you, so I couldn't tell her."

"There then, you see. I don't discount her feelings, and I'll pay them a call first thing in the morning. But if you can imagine what Mistress Diana has to fear from your brother, your imagination is better than mine."

That was not strictly true, for he suspected that Diana was going to her mother: If she was, and if Duncan followed Neil, hoping to connect him to someone else from the raid who might testify against the lad, Duncan might well discover that an even greater prize lay within his grasp. If he managed to track down Lady Maclean and turn her over to a magistrate in Fort William or Inverness, there would be little Rory could do to protect her.

Leaving Ian with protests still spilling from his tongue, Rory went to waken Thomas. "Get me up before dawn," he said, "and put a clean shirt and a brush or two in a kit for me. I may only ride to Maclean House, but if I have misjudged things and the birds have flown, I'll want another shirt with me."

"If ye'll need a shirt, ye'll be needing me as well," Thomas muttered.

Rory did not argue, although he thought both precautions unnecessary, but when he and Thomas reached Maclean House the following morning, an anxious Mary met them at the gate.

"They left two hours ago," she said. "They're bound for Glen Drumin. It lies off the old road General Wade built over the Corriearrack from the Great Glen."

"I don't know exactly where that is," Rory said, "but I do know Spean Bridge, and we ought to catch them before they reach it."

"And if you don't?"

"I'll deal with that problem when I meet it, lass. Have courage. I'll see that no harm befalls them."

They left her standing in the yard and made for the Ballachulish ferry. Once on the Lochaber side, Rory set a punishing pace. He did not believe Diana and Neil would ride fast enough to draw undue attention, but even if they maintained an ordinary pace, they would still be at least an hour ahead of him when he reached Fort William. Spean Bridge lay only eight or ten miles beyond the fort.

Thirteen

Diana and Neil had risen long before sunrise, and they reached the Ballachulish ferry well before the starless darkness began giving way to twilight. The ferryman was awake when they arrived, and they reached the Lochaber side without seeing a sign of Black Duncan or any other Campbell.

That they had seen no one, Diana knew, did not mean there was no one to be seen. Just as darkness hid their movements, so too might it hide the movements of others, and daylight was increasingly near.

She had left the village festivities the previous night soon after parting from Calder, and had made Neil return to Maclean House with her. Mary stayed longer, with Ian and some friends, and since Morag and her brother Gordy also stayed, Diana had not objected. Better that they all be seen having fun, she had thought. Then she and Neil might not be missed.

As the darkness lifted, she noted with misgiving that the sky was overcast. Riding alongside the narrow upper end of Loch Linnhe, they met other travelers, including occasional red-coated soldiers, but she could detect no sign that anyone followed them. Uneasy, she kept looking back over her shoulder.

"Relax, Diana," Neil said the third time she had done so. "Anyone who sees you looking back like that will think we are eloping or some such thing."

"I know," she said. "I just wish this road were not so public."

"Well, it will be so until we pass Fort William," he said. "That is why I told Dugald not to meet us before Spean Bridge. He can get there easily without drawing notice, and once there, no one will pay heed to our meeting him."

"I hope he does not fail us," Diana said, suppressing the urge to look back again. "We'll need him to show us the way to Glen Drumin. I hadn't thought of it before, but I don't know the area well enough to be sure we can find it on our own."

"Nor do I, unless we go all the way to Fort Augustus," Neil said. "The old road over the Corriearrack begins near there, and from that road, I can find Glen Drumin. Dugald will take us a much faster way, of course, straight through the mountains from Spean Bridge. Still, I don't think we'll get there before dark."

"Goodness, I don't see how we can," Diana said, amused. "We're not carrying much, to be sure, but it must be nearly fifty miles, Neil."

"It's only half past seven now," he protested, "and at this pace—"

"We won't be able to maintain this pace once we head into the mountains. Father used to say that one should never count on making more than five miles an hour on horseback, and that is for ordinary travel."

"Well, but still, that is only—"

"We will have to rest the horses, too," she went on firmly, ignoring the interruption. "We cannot afford to hire others. Indeed, since we want to draw no notice, I think we'd be wise to avoid Fort William. There must be a way around it."

"Well, I don't know of one," he said. "In any event, if you want to make speed, we must keep to the main road until we meet Dugald."

"Very well, then." She glanced up at the dark gray sky and

drew her cloak more closely around her. "I just hope it does not rain before we find him."

Neil smiled. "'Mist in the hollows; fine weather follows.'"

"Aye, but there's mist on those hills, too," she pointed out. "That will bring 'water to the mills' before your fine weather, I'll wager."

The rain still had not made good its threat forty minutes later when they approached the village of Maryburgh and got their first view of Fort William. One of three Highland forts commanding the Great Glen, it was the only one that never had fallen to a rebel attack. At the moment, thanks to the deepening gloom, its high walls looked forbidding. Diana put up her hood and pulled it forward.

Lying south of the fort, the village existed chiefly to supply its garrison. Cottages and shops lined both sides of the road. Pedestrians, other riders—including a small patrol of soldiers—and even a rackety old coach, added to the traffic. Diana eyed the soldiers warily, but none seemed to pay them heed.

Ten minutes later, rain began to fall lightly as she and Neil left village and fort behind. There were still others on the road, however, and she realized that the main route from Fort William to Fort Augustus and Inverness was used no less than that from Ballachulish to Fort William.

They entered a thick wood, and for a time the interwoven branches overhead sheltered them from the rain, but there was less light, and they slowed their pace accordingly. Whenever they passed through a clearing they received a shower, and twice they took shelter for a time with other travelers to let the rain ease before continuing on their way. When they emerged from the woods at last, they could see in the distance the high bridge spanning the River Spean's deep gorge.

As the site of the first shots fired in the Forty-Five, the bridge stirred Diana's emotions, but her feelings were undeniably mixed. The Jacobites had won that skirmish, but in the end their cause had been lost, and many people, even friends, now questioned both the sense and the value of the uprising. Since she still believed that a German-born king had no right to rule

Scotland, it struck her as ironic and sad that she was on her way to persuade her mother to swear fealty to him.

It was nearly noon, and by her calculation, they still had twenty miles or more to go through the rugged mountains of the deepest Highlands. Sighing, she hugged her cloak more tightly around her and urged her horse on toward the bridge, where she could see the small patrol of red-coated soldiers crossing.

Rory and Thomas encountered a setback at Maryburgh. Rory had expected to change horses there easily but soon discovered that Maryburgh did not boast a posting house like those found along most well-traveled roads. Directed to Fort William by a helpful citizen, he learned that the fort had few horses to spare, and no stalls for hire. He learned as well that Duncan and his men were ahead of them.

He and Thomas had entered the fort through the main gate, and he saw at once that the place was nearly deserted. At one time, he knew, it had contained upwards of twelve hundred men, but it now contained less than five hundred, and many of those were out with patrols. The fort's primary purpose now was policing the Highlands. He was beginning to think that a great deal of time, manpower, and money were wasted looking for and chasing Highlanders who dared to wear kilts. Worst of all, according to Patrick, the red-coats rarely caught their prey.

The young soldier who had told him about the lack of horses was a chatty sort, interested in where he had come from and where he was bound. Not wanting to draw attention to Diana or Neil, he said only that he had come from Balcardane.

"Och then, ye be the second lot the day," the young man said. "The young master o' Balcardane were here wi' his men nigh onto an hour since. Asked if I'd seen a young woman and a lad pass this way. Now, I ask ye, would I be likely tae notice one lass amongst many on yon road, me wi' me work and all tae do?"

"No, and I'll ask you no such questions. However, I have

not been in these parts for years. Shall I meet with any new roads betwixt here and Spean Bridge?''

"Nay, me lord, but beyond the bridge ye must keep left if you're bound for Fort Augustus. The other way will take ye tae Dalwhinnie. 'Tis sorry I am aboot the horses, sir, but when Black Duncan ordered up four and the captain from Castle Stalker said he should have them, I couldna say him nay.''

"Of course not. So Patrick Campbell is in the area, is he?''

"Aye, sir, wi' a patrol. He said if Black Duncan can put a few reivers out o' business, he'll thank him for it, so I warrant they be chasing cattle raiders again.''

"I see.''

"I can scare up two horses for ye, sir, but I canna promise they'll be good ones. Most o' these I've got are not full rested yet.''

"I'll take just one, so find me the best you've got," Rory said. Turning to Thomas, he said, "I want you to stay with our horses. Rest them for at least four hours and then follow me to Spean Bridge. I'll manage to leave word there for you, or get a message to you somehow so you'll know which way I'm bound.''

"Aye,'' Thomas said gruffly. " 'Tis nae more than I expected. But ye'll mind yer back, master. 'Tis no from the wench that the danger will come.''

"Now you sound like Mary Maclaine,'' Rory told him. "Have you acquired second sight since we came into the western Highlands, Thomas?''

"I have not. What a daft thing to say!''

"I suppose I'll offend you even more if I tell you that I wish that one of us had it,'' Rory said with a sigh.

Crossing General Wade's high bridge over the deep gorge that contained the roaring River Spean, Diana looked down only once, gulped hard, then kept her eyes fixed resolutely ahead. Safe on the other side, they turned east and at once began watching for Dugald. The rain had stopped, and behind them, the western sky looked lighter and less threatening.

The winding gravel road ahead lay empty, for most other travelers seemed to have gone up the Great Glen toward Fort Augustus. As they rounded a bend, a small clachan appeared, its thatched-roof white cottages scattered like sheep in a damp green meadow above the roadway. Since the road followed the edge of the river gorge, the mountainside plunged steeply away on their right.

Just ahead, a big, fair-haired man stepped onto the road from behind a large boulder and lifted a hand in greeting.

"There he is," Neil said unnecessarily. "Ho, Dugald!"

They rode to meet him, and as they halted their mounts, Diana glanced back and saw four riders coming toward them at a canter. "Neil, look!"

"I see them," he said grimly. "Those are no ordinary travelers."

"Black Duncan?"

"Aye. Dugald, they mustn't catch you."

"Nay, lad," Dugald said. "I've naught tae fear, for he doesna know me. Best if we look like we just stopped tae speak o' the weather."

The four riders came up to them with Duncan in the lead. He said, "So now we see whom you have come so far to meet."

"Have you been following us?" Diana demanded.

"Keep your temper, lass, and introduce me to your companion."

"You know Neil perfectly well."

"I do, but I do not know his friend."

She was about to tell him to mind his own business, but Dugald said in a cheerful voice, "What might ye be wanting wi' poor auld Dugald, me lord?"

Duncan gave him a long look, then said, "I'm hunting reivers, and in view of the company you keep, I suspect you might be one. What do you say to that, eh?"

Dugald's eyes widened and his mouth dropped open, giving

him a look of vapid stupidity that under other circumstances might have made Diana grin with appreciation. At the moment, however, she did not feel the least bit amused.

Dugald said, "Reivers, is it?"

"Now, look here, Duncan," Neil began indignantly.

"You be silent. I'll deal with you in a moment."

Diana snapped, "You won't deal with anyone. There is no law that I know about against traveling out of Appin country, and in any event, what we do is no business of yours. As for harassing this poor man—"

"I'll be glad to discuss that with you at length," Duncan interjected. "I have had men watching your little brother for days now, my dear, in hopes that he would lead us to his cohorts. I confess, however, that I did not expect to find you involved with them. What shall we do about that, I wonder?"

"I have done nothing wrong," she said. But thinking of the pistol she carried in a cunning holster attached to her saddle and covered by her skirt, and the little *skean dhu* in its garter sheath, she felt color rush to her cheeks.

Duncan's dark eyebrows shot up in sardonic disbelief.

He had guided his horse next to hers so that she was on the outside of the road, too near the edge for comfort, but she was determined not to let him see that he frightened her. When he smiled, letting his gaze meet hers, it occurred to her that she might have more reason to be afraid than mere proximity to the precipice.

Her pistol, though not as awkward to reach as the *skean dhu,* lay beneath her skirt, and she could not easily snatch it out. She was no match for him in strength, and more than she feared for her safety did she fear for Neil and Dugald. Both men would try to protect her, and if they did, heaven alone knew what could happen.

Duncan said to his men, "Take these two round the next bend and have a chat with them, lads. I want to know where the big one was the night our herd was raided. I already know where the other one was," he added with a grim smile, "but I'd like you to hear his tale all the same."

"No," Diana exclaimed, trying to urge her horse forward as his men hustled Neil and Dugald away.

Duncan stopped her simply by reaching out and catching her horse's bridle. "You'll stay with me, lassie. We are going to have a little talk, just the two of us."

While he still leaned forward, holding her bridle, she reached under her skirt and jerked her pistol from its holster. Pointing it at him with a shaky hand, she said in a low but grim tone, "Let us go, Duncan, or by heaven, I'll shoot you down."

She expected to startle him, even to frighten him, but he looked at her calmly and said, "So you've done nothing wrong, have you? Do you know the penalty for a woman caught carrying a weapon? Over and above the fine and the imprisonment she suffers until the fine is paid, she must endure six full months in the Tolbooth."

Panic surged within her, but she said stoutly, "I don't care. Tell your men to let Neil and Dugald go."

"Perhaps we can strike a bargain," he said. His voice was low, almost lustful, and a shiver raced up her spine. As she opened her mouth to tell him what she thought of him, he reached out and wrenched the pistol from her grasp. "Now," he said in a much harsher tone, "I think you will be more civil."

"I doubt that," she snapped. "If you think for one minute that I would let you touch me, Duncan Camp—"

The words ended in a shriek when he grabbed the front of her cloak with his free hand and hauled her close, putting his face right up to hers. Measuring his words, he said, "You are in no position to bargain, my lass. If I were interested in your body, I'll wager I'd soon have you begging me to take you in exchange for your idiot brother and his friend. As it is, it will give me far more pleasure to see you hailed before a magistrate and soundly punished for your sins. I need only order one of my men to blow the horn he's carrying to bring soldiers to deal with you. They rode on ahead, you see, so that we could trap you between us."

"You are despicable," she said. "You and every other of your ilk."

"Does that include my cousin Calder?" he asked with a sneer.

"I hope not," Calder said from behind them.

Duncan jumped as if he had been shot, releasing Diana. So intent on their exchange had they been that neither had seen Calder approach. Nor had they heard him, for the roar of the river, though muffled by the depth of the gorge, was yet loud enough to cover the sound of his horse's hooves on the wet gravel road.

Overjoyed to see him, and relieved, as well, Diana said urgently, "His men have taken Neil and our friend Dugald round that bend, sir. He said they were to question them, and I'm afraid to think about how they might be doing so."

"Call your men, Duncan," Calder said. "You have made a mistake."

"I'll be the judge of that. I've just caught two of our cattle thieves."

"Call them."

Duncan glared at him, and for a moment the matter seemed to hang in the balance, but then with a shrug he let out a piercing whistle.

Choosing her words, Diana said, "He told me there is a patrol nearby, sir."

Calder's gaze met hers, but his expression was unreadable. She had a notion that he was angry, but she was not certain if it was with her or only with Duncan. Even as the thought crossed her mind, however, she told herself she was being foolish to think even for a moment that he might side with her for long against his own clansman. Already he had turned back to Duncan.

"Is it Patrick Campbell?"

Diana's tension grew when Duncan nodded. Patrick would very likely recognize her if he saw her, and then the fat would well and truly be in the fire.

Calder said, "Where is he now?"

Duncan gestured with another nod. "Yonder. I told him I'd signal if we had need of him. If I don't, he and his patrol will carry on toward Dalwhinnie."

"Then let them carry on. You have been misled."

"I was not misled by a horse with white stockings."

"Those raiders stole no cattle, Duncan."

"But if I can get the big one to admit that they intended to steal them—"

"You won't do it, and even if you did, intent is not a crime. Moreover, if I say that horse was not the one you thought it, I will be believed, I think."

"Would you lie for a pair of hazel eyes, cousin?"

"There is no need to put me to that test," Calder said evenly. "Mistress Maclean is here at my request, as is her brother. As you well know, I have been learning about the western Highlands. They have influencial kinsmen to whom they have agreed to present me." He smiled at Diana. "I apologize for my tardiness."

"There is no need, sir," Diana said, surprised that her voice sounded normal, particularly since her initial impulse was to deny everything he had said.

Turning back to Duncan, Calder said, "Thomas and I were to have met them at Spean Bridge, but I don't blame them for riding on to meet their man when we were delayed. They want to reach their destination before dark."

Seeing the others returning, Diana found it difficult to breathe normally, for she was certain that either Neil or Dugald would unwittingly give Calder the lie.

He did not give either the chance, however, saying in a hearty tone, "I have just apologized to Mistress Diana, and I will now apologize to you both. It is my error that has brought you to this pass, I'm afraid, for my cousin mistook you for a pair of cattle raiders he has been pursuing. I put him straight, I promise you."

"Pardon me, cousin, if I seem doubtful," Duncan said curtly, "but I should like to hear the tale from their lips, if you don't mind."

"Not in the least, but—"

"Forgive me," Diana said, cutting in before Duncan could demand an answer from Neil or Dugald, both of whom looked bewildered. "I think I can clear this up easily by asking Dugald just one question, if I may."

Calder said, "You may."

Duncan shrugged.

"Dugald," she said calmly, "pray tell Black Duncan who your master is."

Dugald shot her a surprised look, but when she returned it calmly, his eyes began to twinkle. He said with the half-witted air he had affected before, "Oh, aye, miss, I'll tell him that surely. I serves the Earl o' Rothwell, sir. Indeed, I do."

Duncan grimaced and said in a surly tone, "If you seek to impress me with some nobleman of whom I've never heard—"

"But you ought to know him, lad," Calder said with a chuckle. "Rothwell is a powerful English lord. The Crown granted him a Highland estate for his part in planning strategy against the rebels, and he owns vast lands in England as well. He is also a close friend of the British attorney general, and well known to Argyll. Would you interfere with his henchman, Duncan?"

Duncan played his trump card. Holding out Diana's pistol, he said, "What of this, cousin? The wench had it on her person and dared to threaten me with it."

Calder laughed. "She did not shoot you, however, despite what must have been extreme provocation. You may give that thing to me and be glad I don't demand an explanation of your presence here, harassing an innocent young woman and her escort. You would find it difficult after your assault on her party to explain to a magistrate why you believe she has no need to defend herself."

"But that's illegal," Duncan sputtered. "You of all people know—"

"Many things are illegal," Calder said, his voice turning cold. "The more I see of how laws are applied in the Highlands, the more frustrated I become. Have you really nothing better to do, Duncan, than to harass females or chase after men who dare to wear kilts? Do you measure such knives as you find to determine if they are within the ban? It seems to me that you would be doing yourself and everyone else a far better turn to learn to live in peace with your neighbors.''

Duncan's face reddened, and Diana felt a surge of tension, for she knew how dangerous he could be. The pistol he held in his hand—her pistol—was loaded, and for a moment she feared for Calder's life.

He wore a sword, but his hand did not move toward it. He looked at Duncan.

A long moment passed. Diana dared not speak.

To her surprise it was Neil who broke the silence, saying petulantly, ''If you want to fight with Calder, Duncan, get on with it. That sky yonder is getting dark again, and we're all likely to be drenched soon if we stay here talking.''

''Tell me where you are going, Maclean, and why,'' Duncan snapped.

''I told you, they visit kinsmen, and I go with them,'' Calder said, holding out his hand with the palm up.'' Now, give me that gun and get on about your business.''

Certain that Duncan would refuse, Diana watched in amazement as he reluctantly handed the pistol to Calder, but then Neil nearly brought all to ruin.

He exclaimed in dismay, ''What the devil do you mean you are coming with us, Calder? You can't come with us. We don't want you!''

Seeing a smirk begin to grow on Duncan's face, Diana said quickly, ruefully, ''Now you've gone and done it, my lord. I'm afraid I did not tell Neil about our arrangement because I knew he would object, and—''

''Well, of course, I object!''

''Be silent,'' she said sternly. ''You forget yourself. Only think how awkward our encounter with Black Duncan would have been had I not taken this precaution. You recall that Mary warned us of danger.'' Catching Neil's angry gaze and holding it, she was glad when no one else spoke. She dared not look at Dugald.

She could trust the big Highlander to keep his thoughts and feelings hidden from Duncan, but she knew he would have something to say to her presently. She would have a few things to say herself, come to that.

Neil grimaced fretfully, but he did not argue.

Calder said, "We will bid you farewell, Duncan."

"Oh, aye, have it your way. The wench has you twisted right round her thumb now, but when some fisherman pulls your body from the River Spean in a few days, don't say I did not warn you."

"If that's the case, I'll have naught to say at all," Calder said with a wry look.

Unamused, Duncan whirled his horse and rode away, leaving his men to follow as they could.

Watching them go, Diana said, "We owe you our deepest thanks, sir, but you cannot come with us, all the same."

"Don't start with me, lass," he said. "You don't want to know what I think about this. I'm coming, and that's that."

"The devil you are," Neil said hotly. "Dugald, tell him!"

Dugald watched Diana.

She glared at Calder, but when he returned the look steadily, she felt a tingling in her midsection that on one hand gave her pause and on the other instantly reminded her of his lips touching hers. He did not look the least bit lustful at the moment, yet she was trembling as if he had touched her. This would not do.

Collecting her wits, she said, "You can scarcely force your company on us, sir. If you think you can follow us, let me remind you that once darkness falls we can easily lose you in the mountains."

"That would not be wise, mistress. Not only do I know your destination, but you forget what more I know of you and your friends. I daresay that this fellow"—he indicated Dugald— "was with you in Edinburgh and at Castle Stalker, and doubtless has been up to more mischief since. Moreover, you may recall my mentioning to Duncan that the Earl of Rothwell is known to his grace of Argyll.''

"Aye," she said warily.

"It might interest you to learn that he is known to him not just because of his power, but because he is said to have killed a kinsman of the duke's.''

"If Rothwell killed a Campbell, he deserved killing," Diana said stoutly, but the news shook her.

"No doubt, but that Campbell was an agent of the Crown, and they replaced him with an English bailie instead of one of ours. Argyll is no friend to Rothwell.''

"So you want to spy on him," Diana said angrily. "I should have known you had a detestable Campbell motive for helping us.''

"Aye, perhaps you should," he said, "but if I turn back now, it won't be long before Duncan recalls your mother's escape—not to mention that of Allan Breck—and realizes that one or the other might be found by following you. As it is, you'd best hope it doesn't occur to him before he is too far away to pick up our track.''

"He willna do that," Dugald said confidently, "but we'd best be going.''

"Can we take the horses?" Calder asked.

"Aye, for all but the last bit. We'll leave them just below Wade's road over the Corriearrack. A pair of our lads can fetch them round in the morning.''

"I've a man following me. Can someone show him where he must go?''

"Aye, I'll leave word for him in yon clachan, and someone will see that he meets wi' the other lads come morning. They'll bring him along up the glen.''

"Then you and Neil ride on ahead of us," Calder said. "I would have words with Mistress Diana.''

"Best make them quick, my lord," Dugald said. "We'll no be safe till we're beyond sight of this road.''

"Lead on then. I can wait.''

Diana, stifling another of the odd tremors that shot through her body, said defensively, "I have nothing to say to you, sir."

"Then you will listen," he said, "for I have much to say to you."

She could think of nothing more to say but was intensely, and rather uncomfortably, aware of his presence as they rode along together.

Pausing only to leave a message for Thomas with one of the cottagers, they headed straight up the hill behind the clachan, following one river and glen after another until the way grew exceedingly steep and rockbound.

The horses, all Highland bred, picked their way with dexterous skill, but black clouds thickening overhead again gave warning long before the rain started that it would be no simple shower this time. Sheet lightning lit the western sky as they reached the top of a low pass and started downhill again. When mist turned to drizzle, making the granite slope treacherous for the horses, Dugald called a halt.

"The road's above," he said, looking up at a tumble of granite boulders that seemed to stretch on as far as the eye could see. "We'll leave the horses here and go on foot. It's no but aboot three miles tae the glen now."

Soon they were climbing over shadow-draped rocks without a vestige of a trail, and when the rain began in earnest, Dugald hurried them toward a cavelike formation of boulders. "We must take shelter till the rain passes," he said.

Calder said, "You and Neil take that place. I see another that will suit me and Mistress Diana. No, don't argue," he said when Dugald protested that all four could fit well enough and Diana opened her mouth to do likewise. "That space is too small. Moreover, my lass, you and I are going to have our talk now."

A chill shook her, and she knew it was not from the rain. It occurred to her that she was in more danger now than she had been in with Black Duncan.

Fourteen

The cave Calder found proved to be deeper and dryer than Diana had expected. It was also dark inside, and rather chilly.

"Take care that we don't find ourselves in a wildcat's lair," she warned with a shiver. His hand felt tight around her arm, as if he did not intend to let her go.

"I don't fear wildcats, lass. Mind your head. There's an outcropping here."

Ducking obediently, she said impulsively, "Do you fear anything?"

He chuckled, and the sound warmed her, but all he said was, "I don't think I'll tell you what I fear most, lassie."

She felt an impulse to remind him that she had not given him permission to speak so informally, but guilty certainty that he had done so before without censure told her that under the circumstances she would be unwise to attempt it.

"We could use some light," he said, edging forward. She could barely see his shape now, but she knew he was groping ahead as they moved deeper into the cave. "I didn't expect to find more than a shallow cavity in the rocks here," he said.

"Neil and Dugald would be more comfortable here, too, I think," she said.

"I agree, which makes me wonder why Dugald did not— Ah ha!" Amusement colored his voice when he stopped where he was and added with exaggerated politeness, "Would you like to take a seat, Mistress Diana?"

Bewildered, she allowed him to draw her forward, not objecting even when one of his large hands cupped the top of her head protectively to keep her from bumping it against the sloping rock ceiling. To her astonishment, when he guided her hand, she found herself touching wood, then metal. When she felt with her other hand as well, she too began to chuckle.

"Kegs? Whisky kegs?"

"Aye," he said. "I'll wager that's just what they are, and full ones at that if you've got a thirst. There seem to be about a half dozen of them, which explains why Dugald did not lead us here in the first place, and why he was loath to see us come here. I daresay he is sitting in the other shelter right now, begging his Maker to see that we proceed only far enough inside to get out of the rain."

"For that matter, sir, why *did* we come so far?"

"Because I possess a curious nature," he said. "And don't suggest, lassie, that I should call Dugald over here now to explain this."

"Are you angry with me?" she asked bluntly.

"I am."

When he said no more, she realized that her heart was pounding again, harder than it had years before when her father had called her to account for some childhood misdemeanor. She wanted to explain herself, to soothe away his anger. As it was, she could not even obey his suggestion that she sit on one of the kegs. They were small, and the ground in the cave was uneven, making them tipsy. As a compromise, she sat on the sloping floor with her back against the rough wall. When he sat beside her, a disconcerting quiver shot through her body. She edged away, glad when he made no move to stop her.

Drawing courage, she said, "You have no cause to be angry, sir. I do not answer to you."

"More's the pity," he said. "How came you to be so foolish as to travel out of Appin with only that idiot brother of yours to protect you?"

"We had Dugald as well," she said, affecting dignity.

"From what I understood Duncan to say, you had only just met the fellow."

Unable to contradict that fact, she kept silent.

"Well?"

"Very well, that's true, but it is still no concern of yours."

"Was it Dugald who organized the cattle raid, or Allan Breck?"

"What would I know of cattle raids or of Allan Breck?"

Barely aware of movement before his fingers dug hard into her shoulders, she found herself jerked forward. For a moment, she feared that she would be violently shaken, but he only held her tightly.

His voice was fierce though when he said, "Don't duel with me, lass. I've kept my temper with you till now, but it's a near thing. I know now that Allan Breck is your cousin. Thus, what little doubt I may have held that you bear no responsibility for his escape disappeared long ago."

"Then why did you not report me to the authorities?" Her voice sounded harsh, and she wanted to clear her throat, but to do so would imply a weakness, and she had no desire to reveal weakness to this man.

"I did not report it," he said, "because I lack evidence to prove it to anyone else. Many would take my word over yours, however, so do not tempt me." The words sounded measured, as if he were determined to control them. He went on, "Surely, you realize that your cousin may well take you down with him when he is caught. And he will be caught, lass. Have you any idea how flagrantly he flaunts his presence, whether he is in Rannoch, Lochaber, or Appin?"

He had not eased his grip on her arms, and she knew his fingers would leave bruises, but it was not pain she feared. Her unexpected physical and emotional reaction to his nearness frightened her much more. Ignoring her pounding heart and tingling nerve endings, she forced herself to focus on what he had said. "We hear different tales every day about where he is," she muttered. "They are but rumors."

"Not all of them. Your cousin drinks too much, lassie, and his mental powers grow as befuddled as any other man's when he is inebriated. People remember not only which alehouses he honors from night to night, but what he says at each one. He seems to have put off that silly French uniform and red waistcoat of his of late, but most ale-drapers know him whatever he wears, and he shares his low opinion of the British government with far too many people."

"His low opinion of Campbells, as well, I'll warrant."

"That, too. I said he is unwise. He has threatened Glenure more than once. Indeed, I'm told he even tried to convince a man to bring him Glenure's hide in exchange for two pecks of meal."

"That's all grog-house talk," she said, horrified that Calder had heard the same tales she had. "My brother has threatened Red Colin, too, and so have I. I daresay even Mary would like to throttle him for trying to turn us out of our home."

"You had best not repeat such threats to others, however," he said grimly.

"Why? Because I am a Maclean? It is all right for Campbells to issue threats but never for a Maclean or a Stewart to do so?"

"I did not say Campbells can issue threats with impunity."

"Fiddle-faddle, you distort the truth, sir. Ian says Black Duncan has even threatened to murder *you!* He frequently threatens to murder Ian, and for all I know, he's threatened Red Colin, too. Duncan loathes him. That's plain fact."

"We were talking of your cousin, not mine," he said, adding before she could utter the retort that sprang to her lips, "In fact, we were speaking of you."

"Let go of me."

"Not before you hear what I have to say to you."

She nearly told him that he was hurting her, but she could not seem to say the words. She could smell the damp wool of their cloaks, and something more, a light citrus scent that was strangely his own. It was tantalizing, different from any fragrance she knew, and it seemed to make her dizzy, although she had never known any scent to affect her so before.

His next words brought her quickly to her senses. "It is a pity your father is dead," he said harshly.

"How dare you! What a thing to say!"

"Be silent and listen to me. You made a bad enemy in Duncan, and no less of one in Glenure. Just where do you think you will live if he does throw you out?"

"I don't mean to let him throw us out."

"Even if you can stop him, what do you think will become of your mother if Duncan learns where she is? And before you say the words itching to leap from your tongue, think what will happen to anyone he finds harboring her."

"My father still being alive would not help," she said bitterly, unable to repress a shudder. "Black Duncan would just want to hang him, too."

"Nonetheless, a father might shake some sense into you. What stirs you to risk your life like you do? Why did you not heed your cousin Mary's warning about the danger of leaving Appin today?"

"I thought she meant only that we must take care along the road."

"Is that all she generally means?"

"She did not have one of her visions. Those are dreadful. I know, for she said she had horrid ones when her brothers and my father died at Culloden. She saw the faces and heard their cries as if she had been with them. Then she collapsed. It was days before she was herself again, she said. This feeling was nothing like that."

"I see." His grip eased, but he did not release her.

"Why do you care?"

He was silent for so long that she thought he did not intend to answer her. She was about to try to change the subject when he said quietly, "I wish I knew, lass." The atmosphere altered subtly then, and she found herself more aware of his touch than when his fingers had been bruising her arms.

Swallowing carefully, she felt suddenly as if they were alone in the world, as if no matter what happened next, no one would come to her aid, or his. She knew that if she did not move or protest, he would kiss her again. Breathless, she waited.

One of his hands slid to her shoulder and around to her back. She did not resist, nor had she any wish to do so. Distantly, she heard thunder, but it was as nothing to the thudding of her heart. She could taste his breath before his lips touched the left corner of her mouth, kissed it lightly, then moved to kiss her more possessively, more passionately.

Hunger leapt within her, and although she wondered vaguely what power he held over her, and why she found him irresistible, his kisses soon consumed her every thought. He had clearly practiced the art.

That thought gave her pause, and her fingers curled to claws at the mental vision of another woman in his arms. Then his tongue invaded her mouth and she felt his hand at her breast. Flames ignited within her body, banishing rational thought. No man had ever touched her so or kissed her so. No man had ever dared. Yet she made no protest. Indeed, she pressed nearer, kissing him back, her hands reaching for him, touching him, her senses reeling with his caresses, her passion urging her to return them.

"The rain has stopped, your lordship."

The sound of Dugald's voice echoing through the cave startled them both, and Diana heard Calder groan with irritation then grunt with pain when his head made unexpected contact with the rock wall. He released her at once.

"That's good," he said in what sounded like his customary tone. "I'll be right glad to get out of the dark."

"As to that," Dugald said, eyeing him warily as they emerged from the cave into gray light, "daylight is near gone, me lord. We should make it to the top o' the road afore darkness falls, but it will be full dark, I'm thinking, afore we reach the glen, and there willna be any moon the nicht."

"Then we must make haste," Calder said.

Visibly relieved, Dugald shouted to Neil to come along, and the four began making their way up the steep slope. Diana's skirt constantly got in her way until she bunched it up a bit in the front and tucked it beneath her bodice, deciding that her stockings and boots covered her legs decently enough to avoid censure.

As she climbed, her thoughts remained fixed on the incident in the cave. By daylight, such as it was, she could not imagine what had possessed her to submit so easily to his lordship's kisses. Had she gone daft, she wondered, or was she merely besotted with a handsome face and manly figure? Whatever the case, she had allowed him to take liberties with her person that no decent woman would allow a man who had not already committed himself to marrying her.

The last thought brought her up short. Marriage with any Campbell being completely out of the question, she decided that she must indeed be going daft.

Rory was also questioning his impulses. From the moment of learning that Duncan was on her trail, especially since she had left Appin with only her brother to protect her, he had fully intended to give Diana Maclean the tongue-lashing of her life. She still deserved to have her idiocy brought home to her in no uncertain terms. However, when he had come upon them and seen Duncan's hand on her, and Duncan's face threateningly close to hers, he had experienced such a strong desire to murder his cousin that it had taken all his strength of mind not to do so. Still, the wish to shake Diana until her teeth rattled had also remained strong, right up to the moment when the opportunity to do so had presented itself.

He had no sooner touched her, however, than an even more basic, less destructive urge had swept over him. Holding her in the darkness within the cave, he had wanted to possess her completely, to make her his own, to be certain that in future he would have every right to protect her, even if the threat came from another Campbell. What, he wondered, could he have been thinking?

Seeing her look back now as she followed Dugald up the step, rocky slope, as if to be sure no one were tracking them, he felt warm pride in her strength and competence. She was no ordinary woman, this daughter of the Macleans. She would make a fine match for any man. If only she were not a Maclean.

But she was. He heard rocks rattle as Neil briefly lost his footing, then Diana's command—for he could call it no less— to take more care. She was as sure-footed as a goat, and yet much more graceful to watch. When they had left the horses, she had picked up her small satchel and slung it over her shoulder. She carried it easily now, as if it held only feathers.

Surely his appetite for her stemmed from being too long without ordinary feminine company, augmented by a mild infatuation. But even if that were all it was—and he was having a hard time convincing himself—his Balcardane relatives had discerned his interest, and they clearly did not approve. What Argyll would say when he learned of it, as doubtless he would, Rory did not want to imagine.

He could not deny that his impulsive desire to protect Diana and her family conflicted with his loyalty to his clan. He had already drawn deserved censure from Duncan, and would doubtless draw more, thanks to this last confrontation.

These thoughts and others like them passed through his mind as he climbed, following Diana closely in case she happened to slip. It was getting dark when she stopped, and he nearly bumped into her before he heard Dugald's hushed voice.

"Whisst now," the big man warned. "The road lies yonder, but there be someone a-coming up along it the noo. They've horses, too."

"How much farther to Glen Drumin?" Rory asked, keeping his voice low.

"We go up a mite, then down some," Dugald muttered. "This be the Great Glen side o' Wade's road over the Corriearrack. The track into Glen Drumin lies north of it halfway tae the summit from here. But whisst now. They come.''

The four of them had scarcely taken cover behind large boulders before Rory heard masculine laughter and voices, one of them less cheerful than the other.

"We searched every cart, sir," that one said indignantly, his voice carrying clearly through the evening stillness. "From morning onward, we had a steady stream o' carts. We searched hay carts and turnip carts, carts full of sheep, and carts full of wool. But although we examined each and every one with infinite care, sir, nary a dram of whisky did we find.''

"I tell you, the whisky went through," the other voice said with a chuckle.

"I say it did not. I did think it would be in that dray full of oats, the one that made a dash for it when the funeral cortege held everything up. Lord bless me, what a mess that was, stopping everyone for such a time while the box parade passed by! But we caught that dray and searched it front to back, to no avail. The queue of carts continued till long past five, but we found nothing worth our time or trouble.''

"Well, Goodall, you and I are well acquainted now, and you know that my word's as good as your own. I told you I'd fetch a firkin of whisky along the north road under your very eyes, and that it would be on the road between Foyers and Inverness betwixt nine this morning and five o'clock this evening, did I not?''

With a chuckle, Dugald said, "That's the laird, that is." Standing, he signed to the others to follow and scrambled toward the road.

As the two horsemen approached, the one called Goodall said, "I'm telling you, MacDrumin, there was no whisky. That you keep saying there was does not convince me. I did think you a man of your word, but now—'' He broke off, gaping, when Rory and the others stepped onto the road, then added in a startled tone, "Lord bless me, where did that lot spring from?''

MacDrumin had also seen them, and he called out cheerfully

to Dugald by name, adding, "A good evening to you, lad, and to your companions, as well."

"A fine good evening tae yourself, laird, and tae you, as well, Bailie Goodall," Dugald said. "I ha' brought Mistress Maclean, her brother, and Lord Calder by the short way, laird, so as tae get them tae Glen Drumin afore midnight."

MacDrumin bowed to Diana from his saddle and smiled, revealing a missing eye tooth. His bow was graceful, however, and his manner polished when he bade her welcome. Then bending toward Rory, he extended a hand, saying bluffly, "I don't believe we have met before, my lord."

Rory judged him to be of middle height and some fifty years of age. His grip was firm but not overly so, although he was powerfully built. He bore a decided air of audacity, and his eyes twinkled each time his gaze met Dugald's.

From Rory, he turned to Neil and shook hands with him too. As he did, he said dryly, "Good manners demand that I present Bailie Goodall, I expect, though it fair goes against me grain to do the polite for a government man."

Rory smiled at the bailie. "You represent the Crown in these parts then."

"I do, sir, although it is a thankless task, I can tell you. Here's MacDrumin playing off his tricks again this very day, and still insisting he's a man of his word. It's not the playing of a trick on me that I mind," he added, looking sorrowfully at MacDrumin. "It's that you broke your pledged word, Andrew. I trusted you."

"Aye, but I kept my word," MacDrumin said, "and the whisky's well on its way to Inverness. I'll not let you cast doubt on my integrity, you English villain."

"Then you still insist that you sent a firkin of whisky along the north road toward Inverness between nine and five. Have you any witnesses, sir?"

"Aye, there's yourself. Man, you took off your hat to it!"

Mouth agape, Goodall stared at him for a long moment before he collected himself enough to say, "You devilish old sinner!

The Lord ought to smite you where you stand. You hid that whisky amidst the funeral cortege!''

''I did, and it's long gone now,'' MacDrumin said cheerfully.

Clapping a hand to his head, Goodall said, ''I don't want to believe it, but it's as plain as dirt that's what happened. Well, you'll not catch me that way twice.''

''I never do anything the same way twice. Will you ride with us?''

''Not the whole way. I'm spending the night in Glen Tarff. But mayhap the lady would care to ride my horse until we part company,'' he added generously.

When Diana politely declined, both riders dismounted and the entire company walked along together until Goodall left them at a track leading to a cut in the wooded north-facing slope.

Rory had noted that the northern side was different from the one they had climbed. Where smooth granite slabs, huge boulders, and scree defined the latter, punctuated by occasional dry grassy meadows and thickets of trees, the northern hills, valleys, and glens were lushly green and thickly forested. He could hear water rushing through nearby brooks and rivers.

Full darkness had fallen by the time Goodall left them, and by then Rory found himself with yet another dilemma to pit duty against instinct. He had heard clear evidence of lawbreaking. Worse, the bailie had obviously turned a deaf ear. He had treated the incident as no more than a prank or a childish game.

Rory could think of no way now to stop the funeral cortege with its illicit, duty free whisky, but he would have to do something about an officer who allowed such crimes to go unpunished within his bailiwick. Odd though it was to find an Englishman corrupted by a Scot, Rory could not allow it to continue.

To make certain of his facts, he said casually, ''I collect that your success against Goodall means that you've distributed your whisky duty free, MacDrumin.''

The older man chuckled. ''Aye, sure. That duty is an abomination the British government visits upon us poor Highlanders.

German George has no right to claim it on a product we've been producing in the Highlands since the dawn of time.''

Diana said hastily, "Perhaps you do not realize it, sir, but Lord Calder is a Campbell. He is more generous than most, and I know he would never so far forget his duty as a guest as to inform on his host for any perceived . . . uh . . . misdeed—"

"Misdeed, is it?" MacDrumin chuckled again. "Did I no just tell you, lass, there was no misdeed. German George is not entitled to one penny from my whisky, and that's all there is about it. Here's our turning now. You'll be glad to find beds awaiting you, I'll warrant, and to get some good hot food into your bellies."

"Aye, sir, we will," she said, but Rory, meeting a look of concern mixed with speculation, read her thoughts as easily as if she had spoken them aloud to him.

He said nothing, for there was nothing to say. He was a man of law, and as such, he could not ignore activities like MacDrumin's, guest or no guest. As soon as possible, he would have to let Goodall's superiors know the man was ineffective, and order a search made of MacDrumin's estates. If the man had illicit stills, Rory's men would find them and put him out of the whisky business. That he and the laird would break bread together before that was unfortunate, but it could not be helped.

Diana, watching Calder, was dismayed to think that by allowing him to accompany her, she had betrayed MacDrumin. The Crown allowed Highlanders to produce whisky for sale only if they paid for the privilege, and she knew well that MacDrumin delighted in thumbing his nose at the rules. She knew, too, that Calder would feel obliged to do something to end the illicit whisky trading.

When the opportunity presented itself, she moved to walk beside MacDrumin, saying quietly, "I am glad to meet you at last, sir. My mother has spoken of you often, and we are mighty beholden to you now."

"Whisst, lassie, you've naught for which to thank me. I like your mother."

Glancing back to reassure herself that Calder was conversing with Dugald and Neil, she said, "I wish we had not had the misfortune to meet you whilst you were riding with the bailie. Pray, sir, accept my apology for that."

"Nay, lass, there is no need. I have naught to fear from Goodall or your tame Campbell. You must trust that one, or you'd not have brought him with you."

"That's just the problem, you see. I did not invite him. We met with a spot of bother along the way, and he was kind enough to give us his aid."

With concern in his voice, MacDrumin said, "Who dared to accost you?"

"Lord Balcardane's son Black Duncan," she said.

"But Balcardane is a Campbell. Is he not Calder's kinsman?"

"Aye, his uncle."

He was silent for a long moment, and Diana wondered what he was thinking. She had heard much over the years about Andrew MacDrumin of that ilk, chief of the MacDrumins. Her father had admired him greatly, and her mother showed more respect for MacDrumin than she had for any man since Sir Hector Maclean.

Some tales Diana had heard seemed apocryphal, but if even a small percentage of them were true, the MacDrumin had enjoyed a long and fruitful career, tweaking the noses of British authorities. She believed that he had fought at Culloden, although apparently the English had failed to find any Highlander willing to state without equivocation that MacDrumin had taken any part in the rebellion.

When she decided that he was unlikely to say more about Calder's relationship to Balcardane, or to inquire more fully into the incident at Spean Bridge, she said quietly, "Did you know my father well, sir?"

"Aye, lassie, a fine man he was, too. I saw him fall, I'm sorry to say."

Gasping at such a revealing statement, she looked back over her shoulder.

"So you don't trust Calder much, then."

Put that way, as a bare statement of fact, the words were too harsh. "I don't really know," she said. "Until I do, perhaps the less said about such things, the better, but I am glad that if you saw Papa fall, you lived to tell others about it."

"He was a brave man, your father. He was fighting three of the villains single-handedly when he fell."

Feeling a pricking of tears in her eyes, she brushed them away with the back of one hand and said with forced cheerfulness, "What do you hear from Maggie?"

"That she will be in the glen Monday, and 'tis a pity, that, for we did not expect them for yet another month."

"A pity! You sound as if you don't want your daughter home again, sir. I cannot believe that is true."

"Nay, I'll be glad to see the lass. But she's expecting another bairn, so I don't doubt she'll be right skittersome, like most women at such times. I don't envy Rothwell dealing with her, I admit, but he ought to have kept her in England another sennight at least. I've got kegs to move."

She recalled the ones they had found in the cave. "He does not approve?

"Och, well, I'd not go so far as to say he *dis*approves, but 'tis better when he knows naught about some things."

Struck by a sudden, dismaying thought, Diana said, "Faith, sir, I can see that you will want Mam to leave if his lordship is coming. But things have come to an unfortunate pass at home, and I do not know if it is safe yet for her to return. We need to speak with her, which is why Neil and I have come to Glen Drumin."

"Campbell trouble?"

"Aye, one of them wants to turn us out of our home and set us to serving the new tenants as common drudges."

To her surprise, he chuckled. "Lady Anne Stewart, a drudge? You're all about in your head, lass. It won't happen. She'd snatch any mistress bald-headed the first time she wanted a dust mop. No wildcat is a ruthless as that woman.''

"I shot at a wildcat not long ago,'' she said. "It was attacking Calder.''

"You didna let the animal maul him to bits? You are either not your mother's daughter, lass, or you must be hard smitten.'' He chuckled again. "Come to think on it, he didna let you fall victim to his cousin, so he must be smitten, too.''

"I don't know about that,'' Diana said, but her thoughts whirled. It had suddenly occurred to her that she might keep Calder from betraying MacDrumin's activities to the authorities if she could keep his interest fixed on her.

The thought stirred an anticipatory tingling in her nerve ends again, but she ignored it, telling herself firmly that if she decided to seduce his lordship, it would be because she had a duty to protect MacDrumin. Thus, such a decision would be sensible— nearly patriotic, in fact—and certainly not derived from mere animal lust.

Fifteen

The golden glow of candlelight spilled into the yard through the open doorway of Glen Drumin House when they arrived. Men called to one another in the stable yard, and Dugald shouted to someone named Geordie that he had another task for him after they had put the laird's horse away.

Diana, waiting impatiently for her host to move toward the house, watched the doorway expectantly. She did not have to wait long before a familiar figure appeared there and a familiar voice exclaimed tartly, "Is that you at last, Andrew? We had begun to think you must have fallen off a mountain. Do you consider no one's wishes but your own, sir?"

"Mam!"

"Diana? Bless me, child, is that really you?"

A moment later, Diana was in her mother's arms, hugging her tightly. "Oh, Mam, I think I've missed you even more these past weeks than when you were in prison. How can that be?"

"Don't be absurd, child," Lady Maclean said, hugging her back. "I am far happier here than I was in Edinburgh, I promise you."

"I'll warrant you are," Neil said with a laugh, coming up to them.

"Neil, you too? But how so? Is aught amiss at home?"

"That's why we've come," Neil said. "Diana thinks—"

Cutting him off without hesitation, Diana said, "This is not the time or place to discuss our reason for coming. Wait until we can be private with her."

"Oh, aye, if you like, but Calder's gone somewhere with MacDrumin."

Lady Maclean said, "We ought not to stand in the doorway, at all events. Come in, children, and have something to eat. Kate, my dear, tell them to bring more food. We have guests!"

A smiling young woman came forward to greet them when they entered the cavernous, candlelit great hall. Her hair was pale blonde and fine, her features small and neatly etched. She went on smiling politely as Lady Maclean made the introductions, and Diana found it hard to believe that this was Dugald's cousin Kate, who had grown from a barefoot girl of the glen to become sister-in-law to a powerful English earl. It was even harder to imagine that this dainty, well-mannered creature had once been known as Mad Kate MacCain, but so Dugald had told her.

"How do you do, ma'am," Diana said.

"Very well, thank you," Kate replied with a twinkle.

Lady Maclean said, "Kate's husband is presently somewhere in the northern Highlands, tending the sick. He is quite skilled with his remedies, I'm told, though I have not been privileged to see him at work. I have told him and Kate about our Mary, however. I do trust she is well."

They reassured her, taking seats near a fireplace large enough for six grown men to stand upright and abreast. A medium-sized fire blazed there now, and they warmed their hands and talked of domestic matters until the other men came inside. Then there were more introductions.

Upon hearing his name again, Lady Maclean eyed his lordship askance. "Calder? That would be the Cawdor branch of the Campbells, would it not?"

"It would, ma'am," he said.

Watching him closely, Diana could not tell from his expression what he was thinking, but at least he did not immediately order her mother's arrest.

"Your father was first cousin to Argyll, then," Lady Maclean said. "That does not recommend him to me, sir. What business brings you to Glen Drumin?"

"He has come to try our whisky," MacDrumin said cheerfully. Then, to a maidservant who was putting food on the table, he added, "Bring out a half dozen chopins and a good large jug, lass."

"Aye, laird, they are here," she said, gesturing to a tray already on the table.

"Good lass. Here, Calder, I'll pour the first one for you myself." He poured a generous amount into a large mug and held it out. "Try that, will you?"

Calder sipped cautiously, then sipped again. "Excellent stuff," he said.

"Aye, it is," MacDrumin said with a grin. "Ye'll no find better anywhere."

"I don't doubt you, sir, although I think I have tasted it once before, on a ridge top in Appin country. All the same—"

"Dugald gave some to Bardie," Diana said hastily. "May I try some?"

"To be sure, lass," MacDrumin said, pouring a mug for her.

"Take care, Diana," Lady Maclean warned. "The world has a tendency to tip after a few swallows of that brew, and it feels like fire going down. Won't you all sit down? Kate and I tired of waiting for Andrew, so we've eaten, but we'll sit and talk with you. Tell us about your journey. You must have got wet, I should think."

"We nearly didn't get here at all," Neil blurted. "Oh, don't look at me like that, Diana. We'll be telling them soon enough, and if Calder don't want to hear it, he can just shut his ears. It was Black Duncan, Mam! He stopped us just this side of Spean Bridge, and he looked as grim as death. If it hadn't been for his lordship here intervening, we'd be there yet, or dead from being flung into Spean Gorge."

"Most likely in prison," Diana said. "Duncan thinks Neil took part in a cattle raid at Balcardane a sennight ago, Mam, and although he's got no proof, he wants to hail him before a magistrate."

MacDrumin regarded Neil with more interest than he had hitherto shown in him, and said, "Did you now, lad? A cattle raid. 'Tis an ancient and noble pastime, that. Good sport, too."

"Dangerous sport," Lady Maclean said, grimly eyeing her son.

"Och, you take too dim a view," MacDrumin said. "God put cattle on this earth, not man, and they take their food from land on which man has done no labor. Therefore, they belong to all of us in common. If we steal our neighbors' cattle today, they'll steal ours tomorrow, which makes us quits, as I see the matter."

Calder said evenly, "I should still call it theft, myself."

"You sound like a Sassennach," MacDrumin protested. "Them in the Lowlands forget that their land once belonged to our forefathers. They refuse to understand Highland men who take their prey where they find it. But, as I see it, it's up to them to try to prevent us from succeeding if they do not like our ways."

"Or pay blackmail," Calder said evenly.

"Aye, 'tis a time-honored way to protect themselves," MacDrumin said, grinning. "Why, I can recall a time when men expected the heir to any Highland chiefship to have led at least one cattle raid before his succession."

"So you have led raids yourself, I expect."

Laying a finger alongside his nose, MacDrumin said, "Now, that would be telling. And considering your position on the matter, I think I'll hold my tongue."

After a pause, Lady Maclean said, "I don't want to talk about Black Duncan Campbell or about foolish cattle raids. Are all our people well, my dears?"

Flushing, and avoiding his mother's gimlet eye, Neil turned

his attention to the mug MacDrumin had filled for him, but Diana said, "They are, Mam. I've taken care to visit as many as I can each week, just as you would. They all ask after you, and Granny Jameson pounded her stick on the floor when I told her I couldn't say where you were. James of the Glen sent oatmeal to some of the folks on the island, saying it was what Ardsheal would want him to do. I doubt that's so, but it was kind of James all the same, especially in view of how busy he has been."

"It was indeed thoughtful of him," Lady Maclean agreed. "He is always busy, however, so I do not think you need refine upon that."

Diana exchanged a look with Calder.

"That mug of yours is empty," MacDrumin said to Calder. "Let me fill it for you. Here, everyone, bring your stools and benches to the table. The food's going to grow cold. Dugald, when you've finished eating, go along and speak to the lads, will you? There's work to be done yet before Rothwell and Maggie arrive."

Diana glanced again at Calder. Seeing the speculative gleam in his eyes, she knew he had guessed as easily as she had that MacDrumin intended to move more whisky, possibly the kegs in the cave below the Corriearrack road.

"Mam," she said, "Lord Calder may well have saved our lives today, or Neil's, at least. He does not realize, I think, what danger he was in. I am fast coming to believe that Duncan is as much our enemy as Red Colin of Glen Ure."

"We can talk of that later, darling. Eat your supper now."

"Try some of this lamb, Diana," Kate said, passing a platter to her.

Diana thanked her, helped herself to a slice of lamb, then passed the platter to Neil. Having taken note of the size of the house, she had expected a host of servants, but the service was much the same as it was at Maclean House. She wondered if that state of affairs would change when the earl arrived.

"Mam, if Rothwell is expected, surely we must make arrangements for you to go elsewhere before he arrives."

Lady Maclean glanced at Calder, then at her daughter, before saying cautiously, "Andrew assures me that I have nothing to fear from Rothwell."

"Nor do you, madam," MacDrumin said. "That lad has better sense than to interfere with a woman of your stature over a few silly trees."

"There's a bit more to it than that, Andrew, as you know full well."

"Calder knows, too, Mam," Diana said. "I . . . I met him in Edinburgh."

Feeling all eyes on her, she realized suddenly that she did not want the whole history of that episode to come out in this company. Although MacDrumin's reputation for mischief was legendary and she had heard similar tales about Kate's adventures, it was hard to imagine either of them helping a Crown prisoner escape.

Lady Maclean eyed her narrowly. "What do you mean, you met him in Edinburgh?" Turning to Calder, she said, "Were you at the castle when I was, sir?"

"Aye, ma'am, I was. I had the honor to meet your daughter the day you left."

"I see." She was silent for a moment, then grinned at the openly curious MacDrumin. "I think Diana means to say that she met him in prison, Andrew, and I doubt very much that he was a prisoner."

MacDrumin chuckled. "Have some more whisky, lad."

Calder put a hand over his mug. "Thank you, sir, but I'll wait till I've got a bit more food in me if it's all the same to you. In point of fact, Lady Maclean, my purpose in visiting the castle was to meet you. I had some reservations about your imprisonment. But as it chanced, I arrived a few hours too late."

Now she chuckled, too. "I don't believe I'll apologize for that, sir. I was glad to get away, I promise you."

"I daresay you were, ma'am, but there are some few details still to be sorted out, you know." He spoke calmly, but every eye turned his way now.

Kate said, "I thought Diana's plan was clever. What made you suspect she was not all she claimed to be?"

"Mere chance, ma'am," Calder said. "I encountered her unexpectedly just after another prison escape."

Kate clapped her hands. "Another one! We hadn't heard. Who was it?"

There had been a note in Calder's voice that made Diana bite her lip and avoid his gaze, so it was Neil who said, "We got Allan Breck out of Castle Stalker. Diana slipped him a message, and he put her scarf out the window, so Bardie—"

Jerked from her reverie, Diana said hastily, "Button up, Neil. You must never name names or speak so openly of such things. Will you never learn?"

Looking cross, Neil turned his attention back to his food.

Calder said thoughtfully, "So Bardie did help. I wondered if he had, but I never suspected he might have done more than help with the planning."

"Who's Bardie?" MacDrumin demanded. "No, wait. We'll have a bit more whisky, and then I'll send the wench away, so we can talk plainly."

Having arranged matters thus to his satisfaction, and having sent Dugald out to attend to unspecified other matters, he demanded details.

Neil revived as a result of MacDrumin's enthusiasm, and when Lady Maclean only shrugged in response to Diana's mute look of appeal, he launched into a frank description of Allan Breck's escape from Castle Stalker.

At hearing of Calder's undignified departure from his saddle, and the reason for it, MacDrumin roared with laughter, clapping him on the shoulder and offering mock commiseration. Then he collapsed in gales of new laughter.

"To think of a man your size unhorsed by a dwarf!"

Calder was not amused. His lips pressed together in a thin, straight line, and a muscle jumped in his cheek. But his irritation was no match for MacDrumin's infectious laughter. Before long, the hard lines in his face softened. When he looked at

Diana and smiled wryly, warmth surged through her, and she smiled back.

Relaxed by the whisky, she found that she no longer objected to her brother's candid account of the incident at Stalker, but the telling revived other memories.

Calder's gaze glinted like kindled tinder, and she knew he was remembering, too. He stirred uneasily, as if he were too hot, but she knew instinctively that the heat disturbing him did not come from the nearby fire. Sensing a power she had not known she had, she let her smile widen, feeling sensuously warmed all through.

"I will not allow you to tease him, sir," she said to Mac-Drumin while still looking directly into Calder's eyes. "No man could have stayed in his saddle under such circumstances. Bardie is very powerful, and he never saw him coming."

"The way Neil tells it, he never saw him leaving either," MacDrumin said, lapsing into another fit of laughter. "I think I could make good use of your Bardie."

"He is something of a rogue, sir," Calder said, "not unlike yourself."

MacDrumin chuckled.

Abruptly Lady Maclean said, "Surely, the pair of you did not come all this way to talk of Bardie Gillonie, or to tell me about your encounter with Black Duncan Campbell, which would not have occurred if you had not left Appin. And since you did not know Rothwell and Maggie are on their way until you met Andrew . . ." She paused, her eyes narrowing. "Why *did* you come?"

Neil, who had drunk a good deal more than Diana, said just as bluntly, "Red Colin in going to evict us, Mam."

"What?"

Taking turns, with both sometimes talking at once, Neil and Diana explained.

"That scurvy devil," Lady Maclean exclaimed when they finished. Glaring at Calder, she added, "I know Colin is related to you, but I won't apologize. If I were a violent woman, I'd cheerfully run him through with my sword, if I had a sword."

"It's not so bad as it might be, Mam," Neil said. "James got a paper to stop him, and Diana and Mary went with some others to present it. I'd like to have seen Red Colin's face when he read it, I can tell you."

Lady Maclean nodded approvingly. "Excellent," she said. "I am very pleased with James, and so I shall tell him."

"Aye, Mam, but there's a rub," Diana said. "You've got to take the oath."

Lady Maclean stiffened ominously. "I've got to do *what?*"

"I made no promises," Diana hastened to reassure her. "I thought I might have to speak on your behalf, and I was certain you would not refuse if I said you would not. But Colin never asked me. He was too stunned by the papers saying he could not evict us, I think, to note the condition. But he will have read the whole thing carefully by now. Moreover, Term Day is less than a fortnight away. As tenant, you must take the oath before then if he is not to make more difficulties."

Lady Maclean made a visible effort to control herself, but her expression did not lead anyone to think she intended to cooperate, difficulties or no difficulties.

Calder said gently, "Perhaps you ought to explain, mistress, that Glenure does not mean you to starve. You will be glad to know, my lady, that he has already arranged for you, your daughter, and your niece to take positions as servants to the new tenants. He thinks he has been most thoughtful and compassionate, ma'am."

"Does he, indeed?" She sighed, grimacing ruefully, then said, "I see he leaves me no choice. I have no one else to turn to who would not suffer for helping us, sir, and I won't see my daughter and niece turned into drudges to sustain my pride. What must I do, Diana?"

"Why, I don't know exactly," Diana admitted. "I expect you have to take the oath before a magistrate, or some other person of law."

"I can witness any oath she takes," Calder said easily, "although I would advise you to wait until Rothwell arrives, ma'am. No one will question any oath witnessed by the pair of us, I promise you."

Diana smiled at him and said, "If you swear the oath, Mam, Calder thinks you can safely return home. He believes he can prevent your arrest."

"Is that so, sir?"

"Yes, ma'am. I have certain authority because of my position, you see."

"He is close kin to Argyll and has access to the duke's ear, Mam."

Again Lady Maclean looked rueful. "I doubt that his grace will support my cause, sir. He and I have not generally seen eye-to-eye on matters."

"No, ma'am. I have heard as much," Calder said with a twinkle.

Neil said enthusiastically, "It will be grand to have you home, Mam. We've missed you, and Red Colin won't be so quick to plague us with you there."

"There will be no more cattle raids, young man."

Neil shook his head, grinning, but MacDrumin said, "Now, now, don't be too hard on the lad, Annie. Showed mettle, that did. Showed he's a man. Have a drink, lad. You, too, Calder. I say, sir, do you play golf?"

"I do," Calder said. "Don't tell me you've got a links hereabouts?"

"Aye, I do." MacDrumin grinned. "Some complain about the trees, of course, but I think they add to the challenge. We'll have a game when Ned—Rothwell, that is—gets here. He's a dab hand with a golf club. Taught him myself."

The conversation turned to other matters after that, and they managed to avoid controversial topics until Lady Maclean declared that she was going to bed. Bidding the gentlemen good-night, she took Diana and Kate up with her.

"Here is your bedchamber, my dear," she said, opening a door at the end of a long corridor. "Where did you put Calder and Neil, Kate?"

"His lordship in the first room, near the stairway," Kate

said, gesturing, "and Neil is upstairs. Would you like a maid-servant to attend you, Diana?"

"Thank you. I did not bring much with me, so if I am not soon going to look like something dragged through a hedge, perhaps I should give someone my things to wash and iron."

An hour later, tucked into her comfortable bed with a small fire burning down to coals on the hearth, Diana found herself pondering the strong possibility that Calder might soon arrange for MacDrumin's arrest. Despite the clear liking the two had for each other, she did not think Calder would ignore his clear obligation.

The law was strict, and even factors who were lax about the kilting law or the disarming were inflexible about duty. That was money owed to the Crown, and thus was a most serious matter. MacDrumin could go to prison for a long time.

She owed him much for hiding Lady Maclean from the same authorities who would put him in prison. Such a debt was too great to repay with mere thanks, and MacDrumin, though a cousin, was neither a Maclean nor a Stewart. He was chief of his own clan, related to Lady Maclean through two marriages. Moreover, Diana herself was to blame for Calder's dangerous presence in Glen Drumin.

Somehow she would have to persuade him not to betray MacDrumin. Lying there, unable to sleep, she weighed the possibilities.

Calder had protected her more than once from the conse-quences of her actions and clearly was fond of her, though she did not think it was much more than that. No more than her feelings for him could be. That her heart pounded harder when he was nearby was unfortunate, since he was a Campbell born and bred. Had he been a member of any other clan . . .

But here her innate honesty stopped her thoughts. She could not finish one so patently untrue. When she was with him, nine times out of ten she forgot he was a Campbell. When he smiled at her, she nearly always wanted to smile back. The intense way he looked at her when she talked, as if whatever she was saying was of vast importance, made her feel the same as when the sun came out to lighten a gray day. Just the sound of his voice warmed her. A simple touch of his hand stimulated all sorts of unfamiliar sensations, and all those things acted to make her forget his antecedents. Remembering them now brought a lump of sadness to her throat.

Face to face with Black Duncan, she nearly always felt anger, resentment, and a strong urge to spit in his face, although she had never done such a vulgar thing in all her life. Just looking at Duncan made her want to defy him.

Red Colin affected her the same way, except that she felt more contempt for him. His mother was a Cameron, after all, and although a man took his father's clan, not his mother's, he ought to feel some connection to the latter. He certainly ought to have more sense than to serve the Duke of Argyll and the English government blindly. His mother certainly had taught him better than that as a child.

In contrast to her feelings about Duncan and Red Colin were her feelings for Calder. The first time she met him, she had felt a tug of familiarity, awareness of a bond between them. Something had drawn her to him, and invited her to trust him.

She had known, facing him in Edinburgh Castle prison, that he would not harm her. At Castle Stalker, though the first sight of him had filled her with fear, once she was face to face with him in his bedchamber, she had found herself trusting him again. She had never feared rape, although at the time, his position and her pretended one had made the possibility more than likely.

Remembering her feelings when he had told her he wanted his bed warmed, she felt herself blushing, wondering what it would have been like if she had simply obeyed him. She wondered, too, what would have happened if she had not knocked over the warming pan, if he had not burned himself, if she had not poured brandy all over him. He had cared more then for what Patrick Campbell would think were he to learn that Calder had *not* ravished her, than for his own needs and wishes. He had let her sleep, unmolested, by the fire.

Just thinking of that now sent tremors through her body.

Thoughts of his touch, his kisses, filled her mind, and she made no effort to repress them. Instead, she wondered if she could use her ability to stir his senses on MacDrumin's behalf.

Hearing masculine laughter, she knew the men had come upstairs and were retiring to their bedchambers. Quick as thought, she got up and snatched up a plaid wool coverlet, draping it over her shoulders and clutching it tightly about her. Could she still trust him not to ravish her? She did not want that. She kept telling herself that she just wanted to use his interest in her to influence his actions. Would she have the nerve to approach him, she wondered, or would she prove a coward?

The maidservant Kate had provided had plaited her hair, and she paused long enough to brush the plaits into smooth ebony waves before moving to the door. Putting her ear against the wood, she listened but could hear nothing, and so she opened the door and peeped into the corridor. The glow of a lamp on the landing showed her that it was empty.

She had taken but three steps from her room when the door at the end opened and Thomas MacKellar came out, carrying a large ewer. Diana held her breath, but he did not look her way, turning instead toward the landing.

Barefoot, for she had brought no slippers, she hurried toward his lordship's door, worried now that someone else might appear. Her attention fixed on her destination, she paid no more heed to Thomas until she reached the door. Then, and only then, did she remember that the stairway to the great hall doubled back upon itself. Looking that way, she saw Thomas descending, facing her. He was looking down, however, lost in thought, and she did not think he had seen her.

She rapped lightly, and then before her courage could abandon her, she lifted the latch and pushed the door open.

Calder looked up from a small table, where he sat writing. He frowned. "You should not be here, mistress."

"It is not the first time I have been in your bedchamber, sir," she reminded him. "I want to talk to you."

"We should talk by daylight," he said, getting to his feet

with obvious reluctance. "Regardless of past moments between us, this is not seemly."

"I don't care," she said, shutting the door. "What I came to say to you is important. I . . . I think you care a little for me, sir, and if that is so . . ." She let the words trail to silence, daring him to contradict her.

Looking rueful, he said, "Lass, just being near you makes me crazy. From our first meeting, my head has told me to do one thing, my heart another."

"Your heart?" Her own pounded hard in her chest. She had not expected him to admit so much.

"Aye, my heart. Stay where you are, or I won't answer for my actions. What would you demand of me now?"

Hesitating—for the suggestion that he could not control himself was flattering, and exciting as well—she said at last, "I don't understand my feelings either, where you are concerned. One minute I can think clearly, the next not."

"I know." His voice was low in his throat, and again the sound of it stirred sensations in her body that were beginning to be familiar to her.

She stepped nearer. "Please, I want . . ." She hesitated again, watching him.

"Say my name, lass."

"Lord Calder?"

"Nay, 'tis Rory. I would hear it from your lips."

Certain now that she could persuade him to ignore what he knew about the laird's illicit activities, Diana stepped nearer, releasing the tight hold she had kept on the coverlet draped around her. It fell open, revealing her lawn shift. Reaching toward him tentatively, she said, "Rory . . . please, sir, I would beg a boon of thee."

He caught her hand in his, pulling it hard against his chest, holding her gaze with his own, his eyes like silver fire, his lips parted as if he anticipated kissing her. It was what she had wanted to see, but now, instead of feeling only satisfaction at her success, she felt a sense of confident expectation that threatened to overwhelm her. Nearly forgetting her purpose, she turned her face up to his, her lips parting in invitation as heat raced through her veins.

His lips claimed hers without further ado, burning with pent-up passion, his mouth hot against hers. She could hear his breath rasping in his throat, and when he released her hand to embrace her, she sighed with pleasure, pressing closer, paying no heed when he brushed the plaid coverlet aside impatiently.

"We're playing with fire, sweetheart," he murmured against her lips. "Are you certain you want this?"

She moaned in response, trying to think but unable to cool her passions enough to do so. Perhaps she had drunk too much of MacDrumin's potent whisky, but she did not think so. It was not whisky that stirred her. It was Calder . . . Rory. In her mind, she saw the Gaelic spelling of his name, *Ruairidh*. The letters seemed to be outlined in flames, and those flames warmed her to her soul.

He kissed her harder, and then she felt his tongue parting her lips to explore the interior of her mouth. Her breasts seemed to swell, and she felt the hardness of his body against hers. Her shift was thin, making it feel almost as if his hands touched bare flesh.

"By my faith, what have we here? Fine goings-on, I must say!"

Startled, they jumped apart and turned as one to face Mac-Drumin. Neither of them had heard the door open, but clearly it had, for the laird stood framed on the threshold with his hands on his hips and his feet apart, looking grim. Behind him, Thomas MacKellar stood on tiptoe, peering over his shoulder, his expression a mask of astonished amusement.

Before Diana could think of a word to say, Rory said calmly, "We were discussing marriage, sir, that's all."

Sixteen

Rory met MacDrumin's stern gaze calmly, but in his mind's eye he was seeing Argyll's face. Surprisingly, he experienced a sense of steadiness, as if he had made an important decision, and more than that, a good decision. A glow radiated through him. Then he looked at Diana.

That his words had stunned her was evident. That she intended to conceal her astonishment was equally evident. He saw her swallow and bend down to pick up the plaid coverlet she had worn over her thin nightdress. For the first time he noted that she was barefoot, and he wondered if she was cold.

MacDrumin said evenly, "Marriage, is it?"

"Aye," Rory said, taking the coverlet from her and draping it gently over her shoulders. "Sit on that stool by the fire, lass. You'll catch your death." Turning back to MacDrumin, he added, "We've made no decision, but the subject came up."

"I'll warrant it did." MacDrumin chuckled. "You're a bold lad, my lord, to think you can cozen her ladyship into favoring a Campbell husband for her daughter, but you're a grand sight bolder to trifle with the lass here in your bedchamber, and then only *think* about wedding with her."

''Did you have a purpose in coming here, sir?'' Rory asked with one eye on Diana, who had flushed deeply at the laird's words.

''Oh, aye. You said you like to play golf, and knowing you would not have clubs with you, I came to say you can have a look at mine tomorrow, and see what will suit you. I've quite a good collection. Played for the silver club at Leith, I have, and I go out with the Burgess in Edinburgh whenever I get to the city.''

''I'll warrant then that you're a better player than I am, sir.''

''Oh, I'm a dab hand, I am. Taught Ned to play just so I could get a game in now and again here in the glen. On the whole, the English don't ken what they're missing, but folk hereabouts don't play much either. I'd suggest we play tomorrow, but the parson would have a fit and all if we did, so we'll wait till Monday.''

Still keeping a close eye on Diana, Rory agreed, then said pointedly that he would take a look at the laird's clubs the next day.

MacDrumin did not stir from his place by the door. Rubbing his chin thoughtfully, he looked at Rory again. A twinkle lit his eyes as he said, ''Am I to understand then, lad, that you have promised to marry the lass?''

Wondering why he felt no sense of entrapment, since he understood MacDrumin's meaning perfectly, Rory said calmly, ''I am quite willing to make such a promise, yes.''

MacDrumin chuckled again, then said to Diana, ''From what your mam tells me, lass, you've a devilish unfeminine habit of taking matters into your own hands. Still, your father's dead and in his grave, and that brother of yours don't know how to take you in hand. Moreover, I am that road myself, so I've naught to say. I'll just take myself off now and let the pair of you sort it out.'' He glanced at Rory, then back at her, adding with his impudent twinkle, ''I'm thinking you may have broken off more of the loaf than you can chew, lad.''

* * *

When MacDrumin had gone, Diana drew a deep breath, clutched the coverlet closer around her, and forced herself to look directly at Rory. "I don't understand," she said. "I thought he would send me back to my bedchamber, but he didn't. And why did you say you would marry me? You need not do so, you know. We have done nothing to necessitate so drastic a course, even if our families would allow it."

He shoved a hand through his hair. Then, clearly choosing his words with care, he said, "MacDrumin left so we could get on with the second part of what he thinks he interrupted."

She frowned. "I don't understand, sir. I wish you will speak plainly."

"I will then. It's a matter of law, sweetheart. Scottish law allows several forms of marriage thought unusual in other countries, especially England. But half a century ago, when they created the Union, the English agreed to recognize all Scottish marriages."

"You cannot mean marriage by declaration," Diana said. "I know about that. Both parties have to agree before witnesses that they are married. MacDrumin never asked me if I had agreed."

"The law actually says that if one party makes a declaration before one or more witnesses that the other party does not disclaim, the marriage is valid."

"But you did not make such a declaration! Your simply telling him you are willing to *promise* to marry me—and you know he asked only because he found us in what some people might consider to be a compromising posture—"

"Most would deem it compromising," he interjected mildly.

She made an impatient gesture. "But you and I know that . . ." The memory of the feelings he had stirred in her, and her response to them stilled the words in her throat. She swallowed, adding brusquely, "At all events, you made no declaration, so there is no reason to think you must marry me."

He did not speak at once. Then, slowly, he said, "MacDrumin was not thinking of marriage by declaration, lass. There is a second form, called *promise subsequente copula*—"

"How do you know such things? What does that mean?"

"Essentially, it's one form of marriage by consummation," he said. "In this case, a promise to marry followed by . . ."

"By a coupling, obviously," she said impatiently. "I know what consummation is, for goodness' sake."

"Very well, then. If both the promise and the coupling take place in Scotland, canon law recognizes the couple as lawfully married. The Scottish kirk prefers that a proper ceremony follow eventually, but no ceremony is required for the marriage to be acknowledged as lawful both by the church and by British civil law. You'd acquire all the rights and privileges due to my wife by virtue of the coupling."

Heat flooded her cheeks. "Faith, sir, do you mean he expects us to jump into your bed now that he has gone away?"

When Rory nodded, she felt a sudden bubble of laughter in her throat. Though she had certainly wanted to stir his desire for her, she had meant only to divert him from his intent to arrest MacDrumin. It had not occurred to her that she might manipulate him into marriage. As to the bedding, her body's response to the mere thought amazed her. Every nerve tingled, and waves of desire surged through her. When he reached for her hand, she let him draw her to her feet.

Quietly, he said, "I believe he thinks we have devised a plan to get round the objections of our families. It would not be so odd for him to believe that, you know, for he is one who constantly seeks to circumvent authority. Moreover, I'll wager he can see that we are attracted to each other."

"Are we?" She looked down, oddly unsure of herself.

"You know we are." He drew her closer.

" 'Tis but simple lust, sir, and well do you know it," she said bluntly, but she did not try to draw away, adding with a sigh, "I cannot marry a Campbell. For one thing, it would kill my mother. She loathes Argyll, you know. She has threatened to snatch him bald-headed the moment an opportunity presents itself.''

"Fortunately then for his grace, he already is bald-headed. He shaves his pate so his wigs will sit straight. In any event, I think your mother is far too strong-minded to be undone by any marriage of your making, sweetheart.''

"Aye, well, even if I were willing to marry you, which I'm not, I would never do so in such a conniving way. Furthermore, you don't want to marry me any more than I want to marry you. I just came in here—'' She broke off, unwilling to tell him she had hoped to distract him to protect MacDrumin.

It occurred to her that perhaps that reason no longer existed. Frowning thoughtfully, she said, "If the laird thinks you have trifled with me, he could make trouble for you in certain quarters, could he not, even with Argyll?''

Frowning, he said, "Particularly with Argyll. What's more, I'd not put it past the old rascal to do such a thing, just to make mischief.''

She shrugged, hoping the gesture looked casual, and said in an offhand way, "I daresay that if you don't make trouble for him, he won't make any for you. You have eaten his bread, after all, and he believes in Highland hospitality.''

"He will be expecting an announcement from us, however. When none is forthcoming, what do you suppose he will do?''

"I . . . I don't know.''

"Nor do I. Look here, lass, let's be plain. I know you are thinking that I should keep silent about his whisky, but—''

"After his kindness to Mam, betraying him to the authorities would be a dreadfully backhanded turn, sir.''

"She is not my mother.''

"No, but she is mine.'' She touched his chest, looking up into his eyes. "It would be a horrid thing to do. Please don't. I'll see that he says nothing to Argyll.''

Looking into her eyes, he grasped her chin, holding it firmly, the way he had done at Castle Stalker, and his tone was nearly as stern as it had been that night. "I have a conscience, sweetheart, and a duty. He is breaking the law.''

"Please, Rory." Her fingers tightened on his waistcoat.

He sighed. "The most I can promise is that I won't act until I have spoken to Rothwell. This is his land, after all. He has a right to know what goes on here, and to understand what I am obliged to do."

"Good. Perhaps he can put a stop to it. Then you need tell no one else."

"MacDrumin has broken the law," he said steadily. "From what he and the bailie said, he has broken it many times before. And he must be using his land to produce his illicit whisky, lassie. I cannot overlook that."

"Yes, you can." She felt her temper stir, and firmly suppressed it.

"You must understand my position, Diana."

"I understand that you have broken bread with him and drunk his whisky." Anger crept into her voice. "What manner of man are you that you could so abuse a gentleman's hospitality?"

"There is more to it than that. Perhaps I should explain just what my duty—"

"There is nothing to explain. You said you were willing to marry me," she added, speaking hastily so she would not think about what she was going to say. "You even sounded like you *want* to marry me. Is that so?"

"I could scarcely be such a rogue as to deny it now," he said.

"Tell me this, then. If I agree to go through with what MacDrumin suggested, would you agree to forget about his whisky?"

"No."

"Then good night, sir," she snapped, turning on her heel. At the door, she paused, looked back, and said, "I shall leave you to make any explanation that proves necessary tomorrow. I daresay you will enjoy that."

He made no effort to stop her, and she did not know if she was glad or sorry, but it was a long time after she climbed into her bed before she slept.

On Sunday morning, the household attended service at the nearby kirk, and that afternoon, Diana watched as Rory and the laird made what seemed to her to be a grand production of examining the latter's golf clubs. There clearly were plenty from which to choose.

It rained Monday, forcing the men to put off their golf game, and that evening, the laird's daughter Maggie and her husband, Edward, fourth Earl of Rothwell, arrived in the glen with their extensive entourage.

Maggie was buoyant and cheerful, glad to be home and happy in her new pregnancy. Diana took to her as quickly as she had taken to Kate, and to her relief, Rothwell seemed to take their presence in his house in stride.

Meanwhile, the youngest member of their party allowed his grandfather to cradle him in his arms and talk nonsense to him. Staring up at MacDrumin with big blue eyes, gurgling and blowing bubbles at him, he remained content there until his nurse bore him off to his crib. No one mentioned such uncomfortable subjects as oaths of allegiance or whisky smuggling, and Diana went to bed thinking that perhaps Rory no longer intended to speak to Rothwell, after all.

Events Tuesday morning reinforced that hope. When she descended to the hall to break her fast, the first voice she heard was Rory's, saying to MacDrumin, "No one ever meant for a woman to swear that oath, sir. That's the problem."

" 'Tis a barbarous thing for anyone to swear, I'd say. But to ask a woman to say such things goes right against a man's grain. Don't you agree with me, Ned?"

"I do," Rothwell said, smiling lazily from his place at the long table, near the huge fireplace. He was a large, dark-haired man of powerful physique and chiseled, prominent features. Vitality fairly crackled in the air around him, and Diana thought him distinguished looking, although not nearly as handsome as Rory.

The two men seemed to get along well, but if they had held any private conversation, there was nothing in either demeanor to indicate that they had discussed the laird. Both rose to their feet when she approached, as did MacDrumin.

"Good morning," she said. "I heard you talking about the oath. Has Mam agreed to swear it today?"

MacDrumin said, "Aye, but I've just been saying that they ought not to make her say such things. Ought not make anyone say them, come to that."

"What must I say, Andrew?" Lady Maclean asked, coming down the stairway, her wide skirt sweeping the steps. "I never thought to ask, and I don't believe I've ever read the oath."

Rothwell and Rory exchanged looks before Rory said, "First you must swear allegiance to the British Crown, ma'am. Then you must swear that you do not possess any gun, sword, pistol, or arm whatsoever and never use any tartan, plaid, or any part of the Highland garb. That's all."

"All!" MacDrumin was indignant. "What about the bit where she prays that if she breaks her oath she will never again see her children or relations, or will be killed in battle as a coward and lie without Christian burial in a strange land, far from the graves of her forefathers and kindred. What of—"

"Hush, Andrew," Lady Maclean said, touching his arm. "It is quite dreadful, I agree, but now that I've decided I must do it if we are to keep our home, I just want it over and done." She turned to Rory. "May we get on with it at once, sir?"

"If you like," Rory said, "and if Rothwell will agree to bear witness."

"Certainly, I will," Rothwell said.

"Here's a Bible," MacDrumin said reluctantly, producing a battered copy from a carved and polished box on a nearby shelf.

Taking it carefully, Rory held it before Lady Maclean.

Without ado, she placed her right hand on it and looked expectantly at him.

"Please repeat after me, ma'am," he said, "I, Anne Stewart Maclean, do offer fealty to the British Crown . . ."

"I, Anne Stewart Maclean . . ."

Diana closed her eyes, trying to shut out the words. The oath signified not loyalty but the betrayal of a cause held dear all her life. The Macleans had fought against yielding for nearly a century. Now it seemed as if taking the oath hurt her more than it did her mother. Anne Stewart Maclean had always been strong, nearly as strong as her rebel husband, steadfastly refusing to desert the Stewart kings for the upstart Hanoverians. To hear her speak the words made Diana's stomach turn. That she was repeating them to one so closely connected to those who had brought this day to pass ought to have made it ten times worse. Diana wished she could hate him, but she could not. Her body had defied her, and now so did her mind.

". . . and I do swear that, as I shall have to answer to God at the great day of judgment, I have not nor shall have in my possession, any gun, sword, pistol, or arm whatsoever; and never use any tartan, plaid, or any part of the Highland garb. If I do so, may I be cursed in my undertakings, family, and property . . ."

"Oh, Mam, don't," Diana cried. "I cannot bear it."

Lady Maclean reached out to take her hand. "They are only words, my love, and I have learned much during my time here in Glen Drumin. To cling to lost causes is never wise. The common people suffer most, you see, and we can do naught for them if Colin throws us out. Duty is seldom pleasant, Diana, but we must do ours. What else must I pledge, my lords?"

Rothwell said, "I am quite willing to bear witness to your having sworn the full oath, my lady. The last phrases clearly were intended only for men to speak."

"I, too, have heard enough," Rory said.

"That's settled then," MacDrumin said cheerfully. Shouting for whisky, he added, "When we've drunk a toast, I say we shall play bit of golf. Ho there, lad," he called to Neil, who was descending the stairs, "will ye play with us?"

"I've never played golf," Neil said. "There was no one to teach me."

"Then you must come along with us."

"May I come, too," Diana asked, "or is golf a game only men can play?"

"Don't let my Maggie hear you say that," Rothwell said, smiling at her.

"Your Maggie's already heard," that lady declared from the stair landing, adding as she descended the last flight, "I'll have you know, you lot, that Mary Queen of Scots played golf. So let me hear none of your nonsense about the frailty of women, if you please."

"Will you play then?" Diana asked her. Though she knew that Maggie was with child again, there was little sign of it in her slender figure.

Maggie laughed. "I'll walk about with you, for I want some exercise, but Ned will worry about me enough without my actually playing today."

"Perhaps another morning you can play," Rothwell said. "Our guests are not leaving at once, I hope. We have scarcely begun to know them."

Diana looked hesitantly at Lady Maclean. "We must get back soon, Mam. Term Day is but eleven days away."

"Aye, but there is naught we can do to stop its coming, Diana, and now that I've taken the oath . . ."

"Red Colin does not know that," Diana pointed out.

"He will know soon enough. We can linger a few days more, and still take two days for the journey. We shall have to borrow at least one horse, too, since the one I rode here belongs to Andrew."

"You'll take a horse and welcome," MacDrumin said. "You can take Dugald, as well, and he will bring it back again. Now that's settled, so drink up, lads. We have a game to play."

Rory watched as MacDrumin placed his featherie—a small cowhide bag stuffed tight with feathers—on the mound that formed his starting tee. The laird stood over it, judging his distance with shrewd, narrowed eyes and holding his club as if it were part of him. Clearly, he played the game often, but the course he had laid out was like no links Rory had ever seen. There were far too many trees and bushes, for one thing.

All the links he had seen before had none, but then, most of those lay near the sea on the east coast of Scotland.

The previous day's rain had left MacDrumin's overgrown course damp, and the featherie was heavy and sluggish. They had to take care not to slice it to bits with their clubs, for a new one cost four or five shillings. They were at the beginning of the second hole now. MacDrumin had won the first easily.

The laird swung, connected solidly with the featherie, and sent it sailing straight toward the green. "The devil fly away with the thing," he exclaimed a moment later. "It's hit a sheep! You lads, put down those clubs and chase the pesky critters off. And do it before one of them eats my featherie!"

The boys carrying their clubs obeyed at once, and Neil ran to help them. When the laird strode forward to supervise their activities, and Maggie drew Diana aside to show her a favorite view, Rory found himself standing alone with Rothwell.

He had made no effort to single the earl out before, for after Diana's fury and her charge that he did not understand the rules of hospitality, he had found himself reluctant to press the issue. When MacDrumin had cheerfully agreed—the morning after the incident in Rory's bedchamber—to let him manage his own affairs, Rory's dilemma grew. And it gnawed at him, for despite his unwillingness to deal with Diana as she deserved, he took his judicial duties seriously. He did not think he could overlook MacDrumin's illicit activities, but the more he thought about what duty demanded of him, the less he liked it.

"I want a word with you, sir," he said more abruptly than he had intended.

Rothwell's eyebrows shifted upward. "A serious matter? MacDrumin tells me you've taken a fancy to Mistress Diana, and I have noted a certain amount of tension between the pair of you myself. If you are wondering if I'd recommend such a union, I can say without equivocation that I would."

Rory smiled wryly. "You did it yourself, in fact, since you are English, sir, and married a Highlander. But perhaps your political views were not so unlike."

"Were they not? I seem to recall that they were vastly unlike. She was a devoted admirer of the prince, I'm afraid."

"Bonnie Prince Charlie?"

"Yes. It is not common knowledge, and I'll beg you not to repeat it, but she met him in London when he was there two years ago. Fortunately, he did not live up to the vision she had created of him, which made matters rather easier for me."

Rory decided it would be tactless to suggest that Maggie might have entertained Rothwell's suit because he was wealthy, and marriage meant her father and their tenants could go on living in Glen Drumin. Having taken MacDrumin's measure, he was as sure as he could be that whatever Maggie had thought, the wily laird would have considered that factor carefully. Deftly he changed the subject. "It was not marriage between factions that I wanted to discuss, sir."

"But something of a serious nature, nonetheless."

"Aye. I don't know if you are aware that I have the honor to sit on the Scottish Exchequer Court."

Rothwell nodded. "I did not like to ask, since no one mentioned it, but I did recognize your title and thought I recalled a connection to the Exchequer. The attorney general of England is a good friend, you see, and of course you work closely with Scotland's lord advocate, I believe."

"I do. I'm glad you know, because you will understand that I cannot remain blind to certain of the laird's activities." He watched Rothwell closely. He did not think a man of his reputation would take an active part in smuggling, but he thought it was possible that the earl suspected, or even knew, what MacDrumin was up to.

To his surprise, Rothwell chuckled. "What's the old reprobate up to now?"

"He is smuggling whisky."

"Is he? What makes you think so?"

"I heard him say as much to none other than the local bailie."

"So he tricked Goodall again, did he?"

Rory stared at him. "You knew?"

"Oh, yes, it's Andrew's notion of interesting entertainment, I'm afraid."

"Unlawful entertainment. He has failed to pay duty on that whisky, sir."

"He does not have to pay duty," Rothwell replied mildly.

"Why the devil not?"

"When I took over here, I felt much as you do," the earl said, watching the boys chasing a last rebellious sheep from the green. "I soon came to realize that without means to support themselves, the people here would starve, and few courses of action presented themselves to me. I could let them starve, or I could support them—the last being a very expensive choice, as I am sure you must agree."

"Yes, but—" He fell silent at a gesture from the other man.

"I came to realize in time that the whisky itself suggested a third possibility. It is excellent whisky, as you know, and once I saw that many wealthy Englishmen agreed with that evaluation, I realized we could sell it in London for enough money to keep body and soul together up here."

"But the duty," Rory said. "What of the duty?"

"I was willing to pay it," Rothwell said with a reminiscent smile, "but Andrew sees it as no less than extortion by the Crown, since Highlanders have been making the stuff for centuries. I came to agree with him, and fortunately was able to get one of the few waivers that were going, for Glen Drumin."

"Then why does he delight so in slipping the stuff past the authorities?"

"Because the mental exercise amuses me, of course," MacDrumin said, emerging from nearby shrubbery. "Those dratted sheep. They do an excellent job of keeping the green smooth for putting, but they are a devilish nuisance all the same."

Rory said, "What do you mean, the mental exercise amuses you?"

MacDrumin grinned. "Ned took all the fun away, don't you see? So I make wagers with Francis Goodall, and so far he's paid me a grand sight more than I've ever paid the government in duty. Ned here don't approve, so I try to have all my deliveries finished before he arrives. Nearly didn't make it this time. It's your turn, lass," he said to Diana who had approached with Maggie while he was speaking.

Rory saw that she looked dumbfounded.

"Do you mean to say you were never in danger of being arrested for smuggling?" she said, looking accusingly at Mac-Drumin.

"Nay, lassie. Did you think I was?"

"Aye," she said, looking daggers at Rory.

He could read her mind clearly. She had nearly given herself to him, hoping that by doing so, she could protect a man who needed no protection.

Rory wanted to smile at her, even to take her in his arms and hug her, but he could not do so, and he thought it just as well. By the look of her at that moment, she would rather have killed him than hugged him.

Her cheeks were flushed, her eyes sparkled with wrath, and she advanced upon the tee with an angry stride. He almost felt sorry for the innocent featherie when she whacked it hard enough to send it to the far side of the green.

Diana was furious. She felt as if she no longer knew if she was on her heels or on her head. Knowing she ought to be grateful that MacDrumin was no longer in danger, she felt as if he were the one who had angered her. She had thought she knew herself. Now she was not at all certain about that.

She had heard her mother swear fealty to King George and what amounted to an English government. What other members of the Maclean clan would think of that, she did not want to think about. But worse than that, she had nearly given herself to a man who was loyal to that government and to the Duke of Argyll, and who stood opposed to most of which she had long held dear.

As they walked toward the green, she realized that Maggie

had made matters even worse. As they had stood enjoying her favorite view, when Diana admitted with a sigh that she had never expected to see her mother turn away from the true line, Maggie had said, "I met him, you know—the prince."

Awed, Diana had instantly demanded to know what he was like.

Maggie had shrugged, looking sad. "He was not what I expected, Diana, not in the least. He was drunk, for one thing, and vulgar. He could think only of himself, like a spoiled child. I wanted to smack him."

"Y-you are happy in your marriage." In Diana's mind, the statement had not seemed in any way a *non sequitur*.

"Ned is wonderful," Maggie had replied. "I do miss Glen Drumin, and I don't care much for London. But I adore Ned and would not be happy away from him, so I adapt. Still, it's grand to be back in the glen again."

Recalling her words now, Diana wondered what it was like to adore a man.

"Where's the jam pot?" MacDrumin demanded, pulling her from her thoughts. "This irksome hole is in a puddle from the rain. I'll need to cut another." He already had his clasp knife out, and one of the lads handed him an eagle feather to mark the new hole.

They played golf one other time before the Macleans and Rory left Glen Drumin, and MacDrumin won again that time. But no one minded, and when they took their leave, Diana found that she was sorry to go. She had made new friends in Maggie and Kate, and the impudent laird amused and delighted her. He had said nothing at all about the incident in Rory's bedchamber, and so she had relaxed, thinking that most of her worries were over.

Except for the fact that Lady Maclean contracted a slight cold, the journey back to Maclean House passed without incident. When they rode into the yard, Mary came running to meet them.

Diana greeted her with delight. "How we've missed you,"

she exclaimed as Rory helped her to dismount. Dugald and Neil assisted Lady Maclean.

"Faith, but I'm glad you've come home," Mary said, rushing to hug Diana. "I'm afraid I've got the most awful news for you, though. Red Colin's gone and got the sist rescinded. We're all to be evicted on Friday!"

Seventeen

Neil cursed, and Diana stared at Mary in disbelief. "We're to be evicted?"

Nodding, Mary said, "Colin must have left for Edinburgh the same morning you did, the day after we presented him with the sist. James learned just two days ago, on Monday, that he went there to submit a plea against our sist, and that one of the lords of session agreed to rescind it."

"Just like that? But how could that be?"

"I don't understand the details," Mary said with a sigh. "All I can tell you is what James told me. He was furious."

"Of course he was," Lady Maclean said, coughing. "He has every reason to be. I tell you, it would be a public service if someone would shoot Colin Glenure."

"Mam, please." Diana glanced at Rory and saw him frown. "What is it?" she asked. When he did not respond immediately, she said grimly, "You might just as well say what you are thinking. I know he is your kinsman, and all, but—"

"He is just doing his duty," Rory said calmly. He turned to Mary. "Do you recall exactly what James of the Glen told you?"

"Most of it," she said, frowning in concentration. "Red Colin returned here on Saturday, but he had already left for Maryburgh when James got a letter from his advocate in Edinburgh. That came Monday afternoon. The letter said that after James had got his sist, he apparently carried away something called the Bill of Suspension. Is that important, sir? James was in such a tirrivee when he told me about it that he did not make much sense."

"Yes, it's important," Rory said. "The sist is just the document you and the others presented to him, the court's order to let you stay on this land."

"We know that," Mary said. Diana and Lady Maclean nodded in agreement.

"The Bill of Suspension," he went on, "contains all the arguments James made in court to win that sist. They were written down at the time, then confirmed, and James should have filed the papers containing those arguments with the court. Since they were missing, Glenure was able to present his case to a different judge against an absent defense. By the time James's advocate learned what was happening, the proceeding was doubtless over and done. Where is Glenure now?"

"He and that nephew of his, Mungo Campbell, went to Maryburgh on Monday," Mary said. "They must get formal eviction notices."

Diana said bitterly, "The brass of the man! I'd have expected him to stay here to gloat if he's won so easily. Why must he go to Maryburgh for notices? If the court in Edinburgh has already ruled . . ." Bewildered, she looked at Rory.

"An Edinburgh court cannot order evictions in Argyll," he said. "It can delay such actions or set them aside, but notices must be obtained from the sheriff of the shire where the evictions will take place, or from one of his substitutes."

"You certainly seem to know a great deal about these things," Neil said, looking at him suspiciously.

"He certainly does," Diana agreed.

Rory was still watching Mary. "What has James done about this?"

"Don't tell him," Diana snapped. "He will only pass it on to Red Colin."

Mary's lips twisted wryly. "I daresay it won't matter if he does, you know. As I said, poor James found this out only two days ago. He's been scurrying to and fro ever since, trying to find someone who will help us, but no one is leaping to do so, and Term Day is only two days away. Red Colin will be back here tomorrow."

"How do you know that?" Diana demanded.

"Because yesterday the landlord of the Kentallen Inn, who is himself set down for eviction, received a message telling him he must prepare to entertain Red Colin and his party tomorrow evening."

Diana sighed, feeling deep depression creep over her. "What can we do?"

Lady Maclean said bluntly, "We will fight, that's what. That wretched man is putting people off lands they have owned since the dawn of time, and we are not the only ones with nowhere else to go. He ought to be put down, like a rabid dog."

"Mam, you mustn't say such things! And you should get into the house, out of this wind. She's caught a cold, Mary."

Ignoring her, Lady Maclean looked bitterly at Rory. "I don't care if you do tell your wretched kinsman what I said, young man, Argyll ought to help the people who live in Appin country. It's part of Argyllshire, after all, and none of us can harm him or his odious English friends anymore."

Diana held her breath, but Rory said mildly, "I don't doubt that you are right about that, my lady."

"Red Colin is just trying to show that he is not soft on Highlanders," Diana said with a sigh. "Once he was accused of that, his behavior got worse than ever. I'll warrant that's at the root of all this. If we can manage to hold the land until all the rumors of a new uprising die away, perhaps he will become more reasonable."

"That is what James said," Mary told her. "The man who advised him in Edinburgh suggested as much, and James has decided that we must all refuse to vacate our homes unless they threaten us with military force. He is willing to trust the Barons to set all the evictions aside when next they meet. The one he talked to in Edinburgh assured him that they will.''

"Unfortunately," Rory said, "they do not sit again until mid-June.''

"No, James explained that,'' Mary said. "He hopes that by confronting Red Colin with a formal protest presented by the effected tenants and other persons of standing in the county, we can make him back down for now. Allan says he knows several prominent men who will stand with us.''

Rory said casually, "Allan Breck is here?''

Mary glanced at him, then looked ruefully at Diana and Lady Maclean as she said, "Nay, sir, not now, but he was for an hour or so yester morning. He stayed with James over Monday night. He said James was in such a dither then he did not like to leave him, but once they had worked out what could be done, Allan said, James felt much better.''

Lady Maclean nodded. "It always helps to have something positive to do. I take it then that Allan means to speak to—'' She broke off abruptly, shooting a grimace at Rory. "I, too, forget that we are foolish to speak of such things in front of you. Like it or not, young man, you are one of the enemy. The fact that you are fond of Diana does not alter that fact one whit. Don't you have things to do?''

"I could help, ma'am, if you would let me.''

Diana watched to see if the earnest look of innocence would affect her mother, and when it looked as if Lady Maclean was softening, she said curtly, "Don't fall for that look, Mam. It is one he has cultivated to a criminal art.'' Glaring at Rory, she said, "I told you about our sist, sir. You invited my confidence, and I trusted you. Can you swear that you did not tell Red Colin just what he had to do to counter it.''

"I did not,'' he said, his mouth tightening.

"I don't believe you.''

"Now, look here, I've given you my word—''

"The word of a Campbell,'' she retorted bitterly. "I'd be a

fool in this instance to accept it. I cannot doubt for one moment that you would have advised Colin if he had asked you. Who else hereabouts would have the knowledge to do so? You seem to know much more than most folks do about the Scottish courts.''

"Well, I should, should I not?'' he said as one goaded.

"Just because you are a man and have the advantage of a grand education, and even grander connections? Well, I have had an education, too, sir, and mine tells me not to trust anyone outside my clan. You have already heard more than enough of our conversation. I want you to leave.''

"Diana, don't you know that I can help you, that I'm—''

"I don't want to hear it,'' she snapped. "There is nothing you can say that will convince me to let you hear more of our discussion. Why, for all I know, you wanted Mam to come back here just so Colin could arrest her again.''

"You know that is not so. I can protect her, Diana. If there is any trouble about that, I hope you will not hesitate to send for me.''

"Oh, go away, my lord. If you are so powerful, stop Colin yourself. You certainly have my leave to do that if you can.''

Glancing at the others, and realizing that they would not support him against her, Rory made his farewells rather curtly and mounted his horse. He had realized, to his dismay and chagrin, that Diana did not know he was a Baron of the Exchequer. Tempted though he was to explain at once and force her to listen, he decided he would have better success if he let her cool off a bit first.

He had assumed from the start that she did know, and nothing she had said had indicated anything else. Indeed, even now, he found it hard to believe that they had never discussed his position openly. It seemed as if they had, as if she had said things to him that made her knowledge evident. In any case, many people knew he was with the Exchequer. It was hard to believe that no one had told Diana, but the more he thought about it the more certain he became that he had not done so.

He could not recall just what things she had said to make him think she knew, but he decided it did not matter. What did matter was Glenure's idiocy. How he or anyone else could expect to bring peace to Appin country or any other part of the Highlands by forcing people out of homes their families had inhabited for centuries he did not know. He would have to put a stop to it.

As he rode toward Balcardane, he considered the alternatives and found them limited. He could not act alone in the matter, certainly not now that an Edinburgh court had ruled in Glenure's favor. Nor did he think he would have much luck confronting Glenure on his own.

Diana was right about one thing, and that was that Glenure was determined to show that the Barons had not made a mistake by confirming him in his post. That he had realized Rory had been checking on him grated now. Bad enough that Glenure had seen his visit as an incentive to take a more adamant posture, but the factor's determination now to see the evictions through argued a stubborn nature far beyond what Rory thought anyone could have anticipated.

He doubted that either Balcardane or Argyll would side against Glenure. They were kinsmen, after all, so it was a good thing that Argyll was away and would not interest himself in the matter unless someone drew it to his attention. Even then, he decided, Argyll was likely to prove far more interested in Rory's increasing preoccupation with a young woman from a clan his grace thought obstreperous than in anything one of his factors had done.

Rory grimaced, anticipating the interview that would likely follow Argyll's learning of that preoccupation. First things first, however. He had to think of a way to help, and a way to explain himself to Diana. At this juncture, although he was certain that her feelings for him matched his for her, she was not likely to listen to anything he might say. Therefore, his help must come first.

By the time Rosinante topped the densely wooded rise above Balcardane Castle, and Rory saw Ian striding uphill toward him, he had decided that his best course was to be present on Friday when Glenure presented his eviction notice and tried to enforce it. The "prominent men" Allan Breck had promised to produce would no doubt stare to see him there, but they would accept his assistance. He doubted that even Glenure would insist on pressing the matter then and there with a Baron standing against it. As for Mistress Spitfire, it would not harm her to stew a bit in the meantime, since she would doubtless be pleased with the result and quite willing to hear him out afterward.

Ian shouted a greeting. "You're back! We wondered when we should expect you. Duncan will spit horse nails when he sees you, too, for he said we should not look to see you before Term Day, but I bet him you would return today."

"You must have neglected to tell him Lady Maclean had to swear the oath to retain her tenancy," Rory said mildly. "Glenure can hardly be expected to know she has done so if no one is here to tell him."

"Is that why you are looking so cheerful? Is it all arranged? I haven't seen Mary for days, but she must be pleased about that."

Realizing that Ian had seen him smile at the thought of making Diana stew as mild punishment for her failure to trust him, Rory said ruefully, "It's not settled yet because Glenure's making more trouble. That man is a menace to peace."

"He's not really, you know," Ian said, turning to walk beside Rosinante. "He just flares up whenever anyone pokes at him. What's he done now?"

"I'm surprised you haven't heard. He went to Edinburgh and overturned the sist that your Mary and the others presented to him before I left."

"That was clever," Ian said thoughtfully. "I wonder who advised him."

"Your irritating brother or your father, most likely."

Ian glanced up at him. "Are you at outs with Duncan again?

He was gone for several days about the same time you left, and he's scarcely said a word since he got back, except to warn me to choose my friends more carefully. He is always saying such stuff though. I scarcely heed him anymore. Are you vexed with him?''

"I've yet to see him," Rory pointed out, seeing no reason to make Ian choose sides over the incident at Spean Bridge. "I've been away for nearly a fortnight, after all, but if he did advise Glenure to seek countermeasures, he did no one any good. Colin is making far too many enemies. Since it's my duty to see that he manages his lot of forfeited estates without undue strife, I could wish that he had sought my counsel before he dashed off to Edinburgh."

"Can't you just tell him to stop being a fool?"

"According to Mistress Maclaine, he's gone to Maryburgh to get proper eviction notices. Moreover," Rory added, "he seems to have announced his itinerary to all and sundry, for she told us he sent word to the landlord at the Kentallen Inn to hold rooms for his party tomorrow night. By now, half of Appin must know when he means to return, and anyone who tries can predict his route with near certainty, because he'll have to take the ferry across the narrows."

Ian frowned. "Are you suggesting that someone might interfere with him?"

"He's irked a lot of people, lad. Someone might try to teach him manners."

"Should we send someone to warn him?"

Rory thought for a moment. He was, after all, teaching Diana a lesson, and Glenure deserved one more than she did. If one or two Highlanders attempted to frighten the wits out of him, who was Rory to interfere? "He'll be traveling with an escort, so I doubt there's any real danger," he said comfortably.

"Aye, Colin of all people knows better than to travel alone anywhere in Argyll. Like as not, they'll be armed, too, so he'll be safe enough."

* * *

Diana did not worry in the least about Red Colin's safety. If she thought about it at all, it was to hope he would fall into the narrows and drown before he could carry out his horrid evictions.

No one wanted to talk about them. Even Lady Maclean changed the subject when Diana tried to bring it up at supper that evening; and the following morning, when Neil said he was going to walk up the glen, and Diana begged him to stay and talk about what to do, he snapped at her in a way that was most unlike him.

"I've no wish to talk about absurdities," he said. "I'm going out because I've naught to gain by staying and I'm sick to death of fretting about what might come. If Colin wants to evict us, he will, and there will be no mending it."

"Neil, really—"

"I'm sick of talk, Diana. If it isn't you begging me to talk about what I've no control over, it's Allan telling me I'd like being a soldier in France, which I'm very sure I would *not* like. I just want everyone to leave me alone!"

Lady Maclean said, "Has Allan tried to talk you into joining his regiment?"

"Aye, and he was at it again last night at the inn till I just up and left with Kath—Never mind that," he added hastily, looking from his mother to Diana. Then, belligerently, he added, "If you go for me over her, I just might sail with him after all. Now, leave me be, everyone. I'm going up the glen."

Diana said tartly, "Have a care that her father doesn't take a whip to you."

"Even if that were where I was going, Maccoll has too much respect for my rank to touch me," Neil said scornfully.

"You can't expect him to respect it more than you do," she retorted.

He left without another word.

"So he is still seeing his dairymaid," Lady Maclean said,

stifling a cough. "Well, perhaps it may prove a blessing if she can keep him here when Allan sails."

There was nothing to say to that, and after her ladyship indignantly rejected a suggestion that she spend the day coddling her cold, all three women busied themselves through the morning with their usual chores.

By eleven even Lady Maclean seemed to find the work senseless. With a sigh, she said, "Put the kettle on, Morag. Some tea and a bit of that mutton we had last night will do us more good than pretending things are normal today, when we may be put out of this house altogether tomorrow."

Diana put down the rag she had been using to polish the sitting room mantel and moved to help Mary and Morag fetch out the food. They were setting plates on the table when Neil walked in.

Smiling, he said, "Is there enough for me?"

"Of course," his mother said. "Take down my tea chest, will you, please?"

As he reached to take the chest from the high shelf where it lived, Diana put a mug out for him, saying, "Your walk seems to have done you good."

He made a face at her over his shoulder and said, "I told two women to keep their cattle off Ardsheal land and sent a fellow about his business who was creeping through the woods above Kentallen. Nasty piece of work, he was. Must have been a Campbell. It gave me great pleasure to chase him off, I can tell you."

"I'm going to take some fresh-baked bread to Granny Jameson this afternoon, and perhaps visit Bardie," Diana said. "Would you like to come?"

"Can't," Neil said, avoiding her eye as he took his seat at the table. "I'm meeting someone."

Lady Maclean had unlocked the tea chest. Glancing up as she lifted the lid, she said, "Who?"

"Just some friends," he said. "In point of fact, Diana, I can walk part way with you, because I'll be going toward Kentallen

Inn. If you like, I can ask the innkeeper to join us tomorrow when we meet with Red Colin.''

''Yes, please do,'' she said. ''The more people we can gather, the better.''

''Tell me more about your visit to Glen Drumin,'' Mary said.

Diana knew her cousin had changed the subject so no one would press Neil to tell them more about his plan for the afternoon. Mary disliked contention unless she stirred it herself, and she doubtless wanted to keep Neil in good humor. Certain that he meant to visit Katherine Maccoll and fully intending to winkle a confession out of him while they walked toward Kentallen Inn, Diana soon excused herself and went upstairs to change into a rust-colored walking dress more suitable for the afternoon ahead than the old frock she had worn to do her chores.

An hour later, when she mentioned Katherine as they walked along the shore road, Neil said, ''Leave it, Diana. I'm old enough to decide things for myself, and I don't want anyone telling me aye or nay just now, if it's all the same to you.''

It was not all the same to her, for she was accustomed to demanding satisfaction for her curiosity, and she wanted to know whom he was meeting. In his present mood, however, she knew he would not tell her. Moreover, he had not questioned her plans for the afternoon, and for that she was grateful.

Though she had said she might visit Bardie, what she really meant to do was to wander along the ridge toward Ballachulish in hopes of catching sight of a large gray horse and its rider. She suspected that Rory might attempt to intercept Red Colin on his way to the inn, and while it would infuriate her if he did, she nonetheless wanted to catch at least a glimpse of him.

She felt unhappy about the way she had ended things the day before. He had treated all the Macleans with unexpected kindness. He had even assured MacDrumin that he was willing to marry her. And she had encouraged him, for reasons she did not want to think about now, to believe she might agree to such a union. She did not know, for she had never asked him, how he had explained to MacDrumin the lack of any announcement. She knew, to her private sorrow, that there never could be one now, but she did not want Rory for an enemy.

Red Colin would be in no hurry, she decided, since he had told them at the inn to expect him in the late afternoon or evening. Therefore, the most likely place for the men to meet was at the inn or the ferry landing. She thought Rory would choose the latter for greater privacy, especially since the inn's landlord was one of Colin's prospective victims.

Parting from Neil near Inshaig, she walked up through Glen Duror in search of James, but he was not home, so she went on to Granny Jameson's. After visiting with Granny and others nearby, and acquiring several promises to support them at the meeting with Red Colin, she walked along the ridge until she could see beyond the forest below her to the ferry landing.

The sun was low by then, and she knew she ought to turn back. But seeing no gray gelding, let alone any sign of its rider, she sat on a natural cushion of heather and grass to enjoy the view for a few minutes more before starting home.

The cerulean sky was alive with drifting, puffy white clouds. From her vantage point, the green and purple hillside fell steeply away, and she looked north over Lochaber and east the length of Loch Leven. To the north, she also had an excellent view of the upper part of Loch Linnhe, and for a time she sat thinking about their misty, rain-filled journey to Glen Drumin.

The loch waters, darker blue than the sky, looked deceptively calm. She could see the ferry moving away from North Balla-chulish, and idly she watched it make its way across to Appin.

Four men disembarked and followed the margin of Loch Linnhe for about a half mile. They were soon strung out in a long line and appeared to be in no hurry. The leader was on foot, the others on horseback.

When the middle rider took off his bonnet and revealed a mop of red hair, she was certain it was Colin. They veered to their left up the narrow, rocky track through Lettermore Woods soon afterward, and she could not see them as clearly, but when she got to her feet and began to retrace her steps along the ridge, she caught occasional glimpses of them through gaps in the birches and conifers.

She had been walking for several minutes when a gunshot cracked the silence of the woods. Stopping in her tracks, she heard a man cry out, and then she was running downhill, soon crashing through the thicket, flinging branches aside, as she fought her way down toward the commotion.

"Oh, I am dead!" It was Red Colin's voice, she thought, becoming sure when she heard, "He'll shoot you, too, Mungo. Take care, lad!"

Through a gap in the foliage, Diana saw Mungo dismount. He rushed back to help the stricken factor off his horse, and as he laid him down to unbutton his waistcoat, Mungo looked up toward the ridge at Diana's right. Instantly, her gaze followed his, but surrounded now by trees and shrubbery, she could see nothing.

Evidently he did, for he leapt to his feet and plunged up the hill.

Afraid he would see her, Diana shrank back, but even as she did, she heard another shout. Looking back toward Colin, she saw that the third horseman had joined him and was staring straight at her. Terrified, sure that the woods would soon be crawling with bloodthirsty Campbells, she turned and fled.

Eighteen

Scrambling through the woods as fast as her feet could carry her, Diana tried to think which way she should go. If she followed the ridge above Glen Duror, she would soon come to Bardie's cottage, but she might also meet with Campbells coming from Glen Creran and Glen Ure. If they saw her running, they would be bound to think the worst.

It would be safer all around if she went home. Even if she met Campbells on the way, they could scarcely accuse her of anything more than of being out walking near the end of a fine day, unless they found her before she was clear of Lettermore Woods. That must not happen.

Collecting her scattered wits, she slowed down, picking her way with more care. After a few moments she stopped altogether, crouching behind a tree to look back the way she had come.

The woods were silent. Not a bird chirped nearby. She heard the distant cry of a gull, and the breeze whispering in the leaves, but no human voice or that of any woodland creature disturbed the silence.

She knew the one man must have seen her, but what had he

seen? Could he recognize her again, or had she appeared to be no more than a rust-colored shadow? She had seen him clearly, for she had been close enough to hear Red Colin's words, after all, and his companion had stared straight into her eyes. She realized then that she had not seen the man who had walked ahead of them earlier. Where was he?

Was Colin really dying? Was he perhaps already dead? In the event, surely, they could not seriously suspect that she had killed him. For once, she was not even carrying her pistol. After the incident with Black Duncan, she had been afraid to carry it in Appin country, fearing that if she met him he would demand that she be searched. She did carry her *skean dhu,* however, for she wanted to be able to protect herself, and had confidence that the small knife did not fall under the ban.

With a sharp eye out for movement in her vicinity, keeping to the forest and away from well-traveled tracks, she made her way slowly but much more surely toward Maclean House. The sun had disappeared behind the western mountains before she arrived, and lamplight glowed from the parlor window as she crossed the silent yard. Overhead a few early stars winked in the graying sky.

Morag was in the scullery when she let herself in at the yard door. "Where is everyone else?" Diana asked her.

"Yer mam is in the parlor. Her cough is worse, and Miss Mary's gone to pick gorse by the roadside to brew her a composer."

"And Neil?"

"I've no seen the lad since he walked off wi' ye this afternoon."

Diana felt a distinct chill. Where was Neil? Whom had he met? And why? Though she had suspected an assignation with Katherine, now she was not so sure.

"Diana?" Lady Maclean stood in the doorway on the far side of the kitchen. "Lord bless me, child, you look as if you've been dragged through a hedge backward. What have you done to yourself?"

"Mam, someone shot Red Colin," Diana exclaimed. "I saw it!"

"You saw it?"

"Well, I heard the shot, and I saw that he was hit. He cried out that he was dying. I heard him plainly, Mam. And then Mungo saw someone—" She broke off when the yard door at the end of the scullery opened, then said with relief, "Oh, Mary, thank heaven it's you."

"You're as white as chalk," Mary said, coming in and shutting the door. She dropped the bar into place. "Who did you fear it would be?"

"Campbells," Diana said. "Someone shot Red Colin in Lettermore Woods."

"How dreadful! But I thought you took bread to Granny Jameson. Whatever were you doing in Lettermore Woods?"

"That doesn't matter. I visited others after Granny, looking for people to go with us to confront Colin tomorrow. Then I just walked. I heard the shot, and when I ran and looked, I could hear Colin shouting at Mungo. Then Mungo saw someone on the hillside and ran after him."

"Did you see anyone else?"

"Not a soul, but another man who was with them looked up and saw me. At least, I am nearly certain that he did."

"Dear God," Lady Maclean said, clutching the door frame. "Where is Neil?"

"Mam, he didn't do this."

"But where is he?" She coughed.

"I don't know," Diana admitted. "We parted near Inshaig sometime after two o'clock, and I've not seen him since."

Mary moved past Diana into the kitchen and said over her shoulder to Morag, "Fetch a large panful of water, will you, please, Morag? And I'll want to put this over a low fire, so shift some of those coals away from the hob." Laying the gorse she had cut on the table, she began to pluck off the yellow flowers.

Indignantly, Diana said, "How can you think about that gorse now?"

"What else should I think about?" Mary asked reasonably. "Are you afraid that Neil shot Colin? I shouldn't think he would, myself. It's much more the sort of thing Black Duncan would do, or Allan Breck. Or even Dugald Cameron," she added. "He left with MacDrumin's horses this morning, but I suppose . . ."

"That will do, Mary," Lady Maclean said firmly. "We will not speculate on who might have done such a terrible thing, particularly not about our own. Allan is a Stewart and Neil a Maclean. As for Dugald . . . Bah! None of them would shoot a man from ambush." She coughed again, covering her mouth with her hand.

Concerned, Diana said, "You should be sitting by the fire in the parlor, Mam. Mary, I'm sorry I snapped before. How long will that decoction take?"

"It's got to simmer down over the fire," Mary said. "Aunt Anne has already taken a bit of honey in whisky, though, so—"

Diana raised one eyebrow. "In whisky?"

"Andrew sent several bottles home with us," Lady Maclean said with a little smile. "It is his belief that whisky will cure anything, including the plague, so I thought I would give it a chance to cure this little cold of mine."

"I warrant it could, too," Mary said, "but the gorse will do more to ease that cough, and in any event, I'll add a glass of whisky to the brew. I generally do, you know, but there's no sense befuddling your senses by giving you more now, ma'am. Diana, what are you doing at the window?"

Diana had been peering out into the yard, expecting to see Campbells erupt from the shrubbery. As she began to turn away, movement caught her eye from the far side of the yard. "It's Bardie," she said a moment later, hurrying to the scullery to let him in. "Pray God he knows something."

"Ye've heard about Glenure then," he said after a swift glance at her face.

"Aye, I was there. Come in. Mam and Mary are in the kitchen."

Lumbering through the scullery, he said, "Did ye ken he were dead then?"

"No, is he?" Her breath caught in her throat, and her heart began to pound.

"Aye." Twisting awkwardly, Bardie looked back at her. "Here now, are ye all right, lass?"

"Bardie, I think one of those men saw me on the hillside."

"Aye, that would be Donald Kennedy, the sheriff's man," Bardie said matter-of-factly. "They do say he saw a lass run away up the brae."

Mary said, "Take Bardie into the parlor, Diana, and make Aunt Anne sit by the fire. I'll join you when I've put this on the hob, and Morag can call me when it's ready to strain."

By the time Diana had got Bardie settled on his favorite stool with a glass of whisky, and her mother seated by the fire with a coverlet over her knees, Mary had rejoined them.

After a sip of whisky, Bardie began his tale. "I was in Glen Duror, ye see, when a whole pack of Campbells invaded it, coming from the Kentallen road."

"A whole pack?" Mary tilted her head and smiled at him.

"Well, three or four, at least. Big loutish ones, o' course. Not folks a man o' my character would choose tae break bread with, at all events."

"Tell us what they said, Bardie," Diana said impatiently.

"Aye, sure, if ye can believe them. Glenure and his lot had proceeded from Ballachulish ferry along the margin of the loch, they say, then onto the path through the wood. Seven or eight minutes later, the assassin's shot put an end tae Glenure's devilish mischief forever."

"Yes," Diana said slowly, "that matches what I saw and heard."

"They say men from Glen Duror were with the body by the time any o' them Campbells saw it," Bardie said. "One of James's servants was there. James himself were absent, however."

"He was away when I stopped at his house earlier, too," Diana said. "What else did they say?"

"Diana said she thought Mungo chased someone," Mary said.

"Aye." Bardie nodded. "According tae them, he saw a man in a dun-colored short coat and breeches fleeing up the brae. The man carried a gun, but the distance was so great, Mungo did not think he could ha' fired the fatal shot."

"Did Donald Kennedy see that man as well?" Lady Maclean asked.

"Nay. They say he were too took up wi' Glenure and all the blood. Glenure's man had gone ahead of the others and thought nothing o' hearing a shot, but he soon came back tae see what were keeping them. They sent him a-running tae Kentallen Inn. Then when they knew Glenure was dead, Kennedy went back tae Ballachulish for more help, and Mungo stayed alone with Glenure." He grinned. "That must have been fun for him, all alone wi' a dead body in the midst o' Stewart country."

"You did say that Donald Kennedy saw me," Diana reminded him.

"Aye, but I dinna ken if he knew it were you, lass."

Morag said from the doorway, "That decoction be ready tae strain, Miss Mary. I've got the muslin ready, and all. Do ye want me tae do it?"

Mary got up. "I'll come, Morag." She walked to the doorway into the kitchen but stopped in her tracks on the threshold, stiffening. "What are you doing here?"

Without answering, Allan Breck brushed past her into the parlor and said to Lady Maclean, "You'll have to forgive me if I'm disturbing you. I'm afraid I've stirred up a nest of Campbell hornets, and it's quite likely they'll follow me here."

"What have you done, Allan?" Mary demanded.

"I've done nothing," he said, glaring at her, "but someone shot Glenure, in case you haven't heard, and there are irate Campbells under every rock and behind every tree. I came out of the Inshaig alehouse, and walked straight into a brace of them. It being clearly unwise to take to the hills without knowing what

I could expect to find there, I thought I'd go to ground. This was the closest bolthole.''

"So you put us all in danger," Mary said. "Do you think only of yourself?"

"I've had precious little else to think about for six years," he retorted.

"That's enough," Lady Maclean said sharply. "Diana, help Allan find a place to conceal himself till the danger is past. Mary, go attend to your decoction. If they do come, and everything here seems normal, they will simply go away again."

"But I think Mary is right," Diana said, exchanging a look with that young woman. "Allan should have had better sense than to lead them here."

"This isna the time for argle-bargle," Bardie said. He had moved to a window and now drew the curtain aside just far enough to peek out. "Like his nibs said, they're coming, lass. Ye'd best get him stowed under a bed or somewhere safe."

As Diana grabbed Allan by the sleeve of his black great coat, he said smoothly to Mary, "I know you'd like them to shoot me, sweetheart, but I don't mean to let that happen yet a while. Just keep that sharp little tongue behind your teeth, because if they learn that I'm here, I won't have to think hard about who told them. You won't like what will happen next."

"Don't talk to Mary like that," Diana told him. "If she does not like you, you have only yourself to blame. Moreover, if they learn you are here, you will be in no case to do anything to her."

"Aye, lad," Bardie said over his shoulder. "If they find ye, ye'll soon be hanging from the nearest tree. Get on now. They're halfway across the yard."

Quickly Diana took Allan up the narrow stairs to her mother's bedchamber. "Hide in the wardrobe," she said, "and try not to destroy any more of Mam's clothes than you must."

"I'll try not to destroy any, but it's going to be a tight fit."

"I can't help that," she said, listening for sounds from below. "I don't think they'll demand to search the house unless someone saw you come here, but if you hear them on the stairs, that window next to the wardrobe opens onto the scullery roof. You can drop to the ground from there.''

"They'll most likely leave a guard outside. I would if the circumstances were reversed. Just don't let them come up, lass. I rather fancy this skin of mine.''

Hearing men's voices downstairs, she snatched up a coverlet from the bed and hurried back to the parlor. "Here, Mam, I've brought you the one from—'' Breaking off when she saw Black Duncan, Lord Balcardane, and two other men in the parlor, she added in a puzzled tone. "Faith, sirs, what's amiss?''

"We're searching for villains, lass,'' Balcardane said.

"How dreadful, but won't you take a seat, sir? All of you standing like this makes the room seem too small to hold you. Morag, fetch our guests some whisky from the bottle Mary is using for her decoction. I'll warrant they must be thirsty.''

"Aye, lass,'' Balcardane said, rubbing his hands together. "I won't turn down a dram, now that you mention it.''

"Where's your brother?'' Duncan demanded harshly.

"Mind your manners, lad,'' Balcardane said testily. "There's time enough for that. I want a drink, and it won't hurt you to have one as well. Sit down, sit down.''

Paying him no heed, Duncan looked directly at Diana. "Have you been wearing that red dress all day?''

Realizing belatedly that she had not given a thought to changing her gown, she raised her chin and said, "What business is it of yours if I have?''

"No time for whisky, has Black Duncan,'' Bardie murmured provocatively, "but the man always has time tae note what a lovely lass be wearing.''

Duncan turned on him with a near snarl. "You keep your mouth shut, or I'll make you sorry you did not.''

"Always a fierce one, from the cradle,'' Bardie said to no one in particular as he drew his stool nearer to the wall and sat down. "Expects tae wield the same influence here as he does on his own great dunghill.''

Duncan took a menacing step toward him, "Now, look here,

you misbegotten, short-legged nuisance, you button up your impudence or I'll teach you a lesson you'll not soon forget.''

"Aye, *and* answer tae Parson for it,'' Bardie reminded him, leaning against the wall with his arms crossed over his chest. "Ye mind your manners, ye great mallagrugous malcontent, or I'll tell him ye've been mocking me again, *and* I'll add that ye've been tearing the wings off butterflies again, too, for good measure.''

Balcardane said, "I doubt that Duncan has ever torn wings off butterflies.''

"Nae matter,'' Bardie said, eyeing Duncan warily. "In such a good cause, I dinna mind telling a wee falsehood or two.''

Lady Maclean said calmly, "Have you gentlemen got business here, or did you merely seek to assure yourselves of our safety? We heard that someone shot Colin Glenure in Lettermore Woods.''

Balcardane grimaced. "Now that's a pity, that you've heard already, for we had hoped to get here ahead of the news.'' He glared at Bardie. "I expect we've no need to ask who told you. I heard that Bardie here was seen near Glen Duror.''

"He's not the only one they saw,'' Duncan said, his gaze fixed on Diana. "There was a woman in a red dress, as well. What if I were to tell you that when they searched the nearby area, they found evidence that could hang the murderer?''

Diana felt faint. "What evidence? What could they possibly have found?''

"I don't think I'll tell you that. Where are your brother and your cousin, lass, and James of the Glen?''

"M-my cousin is—''

"I'm here,'' Mary said from the doorway. "I have been standing here these past two minutes, unable to believe my ears. What possessed the pair of you, Duncan Campbell and Bardie Gillonie, to exchange insults in a lady's parlor? And both of you pretending to be civilized men!'' She turned to Balcardane, adding, "I have instructed our maid to bring you a mug of whisky, sir, so won't you draw that other chair near the fire and sit down now? It's getting chilly, I believe.''

"It is that, lass," Balcardane agreed.

"Never mind all that," Duncan snapped. "Where the devil is young Neil and that scoundrel, Allan Breck? By God, I've a good mind to search this house."

"Neil is not here," Lady Maclean said tartly. "We do not know where he is. As to searching my house, do you dare to doubt my word, young man?"

"What about Allan Breck?"

"I do not know where he is either," Lady Maclean said, looking him in the eye. Then, just as he was about to speak again, she fell into a fit of coughing.

Diana turned on him angrily. "There, see what you've done! We just got her settled down, and she was breathing more easily. Now you've upset her again. Go away, Duncan Campbell."

"I'm not going anywhere," Duncan said. "Donald Kennedy saw a lass in a red dress running from the murder scene. I think we'll send for him to see if he recognizes you as that lass."

"And what if he should say that he does?"

"Diana," Mary exclaimed, "how can you suggest such a thing?"

"Easily. I believe that this Kennedy person will say whatever Duncan commands him to say." Avoiding Mary's eye, she draped the coverlet she had brought downstairs atop the one that already lay across Lady Maclean's knees.

"Here now," Balcardane protested. "I don't think Kennedy would lie, you know. He is an honorable man."

Wanting to end the dangerous discussion, Diana straightened and said impulsively, "If you send for Kennedy, then pray, sir, send for Lord Calder as well. At least he seems to have some small notion of fairness, which makes him unique amongst Campbells. Moreover, I won't answer any questions unless he is here."

"Now, that's fair enough," Balcardane said. "As it happens, he was with us earlier in Kentallen, Miss Diana. He and another chap rode into Glen Duror to have a word with James of the Glen."

"Lud, sir," Mary said, "what do they want with James?"

Duncan said, "We want to ask him a few questions, too." To Diana, he said, "I don't mind waiting while one of the lads fetches Rory, but if you think he'll help you tonight like he did at Spean Bridge, you'd best think again." Then, turning to one of the men with him, he said, "Fetch his lordship here at once."

Watching the man leave, Diana gathered her dignity and said, "I don't expect him to help. Most likely he will side with his own Campbells as usual, just as I will side with the Macleans and Stewarts. But he has shown he is capable of hearing both sides before he acts, which is more than one can say of most Campbells."

"He has a duty to listen to both sides of a dispute," Duncan said. "That does not mean he's a fool."

"What do you mean?"

"He knows which clan he belongs to, lass."

"But that's not what I—"

"We'll send for him," Duncan said, cutting her off with a gesture. "I'll even drink a glass of whisky while we wait, but when he gets here, I believe he'll agree that we'd be wise to search this house."

Trying to remain calm, Diana shrugged. "If you want to search the house, of course you will do so. We can hardly stop you."

"Perhaps we should begin with your person, mistress," Duncan suggested. "I seem to recall that you were carrying a banned weapon the last time we met."

Having been on his way to intercept Glenure at Kentallen, Rory learned of the murder soon after it occurred. He rode first to Lettermore Woods, but by the time he arrived at the murder site, others had the matter in hand and had already decided to remove the corpse to Kentallen Inn.

There were more Stewarts and Macleans there than Campbells, which was not odd, considering that they were in the midst of Stewart country. Nonetheless, when Rory heard a man say that someone ought to tell James what had happened, and a man named MacKenzie offered to go, Rory decided to go with him.

When he announced his intention, Mungo Campbell looked sharply at him and said, "Take heed then, sir. They are all thieves and murderers in these parts. We don't want another corpse on our hands tonight."

"I should think James would be glad of a Campbell witness to the fact that he is safe at home and has been there yet a while," Rory said calmly.

"Aye, that's so," Mackenzie said. "Come along then, my lord, and welcome. I'll stake my life that James o' the Glen dinna ha' aught tae do wi' this."

They did find James with his family, but when MacKenzie told him Glenure was dead, he exclaimed, "Lord bless me, was he shot?"

Rory remained silent, careful not to react, for he was aware that he would learn more by listening than by talking. Nevertheless, he thought that if James had wanted to condemn himself, he was going about it efficiently.

Mackenzie glanced sharply at Rory, but he looked back blandly. He had not needed Mungo's warning to know the wisdom of treading lightly.

"He were shot, right enough, James," Mackenzie said. "A single shot from behind, they say. A right cowardly thing, that was."

"It's a shocking outrage," James exclaimed, wringing his hands. "We must hope innocent people are not brought to trouble for this." He glanced at Rory, adding, "I must go to Colin. We were friends for a time, and I owe him respect."

James's wife spoke up anxiously in Gaelic. Rory understood her to say that she did not want James to go, that she feared the reception he would get if he met a host of Campbells at Kentallen Inn.

With a weary sigh, James replied in the same language, "Whoever is guilty, it is I who will pay the penalty."

Now what, Rory wondered with increasing astonishment, had possessed the man to say such a thing?

Mackenzie, still with one eye on Rory, said in English, "Perhaps ye'd best stay here the nicht, James. Ye'll no want the wee woman tae fret." His words were matter-of-fact, but the look accompanying them was compelling.

James blinked but did not argue. "Aye, I will then."

Departing at once, Rory and Mackenzie had reached the shore road again when Rory heard someone shouting his name. Turning, he saw one of Duncan's men, and reined in Rosinante to wait, telling Mackenzie to ride on ahead.

"With Master Duncan's compliments, my lord," the henchman said. "Mistress Diana requests that you come at once to Maclean House."

"Does she, indeed?" Rory murmured, wondering what sort of pickle Mistress Spitfire had got herself into this time, and what Duncan had to do with it. Shouting to Mackenzie that he would be along later, he urged Rosinante to a canter.

Diana looked straight at Duncan, determined not to reveal how much his threat of a personal search for a weapon angered her. "Since you recall the pistol, sir, perhaps you will recall as well that I had good cause to show it and that your cousin took it from you after you had taken it from me. Do you suggest that he then gave it back to me?" Pleased with her choice of words, particularly since she had not actually lied and said that Rory had kept it, she looked him in the eye, wondering if he would accuse his cousin of allowing her to break the law.

A little to her chagrin, Duncan only smiled.

Quickly, before her courage could fail her, she said, "You mentioned evidence earlier. Are you trying to pretend that you found my pistol at the scene?"

Lady Maclean gasped, and Mary clutched a hand to her breast.

Before Duncan could reply Balcardane said, "Naught of the sort, lass. They've found nothing at all helpful yet, I'm afraid, but they'll guard the area tonight and search it much more carefully come daylight."

Diana glared at Duncan, who smiled back serenely. She would have liked very much to think of a scathing remark to make, but she had a feeling that under the circumstances she would be wiser to keep silent.

Morag came in, bearing chopins and a jug. "The barley sugar be melted, Miss Mary, if ye want tae give her ladyship a dose while the men ha' their whisky."

Mary glanced at Diana, then went into the kitchen.

Diana was tempted to follow, for she was eager to share her thoughts and feelings and see if Mary could suggest some course to ease them through what lay ahead. But she knew she must not submit to the temptation. Duncan would like nothing better than to find the pair of them whispering in the kitchen, if he would let her leave the parlor in the first place.

Not wanting to put him to that test, she drew a seat near her mother, noting as she did that Lady Maclean had regained much of her natural color.

"What brew would that be?" Balcardane asked, paying little heed to Morag but looking suspiciously toward the doorway through which Mary had gone.

Diana said, " 'Tis a decoction for my mother's cough, sir, no more than water in which Mary has boiled a few gorse blossoms. She adds a handful of barley sugar and a bit of whisky, and I promise you, it is very effective."

Looking nervously at Duncan, Balcardane said, "I don't suppose she'll try to slip away."

"She would not get far if she did," Duncan said. "I've got four men outside the house." He took the mug Morag handed him and drew up a chair for himself.

Diana wished she dared have a dram of whisky with the others. She had a notion it would calm her unsettled nerves. On the other hand, it might loosen her tongue, and that she could not afford.

Mary came back with a glass of steaming amber-colored

liquid that she handed to Lady Maclean. "Sip it slowly, Aunt Anne, and let it relax you. No harm will come to us tonight."

Looking into her eyes and relaxing visibly, Lady Maclean said, "Thank you, my dear. You take excellent care of me."

Duncan said, "It is no doubt tactless of me to point out, madam, that you may be in as much trouble as your son, your daughter, and your nephew, not to mention James of the Glen. Not only have you been heard to utter threats against Colin Glenure but you have yet to answer for your escape from Edinburgh Castle."

Indignantly, Diana said, "Calder promised that if she took the oath of allegiance, there would be no more trouble over that. He did not think she should ever have been imprisoned in the first place, which just shows he can be sensible."

"It shows, more likely, that he does not know all the facts in the case."

"But you *must* know that Red Colin just wanted to prove he could be harsh. Someone warned him that he must not look as if he were being lenient with rebel families—his mother being a Cameron, and all—so he punished Mam."

"Rory was one of those who gave him that advice," Duncan said gently.

"What reason could he have to do such a thing?"

"His position dictates the reason," Duncan said.

"Because he is close kin to Argyll? But—"

"I refer to his seat on the Barons' Court," Duncan said with a mocking smile. "Rory is responsible for administering western Highland estates that were forfeited to the Crown after the last uprising. He came to Appin country to see how well his factors and bailies were managing them."

Diana stared at him in shock. "Do you mean to say he had authority over Red Colin, that he could have ordered him to withdraw those eviction orders?"

"As to that, I—" Duncan broke off at a sharp rap on the front door.

One of his men opened it at once, and Rory entered, his gaze sweeping the room and coming to rest on Diana.

Glaring at him, she said furiously, "How foolish I was to send for a Campbell when it is a Campbell who's been murdered! Go away, sir. I was stupid to trust you, and I don't ever want to see your face again!"

Nineteen

Rory stood where he was, looking in bewilderment at Diana, unable to understand her fury. Duncan's man had told him only that Balcardane wanted to learn the whereabouts of Sir Neil Maclean and Allan Breck, that therefore, he and Duncan had called at Maclean House, only to have Mistress Diana demand that they send for Lord Calder before she would answer any of their questions.

Glancing at Duncan now, he saw his cousin smirk. Having already seen four of Duncan's men in the yard, Rory deduced that whatever Balcardane's intention had been, his elder son had been amusing himself by stirring up trouble again.

Balcardane said, "Come in, lad, and let that fellow shut the door. Do you think her ladyship is burning good peat to warm the yard?"

Ignoring him, Rory moved toward Diana, who still stood with her hands on her hips, glaring at him, her soft breasts heaving in anger and indignation.

Maintaining his calm, he said, "Why do you want me to leave, lass?"

Her jaw tightened, and she shot a swift oblique glance at

Duncan and Balcardane, but although her throat moved convulsively, she said nothing.

Feeling his temper stir, he suppressed it, saying, "Come now. Are you afraid to speak? What's amiss here?"

Cheeks reddening, eyes flashing fire, she snapped, "What's amiss? You dare to ask me that when Red Colin is dead and your cousin has accused my brother and cousin—aye, and me, as well, if you please—of having murdered him!"

"Now, lass, surely—"

But having begun, she went on as if he had not opened his mouth, "You pretended to care about us! But now I learn that you possessed the power to stop those eviction notices without James's ever having had to go to Edinburgh, or . . . or—" She broke off, clenching and unclenching her fists in frustration, as if she simply could not summon up all the words she needed to express her fury.

"I could not have stopped the notices," he said evenly.

"Fiddlesticks, your secret is out, sir. Duncan has just told us that you are a Baron of the Exchequer, responsible for administering the forfeited estates here. Certainly you could have stopped them."

"Not alone," he said, but he might as well have spared his breath.

"To think that you professed to care about me, about my mother! You probably lied through your teeth when you said she would be safe here now."

"She *is* safe, and I do not lie. Until yesterday I thought you knew—"

"How could I know? People spoke of your power and position, to be sure, but I assumed they meant your close kinship to Argyll. As to Mam's safety, Duncan has just flung it in her teeth that she is still a fugitive, so whatever you may say—"

"I think we should talk privately," Rory said curtly.

"I don't *want* to talk privately."

Balcardane said, "You know, lad, although we are looking to lay Colin's murderer by the heels, what Duncan said about her ladyship is true. She is still a fugitive. Escaped from prison, didn't she? Odrabbit it, ma'am,'' he added, turning to her and raising his glass, as if he had not just been encouraging her arrest, ''this is excellent whisky. I'll warrant it cost you a pretty penny.''

Lady Maclean gasped, but before she could voice her outrage, Duncan said in irritation, ''Never mind the damned the whisky.'' To Rory, he added, ''However much you may wish it otherwise, cousin, her ladyship *is* a fugitive. Furthermore, she has been thick with the rebels hereabouts for years, so if she was not hand in glove with the murderers, you may be sure she knows who, and perhaps even where, they are. We should take everyone in this house into custody.''

Lady Maclean's indignation had increased visibly, and now, looking straight at Duncan, she said, ''Young man, if you know aught to my discredit, let alone that of my daughter or niece, I shall own myself amazed. I have had nothing to do with murder. As to those trumped-up charges that put me in prison—''

''They were exaggerated,'' Rory said when she broke off, spreading her hands as if she need say nothing more. ''Moreover,'' he added, shifting his gaze to Duncan, ''as far as I know, even Argyll is no longer lusting for her ladyship's arrest. We have more important items on our plate, cousin, and we can get to them just as soon as I have had a private word with Diana.''

''We are not going to have private words,'' she retorted.

''Oh, yes, we are,'' he said grimly. ''You can come with me quietly, or I will carry you, but I will not let this business stand as it is any longer.'' When she just glared at him, he folded his arms across his chest. ''Well, lass, which will it be?''

She looked uncertain for a moment, glancing around as if she hoped for aid from one of the others, but no one said a word, not even Bardie.

The generally irrepressible dwarf sat on his stool, leaning against the wall with his hands clasped lightly in his lap, observing the others.

Mary stepped forward, making a gesture as if she would speak, but when Rory caught her gaze, she let her hand fall to her side and stepped back.

Lady Maclean still glared at Duncan as if she would like to treat him as she had once threatened to treat Argyll, and snatch him bald-headed.

After a long moment of tense silence, when Diana still had not said a word or stirred from her position, Rory lowered his arms and took a step toward her.

Stiffening, she said through clenched teeth, "Very well, I'll go with you, but don't think for one moment that you are going to influence me with soft words."

"I've warned you more than once about making trouble, lass," he murmured for her ears alone. "You've more likely earned yourself a scold than soft words."

When she looked swiftly into his eyes, he gazed sternly back until she looked away again. He preferred to keep her off balance, for the last thing he wanted was a shouting match in the yard, where Duncan's men would hear every word.

As they were leaving the house, Rory saw Mary turn toward the kitchen. He hoped she would not try to slip out to warn young Neil or anyone else, but at the moment he did not much care what she did. He could think only of Diana.

Looking down at her glossy curls as she strode ahead of him, he wondered what, if anything, she had had to do with the murder. That she had held Glenure in contempt was certain. That her mother, her brother, and her cousin had each threatened to put a period to the factor's life was also a fact. But what frightened him most was the knowledge that, more than once before, Diana had taken matters into her own, clearly capable hands when she had felt a strong need to do so.

Outside in the shadow-filled yard beneath a dark sky rapidly filling with stars, when she stopped near the gate, he said, "Out with it now, lass. You may say what you like to me. I ask only that you keep your voice down. There is no need to entertain Duncan's men with your assessment of my character."

She turned to face him, and in the dim glow of light from

the house, he saw anger in every rigid line of her body. "You lied to me."

"I did not lie. I thought you knew I was a member of the court."

"How could I know?"

"Many people know, sweetheart. I have not kept it a secret."

"How many know who are not Campbells?"

"James does, and Ian. The lad's a Campbell, but he talks to everyone." He remembered that he had once asked Ian not to noise the information all over Appin, and a hint of that memory must have shown in his expression, for she looked grim.

"James did not tell us, nor did Ian," she said, "and if Ian did not tell Mary, I doubt that he told anyone. Shall I ask him why he did not?"

"I asked him not to puff off my consequence all over Appin," Rory admitted with a sigh. "Look, Diana, I never meant to conceal my relationship with the court. I just wanted to learn the truth about how our factors were managing the forfeited estates without making everyone nervous about my presence. My intention was to prevent trouble, not to create it. The *last* thing I wanted was stir trouble with you."

"You should have told me straight out when we first met."

Gently, he said, "Do you truly believe that I ought to have frightened a simple laundry maid with a complete description of my authority?"

"N-no, perhaps not." She did not look at him.

"What would you have thought if I had told you at Stalker? Recall that you had just helped a felon escape, and that I was more concerned that Patrick might hang you if he learned of your previous activities than I was about explaining my authority. But suppose that I *had* told you then. Would you have been reassured or more frightened than ever?"

She sighed. "I would have been terrified. I was already frightened about what would happen to me if you told Patrick I was reluctant to leap into your bed."

"Our other early meetings were brief, and our minds were generally on other matters. When I found you that first day here in the yard, you were in the midst of a pitched battle with James and Glenure. Both of them knew who I was, but when they saw that you knew me, I daresay they did not think it necessary to recite my titles to you, and I certainly don't recite them to all I meet. Moreover, if I'd thought about it at all, I had reason to believe one of them had told you. I do apologize if I have made it seem that I meant to deceive you. That was never my intention.''

She bit her lower lip, and he took comfort from that, hoping she was sorry she had become so angry. Then she looked straight at him. ''I want to believe you, sir, but although I am not thinking too clearly now, I do think you had other opportunities to be plain with me.''

''I can't deny that, lass. In defense, I can only repeat that by the time it might have occurred to me to tell you, I assumed that you knew.''

''Faith, sir, had I known, don't you think I would have asked for your help?''

''But I've explained that setting aside an eviction requires action by the whole court, and it won't meet again until next month.''

''It might have met sooner had there been a quorum present in Edinburgh when James went there to protest,'' she pointed out.

Rory sighed. ''Diana, most of the others have left the city, too. Even if I had gone with James—which I could scarcely have done since no one told me he was going—the court would in all likelihood still have lacked a quorum.''

''But you might have advised him afterward. If you had discussed the matter with him, you might have discovered in time that he had brought home that thing he ought to have filed with the court.''

''The Bill of Suspension?''

She nodded.

Repressing a stir of frustrated amusement, he said, ''Sweetheart, be reasonable. By the time I learned that James had even *got* the sist, you were on your way to Glen Drumin and Duncan was tracking you.''

''Oh.'' She continued to nibble her lower lip. ''That's true.''

''Aye, and even if it were not, do you think he would have revealed his strategy to me, or expected me to advise him against Glenure? Recall that the Highlands have been humming with rumors of new rebellion, rumors that James certainly knew about, even if he was not party to whatever action was brewing.''

''He wouldn't be!''

''Well, your cousin's recruiting activities seemed to confirm those rumors,'' he pointed out. ''His efforts also made it more difficult for Glenure to prove to some very suspicious men in London that he had not been favoring Highlanders.''

''Your cousin makes as much mischief as mine does,'' Diana said. ''I don't mean Gentle Ian, either.''

''Duncan has been much too busy, I agree,'' Rory said. ''For that matter, I have seen a great deal since my arrival, lass, but no hint of a new rebellion brewing. I'm as convinced as I can be that there is none.''

''If there is, sir, I give you my word, I know nothing about it. I know less about Allan's activities than you know of Duncan's, however. I wish, by the way, that you would step on Duncan again. He annoys me.''

He smiled. ''Tempting though that is, I think I must resist. My uncle is not only grieved by Colin's death but he is consumed with indignation, as well. For me to attack his son would be cruel. I am going to need their help soon, in any case.''

''To find the murderer?''

Her voice sounded small, uncertain, and he wanted to reassure her, but some of his earlier qualms stirred again. He said, ''I shall probably be asked to assist in that task, but I promise I'll be as fair as I can. Will you tell me what you know?''

She shook her head. ''I have learned how easily men can twist words, and I'll not help anyone conjure a reason to hang Neil or Allan, or any of our neighbors.''

''I won't conjure reasons, lass, but neither will I allow Colin's murderer to go free if I can prevent it. I'd best warn you that I do have the authority to order you to submit to a precognition."

"What's that?"

Solemnly he said, "It is a preliminary examination to determine if there are any grounds for a prosecution."

"You would do that to me?"

"You may leave me no choice," he said. "Not to mince matters, sweetheart, you landed yourself in this pickle the day you waved your pistol at Duncan."

"Well, you can ask your questions. You cannot force me to answer them."

"I hope you won't put me to that test."

She looked away, refusing to meet his gaze. "I'm going back inside."

Touching her arm, he said, "Wait. You accused me a moment ago of just pretending to care about you. It is no pretense, Diana, but if you force my hand, you will lose. I cannot step aside now or keep my knowledge of things you've done in the past from affecting my judgment. You'd be wiser to be frank with me."

"I can't jeopardize my family," she said stubbornly. "In the end you'll side with the Campbells against us, and I will side with Macleans. It is sad, sir, but true."

He could not deny it. He was as certain as he could be that once Argyll learned of Glenure's murder, the duke would order him to remain in Appin to oversee the investigation. If that happened, he would have to put his personal feelings aside and let the law take its course.

Diana waited, hoping Rory would deny that he could take sides against her or her family, but he just looked up at the sky as if he hoped to find answers in the stars. After a long moment's silence, she turned back toward the house, only to experience a surge of disappointment when he did not stop her. Not until she neared the front door did she hear the crunch of his footsteps behind her.

She understood that he had not meant to deceive her, that they had both simply assumed things they perhaps should not have assumed. But now events had taken over, igniting new hostility between their clans and stifling the fragile intimacy they had built. She wanted to confide in him. More than that, she wanted to ask for his help, to tell him she was frightened. But she could not. They seemed to stand on opposite sides of an ever-widening abyss.

Inside the house, she saw at once that the atmosphere had changed. Duncan broke off at their entrance in the midst of what appeared to have been a diatribe, and Lady Maclean was clearly having difficulty keeping her temper.

Glowering at Rory, Duncan said, "I've just been telling my father that if you don't apply for the warrants, I will."

"Warrants for whom?" Rory asked mildly.

"Don't be daft. We need warrants to arrest Allan Breck, Sir Neil Maclean, Mistress Silence there, her ladyship, and perhaps Mistress Mary as well. If they were not all involved in Colin's murder, the sheriff and the lord advocate can sort it out soon enough. If they were, we'll have them safely in a cell at Fort William when we want them."

"You're leaping over the hedge before you come to the stile, as usual," Rory said. "Don't you think it would be wise to have some evidence against them before you demand their arrests?"

Diana held her breath, aware that Duncan was watching her. As she had expected, he said, "Ask Mistress Silence there where she was at half past five when Donald Kennedy saw a woman in a red dress on the hillside above the murder site."

Rory looked at her. "Well, lass, did you have aught to do with the murder?"

Grateful that he had not asked what she was doing there, she suppressed a surge of resentment that he had assumed Duncan was right in accusing her, and managed to meet his stern gaze. "I did not," she said flatly.

Clearly bent on doing more mischief, Duncan said, "You know as well as I do that she often carries a pistol."

"And you know as well as I do," Rory retorted in the same tone, "that whoever shot Glenure shot him with a larger weapon. Or are you going to try to convince a court that Mistress Diana hid such a weapon beneath her skirt?"

"We ought at least to search her," Duncan snarled.

"Not without more evidence than you have provided, we won't. Nor will we arrest her ladyship. As for accusing Mistress Mary, you must be daft. Not to mince words, you don't have a prick's worth of proof against any of these women."

Balcardane growled, "You turning against your own, nephew? Our Colin laid down his life while carrying out orders of a government that dared suspect him of treachery. I should think you would want to act on every least hint of complicity."

"Surely, sir, you don't want innocent people arrested."

Diana was not so sure of that. Rarely, in her experience, did the Campbells consider justice before they acted. Rory was unusual in that he seemed able to see both sides of an issue. With a flash of annoying insight she realized that such men were unusual among the Macleans, as well. Fixing her attention on Balcardane, she wondered if he would allow Rory to call the tune.

Duncan said curtly, "We must search this house, at least."

Scarcely daring to breathe, Diana said nothing, and was grateful when Mary spoke from the kitchen doorway, her tone gently mocking. "Next you will say that you saw a regiment of rebels slip in at the back door, Duncan Campbell."

Duncan shot her a furious look, but Diana saw with relief that Rory smiled.

He said to Mary, "I expect he would have mentioned such a spectacle by now if he had seen it, mistress." Then, to Duncan, he said, "You have upset this household enough for one night, I think. If it makes you happy, leave a few of your men nearby to watch for Sir Neil. I doubt that he had aught to do with Glenure's murder, but we should at least learn where he has been."

"You may think he had naught to do with it," Duncan snapped, "but there are others who know better. More than one man heard him threaten Colin. If you try to prevent us from getting warrants to arrest him or that villain Allan Breck, you are no more than a rebel in Campbell clothing, sir.''

''I have not said that you cannot get a warrant for Breck, although it will be redundant since he is already wanted. I expect you can get one for Sir Neil, too. When I left Kentallen Inn, they had already sent for Sheriff Stonefield. He is in Inverness, they say, so it will be Monday before he can get here, but he can attend to applying for your warrants then.''

''We want them straightaway,'' Duncan snapped.

''He has to apply to the lord justice general's clerk in Edinburgh for a murder warrant, I'm afraid, but I doubt that you will be the only one calling for them. There will be many men suspected of this crime, I think.''

''Aye, there will indeed,'' Duncan said. ''That meddling James Stewart, for one, and mayhap a Cameron or two. They've been devilish unhappy with our Colin of late, but I'll wager that at least one of the villains hails from right here at Maclean House. Oh, I know you don't agree, but you are no longer thinking with your head, cousin, and so I shall tell Argyll when we see him.''

Balcardane got up when Duncan opened the door to leave. The earl looked unsteady, as if he still had not taken in the magnitude of what had happened. He was extremely civil to Lady Maclean, treating her with the respect due to her as a woman and a widow, but Diana was certain he meant to demand Neil's arrest.

When he reached the open doorway, he turned back and said to Rory, '' 'Tis barbarous, that's what it is. What manner of villain can shoot a tolerant, unarmed man from behind? Colin leaves two infant daughters and a pregnant wife barely in her twenties. It is a deliberate challenge to lawful authority, nephew. No matter the cost, the villains must be tracked down and hanged, every blessed one of them.''

''We'll catch them, sir,'' Rory said quietly.

''Aye, we will. I've pledged my word on it.'' His expression hardened. ''Argyll will hear of this soon, and what he will think of your refusal to take known felons into custody, or to search these premises—Well, lad, I don't envy you that interview, indeed I don't. But I'll say no more about it now. Duncan's waiting. We're going back to Kentallen Inn. They've taken Colin's body there, you know.'' Without another word, he went out and snapped the door shut behind him.

Diana saw from Rory's expression that he expected to derive no pleasure from an interview with Argyll, but when he caught her gaze, he smiled ruefully.

''I'm sorry, lass. I can't stop them from getting warrants for Neil and your cousin. I had all I could do to stop them from arresting you and her ladyship.''

''We are grateful,'' Lady Maclean said. ''Balcardane is right about one thing. This is barbarous. Before it's done, I fear for us all.''

''That's what James of the Glen said.''

''Have you seen him?'' Diana asked, surprised.

''I have. A chap went to tell him about the murder, and I went along to see if the news surprised him. Don't look like that. Like it or not, I have my duty to do.''

''What else will your duty demand of you, sir?''

''Make no mistake, lass. Once the investigation begins in earnest, it may progress in such a way that I'll have to reveal certain things I know. Therefore, I'd strongly advise you to do nothing more to draw undue attention to yourself.''

Diana said with dignity, ''I shall do what I must, sir, nothing more.''

His smile was crooked. ''I've given you fair warning. I can do no more.''

When he had gone, Bardie said quietly, ''That man does not know himself.''

''What do you mean?'' Diana demanded.

''There he is, six foot something of fearsome Campbell, and he lets a wee scrap of a lass twist him round her thumb.''

''I wish that were so,'' Diana said. ''I could persuade him to leave us alone.''

''Do you really want tae be let alone, lassie? I ha' seen the way ye look at the great creature. Yer eyes go all soft and dwammish.''

''Hush, Bardie. You don't know what you are saying. Go and see if you can tell where Black Duncan's men have hidden. We've got to get Allan out of here before Duncan comes back and searches the house.''

''I doubt he has the nerve tae do that without Calder's leave,'' Bardie said, getting up and carefully turning back a corner of the curtain. ''Move that lamp, lass, so it willna shine straight out at them.''

''Have they gone?'' Allan asked from the shadows of the narrow stairway.

''It's a good thing for you if they have,'' Diana said severely. ''What if someone were still here and heard you?''

''Then I'd take out my sword and run them through,'' he said lightly.

''Don't joke about such things,'' she scolded. ''Mary, whatever are you doing? You keep going back and forth to the kitchen like a nervous cat.''

''Morag took whisky out to Duncan's men,'' Mary said quietly. ''They ought to be nicely relaxed and sleepy by now.''

''Goodness, did you hope to make them drunk? I warrant they are too frightened of Duncan to do anything so foolish.''

''Oh, no,'' Mary said. ''I just want them nicely fuddled. I told Morag to tell them we could not spare them much, but MacDrumin's whisky is potent and very good. Indeed, it is a pity to waste it on them, but when Morag says good-night to us, I don't want anyone thinking clearly enough to wonder where she is going. Most folks hereabouts know she lives here except for occasional visits to her brother.''

''But why is she going anywhere?'' Bardie asked.

Diana caught on swiftly. ''A diversion!''

''Aye,'' Mary said. ''Even if they don't remember that she ought not to be going, they will be suspicious of her, don't you think? At least one of them is bound to demand to see her up close.'' She turned to Allan. ''Do you think you can manage to slip out while the men outside are watching Morag and whoever accosts her?''

''Aye, it will be as easy as kiss my hand, but I'm surprised that you'd help.''

''I want you well away from here, Allan.''

''Be quiet, the pair of you,'' Diana said. Seeing Morag at the kitchen door, she said, ''Do you understand what Miss Mary wants you to do?''

''Aye, mistress. I'm tae look like Master Allan if I can.''

''If you are afraid, one of us can go.''

''Nay, I know those men. They be gormless. Shall I go now?''

''Yes, I think so. Just walk straight across the yard. Miss Mary and I will make a thing of bidding you good-night, but you must not answer.''

''Aye, then, I'm off.''

She put a cloak around her shoulders, pulling the hood forward so that it concealed her face. She was a large woman, and hunching like she was when she went through the scullery, she did look furtive.

''I'll be going, too,'' Bardie said. ''That will give them more tae think about, for I'll go out the front, and her ladyship can make a thing of seeing me off.''

Diana and Mary hurried after Morag, calling good-night from the doorway and waving. The maidservant waved back without showing her face.

As they had hoped, three of the men Duncan had left watching the house hurried to intercept her, grabbing her by the arms and snatching back her hood. One of the men said harshly, ''Here now, lad, who do ye think yer fooling?

At that Morag set up a screech that folks across the loch must have heard, for it sounded to Diana like a banshee's scream, or that of a demented woman. At all events, the clamor brought the fourth man running round the side of the house.

Pandemonium ensued until Diana and Mary hurried into the yard and Diana exclaimed indignantly, ''How dare you attack Morag! Just wait until I complain of your behavior to Lord

Balcardane and Lord Calder. You men should be ashamed of yourselves, setting upon a poor innocent woman like that.''

Since by now it was clear to them all that their victim was female, none was brave enough to question her innocence. Morag declared herself too frightened and upset to go any farther and announced that she would just have to wait for another day to go, whereupon Diana and Mary escorted her tenderly back to the house.

Lady Maclean awaited them in the kitchen. "He's gone," she said. "Bardie went out the front, and when the man watching heard all the row and ran to see what it was, Bardie signed to Allan that his way was clear. By now the pair of them will be safe in the shrubbery on the hillside.''

"Allan is hardly safe," Diana pointed out. "The woods will be crawling with Campbells until they catch the murderer.''

"Bardie will use his own ways, however, and will be able to tell Allan which route is clearest," Lady Maclean said. "Once they catch the right man, things will return to normal, and in any event, I believe Allan is nearly ready to return to France. He said he has been delayed by trouble collecting the second rents.''

"That is hardly amazing," Diana said. "People don't like paying twice. I'll be glad when he leaves though. Too many people think his being here is proof that the rebels are stirring again.

"But who do you think murdered Red Colin?" Mary asked with a frown.

"It is a pity you cannot answer that for us, my dear," Lady Maclean said. "I can tell you only that it was not a Maclean or a Stewart. You heard them say he was shot from behind. No one we know would do such a cowardly thing.''

Mary's expression showed a lack of such confidence, and with sinking spirits Diana realized that her own hitherto blind faith in her kinsmen had weakened.

Twenty

Rory rode back to Balcardane alone. He had intended to return to Kentallen Inn despite the late hour, to see that everything proper was being done there, but he decided he would do better to write a couple of letters instead, one to the duke at Inveraray and another to the Lord Chief Baron of the Exchequer.

At first he dutifully considered what he must write to Argyll, knowing that the rumors that had flown about for months would color any news he imparted. Already he had heard men speculate that Glenure's murder had been intended as a signal to begin the new troubles, and he knew that Argyll, like Balcardane, would view the crime as a flagrant challenge to the rightful government.

He did not want to augment that view. To be sure, Glenure had been a government agent, but his murder did not prove the existence of any conspiracy.

His letter to the Lord Chief Baron of the Exchequer, an elderly, lethargic man appropriately named Idle, would be easier to write. He had small respect for Idle, but in this instance, he thought the man's laziness might prove helpful. The Lord Chief Baron would most likely pass all responsibility for the investigation to the lord advocate and to the Baron who just happened already to be in Appin.

By the time he reached the castle he found himself wondering for the hundredth time how he could balance his growing concern for Diana and her family against his duty as a Baron of the Exchequer and his loyalty to Clan Campbell. That Balcardane would expect complete support was clear. That Argyll would expect him to follow orders went without saying. But Diana would expect—Here imagination failed him. What would Diana expect of him?

At Balcardane he found the great hall empty. A light glowed in the drawing room, but having no wish to exchange small talk with his aunt or with Ian, he went directly to the library, stirring up the fire in there himself.

When a manservant entered, he ordered claret. His uncle kept whisky on a side table near the desk, but Rory knew he needed a clear head to write his letters.

"Beg pardon, my lord," the manservant said when he had poured the wine, "but her ladyship wished to know if you had returned. I told her I would find out."

Repressing annoyance, Rory said, "Please, tell her that I have urgent letters to write. You may also inform her that his lordship and Master Duncan are likely to be late. They may even spend the night at Kentallen Inn."

The manservant bowed himself out, and for some time Rory enjoyed sufficient solitude to write his letter to Argyll. He had decided to state the bare facts without comment, promising to send more information as and when it became available. He was sprinkling silver sand over the letter when the door opened and his aunt peeped in.

"Oh, good," she said, smiling and entering the room as one certain of her welcome. "I hoped you would be finished, and I see that you are, so perhaps you will be kind enough to tell me what, exactly, has occurred to set everyone in such a bustle. I know that curiosity is a sad fault in a female—or, indeed, in anyone of quality—but no one ever tells me anything. I would never ask questions of just anyone—certainly not the servants—as I am persuaded you must know, but when one's husband and elder son get up and leave the house just as they are sitting down to supper, without a word of explanation to anyone, and with such a riot and rumpus following hard upon their departure—Well, it leaves one quite speechless, of course, but I did think that perhaps if you do not quite mind explaining—''

"Someone murdered Colin Glenure," Rory said.

She stared at him in shock. "Who would do such a thing? Why, he was quite important, and his wife is expecting another child quite soon now, I believe. Surely, no one could be so cruel as to kill Colin before the child is even born."

"Red Colin is dead?" Ian stepped in and shut the door that his mother had left open. "Someone said he had been shot, but I didn't know he was dead. Who did it?"

Rory was relieved to see him, for he had not known of a tactful way to be rid of his aunt. He was certain he could rely on Ian.

"We don't know who killed him," he said. "His nephew was with him. He said he saw a man running away, carrying a firelock and wearing a dun-colored jacket and trousers, but he did not recognize the man. I am just writing to inform Argyll and the Lord Chief Baron," he added pointedly.

"Then you don't want us," Ian said at once. "Come along, Mama. We must let him finish his letters."

"But he has finished," Lady Balcardane protested. "He was just dusting his letter with sand when I came in."

"One letter," Ian said. "He has another to write."

"You've written Cousin Archibald then—Argyll, as I should say."

"Yes," Rory said.

"Then he will be coming here," she said, clasping her hands together, "and whatever Balcardane says about expense, I mean to make him comfortable."

Rory nearly told her there was no reason to think Argyll would exert himself to come to Appin, but he held his tongue.

As Lord Justice General of Scotland, the duke might well stick his oar in when he learned of Glenure's death.

Ian turned back to say, "Did Mungo see only the one man?"

"Aye," Rory said. Then before he thought, he added, "A woman in a red dress was seen, too. Your brother is convinced it was Diana Maclean."

"The devil fly away with Duncan," Ian exclaimed. "I know I should not speak ill of my brother, but I tell you, Cousin Rory, there are days when I'd not put it past him to have killed Colin himself just to make trouble for the Macleans."

"Ian, my dear!" Lady Balcardane exclaimed.

"Well, it's just that he's threatened them many and many a time."

Since the same notion had occurred to Rory, he made no comment, and after a moment of tense silence, Ian said quietly, "Good night, sir." Gently taking his mother's arm, he guided her out of the room, shutting the door behind them.

As it happened, Balcardane and Duncan did not stay the night in Kentallen, and unfortunately the following morning Ian repeated his suspicion to his father and Rory just as Duncan joined them in the breakfast room.

"What the devil are you talking about?" Duncan demanded.

"I don't say you did it," Ian said. "I just said that it wouldn't surprise folks much to learn that you had, which is why I thought I should mention it to Father."

"I ought to take you outside and thrash some sense into you," Duncan snapped, taking a threatening step toward him.

"Get your food and sit down, cousin," Rory said sternly. "I'd as lief finish my breakfast without an eruption of violence."

"That's just my point," Ian said, eyeing his brother warily, although Duncan turned without comment and began to serve himself from the sideboard. "You rarely trouble to bank your fires, Duncan. You didn't like Colin much, and you're always making mischief for the Macleans and the Stewarts."

Measuring his words through gritted teeth as he sat down, Duncan said, "You choose to take their side because you are besotted with Mary Maclaine. She has bewitched you till you no longer can see the truth or what danger you put yourself in with such disloyalty to your clan. As for your stupid suspicions, if you paid the least heed to what goes on around you, you would know that the most likely suspect in everyone's mind is Mary's cousin, Allan Breck.''

"He is not her cousin,'' Ian said with a darkling look. "He is kin to Lady Maclean, and you and the others suspect him of killing Colin only because he is a felon. If he is one, it's because he fought for what he believes in. Others have been pardoned for the same crimes, you know, if such things are even crimes.''

"What if I told you that your darling Mary and Diana Maclean were probably hiding Allan Breck last night, that they helped him escape the authorities?''

"I'd say they were protecting him out of fear that he would be captured and hanged as an escaped felon. You must admit that he's a brave fellow, slipping back and forth like he does to bring news of the exiles to their families.''

"He comes to stir up trouble,'' Duncan said, getting to his feet. "Don't disturb yourself, cousin,'' he added when Rory put down his fork. "This young fool needs a lesson, but I've no time to attend to him properly today, and I've lost my appetite.''

Balcardane had been eating steadily, apparently paying no heed to the exchange between his sons. But when Duncan had gone, he shot Ian a sour look from under his brows and said, "You heed what he says, lad. Tempers will be high on both sides, and though I mean to ferret out Colin's killer as soon as I can, you'd best stay close to home till I get things sorted out. You're too trusting by half.''

"I have no enemies, Father,'' Ian said in his quiet way. "Everyone in Appin knows me for a peaceful fellow.''

When Balcardane did not reply, Rory said, "If you are going to Kentallen, sir, I'll ride with you.''

"Aye, I'm going. I sent for a doctor to tell us exactly what killed Colin.''

Ian looked surprised. "Didn't you say someone shot him?"

"Aye, and so they did, but we've only Mungo's say-so and Kennedy's that there was just one shot. The servant heard nothing, so there may have been more."

Rory said, "People frequently give differing versions of what they see and hear at such times. It will be helpful to know what the doctor can tell us."

However, the doctor could tell them little more than they already knew. "Colin Glenure was killed by two bullets that entered his back on each side of his spine and emerged a few inches apart just below his navel," he said when Rory and the earl sat down with him at a table in the inn's dark taproom.

"Two killers then," Rory said, frowning as he signed to the tapster.

"Nay, my lord, I dinna think that. No one heard but one shot, so the musket-balls must ha' been fired at a single discharge. 'Tis common practice hereabouts tae insert two balls into the muzzle, the first larger than the second. Moreover, the proximity of the wounds tells me the shot came from very close by."

"Mungo said the man he saw was a fair distance up the hill," Balcardane murmured thoughtfully.

An unwelcome vision of Diana flashed into Rory's mind before he recalled Bardie's affection for secret forest paths, and wondered if the dwarf owned a musket. He dismissed the thought at once, however. Not only did Bardie seem to be a man who used wits rather than weapons but Rory could not imagine the forthright dwarf shooting any man in the back. Nor would Diana do such a thing. He was as certain of that as he was that the sun would rise again on the morrow.

He was not so certain about Neil Maclean or Allan Breck. Neil struck him as a lad who was both spoiled by his family and frustrated by his situation. He was hereditary chieftain of his clan, but the position gave him no power. The entire clan system had changed in the past six years, leaving men like Neil swinging in the wind. And he had been furious with Colin over the eviction.

As for Allan Breck, Rory believed him capable of anything.

Thanking the doctor for his help and leaving him to deal with the removal of the corpse, he and Balcardane rode to survey the route Glenure's party had taken the previous day. Rory had visited the murder site before, but the light was better now, and men were moving slowly over the hillside, searching for evidence.

Seeing Patrick Campbell astride a fine chestnut, the two rode to meet him.

"Have you found anything?" Rory asked after they had exchanged greetings.

"We think we found where he lay in wait," Patrick said. "I'll show you."

Following as he negotiated his way over tree roots that sprawled across the track, Rory soon saw that a soldier stood by an area where shrubbery was flattened.

Dismounting, the three men moved to examine the place more carefully.

"Look there," Patrick said, pointing.

Kneeling, Rory saw several bits of horn or bone. Picking one up, he saw something red along one edge. Carefully, he scraped a bit off with his thumbnail, examined it closely, then looked up at Patrick, raising his eyebrows in silent query.

"Red sealing wax is my guess," the captain said. "He must have dropped his powder horn, and by the look of that wax, it was not the first time."

Rory nodded. Men commonly repaired cracked powder horns by melting soft sealing wax inside. "You must gather this all up as evidence, Patrick."

"Aye, we will."

"That's right," Balcardane said. "The lord advocate will need such details to build his indictment, but first we must find the villains, and quickly. And though we may not know the shooter, I can tell you who most likely is behind this plot."

"Take care, uncle," Rory warned. "You begin to sound like my cousin. Do you assume that Allan Breck is the villain merely because he has eluded capture for his other misdeeds?"

"I don't say that," Balcardane said. "What I do say is if he did it, he was put up to it by James Stewart. And don't look so surprised. Those two are as thick as inkle weavers and have been since Breck was a lad."

"James of the Glen has an excellent reputation, sir. The people of Appin look up to him and depend upon him. He does not seem a likely party to murder."

"Then you have not learned much in your service to the Exchequer, my lad. James lost the factor's portion of the rents when Colin took the factorship from him. You'll not convince me he gave that much money up willingly."

About to point out that James clearly had enough for his own needs and those of the people he chose to help, Rory held his tongue. Balcardane would never believe anyone could accept a loss of income without protest.

Exchanging a look with Patrick, he said to his uncle, "You still have no evidence, sir. Suspicions, even strong ones, will do you no good in a court of law. If you want justice—"

"Bah," said Balcardane. "Who said anything about justice? If we don't nip this in the bud, my lad, you will have that damned Young Pretender back here in a pig's whisper. I want Allan Breck and the rest of them laid by the heels before they can do more mischief. We're going to hang every man involved in this tragedy."

"But, sir, we still have no indication that more than one person took part."

Pointing to an area some distance up the hillside, Patrick said, "Mungo saw a man running there. Kennedy saw a woman in a red dress near the ridge. Neither one of them could have been the person who hid here. That's three, Rory."

"He's right," Balcardane said, adding for Patrick's benefit, "Diana Maclean wore a red dress last night. Duncan believes she was on the ridge."

A chill shot up Rory's spine, and he had to clench his teeth to keep from telling them they would be fools to suspect Diana. Forcing calm into his voice, he said, "Kennedy did not recognize that woman, and I daresay many hereabouts wear shades of red. It is a Stewart color, after all."

"Aye, it is," Balcardane snapped, "and her mother's a Stewart."

"My dear sir, you cannot arrest people simply because you don't approve of their politics, their antecedents, or their clothing," Rory said. "You need a proper warrant, and to get that, you need evidence you can present against them."

"Oh, I'll have the evidence. I'm making a list for Stonefield of all those hereabouts from whom he'll want to record precognitions." He looked hard at Rory. "I hope you don't intend to interfere with the sheriff in the pursuit of his duty."

"I have no intention of interfering."

He meant what he said, but he was not much surprised to find himself making excuses a short time later to leave his uncle and Patrick to their tasks, nor to find himself riding along the shore road to Maclean House. Two of Duncan's men were still keeping watch, but he paid them no heed. Dismounting near the barn, he tossed the reins to a boy in the yard and strode purposefully toward the front door.

Diana saw him coming. She had been keeping watch for Neil and had heard Rory ride into the yard.

Lady Maclean and Mary, hoping to draw the watchers away, had both gone out walking. Mary intended to visit Bardie and get some herbs she wanted, and Lady Maclean to visit some of the Ardsheal tenants. They had succeeded in drawing off only two of Duncan's watchers, however. Morag was in the kitchen, baking, and the odor of fresh bread filled the house.

Diana had tried to attend to her normal household chores, but she had found herself running to the window at every sound from the yard. Now, seeing the way Rory strode to the house, she felt a surge of panic for Neil, and ran to open the door.

"What is it?" she demanded. "What's happened now? Is it Neil? Tell me!"

He seemed taken aback for a moment, but then he collected

himself and said grimly, "For all I know, your brother is fine. I want to talk to you."

"Have they arrested someone?"

"No. May I come in?"

She stepped aside, and he entered the parlor, filling it as always with his presence. "Where are the others?" he asked.

"Mam and Mary are out. I don't know where Neil is."

"You haven't seen him at all? For how long?"

She hesitated, wondering if she dared be frank with him, or if in telling him anything she would somehow be condemning Neil.

His expression hardened. "I have warned you too many times, lass. Don't play your games with me today. My patience won't stand for it."

"I was just wondering if I could safely say anything at all to you."

"Lord save us," he muttered. Before she realized his intent he grasped one arm and pulled her near, looking stern and dangerous. "You listen to me," he said.

"Let go," she snapped, trying to pull away. "You have no right to—"

He caught her other arm and gave her a shake. "Be silent, Diana, and listen to me, or by heaven, I'll—"

Morag cleared her throat nosily in the doorway, making him bite off the sentence unfinished. She stood there, hands on ample hips, looking steadily at them.

Diana drew a long breath, but her relief was short-lived.

"Get out," Rory said sharply.

"Nay, then," Morag retorted bluntly. "Ye take yer hands from Mistress Diana, or I'll call in the lads tae put ye out."

"If you don't want to see your Mistress Diana carted off to prison, you leave me to deal with her. If I go, and she takes her own road, she's bound to be arrested."

Morag hesitated, looking from him to Diana and back.

"They wouldn't dare," Diana snapped. "I have done nothing wrong. Morag, you know I haven't."

Morag was looking straight at Rory. Her eyes narrowed, her

hands remained on her hips, but he met her scrutiny with a steady look.

"I've got eggs tae collect," she said at last.

"Morag!"

But the woman had gone, and Diana was alone with Rory.

He still held her upper arms. His grasp was firm, and although he would leave no bruises, she knew he would not let her go.

"Say what you came to say then, and go," she said, wishing her voice sounded firmer, more confident.

Grimly, and still with that icy look she hated, he said, "I came to say that you'd better make up your mind to answer any questions they put to you—"

"Who would dare to question me? I've done nothing wrong, I tell you!"

"Look at me then and deny that you were in Lettermore Woods yesterday."

She hesitated, and his gripped tightened convulsively.

"Don't you see, Diana, that I cannot protect you if you act like this? Your silence is as good as a confession."

"Why should you protect me? You wouldn't help us when we needed help before, and now that the Campbells mean to crucify us, you are bound by clan loyalty to aid them. Why should I listen to anything you say?"

He did not reply at once and in place of the anger she had expected to see, she saw frustration instead. His grip relaxed, but she did not try to move away.

As always, he seemed bigger than life, as if there were an aura around him that enveloped her as well. And, as always, she felt drawn to trust him, but she no longer believed she could trust those feelings. Murder had been done, and with a Campbell victim, she dared trust no other Campbell.

At last, quietly, he said, "I cannot order you to trust me. We have discussed your belief that I deceived you before, and I think we both came to realize that we assumed things we ought not to have assumed. We resolved that. If you could just bring yourself to set aside your prejudice against all things

Campbell for a short time, I believe that we can resolve this, too, and that I can help you.''

His voice was low, even gentle. The anger was gone, replaced by powerful compassion, and a tenderness that she could not doubt. Her breathing felt forced, and her body filled with tension. Her heart was beating very fast.

"I was in the woods yesterday," she said abruptly. "I had been in Glen Duror, visiting Granny Jameson and some others, drumming up support for the meeting we were to have today with Red Colin—"

"Wait," he said, releasing her. "Don't tell me any more."

"But you—"

"I am glad you have decided you can trust me, sweetheart, but I don't want you to tell me the details. Sheriff Stonefield will be here from Inverness by Monday. My uncle or Duncan will demand that he take a precognition from you, so—"

"To see if they can charge me with the murder?" She was shocked and for the first time, felt a tremor of fear for herself.

"That is what I have been trying to explain," he said with a rueful smile. "They are looking for more than one person, because they think Glenure's murder is part of a grand conspiracy. That is why you must tell Stonefield the truth without hesitation," he added firmly. "Tell him nothing more and nothing less."

"I don't want to tell him anything," she said stubbornly. "Men have ways of twisting words to suit their own purpose."

"Stonefield is an honest man," Rory said. "He has a good reputation as a man of law. It is his duty to help the lord advocate build an indictment, but he will not twist the facts to do it."

"Still—" She stopped when his hand gently cupped her chin.

"Diana, if you refuse to speak frankly, if you hesitate and seem to choose your words with undue care, they will believe you are hiding the truth to protect yourself or someone close to you. Either course is illegal, so there will be nothing I can do to prevent your arrest."

"Why can't I just tell you then? Won't they believe you if you say you believe me? Or don't you believe me?"

"It is not that simple. I stopped you from telling me the details because they may ask if you have discussed what you will say with anyone else. I don't want you having to say you discussed them with me. Duncan would be certain I had helped you choose the right words to protect yourself. He and my uncle know I am not objective where you are concerned, and I don't want to make it easy for them to prejudice Stonefield against you." He paused, stroking her cheek in a way that made her want to touch him back. Gently, he said, "Please, will you do as I bid?"

"I'll try."

"He smiled. "That's all I'll ask of you, lass, for now."

She licked suddenly dry lips, and while she was trying to think of something intelligent to say, the scullery door banged shut. "Morag's back with the eggs."

"Aye, she is. Now, tell me, where is young Neil?"

"I told you the truth," she said. "I wish I knew. I left him near Inshaig on my way up Glen Duror. He said he was going to meet someone, but I don't know who."

"That's not good. Your cousin Allan was hereabouts yesterday."

She did not want him to ask her about Allan, so she said hastily, "I'm more afraid for Neil. You don't think they've arrested him, do you?"

"I'd have heard if they had."

"He had nothing to do with the murder," she said fiercely.

"I hope not."

He left soon after that, and as she watched him ride away, she wished she could think that he had believed her about Neil. She wished she could be certain she believed it herself. When her brother still had not shown his face at Maclean House by late the following day, she was nearly frantic with worry.

* * *

Rory, too, spent much of the intervening time thinking about Neil Maclean, knowing that the lad's disappearance would weigh heavily against him. Already the name of Allan Breck leapt from gossiping lips all over Appin country, and many folks hinted or declared outright that James of the Glen had been in the plot with him. It would not be long before some suggested Neil as an accomplice.

Expecting word from Argyll, Rory purposely stayed at the castle Saturday morning, and his messenger returned shortly after noon with a letter. As expected, Argyll ordered him to remain in Appin to hold a watching brief. His grace recognized that court duties would recall Rory to Edinburgh in mid-June, but hoped that until then he would keep him informed as events in Appin unfolded.

Knowing he could not expect a reply from the Lord Chief Baron before Monday or Tuesday, Rory wrote a brief note to reassure Argyll of his willingness to remain—albeit not merely because the duke wanted him to do so—and sent it off to Inveraray by the same messenger. Then, ordering Rosinante saddled, he set out to see what more he could learn.

Knowing that young Neil had a ready eye for the lasses, and having heard from more than one source that the lad was enjoying a flirtation with Katherine Maccoll, the dairymaid at James Stewart's farm, he decided to ride up Glen Duror. He reached Aucharn farm in the late afternoon, only to have James's wife tell him that her husband was away at the inn in Inshaig.

"And where might I find Katherine Maccoll?"

"Och, our Katherine be off home tae see her dad for the nicht," the woman replied. "What would ye be wanting with her, my lord?"

Rory saw that despite her glib response she was nervous, and he sought to reassure her by explaining that he was in fact looking for Sir Neil Maclean.

"Och, weel, I've no laid eyes on that lad the day," she said with visible relief.

Taking his leave of her, he rode back toward the clachan near the mouth of the glen. As he approached the alehouse, he saw a group of riders and men on foot closing in on it from the opposite direction.

Recognizing his uncle and Duncan among them, as well as Patrick Campbell, he spurred Rosinante and rode to meet them. "What is going on here?"

"James of the Glen is said to be inside," Balcardane said with satisfaction.

"Aye, so his wife told me, but why do you need all these men?"

"To be sure the villain don't escape, of course," Balcardane said.

"Escape? You cannot be arresting him!"

"That we are, on a charge of murdering Colin Glenure."

"But, I told you, a warrant for murder must be issued from Edinburgh."

"Aye, and I've sent to the lord justice clerk for one this very day."

"You can't arrest the man until you've got the warrant."

"Odrabbit it, lad, don't be difficult," Balcardane snapped. "If we wait, we'll find he's fled to France with that murdering Allan Breck. This way, we'll have him and whoever's with him safely tucked up at Fort William when we want them."

"But that's against the law!"

"In these parts, I *am* the law," Balcardane snapped. "If you think Argyll will tell me to wait for some damned official piece of paper before clapping a murderer into a cell where he belongs, you take it up with him."

Having no doubt that the duke would support Balcardane's position with every ounce of his considerable power, Rory reluctantly held his tongue.

Twenty-One

The women at Maclean House learned about James's arrest the following day from the man who delivered a cask of ale from the alehouse at Inshaig.

"How could anyone think James could commit murder?" Lady Maclean demanded when the ale-man had departed. Her cold was gone, and her usual energy had returned. "James would never have shot Colin in the back."

"I don't think they believe he pulled the trigger, Mam," Diana said. "Calder told me they believe the murder is part of a larger conspiracy, maybe even the start of a new uprising. They could think James a part of that, even its leader."

"He is no such thing," Lady Maclean said, stamping her foot for emphasis. "James went out in the Forty-five, but his participation was so small that he was one of the first men the authorities pardoned. Moreover, he was confident that we would prevail against Colin, so he had no reason to kill him. And why arrest his servant? The poor man did nothing but accompany James to the alehouse for a drink!"

"Duncan's men have gone," Mary said, who had been standing by the parlor window looking into the yard.

Diana was sure the younger girl had been watching for Ian, because they had not seen him since the murder. "Do you see anyone at all?" she asked.

"No, and they were making no effort to conceal themselves before, so I'm sure they've gone now."

Diana frowned. "Either they no longer expect Neil or Allan to come here, or they have stopped looking for them now that they've arrested poor James."

"Where did they take him?" Mary asked.

Easily deciphering the intense look in her cousin's eyes, Diana said thoughtfully, "To Fort William. Do you think—?"

"No," Lady Maclean said flatly before she could finish. "Don't even think of trying anything, Diana, or I swear I will lock you in your room for a month."

Diana smiled. "That did not serve any purpose when I was a child, Mam, so I doubt that it would now, but they will guard James too well for us to help him, I fear. None of the plans we have used before would work to get him out."

Lady Maclean breathed an audible sigh of relief, but it was plain that she was still worried. "I wish Neil would come home," she said.

They still had not seen or heard from him on Monday, however, when Sheriff Stonefield arrived in Appin. Thanks to Rory's warning, Diana was not as surprised as she might have been to learn she was one of the first people the sheriff wanted to question. She was not at all pleased by the news, however.

Stonefield sent two of his men to escort her to the command post he had set up in Inshaig, at the very alehouse where they had arrested James. The sheriff met her cordially and said that he would question her himself.

A corpulent man with a strong air of vitality, he had been sheriff of Argyll for decades. His blue eyes twinkled when he greeted Diana, but when he began the questioning, he did so in a shrewd, businesslike manner. Still, he treated her with dignity and respect, so she found it relatively easy to follow Rory's advice and be truthful. She had half-expected him to be present, and was disappointed that he was not, although she did understand that he could not look as if he were protecting her.

"You say you saw no one lurking in the shrubbery, mistress," Stonefield said thoughtfully after she had answered what seemed like a multitude of questions.

"No, sir, no one," she said. "When I heard the shot, I ran toward the sound. Then I heard Colin cry out, but I saw only Mungo and your agent, Kennedy."

"Ha' ye knowledge of aught else that might aid us in our duty, mistress?"

"No, sir," she answered steadily. She did not know what might aid him, but she knew better than to offer any facts that he had not specifically requested, and she told herself firmly that learning of Allan's visit to Maclean House would not lead him or anyone else to the truth.

Stonefield dismissed her when she had signed the precognition that his clerk had written as she spoke, and she did not tarry. She went straight home.

Late that evening, after Morag had gone to bed, Lady Maclean, Diana, and Mary sat quietly in the parlor. None of them had felt much like going to bed, but Diana was just closing the book she had been reading when Neil came in quietly from the kitchen, startling them all.

"Lord bless us," Lady Maclean exclaimed, clapping a hand to her breast. "Where have you been?"

"Oh, round and about," he replied casually.

Feeling a surge of anger now that she knew he was safe, Diana cast aside her book and sprang up to confront him. "We want to know where," she snapped, hands on her hips. "We have been frantic, Neil. People think you and Allan had something to do with Red Colin's death, and they have arrested poor James."

"I know all about James," Neil said. "The devil of it is that they won't let anyone in to see him, to find out just why they think he was involved."

"Goodness, how do you know that?" Mary asked. "Did you try to see him?"

"No, but others have. They let him speak to his wife after they arrested him, and he gave her a few pounds to give Allan, but Allan needs a good deal more. He also needed his uniform, which he left at Aucharn when he borrowed other clothes from James after escaping from Stalker. His regimentals made him too conspicuous, of course. He had given me a letter to take to James, you see, and—"

"When?" Diana demanded.

"Friday, I think it was or—No, it was Saturday morning, because he wrote it right there in the field where we met." He chuckled, adding, "He used a wood pigeon's feather for a quill, and water mixed with powder from that old horn of his for the ink. I took his letter to Aucharn and gave it to James, and he said he would do what he could, but they arrested him that very night, probably just about the time we—" He broke off abruptly and knelt to stir up the fire with the poker.

"About the time you what?" Diana prompted.

"Oh, nothing. I don't remember what I was going to say."

She did not believe him, but Lady Maclean said, "But, Neil, for goodness' sake, what have you been doing all this time?"

"I told you, I've been out and about. You keep reminding me that I am a chieftain of Clan Maclean, and although I have little to show for it, I did know that I had to do what I could to protect our people and Allan Breck."

"Even so, you could surely have sent word to tell us you were safe. You must have known we would be worried about you."

"I saw men watching the house and thought I'd better stay away. I did not think I could send anyone else without putting them in danger, too."

"Do you think you are safe now?" Diana asked.

"I don't know, but at least I no longer know where they can find Allan. While I did, I couldn't chance being questioned about him. They've clearly decided he's their killer, but he isn't any such thing, of course."

"Are you certain of that?" She hated asking and could see that it made him angry. She did not even glance at her mother.

With forced patience, Neil said, ''The man they saw running away wore a dun-colored jacket and trousers, Diana. Allan has been wearing James's blue checked trews and black jacket ever since he put off his regimentals.''

''You're sure about that.''

''Of course, I am. Do you think our cousin would shoot even a damned Campbell in the *back?*''

''No Maclean or Stewart would do such a thing,'' Lady Maclean said flatly.

''The lines are drawn now,'' Neil said, directing a stern look first at Mary and then at Diana, a look that made him appear suddenly older, more mature, and a bit intimidating. ''The Campbells stand on one side, we on the other, so I forbid the pair of you to have more to do with any of them. Do you understand me?''

Seeing tears spring to Mary's eyes, Diana felt an overwhelming sadness, but she knew Neil was right. Even if he had not been, he was the head of the family and they owed him their obedience. The abyss had grown wider than ever.

Rory learned the details of Diana's precognition soon after she had given it, and to his relief Stonefield, unlike Duncan, seemed not to doubt that she had spoken the truth. Balcardane did not react one way or another.

The investigation was in full force now. Letters crisscrossed Argyll as speedily as messengers could deliver them, summoning law officers, Campbell relatives, and the military to help the investigators. Rory knew that such a huge infusion of manpower to hunt down the killer or killers of one minor official was due solely to continuing rumors that Glenure's murder warned of a potentially more broad-based rebellion ahead. Authorities in London and Edinburgh, like Balcardane and so many others, feared the worst.

The sheriff had taken rooms at Inshaig, but accepting a cordial invitation from the earl, he spent Wednesday night at Balcardane. As the men lingered over their port after dinner, discussing what little they had learned thus far, Duncan said abruptly, "To my mind, the notion that Diana Maclean was in those woods for any innocent purpose is laughable."

Ian said instantly, "She rambles everywhere! You know she does, for she is forever visiting folks to take them food or clothing, or Mary's remedies. Not just Macleans or Stewarts either, Duncan. Everyone likes her."

"Not everyone."

"You don't like any Maclean or Stewart, but nearly everyone has a kind word for Diana. If she says she visited Granny Jameson, that's what she did. And Granny is as much Campbell as she is Maclean. Her mother was born a Campbell."

"This is no time for soft words or generosity toward our enemies," Duncan said harshly. "If you know what's good for you, Ian, you'll take care to show yourself a loyal Campbell, because if I so much as see you near Maclean House, I'll thrash you to within an inch of your life myself. Do you understand me?"

"Your brother's right, lad," Stonefield said. "These are dangerous times."

Ian turned to his father, but Balcardane looked as grim as Duncan did.

"Well?" Duncan said.

Ian grimaced angrily, but he said, "I understand you."

"Good. Do you mean to keep that decanter to yourself, cousin?"

Rory passed him the wine. He had been listening to them with only half an ear, heavily conscious of his growing dilemma. He was not concerned about his safety, but he knew that it would be foolhardy for him to champion Diana or any other Maclean in the presence of his volatile relatives.

As he tried to think how he could reassure Ian without infuriating Duncan and drawing more of that gentleman's angry attention to Maclean House, help came to him from an utterly unexpected quarter.

Lady Balcardane, who had retired to the drawing room sometime before, opened the dining-room door just then and peeped

Amanda Scott

in to say, "Forgive me, all of you, but I have scarcely had an opportunity to say two words, what with all the upset and excitement, and if we are to entertain largely within the next sennight, I simply must order in a great many supplies, and I—"

"Odrabbit it, woman," Balcardane exclaimed, "what are you gabbling about now? More supplies! You spend more than any ten other women as it is. Would you beggar me? Not another penny shall you have. Run along now. This is men's talk."

"But, Cousin Archi—"

"Your cousin Archie can go to the devil for all I care, and take his wife and all his brats with him. A blasted limpet—a barnacle—that's what that man is." Accepting the decanter from Duncan, he looked at Rory to add, "Her cousin Archie descends on us every year with his entire household and expects me to house and feed the whole damned lot of them all for a fortnight or more."

"But, my dear sir, it is not my—"

"Out!" Balcardane roared. "We have *important* matters to discuss."

Visibly reluctant, her ladyship departed, taking care to sweep her wide skirt out of the way as she shut the door.

"Women!" Balcardane snorted. "What were we saying?"

Rory said mildly, "My cousin was warning Ian to have nothing to do with the Macleans, but I cannot help thinking that avoiding them might be a mistake."

"I don't doubt that you would think so," Duncan said scornfully. "Been mighty thick with them yourself, after all."

"Aye, because I believe in knowing as much as I can about anyone with whom I must deal," Rory said. "It seems to me that if we cut all ties with them, we shall be doing ourselves a great mischief."

"Now, that's sound thinking," Stonefield said, pouring himself more wine.

"Yes, it is," Ian said warmly, "and I can—"

"You hold your tongue," Duncan snapped. "I meant what

I said, you know. You are not to go near Maclean House unless you want to answer to me. We'll learn all we need to know without putting your hide at risk.''

''Aye, that we will, and soon, I'm thinking,'' Balcardane said with a look of satisfaction. He leaned forward as if he were about to elaborate, but as he did, he caught Duncan's eye. Flushing, he pressed his lips tightly together again.

''What do you expect to learn, sir?'' Rory asked.

''Maybe nothing,'' Duncan said before Balcardane could answer. ''If we do, Stonefield and you will be the first to hear of it.''

''Very well,'' Rory said, ''but, uncle, I heard that you ordered your men to search James's house after his arrest. Surely you know that the lord advocate can't use any evidence in his indictment that was obtained without a proper warrant.''

''Don't fret yourself,'' Balcardane said. ''We've got our warrant. I received it today from the lord justice clerk, and it's dated for Saturday last, so our arrest of James Stewart is as legal as can be. I've got no patience with these juristic subtleties of yours, nephew. This investigation will proceed as it should proceed.''

Horrified by such an attitude but unable to think how he could combat it, since the Barons' Court had no jurisdiction over murder, Rory did not object when the others changed the subject. Late the following day he discovered what else his uncle had done, when Balcardane came in, chuckling, holding a letter in his hand.

''Now we'll do,'' he said.

''What have you got there, sir?''

''A message I've been expecting from the governor at Fort William, that's what. You'll recall that one of James's servants was arrested with him.''

''I remember.''

''Well, the governor put that chap in a cell with a condemned man, hoping the affinity would soften him up. Then he offered him a wee bribe to tell what he knows about James Stewart's weapons, and the lad cracked like a walnut. Admitted that he and another fellow, Maccoll, hid their master's weapons up the brae after the shooting. I've sent for Patrick Campbell, so we'll go and collect them tonight."

"Then I shall go with you," Rory said.

"Suit yourself, lad. Suit yourself."

They approached Aucharn well after dark, but Rory knew Patrick had sent men ahead to watch the hill above the farmhouse. Balcardane's men dismounted some distance away and moved forward on foot. As they surrounded the house, Rory and the earl heard shouts from the hillside and hurried toward them, to find several of Patrick's men holding a burly man whom he recognized as John Maccoll.

"Look there, my lord." A soldier pointed to the hole full of weapons that Maccoll had apparently just uncovered.

Patrick Campbell knelt by the cache for a moment, then turned and said, "Two muskets, four broadswords. The long gun is loaded, the short one not."

"Have they been fired?" Balcardane demanded.

"Aye, sir, both, but I'd say the short one's the one we want. It's got a larger bore, and can easily hold the two balls the doctor mentioned." Inserting a finger into the muzzle, he withdrew it and held it up for the others to see. It was black.

Rory said, "You cannot know when they were fired, Patrick, and would not any gun stored in such a dirty place be likely to blacken your finger?"

"I don't know, Rory. I'm unused to seeing weapons treated this way."

"Captain," a soldier shouted from up the hill, "we've caught another one!"

Two men hurried down with Neil Maclean struggling between them.

"Caught this lad sneaking about up above, most likely trying to get away," one of the men said. "Doubtless, he were helping that one move yon weapons."

"That's nonsense," Neil snapped. "We just heard the ruckus and came to see what it was all about."

"A likely tale," Duncan said, striding forward. "The Macleans have been hand in glove with these conspirators from the start."

"You're daft," Neil said, trying again without success to free himself.

"Who is 'we'?" Rory asked calmly.

"Katherine Maccoll and I, not that it's any of your business."

"The dairymaid?"

"Aye, that's her father you've got there."

"We found him in possession of illegal weapons," Rory said, "and by the look of things, you knew they were here."

"Even if I did, that's got nothing to do with you."

"Young Maclean's been missing since the shooting," Balcardane said grimly. "That argues strongly that he was art and part of it. Arrest him."

"On what charge?" Rory asked.

The earl shot him a wry smirk. "Illegal weapons and consorting with felons," he said smugly. "Any objection, nephew?"

Rory shook his head. The law required no warrant for either charge, and had not done so since the weapons ban six years before. Moreover, since Patrick's men had found illegal weapons, they had every right to search for more, so he could not object when they joined forces with Balcardane's to ransack the house.

In any case, Neil Maclean's arrest provided a much greater worry, because Rory did not imagine for one minute that Diana would allow her brother to languish for long in a cell at Fort William without making every effort to free him.

"How do I look?" Diana asked Mary early the following Monday morning, as she turned to give her cousin the full effect of her disguise.

"Like a gaberlunzie man," Mary said, chuckling. "That

floppy hat covers nearly all your face, but just wait until Aunt Anne sees you in those men's clothes.''

"I don't mean to wait," Diana told her. "Mam would feel obliged to stop me from going, even to save Neil, and we simply cannot leave him in Campbell hands.''

"They'll only catch him again."

"They must not. He will just have to go to France with Allan, that's all."

"Oh, Diana, I don't think he will. Allan has asked him before, many times."

"He'll go if his only other choice is to let them hang him," Diana said grimly.

"You are not going to Fort William alone, are you?"

"No, Morag's brother Gordy is going with me, and Bardie will come, too."

"But Bardie hates to ride," Mary protested, "and it's too far for him to walk."

"We're not walking *or* riding," Diana said with a grin. "We are taking Neil's sailboat. Here's Bardie now," she added, hearing the scullery door bang shut.

The dwarf lumbered in a moment later, took one look at her, and chuckled. "Ye'll do, lass," he said. "Ha' ye got a pair o' shoon that look new cobbled?"

"Yes, they were Papa's, resoled before he left to follow the prince. His feet were bigger than Neil's, but Neil kept them, hoping he would grow into them someday." She went to fetch them, and when she returned, she found Bardie sitting silently on his favorite stool, watching Mary frown thoughtfully into space.

"What is it?"

"I don't know," Mary said. "I felt a chill, the sort they say means a goose has walked over one's grave. I don't think this venture will prosper, Diana."

"Will it fail?"

Mary hesitated. "I cannot say that. What I feel is like a sense of doom, but in truth, when you talk of your plan to free Neil, the feeling does not alter. Usually, such feelings grow stronger when you speak of what you mean to do. This one feels detached from Neil, as if it is connected to you or to something else altogether.''

''Most likely it's just dread because of the danger and everything else that's been happening,'' Diana said practically. ''After all, James is in grave jeopardy, Ian hasn't been to see you since the murder, and now Neil is in prison.''

''That must be it,'' she said with a shiver. ''I felt another wave of it just then as you were talking. Do take care, Diana. Bardie, look after her.''

''Aye, I'll do that, right enough.''

Soon they were off in the little sailboat, but they had scarcely left Cuil Bay when Diana saw Bardie hunker down in the bottom of the boat, looking green.

''Bardie, I forgot how much you fear the water! Why did you not insist that we travel some other way?''

''Pay me no heed,'' he muttered. ''I'll do well enough if yon lout Gordy can keep this pea shell from turning keel over topsail. Thing is, lass, I canna swim.''

''But your arms and shoulders are so strong! I'd have thought swimming would be easy for you.''

''I sink like a stone.''

''Then you are very brave to have come, Bardie,'' she said, truly moved.

''Ye canna do it alone, just the pair o' ye. Someone must stay wi' the boat, and someone else must be at hand tae bring the lad back after they let him out. Ye willna be with him then, most like, ye ken.''

''That's true,'' she said, ''and the safest escape is by water if we can time it so that darkness falls soon after we get Neil out. You are a dear friend, Bardie.''

Bardie blushed and looked down.

Morag's brother Gordy, a tall lean man with shaggy brown hair, was, like most men living on the loch, an excellent sailor.

Nevertheless, it took them the best part of the day to reach Fort William. The tide was with them most of the way, but the winds were capricious.

They landed below Maryburgh, because they knew better than to land any nearer to the fort, where men kept a constant lookout for trouble from the sea.

Leaving Bardie with the boat, Diana and Gordy speedily made their way through the village to the main gate, where Gordy left her and walked on as if they had merely kept each other company for a time. Diana approached the gate alone, striding as much as she could like the man she pretended to be.

"I have a pair of shoes I have repaired for the prisoner Sir Neil Maclean," she said in Gaelic, pitching her voice as low as it would go. "He ordered them before they arrested him, and they said I could deliver them to him here."

"Who said?"

"I have a letter. Can you read English?"

"I speak a bit," he said in that language, "but I canna read English writing."

"D' ye ken Lord Calder's signature, then?" she asked, switching to English herself and aping his accent. "He's a Baron o' the Exchequer's Court."

"Nay, then, d' ye say his lordship signed yon bit o' paper?"

"Aye, look," she said, showing him. She had worked the signature with care, adding an impressive red wax seal. With satisfaction, she saw his eyes widen.

"If that's real, ye'll ha' no trouble delivering your shoes, I'm thinking," he said. "Come along this way."

Pulling her hat lower, she obeyed, surprised but grateful that he had accepted her word. She felt guilty using Rory's name in such a way, but she had been afraid to use Balcardane's or Patrick Campbell's, and she had not thought a made-up one would serve to fool the governor. She had half expected the guard to insist upon showing it to him, and was profoundly relieved that he had not.

They kept no female prisoners at Fort William, so she was

nearly certain they would not arrest her when they discovered Neil's escape. In the event that she was wrong, and they did, Bardie had sworn he would go instantly to Rory for help.

If he refused—and since he had warned her many times not to meddle, she rather feared that he might—Bardie would send for MacDrumin, Dugald, even for Lord Rothwell if necessary. Diana was certain they would easily manage to rescue her when the authorities tried to move her from Fort William to Inverness or Edinburgh. She felt confident now, almost smug, enjoying the familiar sense of euphoria that nearly always accompanied one of her more daring ventures.

Her intention was to change clothes with Neil just as she had done so successfully with her mother. Following her instructions, Neil would then start shouting at her, and she would shout back, producing a regular slanging match until the guards flung open the doors to see what was amiss. Neil would walk out then, carrying the shoes, his face hidden by the hat. Growling and muttering expletives about his supposedly dissatisfied customer, he would stride forth to freedom.

The jailers would soon tumble to the trick, of course, but hopefully not before Neil was safe aboard the sailboat, out on the loch. With luck, darkness and even a mist would cover his flight.

Her guide had stopped before a heavy wooden door. "Here, cobby, nay doot ye'll soon be shut o' them shoon."

Clearly a hitch, she thought, keeping her head lowered so that her hat would conceal her face. Apparently, she was to see the prison governor first, after all.

The door swung open to reveal a threadbare green carpet on the floor, then the dark square legs of a wooden desk. Her first fleeting thought as she crossed the threshold was gratitude that she did not know the governor personally, but the thought had barely formed before the guard said, "Here be the cobbler tae see young Maclean, my lord, wi' the wee bit o' paper ye signed, saying he might."

Tattered remnants of her euphoria disappeared in a blink,

and she wished the thin green carpet were a magic one that could whisk her instantly far, far away.

Through a roaring in her ears, she heard Rory's voice say calmly, ''Thank you, guard. You may go.''

The door shut with an ominous thud.

Twenty-Two

For a long moment silence reigned, while Diana tried to think of something to say. Clinging to a feeble hope that he would not know at once who she was, she kept her eyes lowered and her head tilted downward.

The floppy hat blocked her view, and the carpet muffled his footsteps, so she did not realize he had crossed the room until she saw his feet right in front of her.

She gasped when he snatched the hat from her head.

"If I had any sense, I'd put you across my knee and beat your backside till it ached for a month," he said evenly.

A tremor shot through her, and she knew from his tone that if she were not very careful, he would carry out his threat. "H-how did you know?"

"I didn't. I knew you would try something, so I had Thomas MacKellar keep a watch. When he said that you had set out in a boat this morning, I rode here as fast as Rosinante could carry me and told the governor I wanted to interview any visitors who asked to see the new prisoners. I didn't expect you to invoke my name in a forged letter, however. For that alone, I ought to make you smart."

"I'm sorry about that. I was afraid to use anyone else's."

"Wise of you." He paused, then said sardonically, "A cobbler, Diana?"

"It would have worked if you had not been here," she muttered, still not daring to look at him.

"Perhaps, but Neil's escape would damn him, you know. Even those who think him innocent would change their minds."

"No one thinks him innocent."

"Not even his sister?"

"I know he is, but no one will heed what I say. If he was at James's farm, he went there to see Katherine Maccoll."

"Ah, yes, his dairymaid. Daughter of the man we caught with the guns."

"Aye, but Neil took no part in Red Colin's murder, Rory. He told me so, and I can always tell when he is lying."

"I believe you," he said, putting a hand on her shoulder. "I have been doing some investigating myself. At best he's been no more than an innocent pawn."

Surprised, she said nothing.

"Will you trust me to handle this, Diana?"

He had not left her much choice, but instinct still warred with nature and experience. "Your uncle and Black Duncan are set on blaming the Macleans and the Stewarts for Red Colin's murder."

"I know they are."

She looked at him. "They will stop at nothing."

"I know that, too. I am a man of law, however, and so is Stonefield. The lord advocate will be guided by us."

"And Argyll?"

"I'll worry about him when I must."

"Can you set Neil free, Rory?"

"I think so, but first we must get you out of here. Who came with you?"

She hesitated, but when her gaze met his, she said, "Bardie and Gordy MacArthur, Morag's brother. Did Thomas not tell you?"

He smiled. "He knows Bardie, but he did not know the other man."

"Gordy is waiting for Neil near the main gate. Bardie is at the boat. He is terrified of the water, but he came."

"You are fortunate in your friends, sweetheart, but they ought to have kept you safe at home."

"Are you still angry with me?" The words jumped out before she knew she was going to speak them.

"I am. We are going to have a very long, very serious talk about this."

"We can't," she said sadly. "Neil has forbidden both Mary and me to have a thing to do with any Campbell, and we must obey him."

"Do you really think that Ian will stop visiting Mary, or that she will tell him he must stay away?"

"She has not seen him since Red Colin's murder."

"Are you certain? I know Duncan ordered him to keep away, but Ian nearly defied him, and I think the lad means to go his own road. If he has to stand up to Duncan to do it, he will."

"Well, I hope he succeeds. Duncan deserves to be bested."

He shook his head but said only, "Come, we must get you out of here." When he put a hand on her shoulder, she began to turn toward the door. He pulled her to him and kissed her hard on the mouth.

Caught by surprise, she gave no thought to his motives, responding instinctively and with a passion that must have astonished him, for he smiled against her mouth. A hand slipped beneath her coat to pull her closer.

She felt his heartbeat and his arousal, and her body tingled in response. At that moment, if he had swept her into his arms and ridden off with her on his trusty steed in the manner of all the best heroes, she would have counted the world well lost. If lust were all one needed for a lifetime of happiness, she thought, she would have done anything he asked of her.

The moment was over too soon. Setting her back away from him and regarding her with a wry grin, he said, "We'd better stop this before someone comes in and wants to know why the devil I'm making love to a cobbler.''

She smiled, but the threat of discovery included the possibility that she might be unmasked and held for punishment, so the smile felt weak.

''Cheer up, sweetheart,'' he said, evidently not misled by it. ''I haven't eaten you yet, and I won't let anyone else do so, because I have quite made up my mind to marry you. Therefore, you had better give some thought to changing your ways, and that includes allowing your husband to protect you. There will be no more of these little adventures once you become my wife.''

''I have not said that I will marry you, sir,'' she reminded him, as desire and temper vied to command her emotions. ''What you want is a Dulcinea who will mold herself to your quixotic fantasies. I am not that woman, and I never shall be.''

''You are certainly no Dulcinea, sweetheart. If you resemble any of Cervantes's women, it is Dorothea, for she is the one with wit and wisdom. However, I am not nearly as quixotic as you are, you know.''

''Nonsense. In any event, our families still won't allow us to marry.''

''We can get round them.''

''I doubt that our promise to wed, let alone a consummation, would shift any Campbell or Maclean from his position even if I were daft enough to agree.''

''What's wrong with me?''

She wanted to tell him the truth, that nothing was wrong, but she could not see daylight through the darkness ahead, so she said simply, ''You're a Campbell.''

The words rang false even to her ears, but he said solemnly, ''I'm rapidly discovering that some Campbells are a bit too villainous for anyone's taste, but all of them are not. I'll wager you know a Maclean or two you don't much fancy.''

She knew several, but she said, ''That changes nothing. I am—''

A rap at the door startled them both, and Rory snatched up

her floppy hat and jammed it onto her head. Hastily, she tucked in the few stray curls that had escaped it, and looked down at the floor.

"Not a word," he muttered. "I'll do the talking. Enter!"

A guard stepped in. "Begging your pardon, my lord, but another of the new lot's got a visitor. His mam, this one is."

"I'll come straightaway," Rory said. "No need to drag the woman back here. As soon as I've seen this cobbler on his way, I'll be with you."

"I'll take him, sir, and I'll show you where I've put the auld woman, too."

Rory hesitated briefly, then said, "Excellent." Then to Diana, he added, "I'll see that these shoes get to Sir Neil, my man. Off you go now."

She tugged the front of her hat and jerked a little bow, then turned silently to follow the guard. Five minutes later, she was outside the gate, looking for Gordy.

Rory dealt with the other prison visitor quickly, then made his way to the governor's spartan office.

John Crawfurd, the lieutenant colonel who commanded Fort William, stood to greet him when he entered. A year older than Rory, he took himself and his duty very seriously. "I trust you have found everything in order, my lord."

"I have, indeed. Has Stonefield arrived yet?"

"Aye, they've put him in the wee chamber I set aside so he can question such prisoners as we've got for him."

"I'll go to him, if you'll have someone show me the way."

"I'll take you myself," Crawfurd said. "That was a fine bit of work we did, was it not, putting our hands on James Stewart's weapons?"

"Only if one was the murder weapon," Rory said, glancing at him."

"We ken fine that one's the wee musket."

"Do we? The servant you threatened and then bribed never

said James shot Glenure, only that they had moved some of James's weapons for him.''

Crawfurd shot him another puzzled look, but Rory said no more. A moment later, the governor stepped past him to open a door.

"Ah, there you are, lad," the sheriff said when they entered the small room. It contained a desk, a chair, and a pair of wooden stools. Stonefield stood to shake Rory's hand, saying, "I've been told you want me to question young Maclean first." Glancing at the governor, he added, "Ah . . . are we all three to question the lad?"

Hastily, Crawfurd said, "I'll leave you to it. I've much to attend to, myself."

When the door had shut, Rory said, "I've been asking questions of my own, Stonefield, and I'm of the opinion that Sir Neil has done no more than try to help certain members of his clan and the clan of his widowed mother."

"I'm told he was present when they found yon suspect weapons."

"He's been seeing the Maccoll wench. Just a flirtation, of course, and it was her father they caught with the weapons, not Maclean. There is no love lost between those two men. Maccoll thinks the lad's been trifling with Katherine."

"As he has," Stonefield said, twinkling. "He'll certainly not marry a dairymaid. But they do say the small gun must be the one, sir, do they not?"

"Stewart's people say it was part of a cache such as many folk hereabouts keep and that they moved the weapons when James was arrested so a search would not turn them up. That is quite a reasonable explanation, don't you agree?"

"Every man was supposed to turn in his weapons—all of them—at Castle Stalker by the summer of forty-seven," Stonefield said with a wry grimace.

"Most of the weapons turned in were damaged or broken. Can you doubt that most folks managed to keep their good ones hidden away?"

The sheriff's eyes twinkled again, but he said, "They should not have done that, and so they should know. Ah, but here's our man now. Come in, lad, and sit down. I've questions to ask you, and I'd advise you to answer them fully and truthfully. This chap who brought you in will write down everything you say."

Unusually subdued, Neil nodded, glancing uncomfortably at Rory before giving his attention to Stonefield.

Rory had brought the shoes with him, and as Neil drew up a stool and sat down, he set them on the corner of the table nearby.

Neil's eyes widened, but he said nothing, for which piece of good sense Rory gave him full marks.

"The cobbler whom you asked to mend these traveled a long way to deliver them," he said mildly. "I told him I would give them to you."

Neil's eyes narrowed. "Did you? That was kind of you, sir, but the cobbler ought never to have gone to so much trouble."

"You must take that up with him," Rory said, meeting his gaze directly.

With a grim look of understanding, Neil said, "Be sure I will, sir."

"In the meantime, I advise you to be candid with Sheriff Stonefield."

"Do you?"

Rory caught his gaze again and held it. "I do," he said sternly.

"That is excellent advice, Sir Neil," the sheriff said. "To begin, just tell me what your relationship is to James of the Glen."

"He is my mother's natural brother," Neil said, "just as he is to the Laird of Ardsheal. Therefore, he is by way of being my uncle."

"What were you doing at Aucharn the night before last?"

Neil hesitated, glanced at Rory again and reddened, then said, "The dairymaid, Katherine, is my friend. We were out walking together."

"Where had you been since the murder of Colin Glenure?"

Again Neil glanced at Rory, who leaned a shoulder against the wall and folded his arms across his chest, gazing steadily back.

Turning back to Stonefield, Neil said, "I have heard men speak of you, sheriff, and they call you a fair man. They do not say the same of the Campbells hereabouts, however. When I learned that a number of them were watching my house, looking for me, I stayed in the hills. Not through any sense of guilt, mind, merely for self preservation."

"Where were you when Glenure was shot?" Stonefield asked.

"If I understand the time correctly, I was with Katherine Maccoll on the ridge above Glen Creran, helping her move a herd to the high pasture. I was with her from half past two till well past six, when we walked back to Aucharn. Bardie Gillonie saw us at about half past three."

"He and Katherine will say the same, you believe?"

Before Neil could speak, Rory said, "They will."

Stonefield's eyebrows shot upward. "Have you spoken with them, sir?"

"I have. They said the same, and I have found no one who claims to have seen Sir Neil elsewhere."

The questions did not end there, but Neil showed no hesitation after that, even when the sheriff asked if he knew the whereabouts of his cousin Allan.

"I do not," he said.

Rory observed from the outset that Neil answered no more than the exact question put to him, but he was not surprised. After the ravages of Cumberland and his men throughout Appin country and the rest of the Highlands, even children fresh from the cradle knew better than to volunteer information to anyone.

Neil's attitude was open and frank, so Rory was no more surprised some twenty minutes later when Stonefield said abruptly, "I'll keep your precognition after you sign it, sir. But unless I meet with facts contradicting what you've told me, I do not think we have cause to keep you locked up any longer."

Straightening, Rory said, "I agree, sheriff. You should release him at once."

"Aye, well, but it's growing dark, sir. Better to release him in the morning."

"I share your concern, but I mean to return tonight, and Maclean House is but a step away from Balcardane. If Sir Neil has no objection, and if we can find him a horse to ride, he can make one of my party."

The sheriff shot him a speculative look. "Do you think that wise, my lord?"

"I do. The lad has some few enemies, sheriff, who would like nothing better than to make mischief for him. They will leave him alone whilst he's with me, and I want no more killing if we can avoid it."

"Aye, well, I'm in agreement with you there, sir."

"Then I'll leave you to arrange for his horse."

Twenty minutes later, as the main gate clanged shut behind them, Neil said quietly, "It's a damned good thing no one asked me to put on those shoes, sir. My feet never did grow as large as my father's."

"It's as well, too, that Stonefield never asked how many were in my party," Rory told him. "You'll do, lad. I don't doubt you could tell us more if you wanted to, but I admire a man who can keep his counsel when it behooves him to do so."

Neil shot him a look from under his brows. "Admire away," he said. "Did she really try to get to me dressed as a cobbler?"

"She did." Rory made no secret of his displeasure. "I think she intended to pull the same stunt she pulled at Edinburgh Castle."

"I will throttle her," Neil said grimly.

"Nay, lad."

"Nay?"

"I have already reserved that pleasure for myself."

*   *   *

The tide was running fast and the wind came from the north, sending the boat skimming over the waves and making Diana glad that Gordy knew what he was doing. Light mist drifted low over the loch, a dusting of stars glittered overhead, and on the dark eastern horizon a pale yellow glow announced the rising of the moon.

Except for a few brief words of explanation, first to Gordy when she found him and then to Bardie at the boat, none of them spoke. Bardie crouched down, keeping as low as he could, and but for the necessity of avoiding the swinging boom, Diana was alone with her thoughts.

One moment she felt angry with Rory for interfering, the next weak with relief that he had not handed her over to the prison governor. She had not known what to expect, but she knew she had instinctively trusted him yet again.

The return journey was swift, too swift, for Diana did not look forward to explaining her actions to her mother. However, the explanation proved easier than expected. Lady Maclean was too relieved to have her safely home again to scold.

Even Morag was still up when they reached the house. Serving whisky to Gordy and Bardie on Lady Maclean's orders, she smiled and chattered more than usual, clearly glad they had returned.

"I won't pretend I am pleased with you, Diana," Lady Maclean said when they had described their journey and its outcome. "I think you are very fortunate that Calder is a fair and sensible young man."

"He's still a Campbell, Mam," she said with a sigh. "In the end he will have to plump for the Campbell side."

"He doesn't always think them right," Mary said. "He often disagrees with Duncan, and he even warned Balcardane that he had overstepped his authority."

"He said that?"

"Aye, when they took James's private papers away from Aucharn."

"But they did that Thursday night, and—Mary, you've seen Ian!"

Mary grew pink but did not look away. "Twice," she admitted. "I met him at the head of the bay on Saturday and again this afternoon. I love him dearly, Diana, but I never thought he could be so brave. He told me Duncan threatened to thrash him if he even comes near Maclean House, as if he were a child, but Ian said he's tired of Duncan always going for him and telling him what to do."

"Ian should know better than to taunt Black Duncan," Lady Maclean said, frowning. "They named that lad more for his temper than for the color of his hair."

"Duncan would never really harm him," Mary said. "Even Ian does not fear that. He says Duncan is always bellowing at him but that it's only because he thinks Ian cannot take care of himself, that he is too gentle for his own—"

"Mary, what is it?" Diana exclaimed. "You've grown white as a sheet!"

Mary pressed a shaking hand to her forehead. "I don't know. I felt dizzy, and my mind seemed to flash all white. The sensation has passed, but I think I'll go to bed. Bardie, you will stay the night, won't you? Tell him he must, Aunt Anne."

"Indeed, you must, Bardie. You can sleep in Neil's room."

Thus, the first person at Maclean House to learn that Rory had kept his word was Bardie Gillonie, who greeted Neil's arrival in the wee hours of the morning with mixed emotions. He was glad Neil was safe, but not so glad to be turned out of his warm bed to sleep on a trundle cot beneath a thin woolen blanket.

Rory had ridden with Neil to Maclean House to see that he got there safely as much as for any other reason, or so he told himself. If he was disappointed to find all the lights out and the inhabitants abed, he kept those feelings to himself.

Bidding Neil good-night and refraining from offering advice he knew the lad would reject, he offered to see that the borrowed horse got back to Fort William, and turned toward Balcardane, leading the animal behind him.

"Thank you, sir," Neil called belatedly, just loudly enough for him to hear.

He waved. "You were lucky to come off with a whole skin, lad, so don't be too quick to risk it again. And don't murder your sister!"

"No, sir. Good night."

It was long after midnight when Rory reached Balcardane. Going directly up to his bedchamber, he found Thomas waiting up for him.

"All manner of riot and rumpus there was tonight," the henchman said, grimacing as he pulled off Rory's boots.

"What's amiss?"

"Aye, ye'll think so, I'll wager. Ye'll ken fine how his lordship fired up about her ladyship's cousin Archie coming tae stay."

"I do recall that discussion."

"Aye, well," Thomas said, looking wise. "Happen it weren't her ladyship's cousin, after all. Seems he never let her finish the sentence and pays no heed to her most times any road. She weren't saying Archie at all. She were saying—"

"Archibald! Good God, she calls Argyll by his given name. I've heard her."

"So it would seem." Thomas grinned, taking Rory's coat and folding it carefully over a stool. "According to her ladyship, his grace will honor us with his presence tomorrow or the next day. He'll be none too pleased tae hear ye've taken an interest in the Maclean fortunes, I'm thinking."

"No, he won't," Rory agreed. "Were you planning to tell him?"

"Nay, not I, and I warrant your uncle will be too caught up counting the groats required tae house and feed a ducal party tae thrust a spoke in yer wheel, but Black Duncan is bound tae tell his grace soon enough."

"It doesn't much matter where he hears it," Rory said with a sigh, "though I'll confess I'd as lief he not hear it from Duncan."

He would have liked to avoid Duncan altogether before the

duke's arrival, but when he entered the breakfast parlor the following morning, he found both his cousins there before him.

Without preamble, Duncan said angrily, "I hear you have interceded on behalf of that scoundrel Maclean."

Keeping his temper, Rory said, "If you mean Sir Neil Maclean, Stonefield took his precognition and decided he had no cause to charge him with a crime."

"And you just happened to be present while Stonefield questioned him, and then you rode back to Maclean House with him."

"You are well informed."

"I've told you before, I have my methods, but there is no great secret about it. You crossed late on the Ballachulish ferry, and one of the men brought me word. You did no good letting him go, you know, for he's hand in glove with James and Allan Breck. Doubtless he will now try to flee the country with Breck."

"Duncan's right, nephew," Balcardane said, entering and joining Rory to examine the dishes set out on the sideboard. "If Neil Maclean ain't in this conspiracy up to his boot tops, you may call me a Dutchman."

"You'll not convince him," Duncan said bitterly. "Our cousin forgets where his loyalty lies. He'll set himself against his own, all for a pair of golden eyes."

"You are being unfair, Duncan," Ian said, spreading marmalade thickly on a chunk of bread he had broken from the triangular loaf on the table. "Rory told you it was Stonefield's decision. He cannot hold Neil if he has no evidence against him. In any event, if you think he is a conspirator, you are an even worse judge of character than I thought. Neil is no villain."

"If you think his release means you can go back to calling at Maclean House, you had better think again, little brother."

Duncan's tone was dangerous, but Ian only shrugged and put the spoon back into the marmalade pot. "I'll be out this afternoon, going about my own business," he said. "If you want to waste your time following me, that is your affair. Not that I can't lose you in the woods any time I want to do so, of course.''

Duncan frowned, but at that moment, Lady Balcardane bustled in, catching her wide skirt on the door latch and pausing to disengage it as she said, ''Did I hear you say you mean to be away this afternoon, Ian dear? You must not, you know, for if Archibald—No, I'm forgetting that you want me to call him Argyll, my dear sir, though I cannot think why I should, for I've known him since I was a child, although in those days I called him Uncle Archibald. Although he is not really my uncle, of course, and no doubt he would stare to hear me address him so now, for I daresay I have not spoken above two words to him in ten years—''

''Silence, woman,'' Balcardane roared. ''You will call him Argyll because I command it. Furthermore, before you order so much as another collop of lamb—''

''Collops? Lud, sir, as if I would serve such poor stuff to his grace. I hope we may do prodigiously better than collops for his supper, and so I tell you.''

Having had, yet again, a surfeit of his relatives' company, Rory excused himself hastily. He found little comfort in the mischievous glint in Ian's eyes as he watched Duncan, but he had no inclination to heed his cousins' squabbles either.

If Argyll truly intended to grace Balcardane Castle with his presence, lamb collops and murder investigations would be the least of Rory's worries. It was high time, he decided, to organize his thoughts and compose his arguments so that he could produce an explanation of his dealings with Diana Maclean that the duke might at least understand if not accept. The last was probably too much to hope.

''Where did Neil go?'' Mary asked as she and Diana hunted eggs in the barn.

''I don't know. All he said—shouted, rather—was that if I ever plan another prison escape, he'll make me sorry I was born, and a lot of other silly stuff. Why?''

"I hope he doesn't do anything rash."

Diana smiled. "It's not like you to worry about him. Will you see Ian today?"

Mary smiled. "Aye, he promised to come, no matter what." Her expression altered oddly and she added, "Morag's waiting for these eggs. Let's go in."

Seeing her shiver, Diana wondered if she was cold.

Archibald Campbell, third Duke of Argyll, no longer enjoyed the vicissitudes of Highland travel, though he still enjoyed many other things. A widower for thirty years, he was, even at the ripe old age of seventy, still noted for his profligacy and his love of power. Some said he loved power too well to hazard it by ostentation and money, so little that he spent it neither to gain friends nor to serve them. Others called him a man of little truth or honor, with no attachment but to his own interest.

Rory was aware of what others said about the man who had so heavily influenced his life, but he had always found him a man of sound judgment with a thorough knowledge of mankind. The duke was also shrewd and argumentative, and he had no doubt as he stood facing him in Balcardane's bookroom that afternoon that his own interests and Argyll's no longer marched in harmony.

Before he had been in the castle ten minutes, the duke had sent for Rory and summarily dismissed both his entourage and his hovering host and hostess.

Now, as Rory stood before the library desk, waiting for him to speak, he felt much like a schoolboy hailed before a harsh headmaster.

"Well?" Argyll snapped.

Not a promising beginning. Knowing he would do better not to equivocate, he smiled and said, "I am glad to see you, too, my lord duke. I trust you did not find your journey too tiring."

"Damn your impudence! What's this nonsense I've been hearing?"

"I am not certain what particular news has upset you, sir, but may I sit down while we sort it out?"

An appreciative gleam showed in Argyll's eyes. He waved to a nearby chair. "Now," he said, when Rory had taken his seat, "I'll be plain. I'm told that I should no longer trust you."

Repressing a surge of anger, aware that more than his reputation rode on this interview, Rory said as calmly as he could, "I have always spoken my own mind and followed my own road, sir. We have disagreed before, and no doubt we will do so again, but I have never given you cause to distrust me, nor will I."

"Well said. What do you make of all this?"

Accustomed to Argyll's abrupt ways, he answered evenly, "It's early days yet, sir. They have arrested one James Stewart, but I am not convinced of his guilt. Until now, he has enjoyed a good reputation and lived an untarnished private life."

"No man who rebelled against his rightful king can be held in high esteem."

Tempted though he was to remind Argyll that the duke's own grandfather and great-grandfather had been executed for high treason, Rory said instead that the authorities had unlawfully refused to let James see his solicitor.

"Don't bother me with his troubles," Argyll growled. "Who's the wench?"

Meeting the basilisk stare, Rory said bluntly, "She is Anne Stewart Maclean's daughter, sir, and I'm afraid I've fallen in love with her."

"Lord save us, that blasted woman again! Am I never to be done with her? I won't have it, Rory. Find yourself another one."

"I'm not willing to do that, sir."

"Damn your impudence!" With that, the floodgates of the ducal wrath opened and the flood washed over its hapless victim.

* * *

"What is it, Mary?" Diana demanded. "For the past five minutes or more you've been pacing the parlor floor like a cat on a hot bakestone."

"I don't know, Diana. I just—"

She broke off, clapping a hand to her mouth, shaking.

"Mary, what is it? What's wrong?"

Mary's face was chalky, her eyes wide and staring blankly. Their irises were almost colorless, their pupils enlarged to black pools. Suddenly, she screamed and threw her arms wide. Her lips moved rapidly but no sound came. Her body grew rigid. Tears welled into her eyes and spilled down her cheeks.

"No," she moaned. "Oh, no-o-o-o!" Then, crying out, as if she were in agony, she collapsed to the floor in a trembling heap.

Diana flew to her side, but although she managed to get Mary to lie on the parlor sofa, she still had not spoken a word an hour later when men came running to tell them that someone had beaten Gentle Ian to death in the woods near Inshaig.

"We found a broken powder horn in the pocket of his jacket," one of them said to a stunned Diana. "He'd mended it with red sealing wax just like them bits they picked up where Glenure's murderer hid in the shrubbery!"

Twenty-Three

Rory was with his uncle when they learned of the tragedy. Having survived his ordeal with Argyll with most of his dignity intact, he had spent the better part of the afternoon escorting the duke to the murder site and then to the alehouse at Inshaig, where Argyll conferred with Balcardane and Sheriff Stonefield.

At one point, frustrated by the fact that his uncle appeared already to have tried and condemned James Stewart, Rory interrupted their discussion to remind the three that James had not yet received the benefit of counsel.

"To let James Stewart talk with a lawyer before we have completed the indictment against him would be damned foolishness," Balcardane declared flatly. "Why make trouble before we've even completed our investigation?"

"Perhaps because the law requires it," Rory suggested mildly.

With a grimace, Balcardane said to Argyll, "You see what comes of elevating a youngster to high position, your grace. He gets above himself. 'Tis damned fortunate this case won't go before the Barons' Court."

"James Stewart will be tried at Inveraray," the duke said firmly.

"You can't do that, sir," Rory protested. "How can the man get a fair trial when the jury will be packed with Campbells? He should be tried at Edinburgh."

Just then one of the duke's men burst into the alehouse, crying, "Murder, your grace! The villain has killed again!"

All four men jumped to their feet, but Stonefield was the first to speak. "Who died? Did they catch the killer this time?"

"Nay, your worship." The man hesitated, looking from man to man, his gaze settling at last on Rory. He said quietly, " 'Tis the lad, my lord, young Master Ian. Halfway betwixt here and Maclean House. He . . . he was beaten tae death."

Balcardane stiffened, his face turning ashen. "Where is Master Duncan?"

Scarcely breathing, Rory waited for the reply. His thoughts had flown to Mary Maclaine and Diana, but the henchman's next words snatched them back.

" 'Twas Black Duncan found the lad, your lordship. When we came upon them, he was shaking him, shouting at him to wake up, but he couldna bring him back from the dead, o' course. Two o' my men stayed wi' the body. Master Duncan, not knowing you was here, sent me tae tell Sheriff Stonefield, whilst he hurried back tae Balcardane. He said he would give them the news there, and fetch men to tend the body. Said he didna want any Stewart or Maclean mucking wi' it."

"Had he none of his own men with him?" Rory asked.

"Nay, my lord. He was alone. There is one more thing." He shot an uncomfortable look at Balcardane, then added reluctantly, "Master Ian had a powder horn in his pocket, a cracked one repaired wi' red sealing wax."

"I don't believe it," Diana said when the men had gone and she was alone with her mother and Mary in the parlor. "They seem to think they've found some sort of evidence against Ian, but someone must have put that powder horn in his pocket, or he found it quite innocently.''

''I agree,'' Lady Maclean said. Having been away most of the day, she had returned minutes after they had received the tragic news. Taking Mary's shawl and draping it over the settle as she worked to make the girl more comfortable, she said, ''I worry less about what they think now than about what they will think later. It will not be long before someone comes looking for Neil, you know.''

''Aye, Duncan will blame him if no one else does.'' Diana glanced out the window, realizing as she did that she was hoping to see Rory. She had kept an eye out for him most of the day, although she had heard that Argyll was at Balcardane, and she knew that most likely Rory was with him.

Neil still had not shown his face when they sat down to their supper. The breeze had stiffened, rattling windows and doors, and stirring shrubs so that branches and leaves hushed against the sides of the house. Throughout the meal, every time a tree branch tapped against shingle or clapboard, Diana started, thinking it might be her brother returning, or someone looking for him.

Mary had taken her usual place at the table, but she moved as if she were in a trance, and did not eat or speak. Sympathetic to her grief, neither Diana nor Lady Maclean tried to draw her from her silence, although both watched her closely.

Morag served their meal, but when it became clear that none of the three was hungry, Diana said, ''You go on to bed if you like, Morag. We'll clear up. That is, if you don't mind, Mam. If I just sit here, waiting, I think I'll go mad.''

Lady Maclean sighed. ''I don't mind. We may all be forced to earn our bread soon, so it's as well to keep our hand in. I'll clear these dishes if you will attend to the hot water and suds. Mary, dear, perhaps you should go to bed, too.''

Mary looked up as if she had just recalled that she was not alone, but she did not speak. The only sign that she had heard was a flickering, empty gaze and new tears that trickled down her pale cheeks.

"I'll look after her, Mam," Diana said. Fetching the wool shawl that Lady Maclean had left on the settle earlier, she draped it over the younger girl's shoulders, gave her a fresh handkerchief, and said quietly, "Come with us into the kitchen, love. You should not be alone just now."

Mary hesitated, resisting silently.

"I promise we won't press you to talk, Mary, but neither will we allow you to disappear into your thoughts. Ian would not like that."

"Why did I not know beforehand?" The question came so quietly that if the wind had not fallen at that moment Diana would not have heard.

She replied in the same matter-of-fact tone she had used before, "You cannot control the gift. You never have. It just happens, or it doesn't."

The only reply was another sob.

"So much has happened that no one could expect you to understand the odd feelings you kept having."

"But if I'd understood them, I would have been able to warn Ian. We must have been talking about him whenever I had them. I just didn't realize."

"You cannot see more than the gift allows," Diana said. "You have explained that to us many times. Wishing it were different will not make it so. Now, come into the kitchen where you will keep warm."

Mary did not speak again, but neither did she resist now when Diana drew her from the sofa and urged her toward the kitchen.

Diana's thoughts were in a jumble, for Ian's death turned everything upside down yet again, and a sudden temptation to run screaming into the night nearly overpowered her. How lovely it would be, she thought, to find herself in a cheerful, sunlit world where everyone was happy and no one fought wars or killed gentle, innocent, loving people.

Her throat tightened, aching again, and the prickling of tears in her eyes made it hard to see, but for Mary's sake, she kept a stern grasp on her emotions.

A pot clattered against the iron stove and then, like an eerie echo, a rattle at the window nearest her almost startled her out of her skin. The breeze had stiffened to a strong wind from the north, punctuated by frequent harsh gusts.

Lady Maclean said, ''We cannot both work in the scullery, Diana. It is too small and cold in this wind, so I'll just put a pan on the kitchen table to wash up what remains. Morag did the pots while we were eating.''

No sooner had Diana got Mary seated in the inglenook than a stronger rattle came from the door leading to the yard at the end of the scullery.

Lady Maclean froze where she stood by the table. She had taken down a big pan for the dishes, and she stood now with her hand resting on its rim, staring toward the scullery. She glanced at Diana, then took a step toward the door.

''Wait, Mam,'' Diana said. ''Let me.'' The huge kettle Morag had left on the hob was belching steam up the flue when she took the poker from its hook on the stone mantelpiece. Pausing just long enough to swing the kettle off the flame, she hid the poker in the folds of her skirt and moved swiftly across the flagstone floor into the scullery, pushing the kitchen door to with her foot. Three more steps took her to the outer door. ''Who is there?''

''Bardie,'' came the harsh response. ''Open up quick, lass. There be Campbells in the wind.''

She reached for the bar, looking back to be sure the other door had shut so no light would spill into the yard. Then, lifting the bar as silently as she could, she pulled the door open and let Bardie slip in.

''Ha' ye food, lassie?'' he demanded. ''I been lying on me belly under a bush these two hours past, to be certain yon stupid Campbell oafs wouldna see me come down tae ye. Nearly stepped on me more than once, they did, but they canna find their ain toes at the ends o' their great flat feet, them.''

''Come into the kitchen,'' Diana said. ''You know about Ian, then. Mam, it's Bardie, and he's hungry,'' she added, as he followed her into the kitchen.

"He's always hungry," Lady Maclean said with a smile. She sliced bread and put it with a platter of meat on the table, then pulled a stool up for him. He swung himself up easily, and as he slapped beef between two slices of bread, she said, "Have you seen Neil?"

"Och, aye." He took a large bite, chewing with obvious satisfaction.

Diana said urgently as she hung the poker back on its hook, "He must stay away from here. Some of them are bound to think he had a part in Ian's death."

"Some do, some don't," Bardie said. "This is good." He was stuffing food into his mouth as if he had not eaten properly in a week, talking around it. When Lady Maclean put a flagon of ale down before him, he grunted his thanks, then downed a third of it in a gulp.

Diana said, "Have you really seen him?"

He nodded.

"Then he is safe for now."

"Aye sure," Bardie muttered. "Safe enough if he keeps his head down, and if Allan Breck don't trip over him."

"Don't tell me Allan is still trying to convince Neil to join Ogilvy's French regiment," Lady Maclean said with annoyance.

"I'm no sure what he's trying tae do." Bardie grimaced. "Young Neil didna want tae come in straightaway for fear some idiot Campbell would shoot him first, then ask afterward if Neil happened tae kill Ian. Still and all, remembering last time, Neil wanted tae be certain ye all were safe afore he takes tae the hills again."

Staring at him, digesting the meaning of his words, both women were silent. Diana recovered first. "Do you mean to tell us that Neil is nearby?"

"Aye, hiding up in the brush. I slipped down tae see that all was clear."

Indignantly, Lady Maclean said, "Do you mean to tell us you have been sitting there stuffing food down your gullet whilst my Neil lies under a bush, starving and chilled to the bone?''

Bardie blinked at her. "It isna so cold as that, and I were fair hungersome.''

Though Rory did his best to get away from Inshaig at once, it proved impossible to do so. Both Balcardane and the duke insisted that he accompany them to where Ian had died.

The lad lay stretched out just off the shore road, near where the River Duror emerged from the glen into the loch. He had clearly taken a beating, but it was not long before they learned that his death had most likely come from hitting his head on a boulder. Rory found blood on the boulder, and a cursory examination told him Ian's head was broken. "It was a fight then," he said, straightening from his examination. He watched his uncle, knowing what the man feared most.

"There's no sign he was shot, then," Balcardane said, his voice tense and filled with sorrow.

Rory shook his head, and one of the men standing guard over the body said, "Master Duncan heard no shot fired, my lords.''

Balcardane muttered under his breath, then said he had seen enough. "Some of you men, find something to put my son's body on, and take it home. The rest of you, go about your business. There is nothing more to see here.''

Stonefield disagreed at once, volubly, but Argyll supported Balcardane, and Rory had no doubt that the pair of them would prevail. He left all three men deep in conversation and rode hard for the castle. Near Kentallen village, he met a group of riders whose leader said Master Duncan had sent them to look after Ian.

Waving them on, he continued to Balcardane, where he found Duncan sprawled in a chair in the bookroom, looking pale and exhausted. He held a half-empty glass of whisky in his hand, but clearly he had not been relaxing, for books, knickknacks, and other articles lay strewn across the room, and glass fragments littered the hearthstones.

"What happened?" Rory asked bluntly, shutting the door.

"The young fool is dead, that's what happened. What else has happened is that I've spent the past hour or more dealing with my mother. I warrant it won't surprise you to hear that she is hysterical. She is not responsible for the mess in here, however. I did all this myself." He sipped his whisky.

Two steps took Rory across the room. Grabbing Duncan by his coat, he yanked him upright. Although the two were the same size, Duncan offered no resistance. "Damn you," Rory snapped, shaking him, "why did you kill him?"

To his shock, Duncan's eyes filled with tears. "That's what they thought when they found me with him. I could see it in their faces."

"You threatened him more than once, and I saw him. Someone beat him, but the blow that killed him came when he fell. Was it an accident, Duncan?"

Tears streaming down his face, Duncan drew a ragged breath, looked at him and said in a firmer tone, "I don't know, Rory. It may have been someone's accident, but I swear to you, I never laid a hand on him. I was looking for him, that's true, because he had as much as said he meant to defy me. But when I got to him, he was dead." He covered his face with both hands then and sank back into his chair. "Why didn't he listen to me? I warned him over and over of the danger, but he would rarely even take a horse. A horse might have saved him!"

"What about the powder horn in his pocket?" Rory asked evenly.

Duncan's hands fell. He stared at Rory. "What powder horn? Ian never carried a powder horn in his life. He wouldn't ever shoot a gun!"

As Lady Maclean stood glaring at Bardie, a steady, light tapping at the yard door drew Diana's attention, and she flew toward the scullery. "There's Neil now, poor laddie. Oh, I hope Duncan's men are not watching the yard again."

She thought she heard Bardie call to her, but she had already shut the door to the kitchen and thought only of getting Neil inside quickly. Unbarring the yard door, she snatched it open, holding it against the wind as she said, "Quick, come in. Oh, how foolish of you to come back so soon!"

"What, are they watching the place again? I swear, I didn't see a soul."

She gasped. It was not Neil but Allan Breck, and realizing— only now—that it might have been anyone, a Campbell, even Black Duncan, made her tremble. She managed to say with a semblance of calm, "I don't think anyone is watching. Bardie studied the yard for a time before he came in."

"Good for Bardie." He shut the door and barred it again, then put a hand on her shoulder to urge her toward the kitchen. Once they were in the light, she saw that he wore his blue regimental coat and red vest over dark trews.

"You cannot stay here, Allan," she said. "It is too dangerous. Someone killed Gentle Ian today, murdered him in cold blood on the road near Inshaig."

"I know," he said, taking the poker from her and hanging it by the hearth. "The news is all over Appin, and the woods are alive with damned Campbells again. A man can scarcely move about without falling over one."

"Then you must know we cannot hide you here," Diana said. "They suspect that you were here after Red Colin's death, and they are still looking for you."

"That's perfectly true," Lady Maclean said sharply. "You endanger us all just by being here, Allan. What do you want?"

"Money, of course. I'm taking my leave of you again— returning to France until it's safe to come back here—but James was to have sent the rent money when they returned my regimental clothes. I got the clothes all right but not the money."

"They arrested James," Diana said. "You must know that. Neil said—"

"Aye, I know. It was just cursed bad luck that he could not

send the money before then. He did send some, but only a few guineas, and I need the rest to take to the lairds in France. My ship is waiting in the Firth, and the devil of it is that I ought to have got off long before now, but I don't want to go empty-handed.'' He looked around. ''Where's your whisky? My throat is dry.''

Without a word, Lady Maclean poured him a large glassful.

''Allan,'' Diana said, aware that Bardie had not spoken a word since her cousin's arrival, ''you swore that you had naught to do with Red Colin's murder, that it was not you or Neil, or James. Did you lie to me then?''

Downing a large slug of whisky, he took bread and meat from the table and put them together as he said, ''Whoever did it performed a public service, my lass, or have you forgotten that? I am not here to chew old business, however, or for any reason other than to get money, a fresh shirt, and some powder.''

''Money? Good gracious, Allan, you can't think we've got any money.''

''You must have some. If it's not enough, jewels will do, and don't tell me you've none of those, for I know you must. Sir Hector told me before Culloden that he'd left you well fixed for emergencies, and this is one, for I've no time left. I'd meant to reach my ship without fuss earlier today, but Ian spoiled that plan.''

Shocked, Diana said, ''How can you blame poor Ian for dying?''

''I blame him for—'' He broke off, finishing his whisky before he said, ''Look, I don't want to argue. Fetch me powder and shot, and be quick about it. You won't pretend to have no arms in this house.''

Eyes narrowing, Bardie spoke at last. ''Lost your powder horn, did you?''

''Threw it away weeks ago,'' Allan said curtly. ''It was beyond repairing.''

''Neil said you used powder and water to make ink a day or two after Colin died,'' Diana said. ''He saw you write a note, using a wood pigeon's feather.''

"Cracked then, was it, your powder horn?" Bardie's eyes glittered. "A few pieces missing from it, perhaps?"

Diana gasped. "They said whoever killed Ian left a powder horn in his pocket, trying to make him look like Colin's murderer, but it was your horn, wasn't it? Yours was old, Neil said. I'll wager it was cracked, then repaired with red sealing wax." Her voice shook. "Allan, you killed Red Colin and Ian both."

He shrugged. "I don't say I did; but even if you happen to be right, what's one Campbell more or less? Now, look lively, Diana. You, too, Mary. I daresay you've got a trinket or two we can sell in France." When Mary did not even glance at him, he peered more closely at her. "Cat got your tongue?"

"Stop it, Allan," Diana snapped. "Leave her be."

He looked surprised. "Lord, did she really care about that Campbell daffodilly? Young Ian wasn't worth a buckle from her shoe."

Mary did not stir, but Diana suddenly sensed danger in the room. Where it came from, she could not have said, but it made the hair on the back of her neck stand up. She saw that Allan's jaw was set.

Dully, she said, "You might as well go. We have nothing to give you."

"Nonsense, where are your jewels?"

"Good God, Allan," Lady Maclean snapped, "do you think I would have let trees be cut on Maclean land if I'd still had jewelry to sell? Six years have passed since Culloden. Only a fool could think we still have jewelry. I suppose we should be grateful you did not need it before now. I dislike having to disappoint you—"

"I don't," Diana said grimly. She looked at him and knew she was seeing him clearly for the first time. "You killed them both, didn't you?"

"What if I did? I don't say I did, mind you—"

"Say it! Or are you just too pigeon-livered to admit what you have done? How could you harm someone as gentle as Ian?"

"I didn't mean to! I told you I could scarcely move without falling over Campbells. I walked bang into him. I was sure he would shout for the others, and I only meant to knock him down and get away, but the young fool hit me back."

"So you beat him to death."

"I'd have sworn I left him alive," Allan said, pouring himself more whisky. "I heard someone coming, so I knocked him down again and ran, that's all."

"You killed him to protect yourself," Diana said bitterly. From the corner of her eye, she caught a furtive motion as Bardie, who had left the table when Allan approached it, inched toward the parlor door, keeping a wary eye on her cousin.

Holding Allan's gaze with her own, Diana said coldly, "You had nothing to fear from Ian. He would not have hurt anyone, for he was kind and loving, not angry like so many others. You had no need to kill him, Allan."

"How little you know!" Abruptly he put down his glass and began opening boxes and cupboards, peering into them. Snatching a leather pouch from a box, he tossed it to Lady Maclean. "Put up some food for me, and when they let you speak to James, tell him to send the money to Ardsheal in France if he has to hire his own courier to get it there. He knows where, and you tell him it's as much as his life is worth if we don't have it by Lammas. That money is crucial to our cause."

"Are you truly leaving now?" Diana asked scornfully.

"Don't look so cheerful, my lass. I'll think you want to see the last of me. Mind now, I am counting on you to mislead them when they come looking for me. If you deny you've seen me, they'll be off about their business." He was still searching for food as he talked, adding things to the pile on the table and glancing at Lady Maclean now and again, to see that she bestowed all the items for him.

She worked silently, not looking at him, her lips pressed tightly together as if she feared she would say more than she ought if she said anything at all.

"Fetch me that powder now, Diana, and any good weapons

you've got at hand,'' Allan said. ''You must have some. Everyone does.''

''I won't do it,'' she said, hands on her hips. ''I won't be party to it anymore, Allan, and don't say I'm being disloyal to my father's cause. I do believe the wrong king is on the throne, but I no longer believe we can do anything about it.''

''We can do plenty more. We've got plans that you know nothing about.'

''So I've heard, but every day more of us turn from the cause, fearing to lose even more than we have. You say we should be willing to starve. Many people *are* starving, Allan. Many more have lost all they own. They can do no more.''

''They are traitors then.''

''No, they are not. Nor am I. Even when all seemed lost, I continued working with you when you were here, and without you when you were safe in France. We rescued you from Castle Stalker when the enemy captured you. I think it is that, above all, that hurts me the most tonight. Though she has never liked you much, Mary helped plan your rescue. In return you killed the man she loved.''

''I should have known better than to expect any woman to understand our position, but by God, Diana, I thought you did. This is not just a difference of opinion. This is the future of Scotland. Do you want us all to kneel to German George and the damned English, and just give up our heritage altogether?''

''I never—''

''That's what you are saying! And don't forget that Glenure was about to put all of you out of this house.''

''We could have stopped him. We had—''

''Don't be daft. You'd *never* have stopped him.''

''Then we shan't be able stop the man who takes his place, either.''

''Oh, aye, his successor will likely try to evict you, but you have a respite, thanks to Colin's killer, and you show no gratitude. You stand there, argle-bargling about the life of some soft Campbell babe-in-arms who would have given me away without a thought. You say he was kind and loving. I say he was a Campbell, and that is all that mattered, because I could not risk his telling them I was there." He glared at her, adding grimly, "For that matter, unless—Look here, Diana, will you give me your word that you'll not tell them I have been here?"

Lady Maclean exclaimed, "Allan, how dare you! Diana is a Maclean."

Though she knew she would be wise to hold her tongue, Diana said, "I won't protect him, Mam, not after what he's done. Clan loyalty is important, but I won't be party to the murder of innocents. Even Red Colin did not deserve killing, for he was only doing his duty, but I can understand that his unfair actions stirred the hatred people felt toward him. However, if Allan killed Ian as well, he is just a common murderer. I will *not* help him avoid the punishment he deserves."

In a sharp tone, Allan said, "Where the devil is Bardie?"

Bardie had vanished.

While Allan dashed into the parlor, Diana snatched the poker off its hook and concealed it again between folds of her skirt. Lady Maclean saw her do it, but Diana had no fear that she would warn Allan. Stewart or no Stewart, if it came to a question of Diana's safety or Allen's, she would never betray her daughter.

Allan came back quickly, saying, "He's gone out the front. I've got to get out of here straightaway, for that damned dwarf don't like me a bit."

"If he does not," Diana said evenly, "you have only yourself to blame. He also helped in your escape, you know, yet you treat him quite shabbily."

"He's a freak," Allan said with a shrug. "Even God treated him shabbily."

"How horrid you are," she exclaimed. "Why did I never see that before? Go on, now. Get out while you still can!"

"I'm going, my dear, but you are going with me." He stepped toward her.

Instantly, she raised the poker. "Touch me and I swear I'll break your arm, Allan Breck. Stand back."

He smiled, reached down to his boot and pulled a dirk from

the top. Then, as if it were a thing he did every day, he stepped behind Lady Maclean and held the dirk to her throat. "Do you think I won't harm her, Diana? Put that down."

Knowing now that he had no compunction about killing, Diana obeyed, leaning the poker against the stone fireplace. With a sigh, she said, "Go, then. Bardie can't move fast enough to bring harm to you." It occurred to her only then that no one had mentioned Neil, so Allan did not know how near he was. Perhaps, if she could keep him talking, Neil and Bardie between them could do something.

"What is it?" he demanded. "What are you thinking?"

"Nothing."

"I doubt that, but we won't stand here discussing it. You'll come with me."

"I won't."

"Your choice is to come with me quietly, or watch your mother die."

She swallowed, but even as she was trying to convince herself that he would not dare kill Lady Maclean, she saw the edge of the blade draw blood. "I'll go," she said hastily. "Please don't hurt her."

"Where is your cloak?"

"Upstairs," she said instantly.

"Then you must do without it. Take that shawl thing Mary's got round her. She won't need it as much as you will."

Gently, knowing she needed some sort of wrap to keep her warm, Diana took the shawl from Mary and put it around herself.

Allan caught her arm in a bruising grip and said to the others, "If you want to see her alive again, stay right here and don't breathe a word of this to a soul. If I see anyone following us, I'll kill her straightaway. Don't think I won't."

With commendable calm under the circumstances, Lady Maclean said, "And if you do get away?"

"Why, I'll set her free, of course," he said, adding carelessly, "Perhaps not right there in the streets of Oban, but once I'm safe aboard ship, we'll put her ashore somewhere or other, and she can make her way back to you. That will happen, however, only if you don't speak a word about this. Come, Diana.''

She had hoped he would put the dirk back in his boot, but he did not, keeping it in hand while he hustled her through the scullery to the yard door.

"Lift the bar," he growled, "and don't make a sound if you want to live. I don't ever regret killing traitors."

She believed him, and found herself hoping that neither Neil nor Bardie would be fool enough to challenge him. However, if Bardie had reached Neil, there was no sign of it. The yard was dark, for there was no moon yet, and filmy clouds blurred the stars overhead. The wind had grown even wilder, hiding any noise they made, and she doubted that anyone could see, let alone follow, them.

He knew the yard as well as she did, and he guided her straight toward the loch. She did not dare cry out or stumble, knowing she was good to him only as a hostage if someone confronted him, and to dissuade the others from following. If she proved too much a nuisance, she feared he would just kill her and run off.

They reached the water's edge without incident, and as he pushed her along the shore path, she wondered where he had tied his horse. Oban lay miles to the south, and the quickest, safest way to get there on such a wild night as this was to ride. She could see better now, for her eyes had adjusted to the darkness and the pounding waves of the loch reflected starlight from overhead.

The wind roared, and she shivered in the thin shawl. She could tell from the way the water ripped at the shore that the tide was running swiftly, but not until they rounded a bend in the path and came upon a cove with a sailboat beached near the tide line did she realize he would take her by water.

Shoving her forward when she hesitated, Allan shouted, "Fergus!"

"Here, master."

"Make haste, man. The sooner we're away, the sooner we'll be safe, but I've brought along a passenger for insurance."

"Ye've brung a wooman! Are ye daft?"

"I am not." Diana heard anger in his voice, but his man ignored it.

"Ye'll never be taking a wooman on yon wee boat!"

"I will. Now hush your gab and help me launch her."

"Aye, but 'tis doomed we are then," Fergus said morosely. "Even He that preserved the Israelites in the Red Sea, and Jonas and Paul, won't bless us wi' a wooman aboard and weather like tae tear us all asunder."

With all her heart, Diana hoped Fergus was wrong, but with such a wind and such a tide, she very much feared that he was not.

Twenty-Four

Rory and Duncan were alone again in the bookroom. The wind howled outside, and Rory had been thinking that his tower room was going to be noisy.

They had talked little after the others retired. After all the upheaval it seemed late, but the hands on the mantel clock showed it was just half past ten when a commotion in the great hall brought both men to their feet. Rory reached the door just as a manservant pushed it open, making him step quickly back.

"Visitors, my lord. I tried to—"

"Never mind," Rory said, cutting the man off when he saw Neil Maclean with Bardie right behind him.

Duncan, peering over Rory's shoulder by then, uttered an angry exclamation and tried to push past him, but Rory held him back.

"What is it?" he asked Neil, his heart in his throat. He could think of only one thing that would bring the young man to face the Campbells in their den, and his first words confirmed that fear.

"It's Diana," Neil exclaimed. "He's taken her, and he says he'll kill her if anyone follows, but Mary says he means her to lie in a watery grave if we follow or not. It's the first time she's seen something before it happened, sir. At least, she was nearly certain it hadn't happened yet, that we—you—can still stop it.''

"Who took her?"

"That devil Allan Breck, that's who, and he's dangerous. He killed Ian."

"Which way did he go?" Duncan demanded.

"Well, he said Oban, which would mean he'd ride straight south, especially in this weather, but Mary said he also mentioned the Firth, and she's sure he's gone by water, not by land. She's not been herself since we learned of Ian, but—"

"I'll find him, by God," Duncan snarled, trying again to push past Rory.

Again Rory stopped him. His own fury urged him to do exactly as Duncan wanted, but he suppressed the impulse. "It won't help to ride off in all directions, tilting at windmills," he told his cousin. "We'll tell your father and Argyll, for we are going to need all the help we can get. Neil, you and Bardie wake up everyone you can find and tell them what happened. Send some men to the ferry and others to search along the Loch Leven road in case they took a different route altogether, but the rest should follow us as quickly as they can. Tell them we're riding to Castle Stalker. It commands all the sea routes into the Firth and guards the road south to Oban, as well. Are you with me, Duncan?"

"Aye, till we put the devil in hell!"

Stars filled the black sky overhead, but the water rushing around the boat was so dark that Diana could not tell how far they were from shore. She could not ask Allan, for he had gagged her in the understandable belief that she would not fear him enough to remain silent.

Fergus had not said another word.

For a time after Allan had dumped her into the boat and launched it, using an oar to fend them off the rocks, the two men had kept busy with rigging and canvas. She could see their shadowy figures now, darker against the stars than against the frenzied water. She saw lights twinkling in the distance from Morven, but they were few, and even as she watched, two disappeared. Most people had gone to bed long since, of course, for working folks rose and retired with the sun.

The boat was not large, but Allan was a good sailor and knew the coast of Loch Linnhe well as he knew the hills and glens of Appin. His life had depended upon such knowledge more than once, as Diana knew.

She did not fear that he might overset them, but sailing blindly into darkness frightened her nevertheless.

Although he had mentioned Oban, she was sure now that he had meant only to throw any followers off their trail. If the French ship awaited him in the Firth of Lorne, near Oban or elsewhere, the shortest route now lay through the Lynn, that narrow span of water between Lismore and the mainland. She doubted, however, that he would dare sail right under the noses of Patrick Campbell and the men at Castle Stalker. At the moment, he was tacking toward the west coast of the loch.

She heard the clink and whoosh of the rigging as the men pulled the main sail and then the jib into place. She sat low in the boat as Bardie had done, and it was just as well, for twice she heard the boom swish by overhead as Allan set his course. Had she sat higher, it might have knocked her into the water.

The sails had flapped wildly at first, then filled and steadied, until the little boat gained speed. Soon it was flying over the waves.

Diana felt Allan move past her several times, and she decided he must have tied the tiller in place. Clearly, he did not expect her to help, and she wondered if she would have. It was one thing to refuse to give him money or conceal him when he had as good as admitted killing Colin and Ian, but to refuse to help when one's own survival was at stake was another matter. Her death would serve no purpose.

She wriggled, trying to get comfortable.

''If you give me your word not to scream, I'll take off that gag,'' he said, bending so close that she could smell the whisky on his breath.

She nodded, but a long moment passed before she felt his hand at the knot behind her head. Then her mouth was free. She did not try to speak, licking her lips and working her jaw a few times to ease its stiffness.

"Will you untie my hands?" she asked at last.

"Not yet." He took the tiller, and for a moment he occupied himself with his course. Then he said, "Mind what I said about silence, Diana, if you don't want me to slap that pretty face and gag you again. I doubt if anyone can hear you over the wind well enough to tell where we are, but I'd as lief they hear nothing at all."

"Where are we going?"

"The ship lies off the east coast of Mull, near Grass Point."

"Will you go through the Lynn, then?"

"Don't be daft."

"It is the most direct route, is it not?"

"On a clear day, perhaps," he said, "but even in a calm, that's treacherous water with currents too strong for any but the best sailors. Moreover, I thought you'd like to take a farewell look at the ancient home of the Macleans."

"A farewell look?" A chill stole into the core of her body, but to her relief her voice sounded as calm as his.

Lightly he said, "I want you to come to France with me, Diana. The others there would be happy to see a friendly face from home. Won't you come?"

Aware that she could endanger herself further with the wrong answer, she said evenly, "Allan, I have responsibilities here, people who depend upon me. Moreover, I simply cannot be a party to the terrible thing you did."

"I did what was necessary," he said. "Now, tell me you'll come. No, wait," he said firmly before she could reply. "Give thought to your answer, and think about it carefully, because it's important." Then he looked up at the sky and, as if he were carrying on an ordinary conversation, added casually, "With the wind as strong as it is, we'll be out of the loch in no time, which is just as well. I'd rather not have to fight the tide when it turns, as it will within the hour."

"I just hope you don't wreck us on the rocks off Lismore," she snapped.

"I've sailed this route more times than you know, lass. I know every inch of the loch and the Firth beyond it. What's more, I can take my direction from the stars, so barring a sudden squall that hides them from view, all will be well."

The wind had decreased, but it was still a considerable force, so when Allan stopped talking, she made no effort to continue the conversation. He needed to keep his mind on the tiller and rigging, or the fierce cross currents near the mouth of the loch could easily swamp the boat when they met with them.

The waves seemed higher and more turbulent even now, and she knew they were near the confluence with the Firth and the Sound. She could hear the wind howling as it swept through the latter, confined by cliffs on both sides, and recognized the sound from her childhood days on the island. The tide was swift, too, nearly at its ebb. It would be turning soon, and Allan would want to be beyond the mouth of the Sound before then. While the tide ebbed, he could easily make Grass Point, but once it turned, the power of the sea would flow against him, creating a tug of war between wind and water for control of the small sailboat.

She purposely kept her thoughts riveted to the present, unable to bear thinking of what Allan had done, or of her worried family at home. Once, without warning, an image of Rory leapt to her mind's eye, but the moment was blessedly brief because the boat picked up speed for a few exhilarating moments, as if they were airborne. Then it settled again and began to move more steadily.

"There's Mull ahead," Allan said. "Can you see Craignure?"

She could not. The dense, looming shadow that was Mull was black, and the last few lights on Morven had gone out. Mixed with the wind, she could hear the roar of the sea crashing against the coast. Far ahead, suddenly, she saw a tiny red light in the blackness. It disappeared the instant she saw it, then flashed again.

Allan grunted in satisfaction. "There's the ship," he said. "Time to choose, Diana. Will you come with me?"

She wondered if he would force her to go. She had believed him when he told the others he would free her when he boarded his ship, but now it occurred to her that freeing her might prove difficult. She did not even know what he meant to do with the boat. He had not said if Fergus was to stay with it or go with him. Perhaps, she decided, it was more than time to ask some questions.

"What will you do if I refuse to go with you?"

"Let's just say you would be wiser to agree," he said.

"Why did you put that powder horn in Ian's pocket?"

"Just to puzzle them a bit."

"You called me a traitor, Allan. Do you really think that?"

"I'm saying you don't honor your duty to your clan. I feared as much before, but I knew it for certain tonight when you refused to help me."

"You asked too much," she said, feeling deep sadness and a prickling of tears. "I could understand someone wanting to kill Colin, for not only was he from an enemy clan but he wielded his power unfairly. Still, I believed you that day when you said you hadn't killed him, that you just had to get away or they would suspect you simply because you were near. But killing Ian is different. You took a part of Mary's life when you killed him, and Mary is one of us."

"She's a woman. What does she know of war and enemies? She would have given herself to a damned Campbell, Diana. For that matter, you're too forgiving of them yourself. You probably think that devil Calder would intercede for any cousin of yours. He wouldn't, but you ought to understand from even thinking he would why I could never have trusted Ian not to give me up to his own brother!"

"Calder's a fair man, Allan. You'd have got a fair trial."

"He's a Campbell, damn his soul. I don't believe I am

hearing this claptrap from a Maclean! He's bewitched you, that's what. The man is the devil incarnate.''

"He may be a Campbell," Diana said bitterly, "but he is more of a man than you are. He doesn't moan about foul play, and he doesn't hide behind women."

"You think I'm a lesser man than some damned *Campbell?*"

"I am disappointed in you, Allan. I expect courage and daring from my kinsmen, not fear and vindictiveness. I expect them to face the consequences of their actions with courage and valor."

"Indeed, my dear," he said grimly, "and are you willing to accept the consequences of giving free rein to that vixen's tongue of yours?"

"I've said only what I believe," she said, fighting back a wave of fear.

"Have you?" he said. "Then you won't object if we leave your fate to the Almighty to decide." Turning toward the bow, he shouted, "Fergus, fend us off with your oar, man. I don't want to knock this boat to flinders." Lowering his voice again, he said gently, "This is where you leave us, Madam Disdain."

Before she realized what he intended, she heard a horrid scraping sound. Billowing canvas flapped as the mainsail crashed down to the boom.

Fergus shouted, "I canna hold her long, master!"

Just as Diana realized that Fergus had jumped out, Allan yanked her to her feet and roughly untied the rope from her wrists.

" 'Twill be a quick farewell, cousin," he said, lifting her and swinging her overboard in one terrifying gesture. Before she had gathered enough breath to scream, her feet touched solid, ruggedly uneven terrain. Giving her a push, Allan added, "You're on the Lady Rock, lass. If you can keep your wits and your footing till sunrise, you'll see Craignure and the ancient Maclean lands to the southwest, Lismore to the northeast, and Castle Stalker beyond."

"Allan, wait!"

He went on as if she had not spoken, "The mainland yonder

is Campbell country, so I'd advise you to stay clear of it. You're only a couple of miles from Mull. Swimming against the tide might make it seem more like ten, but I taught you to swim myself. If you're strong enough, you'll make it. If you aren't, the sea will claim you quickly. The Lord will decide. Jump aboard, Fergus. We're off!''

"Allan, don't leave me here," Diana cried. "The tide is turning. This rock will be covered long before morning!''

"Trust in God," he shouted back, "and mind the Campbells don't get you! Even your precious Calder will think you helped a clansman escape, and are just making up fairy tales to protect yourself and your clan. Farewell, lass.''

She barely understood his last words, for the current speedily swept the boat away. Only then did she realize that the lee side of the rock shot straight down into the sea, and understand how he had managed to put her ashore without wrecking. Even so, he had risked all three of their lives just to spite her.

The sadness that had edged her fear from the moment she realized what he had done now threatened to overwhelm her. For him to accuse her of not showing proper loyalty to her clan, then leave her to die out of simple spite, seemed truly ironic. She would have liked to indulge in a good cry, but when a wave crashed against the far side of the rock, swirling water and foam at her feet, she realized she was not safe even for the moment where she stood.

The rough rock felt wet and cold beneath her fingers. Finding footholds was difficult, but she knew the tide was turning, and although the water would rise no more swiftly than usual, she had little time to decide what to do. Climbing carefully, testing every handhold and foothold, putting all thought of the water's awesome power out of her mind, she inched her way to the crest. The rock had sheltered her from the wind before, but now she stood fully exposed, and it felt much colder now that she was wet from the spray.

She was breathing hard, her gasps audible even above the sounds of wind and surf. A shooting star slashed the heavens. Her ancestors would have taken it as an omen. Wistfully follow-

ing its course, her gaze came to rest on the dense shadow
beyond the tip of Lismore and the Lynn. It was Lorne, the part
of Argyll south of Appin, and she saw a light gleaming in the
darkness at the far north end.

The light seemed to lie beyond Lismore toward the northeast,
about where Castle Stalker stood, but she knew her imagination
was deceiving her. The narrow island looked small only because
she faced its southernmost point. From her low vantage point,
she could not possibly see any land beyond it to the north.

At least she had her bearings. Mull lay behind her, the tip
of Lismore and the mainland of Lorne ahead. As her gaze
drifted right, she saw more lights, a dim cluster of them. She
decided they originated from Dunstaffnage, another infamous
Campbell stronghold, which stood near the town of Oban. That
decision made, she found it easier to pretend that the tiny distant
light in the north came from Stalker.

Unable to bear the chilly wind any longer, she crouched
lower on the rock, seeking a place where she could snuggle
against its rough surface and be sheltered for a time. She had
to think. Staring at distant, imagined castles would do no good.

Though she could swim, she knew she would not last long
in the icy waters of the Firth, certainly not long enough to
swim to Mull where she would be safest. Peering up from
her shelter at the dense black shadow that was her family's
formidable ancient home, she sighed with regret. Even if God
were suddenly to calm the waters and warm them, she was not
certain that she could swim so far.

A roar and crash of water caught her unaware and terrified
her, dousing her with heavy spray, reminding her forcefully
that the sea would swallow her before it swallowed the Lady
Rock. Waves crashed higher and harder by the minute, and the
first one that swept across the top would rip her from the rock,
no matter how good a handhold she had found. Then it would
fling her back and rip her away again, dashing her to pieces in
moments.

She had believed she had hours to decide her best course

before she would face dire peril. Now she knew she had very little time at all.

Although the wind had decreased, waves now broke with more power against her side of the rock. The tide had turned. Shifting upward from her crouch, she tried to keep her feet clear of the rushing water, only to realize that the next large wave could catch her unaware. She would be safer on the north side now.

As she made her way to a declivity that sheltered her momentarily from both water and wind, she wondered if anyone was trying to find her.

Would Neil have gone for help despite Allan's warning? Surely Mam would have made him go. She could not possibly fear Allan more than she would fear Diana's fate at his hands. Or would she? Allan was a Stewart, after all, one of Mam's own clan. Mam would trust him to keep his word to her.

And what of Mary? Diana sighed, fearing she could trust neither Mary nor Neil to act. Neil rarely made decisions on his own, and Mary grieved too much over her loss of Ian to think of anything else. Although Diana knew Mary loved her, she could not be sure her cousin would realize that more danger would come from silence than from sending for help.

Even if someone decided to get help, would they go to Rory? And if they did, would he be able to do anything, or would Balcardane or Duncan call the tune? Would they arrest Neil rather than listen to him? Would any Campbell care that she was in danger? Perhaps they would come though, if only to capture Allan.

She had got that far in her thinking before she realized that even if Rory moved heaven and earth to save her, he would not know where to look. All Allan had said was that he was meeting a ship, not where or when. He had spoken of Oban, but that had been only to throw them off the trail. It would not help them.

Rory would not even know they had taken a boat, so at the least, he would waste time trying to find someone who had seen them, and no one had.

"You are on your own, Diana Maclean," she said aloud. The sound of her voice was comforting, and she went on, "You are clanless now, my lass, abandoned by your own with none to come for you. So what will you do? Will you just sit here helplessly until the Almighty takes you to His arms?"

The wind dropped suddenly, making her last words sound loud. Then a huge wave crashed against the far side of the rock, and she winced as cold water sluiced down her back. More surged up to lap at her boots.

Although nearly ten feet of rock still stood above water, she had no time left to decide what to do, nor any idea how long she had been sitting. Time passed slowly, and although it felt as if she had been there for hours, it had probably not been nearly as long as it felt. The distant light still glowed and when she looked toward Dunstaffnage and Oban she saw the cluster of lights still burning there as well.

She remembered from her time at Stalker that military castles kept lights burning through the night, because there were always guards awake and prowling. Looking back at the first light, she wondered why she found comfort in thinking it was Stalker and decided it was because she would welcome even Campbell shelter now. Not that she would have to go so far, of course. There would be shelter in Lorne, too, if she could reach it. Even her enemies would not turn her away now.

Depression settled over her. First she had to get off the Lady Rock, and there would be no passing fishermen to find her here, the way fishermen had rescued the long ago Lady Elizabeth. She was on her own. She could not swim to Mull against the tide, and she realized even as the thought flitted through her mind that she had dismissed that alternative long before.

It occurred to her then that she had never looked for more signals from the ship. She could see nothing in that direction now. She had seen nothing, in fact, since Allan and Fergus had sailed away. She could not recall hearing even the noise of their sails, or the clink and rattle of the rigging. The wind had been with them, of course, blowing sound away from her. Still, it had been almost like a magician's trick. One moment they had been with her, the next they were gone.

The darkness to the south was no different from the darkness all around her. She could tell land from water, sky from land, but she could see nothing moving, certainly nothing that looked like a ship or a boat. She realized that she had harbored a faint hope that Allan would have second thoughts, that he would make them come back for her, to put her ashore at Mull or farther south, on Jura or Islay.

Biting her lip, she knew she had been indulging a mere wish over reality. Allan would not return, nor would his accomplices allow him to do so. The captain of the ship would rightly refuse to put his vessel and crew at risk, even should Allan voice such a whim, which was more than doubtful.

She was putting off the inevitable. The plain fact was that she could not swim to either shore, nor could she stay where she was. Looking up at the starry heavens, she murmured, ''If it's all the same to you, given a clear choice between drowning and being battered to death on this horrid rock, I think I'd prefer to meet death with dignity rather than wait in terror for it to burst upon me.''

Her mind made up, she knew it was no time to think of enemies or friends, only of giving herself the best chance to survive. Now that the tide had turned, the power of the sea would be with her if she swam toward the northeast. The south tip of Lismore was nearest, so if she aimed for that distant light—at least until she could no longer see it—perhaps the sea would help her swim the distance.

She stood carefully, skirts clinging damply around her legs. The wind had fallen to a gentle breeze, which was just as well, she thought, since being blown over would not help matters. Then new fear washed over her, for she knew that getting off the rock would not be easy. She might die just by attempting it.

Resolutely suppressing the new fear, she let Mary's shawl slip from her shoulders. Her frock laced up the front, so she undid it easily, but her courage nearly failed her when the next large wave crashed against the rock, soaking her thoroughly. White froth pooled just inches below her feet. She had little time left to indulge her terrors.

Letting the frock fall, she pulled off her wet shift. Then shivering in the cold night air, she sat on the wet pile of clothing and tugged off her wet half-boots. She had nearly tossed them aside before she realized she might well hurt one foot or the other trying to jump from the rock. Fear would provide distraction enough without adding pain or loss of blood.

Setting the boots down where they could not slip away, she pulled off her stockings and put the boots back on without fastening them. Then, standing, she debated whether to try to walk around the rock and find a sheltered place to slip into the surging water, or just to jump from where she was and take her chances.

A moment's thought told her she would be foolish to jump without knowing what lay beneath her, and the only place she knew at all was the leeward spot where Allan had put her off the boat. Remembering the steep, nearly straight slope into the sea, she knew that would be the safest place.

Creeping back across the top of the Lady Rock, she faltered at sight of the pounding waves. The tide swept in from the south now, battering that side. Still, she knew it was deep there, and it was the side closest to the mainland.

Watching the water, she soon sensed its rhythm. Waves heaved in, then rolled out again, the water surging up, then down. Occasionally, a much larger wave roared in, sending foam and spray soaring into the air, dousing her with cold water. She was glad it was not winter, when near freezing water would kill her long before she would drown. That might still happen, but not nearly so quickly.

The whole rock was wet now and running with rivulets. She could wait no longer. Timing the rhythm, waiting until a big one hit and fell away, she leapt out as far as she could, feeling the cold water close over her, swallowing her, trying to pull her down and down as the sea eddied back and away from the Lady Rock.

Kicking hard, as much to free her feet from the boots as to propel herself upward, she swam to the surface and struck out hard toward the coast of Lorne. The tide would carry her toward Lismore, toward that distant light, but she could no longer see its comforting glow.

Fighting momentary panic, she forced herself to calm down. She was too low to see the light, that was all, but she could still see the ones at Dunstaffnage and Oban. If she kept them behind her and swam at a slight angle to the current, surely she could reach the southern tip of Lismore.

The thought that the current might carry her into the Lynn of Lorne was not one upon which to dwell. She would be wiser, she knew, simply to accept the fact that she was staying afloat till it pleased the Almighty to claim her for His own.

She concentrated on swimming, on letting the waves carry her. When she tired, she would float, either on her stomach for the few moments she could hold her breath, or on her back. The first time she turned to her back, she recalled with bitter irony that she had been ten when Allan taught her the trick of it.

At first, the feeling of the water on her naked body was almost pleasant, even stimulating. She felt as if she could swim forever. Then, as she grew chilly, it occurred to her that most likely it *was* forever, that it could be her last act on Earth.

It would behoove her, she decided, to pray. The prayers she selected were childhood ones that she could recite in her mind while she swam, for she could not say them aloud. It was hard enough to avoid breathing in salt water when she turned her face up just in time to meet a wave breaking over her head.

She paddled more than she swam, because she found it easier to swim with her head out of water, even if it meant getting a mouthful now and again. The shore seemed to be growing closer, but was still a long way off. Farther away than it ought to be, surely. She had swum for so long.

She turned to her back again, feeling the kiss of the night air on her bare breasts. Her prayers fell silent, replaced in her mind by Rory's image. He seemed to frown, and although she did not see his lips move, she heard his voice say urgently, "Open your eyes, Diana. You must not sleep now."

The voice was so clear that she did open her eyes, realizing that she had nearly dozed off and that she was not ready yet to meet her maker. Turning over, she swam strongly for several moments, then settled back into the paddling rhythm that had served her so well before.

The waves seemed higher. A sliver of moon had risen above the blackness that was the mainland, and there were odd dancing lights on the water now, as if moonlight or the stars reached down to welcome her.

She put an arm out ahead of her, then the other, moving by instinct now, her energy nearly spent. Rolling to her back again, she prayed for strength, but her eyes refused to stay open. The stars vanished, and she smiled, seeing Rory's face again and thinking that if heaven was what it should be, his was the face of God.

Without warning a hand grabbed her arm, and she felt pain when her knuckles banged hard against wood. Her eyes flew open, and she found herself staring into Black Duncan's harsh face.

When she tried to scream, she got a mouthful of salt water. Then other hands were reaching for her. As she slipped into darkness, the last face she saw was Rory's.

"I didn't think we'd find you," he said when she opened her eyes again.

He had wrapped her in something soft, but she felt no warmth. She shivered, and her teeth chattered. Snuggling against him, she sought heat, finding it only when she burrowed her face inside his leather jacket, against his wool shirt, through which she could feel the warmth of his body. Only then did she sense the other hands touching her, rubbing her briskly through the wrapping. She glanced back, remembering then that she had seen Duncan's face first, not Rory's. Two other men, whom she recognized as Campbells, were rowing the boat.

"You came for me," she murmured. "I didn't think anyone would find me."

"We're taking you to Stalker," Rory said. "Dunstaffnage is closer, but we'd have to fight the sea to get there. The tide will carry us swiftly through the Lynn, and Duncan swears he can get us there all in one piece."

"I'm sure he can," she said.

"I will," Duncan growled. "Who threw you in the sea?"

"Allan Breck."

"That devil has much to answer for. Where is he?"

"He must have got away on the French ship that was waiting for him," she said. "He and his man, Fergus Gray, put me on the Lady Rock. With the tide coming in, I knew the waves would soon sweep me into the sea, so I decided to choose my time and meet death head on. How did the four of you find me?"

"There are more than four of us," Rory said gently. "Look about you, lass."

When she did, the pale moonlight revealed boats everywhere. The sea was alive with them, and she realized that the odd blinking lights she had seen were their torches and lanterns. "Campbells?" she said in disbelief.

"Campbells, Camerons, Stewarts, and Macleans," Rory said. "Nearly every man in Appin country who could beg, borrow, or steal a boat. And there are just as many riding the roads between Stalker and Oban, sweetheart. We signaled when we found you, and now word will be spreading over the land. There were no enemies tonight, Diana, only caring people who all wanted you to live."

Twenty-Five

The hall fire roared on the great hearth, crackling and snapping as new sap and soft pine and fir logs fed its flames. Seated in a large wooden chair, wrapped in thick quilts over a soft wool dressing gown, Diana carefully sipped the hot toddy that Rory had given her. The pewter mug had felt too hot at first, as if it burned her fingers, but now it warmed them, and as the potent whisky heated her from within, she felt her body begin to relax.

Seated as she was near the fire with her back to the huge hall, she could pretend she was alone again, that the murmur of men's voices behind her was no more than a whispering wind. She had crossed the abyss.

Rory had not failed her, and she had learned something about herself, and about life in general, too. Remembering that she had once lumped all of Argyll's men together in her mind as fools, she smiled. She would never take any man for granted again. Nor would she put blind faith in anyone again, clan member or not.

The false sense of isolation was oddly comforting, and for

a moment the terrifying hours alone on the Lady Rock seemed to have been only a dream.

"Mind you don't drink that too quickly, lass," Rory said just as she sensed his presence behind her. "You'll fall asleep before we get any food in you."

His voice was low, as if he were taking care not to let it carry to the others. She smiled up at him sleepily, the liquor making her drowsy, chasing the remnants of her terrors away, replacing them with increasing serenity. As he watched her, the look on his face altered perceptibly from concern to amusement.

"Don't laugh at me," she said, her words slurring. "If I am growing tipsy, sir, it is your fault for giving me this toddy without food to go with it."

"I thought you'd prefer meat to porridge," he said, smiling.

She wrinkled her nose. "Porridge?"

"Aye, Patrick thought that being a wee fragile female you would want pap, but I told him you needed to regain your strength and that he should feed you like he would any man who had been through such an ordeal."

She chuckled. "He'll give me raw mutton." Looking over her shoulder, she added with a reminiscent grimace, "Has he recognized me, do you think?"

"No, nor have any of the others. It would not occur to them that the servant girl who ran away weeks ago could be Mistress Diana Maclean. Even if someone noted a resemblance, he'd think it was no more than a coincidence of ancestry."

"Then you won't tell Patrick?"

He grinned. "Never. I've told him you are the woman I mean to marry, so I'd as lief not start a clan war by telling him you are the daft and wicked wench who once released the same villainous prisoner who caused all this strife."

For a moment she could not speak. Not only was the drink making her tongue sluggish but his mention of marriage had stopped the breath in her throat. He had said it before, more than once, but always before she had dismissed the notion as impossible. Now she wanted it to be fact, but she was afraid to believe he really meant it. Telling herself that he had told

Patrick he meant to marry her just to stop his questions, she said evenly, "Will they find Allan, do you think?"

He sighed. "I think he's long gone, lass, and if he's wise he won't return. For a time he may think himself safe if he is convinced that you are dead, but word that you survived is bound to reach France eventually. When it does I'll not be surprised to hear that our Allan has suffered some mysterious but fatal accident. Ardsheal won't approve of his tactics any more than the Macleans, the Stewarts, or the Campbells approved of them. You are well beloved, sweetheart."

The orange and gold light from the fire struck sparks in his gray eyes, but his expression showed no warmth, and she hoped Allan had the sense not to return to Scotland. Despite what he had done, she did not want Rory to kill him, and not because of clan loyalty. She simply did not want Allan's death on Rory's hands.

A serving wench dragged a small table up beside her and put down a platter of beef and a manchet loaf of bread. "Do ye want ale, mistress?"

Diana smiled at her, glad the girl was not one she knew. "No, thank you," she said. "This will do nicely."

"I'll cut your meat for you," Rory said when the wench had gone.

"I am not an invalid, sir."

"Good, then I will allow you to feed yourself," he said amiably.

She did not argue. Indeed, she enjoyed being cosseted. He cut the slices of beef into bite size pieces and hacked slices of bread from the loaf. She was warmer now, her shivers gone, beginning really to relax. Someone on the far side of the hall was strumming a lute, and some of the men began to sing a ballad. Rory pulled a fat pillow from a box near the hearth and sat on it beside her chair.

The beef and bread tasted as good as anything she had ever eaten. Her strength was returning. She still felt sleepy, but her body no longer threatened to collapse. She could barely remember how she had felt when they set her before the fire, when she had felt colder with coverlets wrapped around her than when she opened them to let the fire warm her. Now she was as cozy as she had ever been.

Rory was humming along with the singers now, staring into the fire.

"Have my people given you all you require, Mistress Diana?"

She had not heard Patrick's approach because of the singing, and when she looked up at him, she nearly betrayed her fear that he would know her.

He showed no sign of recognition, however, and she smiled at him. "It is all delicious, sir, some of the tastiest food I've ever eaten. Thank you for looking after me so well."

He chuckled. "It is the least we can do after your ordeal, but I daresay anything would taste good to you now. 'Tis the same after a long day's battle."

"All the same, sir, I am quite content, I promise you."

"Excellent. I don't want Rory complaining that we did not look after his bride-to-be in the fashion he demands. He's got a fearsome temper, I warn you."

"I know his temper," Diana said, adding with a sad sigh, "but I think there is something else you should know even so, sir."

"Don't say it, Diana."

Rory's tone was firm. He looked up at Patrick and said, "She thinks we do not suit, that a union between the pair of us would start another clan war."

"Such a union is more likely to mend things, if you ask me," Patrick said, smiling at Diana. "That is the true way of things, mistress. Men war until one of them finds a lass from the enemy camp who is willing to wed with him. Then all is peaceful for a time. Both sides here would welcome a period of peace, I'll wager, particularly after Glenure's murder." He grimaced at Rory. "If Argyll approves, he might keep the lads in London out of our hair for a month or two, as well."

Rory shot a wary look at Diana.

"Is that why you want me?" she asked.

"It is not." He got to his feet, and in a voice that abruptly stopped the singing, he said, "Lads, listen to me. I have asked Mistress Diana Maclean to do me the honor of accepting my hand in marriage. What think you all?"

Silence fell for a long moment before a lusty cheer broke out.

Rory grinned, then shouted over the din, "She fears that our clans will not approve. Can you put those fears to rest, lads?"

The cheers grew louder, punctuated by clan cries, as men leapt to their feet and began clanging their mugs together, and banging dishes and pots on the tables.

Rory drew Diana to her feet, coverlets and all, and put an arm around her. Bending to speak right into her ear, he murmured, "I think they approve, lassie."

Flushing deeply, Diana moistened her dry lips. She wanted to cry and to laugh all at the same time. She wanted him to hold her forever, to take her away from the din. When the cheers faded enough for Patrick to make himself heard, he bellowed, "The lass thinks he only wants her in the hope of mending fences between us all. Do you think that is his only reason?"

A roar of laughter erupted in the hall, and men began filling their cups and shouting out toasts and ribald suggestions to the lucky groom. Rory handed Diana her mug. "You must drink to every toast, lass. You'll soon be unconscious, I fear."

"I am not so fragile as that, sir." But although she lifted the cup to her lips, she barely tasted the sweet whisky, knowing she had already had enough. Toast followed upon toast, and she soon began to suspect that they intended to make her drunk, but if she was intoxicated, it was not from the whisky. As her gaze moved about the great hall, she saw Campbells arm in arm with Macleans, Camerons, and Stewarts, a sight she had never expected to see. Although the apparent truce might be short-lived, it was heady stuff now, nearly as potent as Highland whisky.

Rory raised his hands, and when the din had died away, he

said with a chuckle, "Having made my declaration, lads, I'll bid you all a good night."

Before she knew what he intended, Diana found herself swept up into his arms, and as he carried her from the hall, a symphony of cheers, more laughter, ribald comments, and equally ribald advice sped them on their way.

Though she was not averse to leaving the hall filled with men, Diana wondered where he was taking her. "Do you know where my chamber is, sir? I don't think this is the way we came when you first brought me in from the sea."

"We're going to my chamber," he said.

"But—"

"Don't argue, sweetheart. This time I mean to consummate matters before you can change your mind, and before those louts downstairs can start a new war."

"But you can't!"

"I can. Before this night is over, we'll be properly married by Scottish law."

"But—"

He bent his head and kissed her, cutting off her protests, and she decided to wait until she could regain her dignity before she renewed her arguments. When they reached his room, he managed to open the door without putting her down, then kicked it shut again behind them. Someone had already lighted a small fire on the grate, but the shutters were open, and a light wind whistled past the open window. He put her down and moved to close and fasten the shutters.

Next he knelt by the fire, adding logs. Then he moved to draw the bed curtains. He closed the ones on the window side first, pausing when he reached the foot of the bed, which faced the hooded fireplace. Smiling, he said, "We'll leave this part open, I think. I don't want you to catch a chill."

A rush of desire swept over her, but she said firmly, "Do I have no say in this matter, sir? I do not recall being properly asked, you know, or do you merely fancy yourself a victor, carrying off the spoils of war?"

Still smiling, he shook his head and moved toward her. "Can

you deny your feelings for me, sweetheart? I have made no secret of mine for you.''

She held her breath, uncertain whether she wanted him to sweep her into his arms again or to reassure her that they were not making a mistake that they would regret for the rest of their lives. He stopped within a hand's breadth of her, and although she wanted him to put his arms around her, he did not.

''Well, Diana?''

''Well, what, Rory?''

''Do you love me?''

''You know I do.'' She looked into his eyes. ''But what if—''

''We cannot live our lives according to *what if* or by other people's expectations, sweetheart. The only thing that counts is now and what we feel for each other. I want you, you want me, and that is enough. In Perthshire, where my home lies, there are few Macleans and even fewer Stewarts. At present I think we can count that as a blessing.''

She frowned. ''I will miss my family, sir.''

''Your mother, Mary, and even Neil, are welcome to live with us if you like,'' he said. ''We can discuss all that later, but unless you say you do not want me, I mean to consummate this union tonight before anything else can interfere.''

''You leave me little choice, sir.''

He said nothing, but she knew he would not take her against her will, or even if she remained the least bit reluctant. Somehow that made the decision both harder and easier to make. Biting her lip, she raised her hands to his shoulders.

He said gently, ''Are you sure?''

She nodded, and when his hands moved to the tie on the wool dressing gown, desire ignited like an ember that had been glowing, hopeful of fuel.

He paused with his hand on the ties, then picked her up without ceremony and carried her to the bed. Putting her down carefully, he spread her covers atop the bedclothes and drew the bed curtains on that side.

There were no candles to snuff. The only light in the room came from the fire. When he stepped out of her view for a moment, she could tell from whispering sounds she heard that he was taking off his clothing.

His boots thudded to the floor, then his heavy jacket hit the wooden chair, making it rock with a clatter against the stone floor. It was almost as if she could see him, but she was not tempted to peek although she could easily have done so.

She heard his bare feet on the stone floor, and then the glowing fire outlined his body for a moment before he climbed onto the bed from its foot. His skin looked golden. He was completely naked.

"You've still got Patrick's dressing gown on," he said, touching her throat, then stroking her skin gently as he moved his warm hand down to the opening of the dressing gown. It parted, revealing her breasts and his hand cupped the right one, his thumb moving lightly across the nipple.

She gasped at the sensations that light touch stirred throughout her body.

"Frightened, sweetheart?"

"Not of you, only of what lies ahead of us."

"Don't think about that. Think only of our happiness, one day at a time."

"You'll expect me to swear an oath of allegiance."

"Only to me, sweetheart."

"What of your family, and his grace of Argyll?"

"I'll expect you to respect my opinions and my family, Diana, just as I will respect you and yours," he said quietly, resting on one elbow to look down at her. "I don't doubt that we will disagree many times, sweetheart, about many things, but the old ways have gone and they won't ever come back."

"I know," she said with a sigh. "It's sad."

"Think of it, and us, as a beginning, lass, not an ending. Those of us who survive and succeed in the future must do so in a new Scotland, and if Scotland is to survive, if any part of our Highland way of life is to survive, then people like us must lead the way. If loving each other can help us learn to live and work together in harmony, we'll be miles ahead of those who cannot do so. We can teach our sons the best of the old and the new, and they can teach their sons.''

''And our daughters?''

''And our daughters.'' He kissed her right breast, and when his tongue touched the nipple, she gasped again, then lay back against the down-filled pillows, her doubts receding rapidly. The bedding smelled of cinnamon and cloves, which she was beginning to think was the most delightful of scents. Drawing a deep breath, she decided that she desired the man beside her far too much to resist his caresses any longer. She wanted him to hold her in his arms forever.

''I must be daft,'' she murmured when his lips touched hers.

''You are beautiful,'' he said. Then he kissed her harder, his arms coming around her, holding her close. His free hand pushed the wool dressing gown off her shoulders. Then, lifting her, he pulled it out from under her and tossed it to the foot of the bed.

She heard it slip to the floor, but she made no protest, for her body had come alive, and she could think of nothing else. He had only to touch her in a new place to ignite leaping flames within her. Moaning, she welcomed his tongue into her mouth, teasing it with her own, easily matching his passion. When he parted her legs and one hand moved gently between them, she gasped, but his touch was sure and stimulating, exciting her and raising her to such a pitch that she was more than ready when he moved to possess her.

He paused, and she knew that he did so with difficulty, for his passions were as untamed as hers, but he kissed her lightly and said, ''I'll be as gentle as I know how to be, sweetheart. I don't want to hurt you.''

She ached for him, and it was all she could do not to beg him to take her. Still, knowing he might hurt her unintentionally, she held her breath, raising a hand to stroke his chest, to tease him as he had teased her. When she heard his breath catch, the sound delighted her.

She moved her hand lower, to his stomach, then moved it

away when he eased himself into her. Her breasts seemed to swell, and her breath came hot and fast, and when he kissed her again, passion blazed again inside her. There was an ache, a brief sharp pain, and then a burning heat that threatened to consume them both. As they clung to each other, no memory of the terrors of the night or the icy sea stirred to quench their ardor.

They moved faster, finding their rhythm, aware of nothing and no one but each other. If this was what it meant to forge new life for a new world, Diana thought when she lay sated in his arms, she was willing to give it her all.

"Are you warm enough?" he asked.

"Aye." But she snuggled closer and did not object when he pulled the coverlets and featherbed over them both. She could hear the waves and the wind again. "Do you hear that?"

"The sea?"

"Aye. Earlier, I thought that whenever I'd hear that sound again, I would think of the Lady Rock. I won't now. I'll think of this moment, with you."

He stiffened, and for a moment she thought that somehow she had misspoken. Then she heard what he had heard, the rattle of a hand at the latch. The door opened and an unfamiliar voice said sharply, "Rory, damn your impudence, sir, are you there?"

She thought Rory growled, but his voice was calm enough when he said, "I hope you will not think me uncivil, your grace, if I point out that you intrude in a most untimely fashion."

Diana wriggled farther down under the covers.

The voice said harshly, "I was told that you had carried off an innocent young woman, sir, and meant to take her to your bed."

"I will murder Patrick for this," Rory muttered. Then in a louder tone, he said, "If it please your grace, your informant apparently neglected to inform you that I have declared my intention to marry this young woman."

A second, much more familiar voice said, "Diana, are you there?"

Having identified the unseen gentleman as his grace of Argyll, Diana had shuddered to think that he might step to the foot of the bed where he would see them both clearly, but Lady Maclean's presence was even more dismaying.

"Mam, what are you doing here?"

"So it *is* you," Lady Maclean said with satisfaction. "They all had to pass Maclean House, of course, coming here to Stalker, and his grace was kind enough to offer me space in his coach"— a distinct growl from his grace indicated that she had perhaps misrepresented the invitation— "and we came with all due speed. I heard before we arrived that you were safe, but what is this? Mary told me it was a case between you, despite all that happened. Do you really want to marry him?"

"Somehow," Diana said with a sigh, "this is not how I had imagined announcing my betrothal."

"Your marriage, lass," Rory said, chuckling. "The deed is done."

"That will be enough out of you, sir," she muttered.

To her horror, he caught up a coverlet, wrapped it around himself, and swept the curtain back. Diana snatched the bed-clothes up to her chin.

"Mistress Diana," the Duke of Argyll said brusquely, apparently undismayed by her appearance, "if he has coerced you in any way, you need only tell me so. I'll not have it said that any kinsman of mine forced this union upon you, for I have heard enough this past evening about heathenish Campbell ways to last me a lifetime, and I do *not* intend to allow him to provide further grist for that particular mill."

"Your grace," Lady Maclean said testily, "if you directed that comment to my account, let me tell you right to your head—"

"Indeed, madam, you have given me enough advice tonight to see me into heaven without so much as a pause at the pearly gates to identify myself, if I follow but a tenth of it. Have done now. I have promised to put this right, and so I shall, although it was in fact one of your clan, *not* one of mine that—"

"Your grace, Rory did not coerce me," Diana said, judging

it more than time to intervene, even if she had to interrupt him to do so.

"Are you certain of that?" the duke demanded. "Because even if he has already possessed you, I can make things right. I can arrange a marriage as much to your advantage, even more so, because when I have finished with him—"

"Now, see here, sir—"

"Do you defy me, Rory? Because if you dare—"

"No, sir, of course not. I merely wish to point out to you—"

"Before you point out anything, I will have an unequivocal answer from this young woman." Argyll looked at Diana, waiting pointedly.

She fought her sense of the absurd, finding it hard under the circumstances to remember that this peevish, elderly man held the power of life and death at his whim, that he was, in fact, the most powerful man in all of Scotland. Sensing Rory's increasing tension, she gathered her wits and said as calmly as she could, "I am content, sir. I love Rory with all my heart. My only worry has been that others might resent our union and cause him harm—indeed, that you yourself might be furious with him if he married me, and would demand a harsh punishment."

Grimly Argyll shifted his gaze to Rory. "I have disagreed with him many times, mistress," he said, "but in this instance I believe he has made a wise decision. To rebuild Scotland, we must unite her. I do not know if this marriage will foster peace. No one can know that, and previous such unions have failed to unite our clans. Still, I believe yours will be a good marriage."

"I can think of one thing that would help foster that peace you speak of, your grace," Lady Maclean said in a much more amiable tone than she generally employed with him. "You have the power, if you will but exert it, to see Craignure restored to the Macleans. Well, not to the Macleans, exactly, but to Diana's child, and Rory's." She paused, watching Argyll.

The silence lengthened. Diana held her breath.

"A wedding gift, you mean?" Argyll looked at Rory. "I don't know that you deserve it, but perhaps we can manage something of that nature. At all events, we'll arrange a proper ceremony immediately, at Inveraray, to show the world that the Campbells and Macleans need not always be at war." Turning to Diana, he added kindly, "I do wish you happy, my dear."

"Thank you, sir," Diana said.

Lady Maclean said, "Are you certain you want this, Diana?"

"Do you object, Mam?"

With a wry smile, her ladyship said, "Would it matter if I did?"

"I love you, Mam. Of course, it must matter, but I love Rory more than I had thought it possible to love any man. What would you have me do?"

"And you, sir, do you love my daughter?"

"With all my heart," Rory said simply.

"Then that is that," Lady Maclean said quietly. "We have intruded enough, Duke. You may take me back to the hall. By now Mary will have learned where Patrick Campbell means to put us, I expect. Besides, I must explain to you again just why you must instantly release James of the Glen."

"Now, see here, madam . . ."

When the door had shut behind them, Rory got up at once to bolt it. "I should have done that before," he said, grinning ruefully at Diana over his shoulder. The firelight played on his body, turning his flesh golden and outlining his muscles with shadows that danced as he moved.

When he turned to put another log on the fire, she said, "Don't be too long, my lord. This bed grows cold without you."

"We'll soon warm it up, sweetheart, never fear."

Watching him walk toward her, Diana knew that for them, love would prevail. For the present, at least, they were free of the past and could look ahead with hope for a future unfettered by clan shackles and blind allegiance.

Dear Reader,

I hope you enjoyed *Highland Secrets.* There is not and never has been a branch of Clan Maclean identified as the Macleans of Craignure. Their history, in large part, is borrowed from the Macleans of Duart and augmented by the author. The ancient history of the Macleans and Campbells, including the legend of the Lady Rock, is based on historical fact and legend, which means that any errors are the fault of yours truly.

There once was a real Lord Calder, but the title did not come into being until 1796, and John Campbell, the man who bore it, spent most of his life in Wales (though his roots were Scottish). He bears no relationship to Rory Campbell, who is fictitious.

Female Jacobite prisoners were all imprisoned at Edinburgh Castle, from which a real Lady Ogilvy escaped in the manner used in this book. The friend who pretended to be a laundress and exchanged clothes with her was afterward allowed to go free.

Scottish law, being generally based on the old canon law of the Roman church, has always recognized so-called irregular marriages. One such form is the famous *marriage by declaration,* which you may recall from *Highland Fling.* A second is the *marriage of promise subsequente copula* described in *Highland Secrets,* where both the promise and the *copula* had to take place in Scotland. A third form is identified as *marriage by cohabitation with habit and repute,* similar to our common-law marraige.

The murder of Colin Campbell of Glen Ure (known commonly as Glenure or Red Colin) occurred as described. Much controversy has been stirred since then by the fact that while Allan Breck Stewart escaped, James of the Glen was arrested and later hanged. Many people then (and now) believed him innocent of all wrongdoing.

My husband and I visited the site of the murder (still an ancient woodland called Lettermore Woods) and the site of James's hanging, both of which have been preserved as historic monuments. We also made a trek to Red Colin's house, Glenure Lodge, one of the oldest privately owned Scottish residences that is neither a great house nor a castle. The road up Glen Creran to Glen Ure is *exactly* the width of an English Ford Punto, with a steep bank on one side and an equally steep drop-off into the river on the other. True adventure for both of us, especially with a righthand-drive car.

If you enjoyed *Highland Secrets,* I hope you will look for *Highland Treasure* in June 1998 from Zebra, in which a villain captures Diana's cousin Mary Maclaine because he thinks he can make use of her gift (second sight) to recover a lost treasure.

Sincerely yours,

Amanda Scott

If you enjoyed HIGHLAND SECRETS, be sure to look for Amanda Scott's next marvelous historical romance, HIGHLAND TREASURE, coming in June, 1998, from Zebra Books. Here's a preview of the passion and adventure to come . . .

Prologue

The Highlands, 1745

Eerie echoes reverberated through the mist-shrouded forest as dirt thudded onto the treasure chest. A second shovelful quickly followed, then a third, as Lord MacCrichton and his elder son, Ewan, hurried to bury the chest.

Ewan's brother, Geordie, a huge man with a childlike demeanor, kept a lookout, holding a spout lantern so that its light spilled into the hole containing the ironbound chest. "Hurry," he said anxiously. "We canna see a thing in this mist."

"Set down the lantern and notch that tree," MacCrichton said to him. He, too, was a large man, though not as big as either of his sons. "It will save time, and since you did not think to bring out another shovel, you can just do it now."

"Aye, that's a good notion, that is. I'll use my dirk. What mark will I use?"

Impatiently, Ewan said, "Must we think of everything, you daft gowk? Use that rattlepate of yours to think for once. We want to be able to find this tree again."

"Aye, well, then, X marks the spot," Geordie said, chuckling as he moved purposefully toward the nearest tree.

For some moments thereafter, the dull thuds of dirt on dirt and the scritch-scratch of metal on bark were the only sounds to be heard, for the denizens of the forest were either fast asleep or keeping their counsel. The air was chilly and damp with mist rising off nearby Loch Creran and drifting over the land in vast, dense patches. But the night would not remain still for long, so they all listened intently for anything out of the ordinary, suspecting that the forest contained more than just forest creatures. The tension seemed to make Geordie particularly nervous.

Suddenly his hand froze mid-stroke, and he exclaimed, "Hark!" When the other two jumped and Ewan glared at him, he said, "Did you no hear that?"

"What?" Then Ewan heard it himself.

A crackling sound, eerily muffled by the mist, came from the direction of the loch. It sounded like a branch breaking and pebbles moving.

"That! Someone's coming. Hurry!" Geordie snatched up the lantern, and just before he shut the spout, its light fell upon the huge X gashed in the bark.

"By my faith," Ewan snapped, "are you truly daft? Anyone who sees that X will be bound to dig here."

"Och, but 'tis why they call him Daft Geordie, that is," Lord MacCrichton said with a sigh.

"But you said to mark it," Geordie protested.

"Aye, lad," Ewan agreed, "but we never thought you'd mark it so bloody damned well." He fell silent, listening. Then, hearing nothing more that was in any way remarkable, he said, "Look you now, Geordie, help us brush pine needles and leaves over this mound so that it won't look fresh dug, and then we'll notch a few more trees like you did this one. The chest is buried deep, so if this one spot don't shriek out to every passerby to take notice of it, we'll be safe enough, I think."

"Aye, that's a fine notion, that is," Geordie said cheerfully. "Plain to see that you got the brains in the family, Ewan."

They worked as silently as possible, halting frequently to listen, and a quarter hour later, MacCrichton said, "That will do. I'm for bed now."

"You and Ewan go on ahead," Geordie said. "I'll notch a few more trees and then bring in the shovels when I come."

"Right, lad," his lordship said. "Don't be too long, though, and don't trip over any damned Campbells whilst you're about it. They've been watching us for weeks now, thinking we mean to follow the prince."

"As we do intend," Geordie said, chuckling again. "Is that no why we're a-burying of this chest, so as to keep the treasure safe till we can return to Shian?"

"We don't want them getting their filthy hands on it while we're away, that's certain. Come along, Ewan. And mind you, Geordie, don't be long."

"I won't." But it was several hours before he returned to Shian Towers, the well-fortified, round-towered castle of the MacCrichtons perched on a knoll above the loch. The next morning when he met his brother in the cluttered breakfast room, he said smugly, "Them damned Campbells will never find our treasure now, Ewan."

"What makes you so certain?"

"Because I've outsmarted them, I have."

Eyes narrowing with misgiving, Ewan said, "What did you do?"

"I notched every blessed tree for a mile or more, that's what I did. No Campbell will ever find it now."

"No, nor anyone else," Ewan snarled as his volatile temper ignited to fury, "How the devil do you think *we* are going to find it again, you daft gowk?"

"But I—"

Daft Geordie did not finish his sentence, however, because with a single, furious blow, his exasperated brother knocked him senseless to the floor.

One

The body of James of the Glen swung gently to and fro in the evening breeze, a stark black shadow against the sun setting beyond the mountains of Morven and the western shore of Loch Linnhe.

The eerie sound of its creaking chains stirred a shudder in the second of the string of ten riders passing through Lettermore Woods in the general direction of the Ballachulish ferry. Not that the party intended to cross into Lochaber, for they did not. They were making for the hill pass into Glen Creran. Mary Maclaine was riding away from her old life into a new one, and already she was having second thoughts.

The effort required not to look at James's body hanging above its lofty grass-topped lump of rock contributed to her depression. The gruesome sight brought back memories of James and of Ian, gentle Ian, whom she had loved so dearly and whose death had been so sudden and violent, albeit not so violent as poor James's.

"Don't dawdle, Mary love," the party's leader said. His

tone was coaxing but held a note of impatience. "We've hours of travel ahead yet, and there's no use looking wistfully at James of the Glen. Wishing won't stir him back to life."

"I know we cannot bring him back," Mary said. "I just wish they would cut him down. It's been more than a year now, after all, since they hanged the poor innocent man."

"No one knows better than I do how long it's been," he said with a teasing look, "but I'll warrant the devilish Campbells mean to leave him there till he rots."

He was a big, broad-shouldered man with curly fair hair, and she supposed most folks would think him handsome. He was certainly charming, for although it had cost him a year's effort, he had charmed her into agreeing to marry him despite her firm belief that with Ian Campbell dead she would never marry any man.

Her gaze shifted involuntarily back to the corpse hanging in chains near the high road. All who traveled between Lochaber and Appin were obliged to pass the gibbet, and its elevated position made it visible as well to folks along an extensive stretch of Loch Linnhe and Loch Leven.

From where she was, she could see the great square tower of Balcardane Castle beyond Ballachulish village, on the hillside above Loch Leven, and the castle, too, stirred memories of Ian, for the castle had been his home. His father was the surly, too-powerful Earl of Balcardane, and his brother was Black Duncan Campbell, a man of whom many folks went in understandable fear. Mary was not one of them, but she had no wish to think about Black Duncan, for although she knew such thoughts were wicked, she could not help blaming him for Ian's death.

"I wish we could just cut James down ourselves, and bury him properly," she said abruptly, forcing her gaze back to her fair-haired companion.

"It would be as much as our lives are worth to try," he said. "That's why *they* are there." He gestured toward the hut where the soldiers guarding the gibbet kept their food and pallets, and could take shelter from the elements. Smoke drifted upward from their cook fire now, and one man stared at them from the doorway.

Mary remembered when they had build the hut, a month after the hanging. Its very presence had been and still was an unmistakable sign that the soldiers would remain a long while to see that no one cut the body down.

Without another word, her companion urged his horse to a canter. She knew he wanted to be over the hill pass before darkness descended upon them, but she could not help resenting his urgency. Had he presented himself at Maclean House that morning as he had promised, instead of waiting until nearly supper time, or had they taken one of the faster routes up Glen Duror or south through Salachan Glen, they would doubtless have made their destination easily before dark. He had been late, however, and had still insisted upon this more circuitous route.

Through habit, Mary kept her resentment to herself. When one had long depended on relatives for one's bed and board, one did not express feelings freely. Instead, one tried to prove useful, to present as light a burden as possible.

Mary was deeply grateful for her Aunt Anne's years of care. Lady Maclean was neither a gentle nor a tender woman, but she was capable, strong, and kind; and she had been most attentive to her niece, for the kinship was a close one. Not only had she been one of Mary's mother's six elder sisters, but Lady Maclean's husband, Sir Hector, had been a member of the same clan as Mary's father, albeit from the Craignure branch, which had long been unfriendly to the Maclaines of Lochfuaran.

Thus, Mary had been double cousin to Diana and Neil, Sir Hector and Lady Maclean's children. After the deaths of Mary's father, brothers, and last remaining sister seven years before—and that of Sir Hector—no one remained to protest when Lady Maclean appeared out of the blue one day to bear Mary away to live with her.

Seven years. Seven long and lonely years of being brave and cheerful and trying not to be a burden, when the very times were burdensome. Men said that luck came and went in seven-year intervals, and Mary thought that might be true. Although she recalled little of her first seven years, living at Lochfuaran on the Island of Mull, she thought they had been happy and generally carefree, but the second seven had been horrid.

Like a bolt of lightning, in her eighth year, tragedy had struck, carrying off her mother and the two of her six elder sisters who were nearest Mary in age. They had all died swiftly, one after the other, during an influenza epidemic.

Her father and other sisters had kept Mary away from the sickroom, of course, but one evening she had seen a shimmering image of her mother, who had said matter-of-factly that she was going to heaven now, and to be a good girl. A few minutes later, Mary's father had come in to tell the shaken, frightened child that her mother was dead. Mary told her family about her vision, but everyone agreed that it had simply been a bad dream brought on by all the anxious activity around her.

The deaths devastated the family, but Mary still had her big, protective father, four frequently cheerful brothers, and four nurturing elder sisters to look after her. Then her sister Sarah had married and died in childbirth, along with her bairn. Her sister Margaret had died the following year of a cut that putrefied, and the year after that, Mary had awakened one night, sitting bolt upright in her bed, soaked with sweat and shaking. Her sister Eliza, who was visiting cousins at Tobermory, had screamed out to her in a dream that she was falling.

In the dream, Mary could not catch her, and thus had she wakened with the certain knowledge that Eliza was dead. She told her brothers and father about the dream the following day, and several hours later word arrived from Tobermory that Eliza had fallen from a parapet while walking in her sleep, and had died instantly.

Years later Mary saw the faces of two of her brothers at what must have been the moment each fell at Culloden, along with a face she later recognized from a portrait as her Uncle Hector. Her other two brothers, her father, and her sole remaining sister had died in the aftermath of that dreadful defeat, at the hands of the man Highlanders called Butcher Cumberland. Mary had witnessed their deaths, too, not by virtue of her gift but from the stable loft at Lochfuaran, where she lay hidden, quaking with terror, beneath a pile of hay. She had never revealed the horrible details of that day to anyone, and now, thinking of it, she shuddered again.

She had been fourteen then, and within a sennight her Aunt Anne had swooped in to collect her. Although the next few years had been bleak, they had proved to be relatively carefree.

When the Crown seized Craignure and Lochfuaran, due to the rebel activities of their owners, Lady Maclean simply moved her little family from the Island of Mull to an estate in Appin country, owned by the exiled Laird of Ardsheal. Ardsheal was Lady Maclean's brother and Mary's uncle, and thanks to him, they had enjoyed shelter, food, and relative peace for a pepper-corn rent.

Then had come the Appin murders, rumors of a new rebellion in the making, and the trial and conviction of James of the Glen, a man Mary still believed had been guilty of no crime other than of being an influential Stewart in a land ruled by the English and the Campbells. The murderer's primary victim had been a Campbell Crown factor hated by most of Appin country's residents. His second victim had been Gentle Ian Campbell.

James of the Glen had been another of Ardsheal's many siblings, albeit one born outside the blanket, so to speak. None-theless, with Ardsheal's help he had educated himself and had grown to be one of the most highly respected men in Appin. It had been James to whom most folks had turned for help with confusing matters of law and finance.

Now James and Ian were dead. Her aunt and her cousin Neil had left for Perthshire a fortnight before to spend the winter with her cousin Diana, married more than a year now and expecting her first child; and Mary was on her way to Shian Towers to marry its master, Ewan, Lord MacCrichton.

* * *

It was after midnight when they finally arrived at Shian Towers. For hours riders carrying torches had lighted their way through the dark shadows of Glen Creran, aided by a half moon riding high above them, haloed by a misty ring. As they approached the castle, sitting high on its forested hill, Mary saw thick mist rising from the loch just below them. Although she strained her eyes, she could see no sign of anything on the opposite shore that might be Dunraven Castle, which Ian had once told her had been the seat of the Earls of Balcardane long before they assumed ownership of the present Loch Leven castle, a prize of war forfeited by a hapless Stewart after the Rising of 1715.

They passed beneath a portcullis, into a torchlit cobbled courtyard.

"Tired, lass?" Ewan's quiet voice snatched her from her reverie.

"A little," she said. "I still don't understand why we rode so far, sir. We must have added nearly fifteen miles to our journey, for we cannot be but ten or twelve miles from Maclean House now. We've ridden right round half of Appin."

"Aye, and if we did?"

A note in his voice held warning, but she dismissed it. She had known him a full year now, and he had been consistently charming and considerate to her. Thus she did not hesitate to say frankly, "I should have thought that having chosen such a long route, you would not have wished to leave Maclean House so late, sir, or that having begun so late, you might have chosen a more direct route."

He lifted her from her saddle, setting her down with a thump, but he did not release her. He was a full head taller than she was, and his hands felt tight around her waist as he said, "Do you find fault with my decision, Mary?"

She could not mistake the warning this time, and it occurred to her with no small impact that perhaps she did not know him very well at all.

"It was not my intent to sound reproachful, sir," she said quietly.

"Good lass." He clapped her on the shoulder, then slipped an arm around her, urging her toward the entrance stairs.

Like other tower houses built early in the previous century, Shian Towers was a tall, handsome combination of stronghold and dwelling house. Built in the shape of an ell with circular towers at every corner and angle-turrets projecting at the gables, it presented an impressive appearance. Shot holes pierced its walls, and projecting above the main entrance, in the angle of the ell, was a device called a machicolation, which Mary knew was for pouring unpleasantness down on unwelcome visitors. The MacCrichton arms surmounted the door, which itself was huge, iron-bound, and located on the first-floor level some twenty feet above the ground, at the top of removable wooden steps.

Ewan hustled her up the stairs and inside, past the stout, woven-iron gate, or *yett,* that could be shut against an enemy attack. As another prevention against assault, the door opened immediately onto twisting stone steps that led up to the great hall and down to the nether portions of the castle, undoubtedly housing the kitchen and some servants' rooms. Holding up her skirt with her right hand, Mary used her left to hold the rope banister as she preceded Ewan and his men upstairs to the hall. The stairs were narrow and wound in a clockwise direction, as Mary knew that such stairs nearly always did, so that a right-handed swordsman would always have the advantage defending his home against an enemy coming up the stairs.

In the great hall, a boy stirred up the fire and one of Ewan's men used a torch to light myriad candles in sconces, revealing a fine, high-ceilinged chamber with dark paneling that Mary saw at once could use oil and rubbing.

"I suppose your family is abed and asleep at this hour, sir," she said, gazing about while she took off her gloves and untied the strings of her long gray cloak. When he did not answer at once, she turned and looked at him.

Ewan glanced from one to another of the three men who

had accompanied them inside. Then, straightening, he said harshly to her, "There is no family here, lass, only ourselves, my men, and a few menservants."

Stunned, Mary exclaimed, "But how can that be? You said you were bringing me here to be married in the midst of your family, that I need not wait for my aunt and Sir Neil to return or for my cousin to recover after the birth of her child. You said—"

"I know what I said," Ewan interjected. "I've said a lot of damned silly stuff over the past year. Not much of it was true, although it is true enough that you are in the midst of my family. There are any number of them buried hereabouts."

"You said you loved me," Mary said, shaken and trying to gather her wits.

"What if I did? Lots of lads say that when it will do them a good turn."

"But what good am I to you? You must know that I have no money or land, that I am completely dependent upon my aunt and my cousin's husband for my keep. I don't even possess a dowry. You said that you did not require one."

"I don't."

"Ewan, I don't understand any of this. Do you *want* to marry me?"

"Oh, aye. I don't want any mistake about things later, and I've got to get myself a proper heir in any event, haven't I?"

"Mistake? What mistake?" She was uncomfortably aware of the three other men in the hall, and of the little boy who had lighted the fire and now squatted alertly near the wall by the stairs, but she had to discover what was going on.

"You don't need to know any more than that you will be my wife, lass, subject to my bidding."

"No, I won't, Ewan," she said, keeping her temper with difficulty. She was too tired to bandy words with him. "I thought I knew you, but clearly I don't. I shall return to Maclean House at first light."

"Well, that's where you're wrong, Mary Maclaine. I have planned this for more than a year, ever since I learned about you, and I won't let you spoil it now. You will be my wife, like it or not, and that's my last word on the subject."

"By the mercy of heaven, sir, you cannot force me to marry you. No parson will perform the service against my will."

He smirked. "I've read the law, I have, and we've no need for any parson."

"You still need my consent, however. A mere declaration of marriage, while legal if I agree, is useless if I contradict you, and even marriage by promise and consummation cannot be forced. A single word of dissent from the bride turns that into rape, Lord MacCrichton." As she said the words, Mary experienced a distinct chill. What good were laws when one was miles from help of any kind?

Ewan's smirk remained unshaken. "You know more than I thought you would, more than I'd expect of any lass," he said, "but that will only make it easier. Scottish law provides for all sorts of irregular marriages, Mary Maclaine."

"I know, for I learned about most of them when my cousin married," Mary said. "Hers was a marriage of promise."

"Well, but you mentioned only two sorts. There is handfasting, as well."

"I am not living with you for a year and a day, just so that—"

"Whisst now, lower your voice, Mary, if you don't want to feel my hand across that vixen's mouth of yours."

"How dare you!"

Ewan slapped her, hard.

Her hand flew to her burning cheek. She was truly shocked, for as a rule Highland men were not violent toward women or children. That trait was unique to Englishmen and Lowlanders—Sassenachs, outlanders. A Highlander might put an erring wife or child across his knee if one needed a stern lesson, but he would never use his fist or lift his hand to any other part of a body weaker than his own.

She stepped back, but Ewan caught her, his hand bruising her upper arms. Giving her a rough shake, he said, "You'll do as you are told, Mary Maclaine. There is one law of marriage with which you are clearly unacquainted, and that is the law of cohabitation. Any man and woman with a habit of cohabitation are presumed under law to be man and wife.''

"That cannot be true," she protested. "Men frequently cohabit with women whom no one pretends are their wives!"

"Only if they come from different classes, lass. You and I are of the same class, however. Moreover, before long, I warrant you'll be only too happy to agree that you are my wife, for I mean to see to that."

A shiver raced up her spine at the look he gave her, but rallying, she said, "I shall write to the Duke of Argyll, sir. You may not be aware—"

"Oh, aye, I ken fine that your cousin Diana married a kinsman of Argyll's. That's one reason I bided my time and exerted myself to charm you, Mary Maclaine. I did not want you complaining to your kinsmen of unwanted attention. I sought you out at the trial of James of the Glen, knowing full well that you cared for the man, and I have exerted myself for a full year to arrive at this exact moment."

"Then you must know that I have only to write . . ." Her words trailed to silence in the face of his confident grin.

"You will write no letters, lass."

"You cannot mean to hold me prisoner! People know where I am. They will expect to hear from me."

"Aye, well, there's a bit of a rub, for you see, I told your maidservant, Morag MacArthur, that we would be traveling into Lochabar for a few weeks to be married from a kinsman's home. That is one reason we traveled the route we did."

"Only one?" She heard the sarcasm in her tone and felt little surprise at the flash of anger in his eyes.

"You will recall that we met one or two folks along the way," he said evenly.

"I do, though we did not meet many."

"My lads told each one that we were headed for a different destination. Then, forbye, it was dark when we passed through the glen. Most folks paid us no heed. We mght have been Campbells or a party of soldiers, for all they saw, and they are wise enough not to venture out without good cause. Then, too . . .'' He hesitated.

"What?"

"I wanted a look at Balcardane to see if Black Duncan was stirring."

"Why?"

"I thought he might take an undesirable interest in the lass that Gentle Ian once wanted."

"Black Duncan takes no interest in me," she said with a grimace. "He did not want Ian to have anything to do with me, which is why we were never properly betrothed. I have told you that many and many a time before now, sir."

"You had best hope that it's true."

"It is. But, Ewan, what do you want with me? This makes no sense."

"'Tis simple enough, and no reason not to tell you the gist of it, I expect. I've a use for your gift, you see."

"My gift?"

"Aye, sure, and you need not look as if I were speaking in tongues, lass. I ken fine that you're a seventh daughter of a seventh daughter, and that you possess the gift of second sight."

"But I still don't understand," Mary said, wholly bewildered now. "What can the Sight have to do with your wish to marry me?"

"Everything," he said flatly. "A seer has told me that the only way to find a certain thing that's been lost to the MacCrichtons is through a seventh daughter."

"But the Sight cannot help find lost articles," she protested. "Truly, sir, you do not understand. I have no control over my gift. All it has ever shown me is the face of a dear one who has died suddenly."

He made a dismissive gesture. "Don't argue with me. You have the gift of healing, for I've heard many speak of it. Men ask you to wash your hands in the water you use to clean their wounds. People with the Sight can find lost bodies, too, for I've heard of such myself. Why should you not find lost treasure, then?"

"Treasure?"

He spread his hands. "Just a manner of speaking, lass. Once I've explained the whole to you, you will understand right enough though."

"I am not going to be your wife, Ewan."

"Yes, you are. You must, for another law I've looked into makes it absolutely necessary."

"What law is that?"

"So long as you are my wife, what you find belongs to me. Otherwise, if you find what I seek, it may be claimed by the Crown instead. I cannot have that. There is no need to talk more about it tonight, however," he added. "The hour grows late, and you must be longing for your bed. I'll take you upstairs."

He signed to the boy squatting against the wall near the stairs. "Bring a torch, lad, and look lively unless you want to feel my whip across your back."

The boy leapt to take a torch from one of the men, holding it aloft with difficulty. Watching him stagger, trying to keep his balance, seemed to amuse Ewan, for he chuckled.

Mary had nowhere else to go at that hour, and she could see nothing to gain by arguing. Her stinging cheek reminded her of what the likely outcome would be, in any case. Thus, she allowed Ewan to take her arm and urge her in the wake of the child up the twisting stone stairway.

"Bar the gates and set a good watch," he said to a man near the doorway. "I think we've flummoxed the lot of them, but it's as well to take care."

"Aye, master."

The stair went up and up, around and around, past other chambers in which Mary saw carpets and elegant furniture but few pictures. She saw few knickknacks of any kind, for that matter. At the top of the stairway was a stout oak door. Ewan pushed it open, revealing a room that boasted a once-bright Turkey carpet, but Mary saw that the carpet was threadbare and old. The furniture needed polish.

"This is your bedchamber, lass. Light candles, Chuff. Then be off with you."

The room was spacious enough. A tall, curtained bed stood against the center of the wall opposite the door. One corner opened into a round tower space, which appeared to be arranged as a powder closet. A small fire crackled on the hearth at Mary's right, and thanks to the little boy, four tallow candles in plain brass sconces soon augmented the firelight. Mary's bundles already lay on the floor.

"Thank you," she said quietly, turning to Ewan. "It seems a pleasant room."

The look of intent in his eyes warned her in the split second before he reached for her.

Skipping nimbly away from him, she said grimly, "If you are thinking of beginning that cohabitation tonight, my lord, you had better think again."

"Why is that, lass?" Grinning, he took another step toward her.

"Because if you lay one more hand on me tonight, I'll cast a spell over the source of your male seed, sir, that will cause it to shrivel up and fall off."

He stared at her in dismay for a long moment, then turned on his heel and strode angrily from the room. The door crashed behind him, but just as Mary was congratulating herself on being rid of him, she heard a key turn in the lock.

Across the loch, at the much larger, far more formidable Castle Dunraven, Duncan Campbell looked across the huge desk in his book room at the messenger whose late arrival had drawn him wearily from his bed.

"You're certain of this news, Bannatyne?"

"Aye, master. Allan Breck has been seen in Rannoch and also in Lochabar."

"He's been seen any number of places this past year and more," Duncan said harshly. 'Still, he never seems to linger in any of those places he's been seen."

"Aye, and that's a fact, that is," the messenger agreed. "No one claims tae ha' seen him more than once, but the landlord at the Swan on Rannoch Moor kens him fine, sir, or so he says. And he says Allan Breck drank a dram o' whisky there not a sennight ago. Said he's here tae collect more money for the exiled lairds, same as before, only this time there be word of a substantial sum available tae him. The name MacCrichton were spoke more than once, the landlord said."

"Not for the first time, either," Duncan said thoughtfully. "The MacCrichtons have long run with the Stewarts of Appin, and with the Macleans—well nigh from the outset of all our troubles. What's more, they seem to have taken advantage of the Earl of Balcardane's long absence from Creran to build their power hereabouts."

"Only on the Appin side o' the loch," Bannatyne said loyally.

Duncan grunted. "They seem resistant to the notion of letting lost causes lie, however. It's time that I had a word with that devil MacCrichton."

"They say he is nay a man tae be trusted," Bannatyne said diffidently.

"Never fear. I don't even trust God." Duncan took a small pouch from the pocket of his coat and tossed it, jingling, to the man. "You've done well, Bannatyne. I'm sorry you had to trudge so far to find me, but it's as well now, I think, that I'm here. Shian Towers lies just across the loch. We'll take boats tomorrow, and I'll pay Ewan, Lord Bloody MacCrichton, a friendly visit."

"You'll nay go alone then!"

"I am not a fool," Duncan said. He spoke quietly, but his tone was such that Bannatyne flushed to the roots of his shaggy hair. "Though my worthy sire decries the cost of my entourage, I am thought to have sufficient men for my needs. But surely you do not expect MacCrichton to be so foolish as to raise arms against me, Bannatyne. That would be against the law, would it not?"

Apparently laboring under the misapprehension that Duncan

required an answer, Bannatyne said, "Aye, sir, that's right, that is. It's nay lawful for any Highlander tae bear weapons, not since the Disarming Act nigh onto six years ago."

"Do you truly suppose that no Highlander carries a weapon, Bannatyne?"

Looking directly at the sword belt that rested on the corner of Duncan's desk, and then at the dirk shoved into his own boot-top, Bannatyne said with a frown, "Nay, sir, I'd nay put m' trust in that."

"Then you are not such a gowk as I thought. Pray, when you seek your pallet send one of the lads sleeping in the hall here to me. I've instructions to give him."

When the man had gone, Duncan got up and put another log on the fire. As he straightened, his dark gaze lit upon the portrait dominating the chimneypiece.

A fair-haired youth attired in the blue, green, and yellow Campbell plaid sat astride a sleek bay horse. The artist had painted the lad laughing, with a bird perched tamely on his shoulder atop bunched folds of the plaid. At the horse's hooves a brown and white spotted spaniel romped, bearing a bright red ball in its mouth, clearly inviting the rider to play.

Duncan's lips hardened into a straight line, and he felt the surge of anger he always felt when his thoughts turned to his younger brother, Ian.

Solemnly now, speaking directly to the portrait, he said, "I will not rest, lad, until the murderous Allan Breck is dead. And may heaven help Ewan MacCrichton if he knows aught of the scoundrel and attempts to keep his knowledge from me."

BOOK YOUR PLACE ON OUR WEBSITE AND MAKE THE READING CONNECTION!

We've created a customized website just for our very special readers, where you can get the inside scoop on everything that's going on with Zebra, Pinnacle and Kensington books.

When you come online, you'll have the exciting opportunity to:

- View covers of upcoming books
- Read sample chapters
- Learn about our future publishing schedule (listed by publication month *and author*)
- Find out when your favorite authors will be visiting a city near you
- Search for and order backlist books from our online catalog
- Check out author bios and background information
- Send e-mail to your favorite authors
- Meet the Kensington staff online
- Join us in weekly chats with authors, readers and other guests
- Get writing guidelines
- AND MUCH MORE!

Visit our website at
http://www.kensingtonbooks.com

The Queen of
Romance

Cassie Edwards